I0576512

Lewis Tappan

The Life of Arthur Tappan

Lewis Tappan

The Life of Arthur Tappan

ISBN/EAN: 9783742813886

Manufactured in Europe, USA, Canada, Australia, Japa

Cover: Foto ©Andreas Hilbeck / pixelio.de

Manufactured and distributed by brebook publishing software
(www.brebook.com)

Lewis Tappan

The Life of Arthur Tappan

THE LIFE

OF

ARTHUR TAPPAN.

His daily life, far better understood
In deeds than words, was simply doing good;
So calm, so constant was his rectitude
That by his loss alone we know his worth,
And feel how true a man has walked with us òn earth.

WHITTIER.

He being dead yet speaketh. HEBREWS xi. 4.

NEW YORK:

PUBLISHED BY HURD AND HOUGHTON.

CAMBRIDGE: RIVERSIDE PRESS.

1870.

PRINTED BY H. O. HOUGHTON AND CO.

CONTENTS.

V.

VI.

VII.

VIII.

8   CONTENTS.

XXVII.

INTRODUCTION.

THE inquiry has often been made, since the death of Mr. Arthur Tappan, When will a suitable memorial of one so widely known and so highly esteemed, be published? The answer has been: *A man's good name is his best monument.* Still the inquiry is reiterated, and an earnest desire expressed, from various sources, that at least some sketch of the life of a man so eminently useful, should be prepared, not only for surviving relatives, and near friends, but for many who knew him only by reputation. We want, say they, to know something of his parentage, his early life, his habits of business, the secret of his success, and the reasons of his reverses as a merchant, his experience as a philanthropist and a Christian. We desire to know something of the inner man, how he appeared in his family, in his place of business, in the walks and conflicts of life.

It is natural that such requests should be made, and it is reasonable that those who make them should be gratified. But it is necessary to bear in mind that he was a man of a remarkably quiet spirit, unostentatious, averse to publicity, and desirous of being felt rather than seen. He had but a common school education, was not a writer, or speaker, and kept no journal of his feelings, or actions. He was seldom seen except at his place of business, in his family, in his garden, in the church, or lecture-room, at committee meetings, and as

presiding officer of public meetings. In all these relations he gave himself to the work in hand. He was
remarkable for seriousness, despatch, impatience at non-
observance of rules, at prolixity, waste of time, or opportunity. He consulted the rights and convenience of
others as well as his own, and reflected that the Master whom he served, required fidelity, diligence, faith-
fulness, accomplishment—few words and abundant
deeds.

It is proposed, with the materials at hand, to give
a narration of the principal incidents in the life of Mr.
Tappan, for his children and grandchildren, primarily,
and with such minuteness as may be of special interest
to them. And also to give a statement of his connection with the benevolent institutions of the times in
which he lived, and in whose doings he participated;
together with the views he cherished on the subject of
moral reform in its various departments.

In doing this, it will be necessary to speak with
plainness of men and measures, defending the right
and condemning the wrong. The truth of history
requires that this should be done, although it is obliga-
tory to "speak the truth in love." That good men, as
individuals and members of benevolent societies, sometimes manifested opposition to the course he pursued, he
did not deny. He lamented the inconsistency of such
persons, but justly considered that it afforded no sanction to what was wrong, either in principle or conduct.
"To err is human." While he made all due allowances
for the frailties of others, he never forgot the duty he
owed to his Maker and his fellow-men, in opposing associations when they acted as if they overlooked sound
principles, and in laboring with men of any class who
appeared to keep them in view. The cause of good

morals and uncorrupted Christianity, requires that in delineating the character of an eminent and successful moral reformer, it should be made to appear that his zeal was accompanied with knowledge, that he had good ground for his opposition to prevailing delinquencies, that he did not spend his strength or his property for naught.

It was not however wholly as an opposer of wrong that Mr. Tappan devoted his energies and money. He also advocated THE RIGHT. He aimed to build up good institutions, while he strove against those that conducted their affairs, as he believed, to the injury of his fellow-men, and the dishonor of Christ.

Had the narrative been prepared solely for the relatives and near friends, a considerable portion of what is said might with propriety have been omitted, but in a portraiture of the man for other persons, his views of reform constitute an important part of the delineation. It has not been the object of the compiler to prepare a popular, so much as a faithful narrative. His desire has been to do good rather than to please fastidious readers. Some of them will peruse a portion, while others, it may be, will read the whole.

An old friend of my brother, an officer of one of the societies, whose conservative policy he felt bound to censure, after a general examination of the narrative says: "I took up the memoir of *Arthur Tappan*, (name ever dear to me,) and . . . . I am *very glad you have prepared it*. It seems to me a truthful, *bona fide* record; and though perhaps in some parts it is too long and minute, I cannot doubt that it will circulate widely and be highly valued, and do great good. . . . . I suspect that, just as the manuscript now stands, most of the readers will fail to see the kindness and true loveliness of his character

as you and I know it to have been; but while I hint
this, I would leave all to your own judgment and discretion. . . . .

"You certainly wish to say many things of Mr.
Arthur Tappan (as you have said in the memoir) for
which our Society would not be the appropriate pub-
lisher. Many such things it would be appropriate and
doubtless desirable that you should say. . . . . Personally I am not displeased with any thing I saw in the
manuscript, and I thought from your standpoint, you
treated the subject certainly without intending to dis-
please those called more conservative."

In copying for the press, the suggestion contained in
the above has been borne in mind. Without any pre-
tension to literary excellence, the compiler has aimed to
make a truthful sketch, with such inferences as naturally flowed from the subject, in honor of a beloved
brother with whom he was intimate from childhood; in
honor of the cause of philanthropy and religion so dear
to his heart; and in honor of Him who raised up, sustained, and blessed him.

I commend the work to the considerate judgment of
all parties interested in the subject of it; and especially
do I implore upon it the Divine benediction.

                                LEWIS TAPPAN.

No. 218 Degbaw-street,
Brooklyn, N. Y., May 22, 1870.

SKETCH

OF THE

LIFE OF ARTHUR TAPPAN.

I.

ARTHUR TAPPAN was born at Northampton, Mas-
sachusetts, May 22, 1786. His father was BENJAMIN
TAPPAN, and his mother's maiden name was SARAH
HOMES.*

Benjamin Tappan carried on the business of a
gold and silversmith, in Northampton, for twenty
years, when he relinquished it to engage in the dry-
goods business, first under the firm of Tappan &
Fowle, and afterwards as Tappan & Whitney. It
was honorable to him, as it is a matter of just pride
to his children, that while all the country merchants
in the place, at that period, sold spirituous liquors,
he always refrained from selling such articles.

The seventh child, who was also the fifth son, of
Mr. and Mrs. Tappan, was Arthur, the subject of
this memoir. His childhood and early boyhood

---

* For genealogical notices see Appendix 1.

were passed in a village distinguished for its many privileges and also for its beautiful scenery.

His father was a man of medium size, of uncommonly fair skin; his head was early gray, somewhat bald, with a long queue and powdered hair. He was a man of sound evangelical principles, attentive to religious duties, holding the clergy in much respect, never forgetting that he was the son of a minister. He loved good men, good preaching, and good books; and was a constant attendant upon public worship. An amusing anecdote respecting this trait was told. One of his townsmen, on coming from the morning service, Sabbath noon, told his wife that neighbor Tappan was dead! The good woman expressed great surprise and concern, as she was an intimate friend of Mrs. Tappan. Seeing her distress her husband said, "I suppose he is dead, for he was not at church." The fact was, Mr. Tappan had returned from a journey on Saturday night, much fatigued, and remained at home the next forenoon.

He was also scrupulous about attending the week-day sacramental lecture, and would lock the door of his store, if no member of his family was present to "'tend shop" in his absence. He enjoyed social intercourse with neighbors and friends, knew all the ministers and good people in the neighboring towns, and met them with cordiality. He was also fond of telling and hearing good stories, but never used profane or indelicate language; and his hearty laugh evinced the pleasure he took in the wit of others, as well as his own. He was not severe with his children, but required strict obedience, and did not spare the rod when he deemed it necessary, and especially when complaints were made of their ill-conduct by their mother. He had great respect for her judgment, and sometimes reminded his children of the gratitude they ought to feel for having so good a mother.

He was very fond of visiting, in a social way, in which respect he was different from his wife, who loved home, and the society of her husband and children. Still, she would put aside her knitting whenever there was an urgent request: "Come, come, wife, let us step over to neighbor so-and-so, and see how they are."

It was the custom, in those days, more than it is now, among refined and cultivated men, to indulge in smoking and in the use of spirituous liquors. He never fell into these useless and pernicious habits, and neither brandy nor kindred drinks were ever seen on his table. At one time he had for a guest a young minister from a neighboring town, who, in the morning, took a flask of bitters from his pocket, saying, "Friend Tappan, if you will furnish me with some water I will prepare a drink for us before breakfast." The surprise and grief that he expressed at this request produced such an impression upon the young preacher, that, in after-life, he reminded the faithful reprover of the incident, and said: "I gave up that bad practice, immediately on hearing your kind and Christian expostulation." That cler-

gyman, during his life, had the training of more
than fifty young ministers, including seven or
eight foreign missionaries, on whom he faithfully
inculcated strict temperance principles. "A word
fitly spoken is like apples of gold in pictures of
silver."

A granddaughter, who lived many years in the
family, and contributed greatly to their comfort,
says: "The time I spent with my beloved grandparents was to me a rich privilege. I was with them
when they died. They were both dead on the Sabbath, and both were left in the house, with no guard
but the blessed angels, while the family attended
public worship. I should not have thought of leaving grandfather in that way if he had not chosen to
do the same when grandmother died. He remarked that if we ever needed the consolations of the
sanctuary it was in the time of affliction. Grandfather loved the Bible, and I think it was his practice
to read in it about two hours each day. After he
was eighty years of age he was requested to teach
a Bible-class in the Sunday-school, and declined on
account of deafness."

While Arthur reverenced his father, he had the
most affectionate regard for his mother, as did all
her children. In person she was small, with a fine
head of dark-brown hair, which in her youth nearly
reached to the ground, and which even in old age
was unmixed with any gray locks. Her eyes were
hazel, her complexion fair, her skin soft and un-
wrinkled to the end of her days. The preaching of

Whitefield in Boston, during her early years, was often the subject of conversation with her children. The discourses of that eminent man, together with some remarkable providences of God in sparing her life on several occasions when in imminent danger, made a strong impression on her feelings, and resulted in her conversion. Led by the Holy Spirit, as she often said, she united with the Old South church in Boston, when she was about twenty-one years of age. She maintained a consistent walk and conversation during her entire pilgrimage.

Her seriousness was not of a gloomy cast. She was affectionate, sweet-tempered, and yet resolute and determined when such qualities were called for. It was her endeavor to gratify her children so far as would be for their good; but it was her especial desire to be faithful to their souls. She was indeed a living example of piety, her unconscious influence shedding light upon the whole household, while valuable instruction was ever falling from her lips. As a remarkable evidence of her respect for public worship, and of her cheerful submission to the divine will even under the most afflicting circumstances, it may be mentioned that on the Lord's day when her beloved daughter had been found dead in her bed that morning, she attended church, both services. To one who afterwards expressed surprise at her doing this, she said: "I could never have done it, if I had not been so raised above self by the overwhelming sense of the happiness of my dear departed child. My first thought when I saw her dead

body was, 'Oh, what a beautiful morning this is to
her,' and this went with me all day."

Arthur's mother, though small in stature, and
quiet in disposition, evinced, when the occasion called it forth, uncommon nerve and resolution. She
was awakened one night by a noise in the sitting-
room, and supposing some one had broken into the
house for burglarious purposes, she arose and con-
fronted the supposed housebreaker, when she found
that he was only a member of the family who had
come home at a late hour.

When the British army, under the command of
General Burgoyne, had entered the state of New
York, menacing the whole country, and men were
called from Massachusetts to repair to Saratoga to
oppose him, her husband among the number, she
was seen buckling on his knapsack and other accou-
trements, and was heard to say, "Hurry off, my
husband; I'm afraid you will be too late."

The child of such parents, it would be strange
indeed if something of their firmness as well as
genial and devout character had not been impressed
upon their son, the subject of this narrative. They
watched over his childhood and youth with tender
and prayerful solicitude, and both lived to see him,
in mature life, an exemplary Christian, a successful
merchant, a man well-known and greatly respected
as a liberal benefactor to benevolent and religious
objects.

Arthur was small in size, of a rather delicate
constitution, and serious minded. He was not averse

to play, but was of a more industrious habit and thoughtful disposition than most boys. From the age of five to fifteen he attended the school in the centre of the town, under the *discipline*, if not instruction, of perhaps a dozen schoolmasters, who were hired by the selectmen of the town by the quarter or year. The sons of farmers and other laboring men generally attended school during the winter months, and the sons of professional men and tradesmen throughout the year.

These schoolmasters were sometimes educated men, often very young and inexperienced, and generally persons whose attainments did not go beyond the most common branches of arithmetic, grammar, and geography. They had no blackboards, maps, or globes, or steel pens! And as the number of scholars was very large, and many quite unruly, the time of the master was occupied to a great extent, in making pens, and feruling or birching the disorderly. The large schoolroom was imperfectly warmed; compared with schoolrooms at the present day, it was more like a prison than a schoolhouse. About once a quarter the minister visited the school, and heard the boys say the catechism.

Arthur was diligent and painstaking in study, and well-behaved. He had the good fortune to escape much chastisement, either at home, or in school. Out of school, he delighted in play, in nutting and swimming. He also did his share of making hay, picking apples, working in the garden, driving the cows to pasture, and such labors as were required of the sons of mechanics and country merchants if they owned, as his father did, fifteen to twenty acres of land in a homestead, orchards, and pastures.

On more than one occasion his earthly career seemed to be near its termination. Once, when quite an infant, owing to some carelessness, the press-bedstead in the sitting-room in which he had been laid to sleep, was turned up by some one who did not know that a little child was in the bed. Soon after the mother or nurse came into the room, and exclaimed, "Where is the baby?" The bedstead was let down, and the almost smothered child was carried out into the open air, where, under a good Providence, the breeze revived him.

At another time, when a small boy, he and other lads in the neighborhood went to the "raising" of a new dwelling-house near by. According to the custom of those days the owner of the frame provided the town's people who assembled on the occasion, with pails of rum and water. At the conclusion the boys scraped up and swallowed the sugar and rum that remained in the pails. The consequence was, some of them became tipsy. Little Arthur was one of the unfortunate ones, and on reaching home fell prostrate on the floor of the shed. His father, in quest of some wood for the next morning's fire, saw what appeared to him in the darkness of the evening to be a log, was arrested by the groan or motion of his son, and was thus spared the horror of striking the axe into his head! At another time, when Arthur was about ten years of age, he undertook to skate from the ferry at Northampton to the lower ferry at Hadley, about a mile on the Connecticut river, when, on nearing the shore, the ice gave way, and he came near losing his life.

His mother related to her children, that during her childhood and youth she had several escapes from death, once in falling from a chamber window to a paved yard, and she thought that if people would record all the wonderful interpositions of Providence in preserving life, it would astonish them, and lead them to exercise more gratitude to God.

In view of such remarkable preservations she often repeated to Arthur and her other children, among the many beautiful hymns she had treasured up in her memory, one, from her favorite author, Dr. Watts, that reminded her of her own thoughtlessness when a child and youth, with admiring wonder at the grace that had spared her life, and pardoned her sins, and given her so good hope, nay a certain assurance, of a blessed immortality. Her children never forgot the deep emotion, with which she would acknowledge her neglect of religion; and the impressiveness with which she would recite the hymn alluded to:

"How sweet and awful is the place,
  With Christ within the doors;
While everlasting-love displays
  The choicest of her stores!

"While all our hearts, and all our songs,
  Join to admire the feast,
Each of us cries, with thankful tongues—
  'Lord, why was I a guest?

"'Why was I made to hear thy voice,
    And enter while there's room,
When thousands make a wretched choice,
    And rather starve than come?'

"'Twas the same love that spread the feast,
    That sweetly drew us in ;
Else we had still refused to taste,
    And perished in our sin.

"Pity the nations, O our God!
    Constrain the earth to come;
Send thy victorious word abroad,
    And bring the strangers home."

He remembered all his days the hymns his mother taught him, and particularly the beautiful one written by Addison, which he learned at her knee :

"When all thy mercies, O my God," etc.

He often repeated it. On his bed of death it was sweet to his memory, and most appropriately was it incorporated into the funeral service.

Sunday, in the last century, was a somewhat tedious, if not gloomy day, especially to children. From Saturday at sundown, to Sunday at sundown, they were kept indoors, except when they went to and from church. They were forbidden to play, or make any noise, and had very few books to read, while the small number in the "bookcase" were ill adapted to the taste and capacity of young persons. In religious families, and probably in most of the families, the children were required to remember and recite the texts, and commit to memory a hymn or two, and portions of the "Westminster Assembly's Catechism." This was the invariable Sabbath-day lesson. Forming a semi-circle around the armchair of their father, Arthur and the rest of the children, with "the girl," recited the hymns and catechism.

There was one practice in the family that redeemed the Sabbath from its austerity, at least for a time. At the conclusion of the "catechising" a nice applepie was the reward for study and good behavior, but the mother so managed as seldom to exclude any child from participating in the treat. Which of the children will ever forget that oblong tin pan, with the luscious pie, particularly those who were fortunate enough to get the corner piece! This portion often fell to the faithful girl, Polly, whose diligent study, and retentive memory, usually gave her the post of honor among the catechumens.

There was no Sunday-school at that time, and parents had not acquired the art of making the Lord's day pleasant and profitable to their children. It is probably even now, a problem difficult of solution, how to keep the fourth commandment—"Remember the Sabbath-day, to keep it holy"—aright, with sufficient license for the exuberant spirits of the young. It may be that too many parents devolve upon Sunday-school teachers the chief government and instruction of their children, instead of teaching them "in the house and by the way" themselves, as their companions when they are not in the Sunday-school. Our forefathers, we think, were overstrict, so as to make religion distasteful to the young. It was probably so. But is there not danger on the other side, in giving a loose rein, and not sufficiently restraining and guiding the young? May God help parents in the arduous work of training up children in the way they should go!

Mr. Tappan had one rule that delighted his children ; he would never whip them on the Lord's day! On the contrary, if he had a supply of the good "Seek-no-further," as he often had, he would take out some of the apples from the bottom of the old clock, and divide them among the children. The mother thought in her advanced age, and acknowledged that rather too tight a rein had been held in family government. "If," said she, " I were to live my life over again, I would allow my children greater indulgence on the Lord's day, especially when I recollect how few interesting books they had to entertain them. I would not confine them to books of a strictly religious character, but allow them to read good moral publications adapted to their capacities."

Sunday evening, as might have been expected after such dilatory hours, was the gayest and most noisy of the whole week. The children were impatient to have the Sabbath over. They might well say, "O sun! I hate thy beams." Watching the declining sun, and seeing who could the soonest exclaim, "The sun is set," the moment the last rays ceased to shine upon the chest of drawers in the kitchen, they would rush out of doors, and, together with all the boys in the neighborhood make the *welkin* ring with their yells and noisy merriment. Strangers in town, who had been accustomed to consider Sunday evening part of the Sabbath, were astonished at this apparent irreverence of sacred time. While some of the boys were trundling hoops, or shouting in the streets, others with their sisters had hilarious times in the house, while the mothers were engaged in sewing or knitting, and the fathers, too many of them, were at the public houses, discussing the news or indulging themselves in smoking and drinking.

The native place of Arthur Tappan was the shire town of a large county, now divided into three counties, Hampshire, Hampden, and Franklin. There were semi-annual sessions of the court of common pleas, and of the supreme court; and both the civil and criminal courts were full of business. The five judges, who composed each court, would walk from their lodgings in platoon form, with cocked hats and powdered hair, preceded by the high sheriff, with his half-uniform, his sword and staff, while the bell was rung until the judges entered the courthouse. Meantime the lawyers would be flocking from all quarters carrying their briefs in green satchels, with their law-books under their arms. August sight!

Saturday was the day for the infliction of punishment upon the the poor wretches who had been convicted and sentenced. A gallows was erected in the public street in front of the schoolhouse, and used for a pillory and whipping post. The prisoners were brought from the prison by the jailer, assisted by the deputy sheriffs, while the high sheriff, often mounted on horseback, rode about the gallows and among the spectators, superintending the execution of the law. Meantime the boys were let out of school, it being considered proper that the rising generation should, for their warning, see, in the punishment to be inflicted, that "every transgression and disobedience received a just recompense of reward."

Some were set in the pillory an hour, some were whipped forty stripes save one, or a less number, on the bare back; others, convicted of manslaughter, were branded M in their foreheads with a hot iron; others had their ears cropped, or were seated upon the gallows an hour with ropes about their necks. Such barbarous punishments were inflicted upon convicted felons in all the shire towns of the commonwealth, until a more enlightened public sentiment induced the Legislature to abolish them, and substitute the penitentiary for the whipping post, the pillory, the knife, and the branding iron.

The effect produced on the boys was very different from the calculations of their fathers. The public exhibition being over, they would assemble in the rear of the schoolhouse, and inflict upon each other an imitation of the punishments they had just witnessed. Arthur was not a boy to take part in such cruelties, but it is not amiss to describe the scenes of which he was a witness. He believed in after-life, that some improvements had been made in society, that men in general were less sanguinary than heretofore, but he considered that the term "penitentiary" was rendered by savage usages in stateprisons, a misnomer, suggesting any thing but penitence or reformation.

One of the most cruel usages of that day was the incarceration of debtors. Not a few honest and worthy, but unfortunate men were shut up in the common jails of the country by merciless creditors simply because they were unable to pay their debts! Taken from their families, deprived of laboring for their support, constantly increasing instead of diminishing their indebtedness, and left to mourn in idleness, in company often with criminals, over their misfortunes and the distresses of their families, they suffered often more than felons who were imprisoned for their crimes. Arthur, with other boys, frequently saw respectable men thus cut off from society, gazing through the iron bars of their cells, in company with malefactors who had made war upon their fellow-men, and were justly receiving the due reward of their deeds. Happily for the country, the imprisonment of men guilty only of inability to pay their debts was, after a severe and protracted struggle, done away.

Some one has said that children ought to live in the country until they are at least twelve years old. It was well for Arthur Tappan that he had the advantages of birth and early life in a country village. Had he been reared in a city he might not have lived to adult years. The wholesome air, the healthful recreations, and the customary employments of the country, conduced to the invigoration of his constitution, while the beautiful scenery improved his taste, invigorated his mind, and was a source of unmixed enjoyment. He had his full share of the frolics, amusements and occupations of boyhood. Simply clad, barefoot half of the year, roaming over hill and dale, swimming in warm weather, or sliding. down hill or sleighing or skating in the winter season, with the healthful exercise of climbing, trundling of the hoop, flying of the kite, ball playing, trout fishing, nutting, berrying, gardening, wood chopping, all these, and the numberless pastimes and employments that occupied his time, gave a charm to his youthful days, and laid the foundation of whatever hardiness of constitution, and general health he enjoyed in after years.

His parents indulged him, as they did his brothers, in permission to keep doves, squirrels, rabbits, chickens, and sometimes a dog, or a fox, and he was never known to treat them cruelly. His disposition was kind and humane, albeit, like other boys at that day, he gathered birds' eggs, and kept them in his chamber on strings, much to the discredit, as we now think of both the pilferers and their parents. There was in those days no kind-hearted Henry Bergh* to keep "watch and ward" over the animal kingdom.

It was a joyful time to the children when they were permitted to throw aside their stockings and shoes, and go barefoot during the summer months.

---

* President of the "American Society for the Prevention of Cruelty to Animals."

"When you can't see any snow on Mount Holyoke," their father used to say, "then you may leave your shoes off." The mountains, both Mount Holyoke and Mount Tom, were daily watched by the impatient boys, who fancied the snow was gone long before their parents did, and many little disputations took place whether that white appearance was snow or not.

Arthur's mother contrived to rear her ten children without much aid from the physician, who once said, "If there were ten such mothers in town I would move away." With Buchan's "Domestic Medicine," and pills made of a decoction of the bark of the butternut-tree, she managed to be the physician of the family, so that a doctor was seldom employed. The pills, made from the bark the boys were sent into the woods to gather, were a panacea for all childhood complaints. The nauseous medicine was hid in preserved quince, and in the presence of the sick child, the good mother seeming to forget the proverb: "Surely in vain the net is spread in the sight of any bird."

One of the wondrous sights of Arthur's boyhood was to see from the belfry of the meetinghouse, the great freshets that occasionally occurred in the spring. At such times the Connecticut river would overflow its banks, and submerge the meadows, thousand of acres appearing like a vast lake. These overflows enriched the grounds Nile-like, and were the cause of great excitement to the inhabitants, and exhilaration to the children.

As the water subsided the shad and salmon fish-ing-place on the banks of the Connecticut, in the meadow, attracted the boys; and as the nets were drawn to the shore the action of the fish in their attempts to escape greatly excited and amused them. The proportion of salmon to shad was very small, and the value of a pound of the former was equal to a full-sized one of the latter. Those scenes are unknown probably at the present day, when dams and factories prevent the fish from ascending the river.

The first death in the family was on October 30, 1793, when the youngest child of the family, little George, a mere infant, was taken away. Arthur was seven years old. He never forgot the solemn scenes; the christening, the death, the funeral, the long pro-cession, the grave, the lowering of the coffin, the heavy sound upon it, and the tolling of the dreadful bell, whose inscription was:

"I to the church the living call,
And to the grave do summon all."

But joys and sorrows are mingled, not only in the hearts of children, but of adults also. The same year was the first wedding he attended, that of a sis-ter very dear to him. The scenes attending it were also engraven upon his memory. After the cere-mony, the singing, the congratulations, the enter-tainment, a procession was formed according to pre-vailing custom, that moved from the dwelling of the bride, to the house of the bridegroom. Little Arthur brought up the rear with some boy or girl of his own age, while the two younger children could hardly be pacified to remain at home when all seemed to have gone away to enjoy themselves.

When a lad, his mother held up to him the example of his schoolmaster—one of the best he ever had—Mr. BANCROFT FOWLER, then in a law office, and subsequently a minister of the gospel in much estimation. Being somewhat intimate in the family, she had knowledge of a set of rules he had written down for his own guidance. One of them, "DARE TO BE SINGULAR," particularly pleased her, and she recommended it to her son as a valuable rule for him in the journey of life.

These items have an interest for young persons, at least, and especially for the descendants of him whose life is herein sketched. Wordsworth says:

"The child is father of the man."

And they may see, in the preceding narrative and what follows of the youth of Arthur Tappan, the germ of the man.

In after-life his native town was never forgotten. The scenes of his childhood were dear to him, and the companions of his youth were ever in his memory. He loved play, took a full share of the hilarities of his playmates, and cheerfully did his part of the small labors that devolved upon him. In his view there was never such a delightful place. Well might he say then:

"These were thy charms, sweet village! sports like these,
With sweet succession, taught e'en toil to please."

He retained all his days a peculiar love of the

country, and praised its streams, its trees, its flowers, its woods, its roads, its hills, its mountains, with
almost youthful delight; and he mourned that children reared in cities could not in their early years
have the enjoyments and healthy pursuits of a
country life. It seemed to him that Providence
had so ordered it that his life was to be spent chiefly in the city, and he submitted to the necessity, endeavoring to make the best of it, while his choice
would have been a rural residence.

II.

ARTHUR's brother John, five years older than himself, was a clerk in the wholesale importing store of
Sewall & Salisbury in Boston, and had made arrangements by which he was admitted as an appren-
tice, as clerks were then called, in the same establishment. It was in the spring of 1801, when he was
nearly fifteen years of age, that he left his father's
house, and, mounted on a horse belonging to one of
his employers, that had been kept during the winter
in the country, proceeded to Boston. His parents
had confidence in him, as they had trained him in
the way he should go, and confided in a covenant-
keeping God. His mother had said, "I never knew
him tell a lie." With their small means to give him
an outfit they might have said, "Silver and gold
have we none, but such as we have give we thee—
our benediction and prayers." When he was presented to Mr. Sewall at No. 16 Merchants' Row, near
Faneuil Hall, that gentleman, who was himself below the medium size, gave him a scrutinizing look,
and said, "You are smaller than I expected." The
fragile little fellow in aftertimes, on mentioning this
reception to one of his children, said, "I straight-
ened myself up and looked as tall as I could."

Boston was his mother's birthplace. At no great
distance from the store where he was to be employed, was the shop where his father had served his

2*

apprenticeship, just forty years before, with William
Homes, the "honest goldsmith," as he was called,
and the father of his future wife. Boston was a
small town then, containing about thirty thousand
inhabitants. His uncle Homes now occupied the
same shop, and also pursued the goldsmith business.

There were two departments in the store of Sewall
& Salisbury, the hardware and dry goods. Arthur
was placed in the former. His employers put him
to board in the family of Colonel Joseph May, whose
wife was a sister of Mr. Sewall. The young clerk
had the privilege of visiting in the family of Mr.
Sewall, and it was a privilege he highly valued. Often did he speak of the intelligence and amiability
of this family, of the affectionate intercourse between
the parents, and between them and their children.

In Col. May's family he had many advantages.
From daily intercourse with a man of so much practical wisdom, he doubtless received impressions that
were useful to him in subsequent life. It is said in
Freeman Hunt's "Sketches of Public Characters,"
that Col. May, having failed in business at the early
age of thirty-eight, gave up all his property, "even
to the ring on his finger, for the benefit of his creditors;" that "he resolved never to be a rich man,"
preferring to take a moderate salary as secretary of
of an insurance company, being there and elsewhere,
remarkable for his "love of order, his methodical
habits, and his high estimate of the importance of
punctuality."

For upwards of two years, young Tappan was in

the employment of the firm, and afterwards to the end of his minority, the clerk of their successors, Sewall, Salisbury & Co., his brother John having been received as a partner in 1803. They occupied the same store, and his board was paid by his employers from the first, while the perquisites of the store divided among the clerks, were sufficient for his other expenses. "My brother John," he once said, "was like a kind father to me. I attended evening school, and studied all my spare time. As the youngest clerk, I had to clean and fill twenty-four oil lamps in the store. Another boy, who afterwards became an eminent merchant, I used to meet trundling home goods in a wheelbarrow. I was troubled with a chronic headache, and when it was more severe than usual, and I was tired, I occasionally crept upon a shelf behind a pile of goods to rest my head and get a little sleep." He was subject to this headache daily, during his whole clerkship, and, indeed throughout his life; but although its effects were discernible in his countenance and manners, he seldom made any complaint, or even allusion to it. He strove hard, and with much success, to combat its influence on his nervous system, and his social intercourse.

Besides making himself master of the hardware business, he acquired a knowledge of dry goods, as opportunity offered, and also learned book-keeping by the Italian or double entry system, which was about that time introduced into the business-firms of Boston.

During the early part of his residence in Boston, he attended public worship on the Lord's day, there being no week-day services among Congregationalits, at the Old South church, where his parents and grandparents had been members. On the settlement of Rev. William E. Channing, as pastor of the Federal Street church and society, in the latter part of 1803, he attended there, sitting in his brother John's pew. Mr. Channing was considered at that time an evangelical minister, or something very near it. In the pulpit he was the "beau ideal" of the poet Cowper's preacher, and discoursed with earnestness and eloquence. In society he was greatly beloved, remarkable for his self-respect, and for maintaining the dignity of the ministerial office. His preaching, though afterwards considered deficient by evangelical people, in and out of the congregation, was characterized by fervor and seriousness. His favorite themes were the paternal character of God, and Jesus Christ as a moral and spiritual instructor. In his theological views he was an Arian. His youthful hearer, the subject of this narrative, ever acknowledged the interest he took in the preaching, and in the preacher. And his reverence and affection were revived and strengthened, when in afterlife, Dr. Channing took a decided part in the anti-slavery agitation, in favor of free speech, and the deliverance of the country from its chief curse, human bondage.

During the largest part of his minority he had the gratification of frequently visiting his sister, the wife of Rev. John Pierce of Brookline. It was his custom on such occasions, to walk from his residence in Boston to the parsonage, about five miles, on Sunday morning, and return in the same way at night. In that happy and hospitable family he spent many delightful days, and had the opportunity of hearing a large number of clergymen in their exchanges with the village pastor. He had also the privilege of occasionally visiting his uncle, Rev. Dr. David Tappan, professor of divinity in Harvard College at Cambridge, until his death, August 27, 1803.

Every year he had the opportunity of visiting his parents at Northampton, and at intervals of welcoming them in Boston. His father came to Boston once or twice a year to make his purchases of goods, and his mother sometimes accompanied him. At one time he went with his father to see his aged grandmother at Manchester, Mass., and greatly prized the opportunity of paying his respects to the venerable woman.

His mother wrote to him May 9, 1805: "I doubt not you are deeply affected with the situation in which your dear brother John has been placed. By an overruling providence God has returned him to his friends, laden with abundant experience of his great power and wonderful mercy." She alluded to the shipwreck.

He was passenger in the ship Jupiter, which sailed from London to New York, in the early part of 1805, with seventy-two passengers. On the sixth

of April, a great field of ice was seen, and before
night no way could be found through it. At mid-
night the first mate was so intoxicated that he fell
upon deck, and the captain being upon the bowsprit
looking out for the islands of ice, the ship struck an
iceberg, and began to fill very fast. The boats were
got out, and all but twenty-seven sprang into them.
But the boats could hold no more, and all the rest—
men, women and children—went down in the ship,
in less than an hour after she struck the ice.

One man and his wife and nine children, were
among those that were lost. Another man lost his
mother, brother, sisters and two nephews. One of
the passengers was a clergyman, who was emigra-
ting to the United States with some of the people
of his charge. As the yawl left the side of the ship
he was heard talking to his two little sons, with
whom he was walking the deck to and fro, saying,
"We shall soon be in heaven, dear children!" The
deck of the ship was then but a foot or two above
the water. John Tappan was providentially saved,
with forty-five others, one of them a babe but six
months old. He was in the yawl, which, together
with the long boat, was on the ocean, a thousand
miles from land, three days before they saw a vessel. They were taken up and brought safely to the
United States, having suffered somewhat by being
frozen.*

During Arthur's clerkship, his cousin, Robert
Homes, died in Boston. He was a merchant, and

---

* See "Memoir of Mrs. Sarah Tappan," p. 50.

died at an early age. Arthur attended the funeral.
Funerals at that time, and for several years afterwards, were usually conducted in this wise. The
relatives, acquaintances, neighbors, and other persons after assembling at the dwelling-house of the
deceased, and attending to the prayer offered by the
pastor, were treated with wine, carried about on
waiters. A list of the names of persons to walk in
the procession was meantime prepared. Neither
carriages nor hearses were used, but the mourners
and friends followed the bier that was borne on
men's shoulders. As their names were read off by
the conductor of the funeral ceremonies, they left
the house and formed a procession in couples, walking through the streets to the place of burial in the
town, as it was then called.

The list included, if practicable, all the persons
who attended the funeral obsequies, and it often
happened that a young man and maiden were called
off to walk together who had never seen each other
before. Solemn silence prevailed at the grave, and
when it was sodded over, the pall-bearers returned
to the former residence of the deceased with the relatives to receive refreshment of some sort, while the
rest of the company went to their several abodes.
It was customary for the gentleman to wait upon
the lady with whom he walked, to her abode; and
it not unusually occurred that the transient acquaintance of the parties terminated in a lasting friendship, "for better, for worse," that continued the
whole life.

There was living in Boston at this time, an old lady, Mrs. Abigail Waters, an aunt of Arthur's mother, being her mother's sister, nearly ninety years of age. She retained her faculties to a remarkable degree, attended the Old South church every Sabbath, enjoyed the calls and conversation of both old and young people, and occasionally went to little family parties. She had considerable wit; and her piety was beyond a question. It was entertaining to Arthur, her grand-nephew, to hear from the lips of this venerable woman of the youthful days of his parents and of their parents, and of Boston and its surroundings, in the early part of tho preceding century. This aged mother in Israel, though in unusual health for a person of her advanced age, used to speak of her departure with cheerful trust and confidence, as one about to set out on a pleasant journey. She said to one of her youthful visitors one morning, "I woke up last night and thought that I was dead, but when I found that I was not, I felt, oh, how sorry!" She died November 22, 1816, in the ninety-sixth year of her age. The last words uttered by her were—"Open to me the gates, that I may enter in!"*

For nearly seven years he was, as we have seen, in the service of the mercantile firms above mentioned. During the whole period he was distinguished for his industry, good habits, and exemplary devotion to the interests of his employers. He had

---

* See "Memoirs of the Life of Mrs. Abigail Waters," by Rev. Joshua Huntington, pastor of the Old South church, Boston.

but few associates out of the domestic circle, and
shunned all companionship with frivolous and vicious
persons. When not engaged in the store, he employed
his leisure in useful reading and study, or in healthy
recreation. His father had advised him to be out
in the open air as much as possible, and accustom
himself to walking and bathing frequently, as it
had been his practice in his youth. He did not
fail to comply with this advice, which well suited
his natural inclination.

His brother John has recently said of him : "He
was remarkably correct in conduct, he acquired
knowledge by digging hard for it, and though the
least sprightly, he was the most serious of the brothers." It is not intended that, at this time, he had
experienced the regenerating grace of God. The
instructions and prayers of his parents, and the
other religious teachings in his boyhood, though
they had some effect upon his conscience, had not
induced him to secure "the pearl of great price."
And the religious teachings during the after years
of his minority had influenced him to think a change
of heart was unnecessary, that a good moral character was about all that was required.

He aimed to be moral, and could probably say
with the young man in the gospel, as to his observance of the second table of the commandments,
"All these things have I kept from my youth up."
Without filial trust he felt an awe of the Almighty,
and might also have truly said of himself, as did
MILTON in his youth : "I again take God to witness

that, in all places where so many things are considered lawful, I lived sound and untouched from all
profligacy and vice; having this thought perpetually with me, that, though I might escape the eyes of
man, I certainly could not the eyes of God."*

He recoiled from vice and from vicious persons,
and no one, it is believed, ever heard him utter an
impure or profane word. He avoided also the
"secret sins," as well as "presumptuous transgressions" that too commonly assail and defile the
young, to the injury of both body and spirit. Abstaining from fleshly lusts and impurities, that "war
against the soul," he was remarkable for PURITY.
The advice of the poet to his youthful friend was
not unheeded by him :

> "The sacred lowe o' weel-plac'd love,
>   Luxuriantly indulge it ;
> But never tempt th' *ilicit rove*,
>   Tho' naething should divulge it :
> I wave the quantum o' the sin,
>   The hazard of concealing ;
> But och ! it hardens a' within,
>   And petrifies the feeling !"

It may be truly said that he had an *aversion* to
the besetting sins of youth, in the sense defined by
the Rev. Rowland Hill, the celebrated eccentric
preacher in London : "You ought to feel an AVER-
SION to sin," said he to a youth with whom he was
conversing.. "What do you mean by that?" inquired
the young man. "I mean," said Mr. Hill, "you

* See the "Account of Milton's Tour through France," in 1639,
after an absence of fifteen months.

should feel toward sin as you would if putting your hand into your pocket, you touched a toad?"*

* Mr. Tappan had the curiosity to hear Mr. Hill when in London, in 1810. The audience was large, and the minister full of animation. His erect figure, peculiar gesticulation, and forcible language were not soon to be forgotten. Neither was the occasional coarseness of his illustrations. The subject that evening was, "The superiority of the light of revelation over the light of nature."

III.

WHEN he was in his twenty-first year, he and his brother Lewis were drafted into the United States' service, as part of one hundred thousand militia ordered out by President Jefferson, in view of the possibility of a war with France. Only twenty-six soldiers were drafted from the eighth ward, which was one of the largest in Boston, and it seemed singular that the two brothers, out of the large number enrolled, were both drafted. They were accustomed to "train" in the militia company, composed of men between the ages of eighteen and forty-five, of the ward in which they boarded. The twenty-six, under the command of an ensign, were paraded at the foot of the Common, went through the manual exercise, were marched to and fro without music, and at length dismissed, to hold themselves in readiness whenever their services should be required! But they never were required, and the preposterous notion of mustering such a body of militia troops to defend the nation against a foreign country became a subject of derision, especially on the part of opponents of the national administration.

In the autumn of this year (1806) he visited Montreal, with a view to ascertain, by personal observation and inquiry, whether it would be a suitable place for him to commence business the ensuing year, as his employers had determined to set him up in trade, with another clerk, in testimony of their appreciation of their long and faithful services. In a letter to his sister, four years younger than himself, he gave an account of his journey, which at that day was a slow and tedious one. He described Montreal and its surroundings, mentioned persons he had known in his native town, who had become residents of that city, and spoke of the hospitality shown him by them, and those to whom he carried letters of recommendation. Though favorably impressed in many respects, he thought there was not much hazard, to use his own expression, "in predicting that Montreal would not be the place for him to settle in." Still he seemed to have an idea that he might, at some future time, take up his abode there, in the midst of the French and English population, as appears from another letter to the same sister, dated Boston, February 9, 1807, in which he says:

" . . . . . I have now commenced the study of the French language, and, that none of my time may be lost, I allow myself but five or six of the twenty-four hours for sleep. This I am told by those who are too indolent to imitate my example, will injure my health, but feeling no ill-effects from it, I have no reason to think it correct, but am more and more confirmed in the opinion that most people spend twice the time in sleep that is necessary."

The spring following, having arrived at the age of twenty-one, he made preparations to go into the dry goods importing business at Portland, in the "District of Maine," in Massachusetts, so-called as it had not then been admitted into the national union as a state. His partner was Henry D. Sewall, son of Chief Justice Sewall, and nephew of Mr. Joseph Sewall, his late employer. The new firm was Tappan & Sewall. A competent capital was furnished them by Sewall, Salisbury & Co., which was afterwards gratefully repaid with interest.

The following affectionate and faithful letter was written to him by his mother, after he had made one of his annual visits to his parents, at the termination of his clerkship, and when he was about commencing business at Portland.

NORTHAMPTON, June, 1807.

MY DEAR SON: I cannot feel willing you should leave me without saying more to you than I have; and, as I have not the opportunity to speak, I think best to write. Your happiness, as that of all my children, lies near my heart. I would not, on any account, give them unnecessary pain. It is your happiness I seek, and fain would I assist you in building it on a sure foundation. "*Other foundation can no man lay than that is laid*, which is Jesus Christ." 1 Cor. 3:11. Build on Christ Jesus, as the chief cornerstone.

I fear you have imbibed some errors, from what you dropped last night respecting the new birth. There are many loose writers, and it is to be feared, unsound preachers in our day. But the word of God is plain. He that runneth may read. Study it attentively, with sincere and fervent prayer for the outpouring of the Holy Spirit to enlighten your darkened understanding, and make your path of duty plain. God is a prayer-hearing God. He has not said to the seed of Jacob, seek my face in vain. The Bible is full of encouragement to those who diligently seek for true wisdom, and assures us that all her paths are peace, and her

ways pleasant; and, from forty years' experience, I can subscribe to the truth of it.

O taste and see that the Lord is gracious, full of compassion, not willing that any should perish.   Hear him say in
his word, "Turn ye, for why will ye die?   Seek, and ye shall
find; knock, and it shall be opened unto you; whosoever
will, let him come, and take the water of life freely, without
money and without price."   "Believe, and take the promised
rest."   Pray for an entire change of heart and pursuits; that
you may love God supremely, and place your chief happiness in obeying his precepts.   Hate sin sincerely, and strive
constantly to overcome every evil propensity; and this not
in your own strength, but relying on promised assistance
from Him who hath said, "My strength shall be made perfect in your weakness, and my grace is at all times sufficient
for you."   We have abundant reason to believe that if we
are sincere in seeking for mercy, we shall have God on our
side.   If God was not more willing to save us than we are
to be saved, he never would have given up his Son a ransom
for sinners, nor informed us of it in his word, nor sent the
Holy Spirit to convince us of sin, and urge us to repentance.

From my own experience I firmly believe the Calvinistic
doctrines to be Scriptural.   I would not willingly consent to
abrogate one of them.   I love to acknowledge myself nothing, that God may be all.   I feel that I am depraved in the
whole man; that in me naturally there is no good; that all
my sufficiency is of God; and it is my happiness that I may
go to him as a guilty, weak and helpless creature, and cast all
my cares upon him.   He has promised never to leave nor
forsake me, and I can trust his word.   It is this comfort, my
dear child, that I wish you to enjoy.   It is what the world
can neither give, nor deprive us of.   Oh, seek first the kingdom of God, and all other things shall be added unto you:
that is, you shall be fully satisfied with the allotments of
Providence; and how can it be otherwise if you believe the
promise, "that all things shall work together for good to
them who put their trust in him."   Therefore in all your
ways acknowledge him, and he will direct your paths; trust
not to your own understanding, it will deceive you. . . . . . .

That you may be made to see your lost, undone estate, by
nature and practice, and directed to rely wholly on the merits
of a glorious Saviour; that you may be filled with the divine
influences of the Holy Spirit, sanctifying and purifying your
nature, and live to the glory of God, is the sincere prayer of
your affectionate mother,   SARAH TAPPAN.

As was the custom in those days with young
merchants about to commence business, he and his
partner, before occupying their store in September,
1807, hired a horse and chaise to visit the different
towns in New Hampshire and Vermont, to inform
country merchants of their intentions, and solicit their
custom.   During their excursion they went to the
White hills, as the White mountains were then called, hired a guide, and ascended to the top of Mount
Washington, an exploit almost equal, at the time, to
an ascension of the Alps at the present day.   There
was then no road, and not much of a path, and the
ascent had been rarely made.   The pedestrians
were out two nights, losing themselves in a fog, but
being amply recompensed with a magnificent view
when the sun shone out.

After being in business about two months, he
wrote to his sister from Portland, under date of October 25, 1807, giving a brief description of the town,
and his boarding place, which, he says, "is at the
house of a merchant recently reduced to bankruptcy,
and now keeping boarders for a livelihood."   He
adds:

"When I behold such a picture, my mind recoils
at the view, and a resolution half escapes me, to
avoid the possibility of ever sharing a similar fate,

and beholding those who would be endeared to me by the most tender ties reduced with myself to struggle with misfortune. But should we reject a certain good from an apprehension of evil? Should we not brand that person as an idiot, who refuses to buy an estate because it would increase his cares and subject him to greater losses, when the possession would extend his means of benevolence, and enable him, by giving happiness to others, to enlarge the bounds of his own. No less is that person to be despised who denies himself the enjoyments of a family and the opportunities such a situation gives of doing good, from the cowardly apprehension of misfortunes which ten thousand chances to one, never happen. But what am I writing? You will, I believe, be no less puzzled than myself to answer this question, so wishing you success I am your most obedient and most affectionate brother,

"ARTHUR TAPPAN."

The following letters to his sister were written in the ensuing year.

POLAND, April 2, 1808.

After mentioning that an overture had been made to him to remove his business to Boston, which, after reflection both he and his partner had declined, he says:

" 'T is not so much on the place or the circle of acquaintance that our happiness rests, as on ourselves. A contented mind is a source of enjoyment within the reach of every person, and which it is our duty to possess. I do not mean that we should be satisfied with our mental acquirements, or advancement in piety, but with the dispensations of Providence. - The numerous sources of enjoyment which encircle every one, may be embittered or made productive only of misery, by an unhappy temper, while a firm reliance on God will promote a disposition to enjoy his bounties and sweeten every occurrence of life. Since, then, I can have little hope of again residing in Boston, it will be my study to know and appreciate the advantages of my present situation."

Being on a short visit at Boston he writes to his sister at Northampton, his views of the circus, especially its influence on young women, and then sarcastically says:

"BOSTON, May 14, 1808.

"But I know some who, *too little refined* to relish such amusements, have had the independence and good sense to resist the allurements of fashion, and form a just estimate of this ennobling entertainment! We seem fast progressing to that state of purity of manners and perfection of tastes which delight in exalted pursuits, and to that time when bull-baiting and other amusements *equally characteristic* of a polished age will be encouraged by the fashionable world. Fashion! Fashion! How much is society influenced by this little word; how few are able to resist its potency. To be wholly insensible to its power is perhaps not desirable, but those are surely to be pitied who allow its influence to predominate over nature and over reason."

After living at Portland about two years, they made up their minds that Montreal was probably a larger field for business, and therefore closed up their affairs, and opened a store in that city, with the hope of soon realizing a moderate fortune. In a community where so many of the inhabitants and people with whom he should transact business spoke the French language, he deemed it best to board in a French family. He derived both instruction and amusement while living in this way, but after a while thought it best to reside with his own countrymen.

The following letter was written to him by his father:

"NORTHAMPTON, Jan. 17, 1809.

MY DEAR SON: I received a letter from you dated the 15th of May, and since that time have heard from you by the way of Charles, in a letter he wrote at Walpole on his return from Canada. I hope that your goods have arrived before this time, that you may make it profitable to do business in that region.

I understand by a line from Lewis, that Charles is now on his way to make you another visit. I hope to hear from you by him, and to have news that will gladden the hearts of your parents. Your temporal, and especially eternal interest, will ever lie near our hearts, and we charge you, my dear son, to make religion your business, and to attend to the concerns of your soul without any delay. Seek the one thing needful, and choose that good part which shall never be taken away from you. Be not, my dear son, too much taken up with the world, and things that are seen and temporal, and neglect the more important concerns of another world. We are all hastening out of time into eternity, and must give a strict and impartial account of our own improvement of the day and means of grace. We are anxious for you, my son, lest, living among the profane and worldly, you lose any serious impressions you may have had heretofore, and live without God in the world. Your parents were sorry to have you leave Portland and go to Montreal, principally because of the want of religion there, and the abounding of wickedness among the inhabitants, the name and day of God openly profaned, or rather, as we hear, little or no regard paid to the Sabbath and the ordinances of the gospel. We know the depravity of the heart of man, and how prone we are to cast off fear and restrain prayer, even where religion is supported and countenanced. What then must be the danger of a youth who has no examples set before him but those that are bad, and is under no restraints but those of his own conscience. Temptations are always ready to assault the young, and unless restraining grace is given, they will be likely to fall into sin and perish.

Oh, my son, be upon your guard; shun as much as possible evil company; go not with the wicked and profane of either sex, but, if possible to find any such, associate with the virtuous and good, and make such your chosen companions and most intimate friends. Pray to God, my Son, both morning and evening, to sanctify you, and keep you from sin and all evil, to make you holy, that you may be happy. Live a life of religion; live above the world, and be not conformed to the maxims and practices of it, that are sinful and displeasing to a holy God, but abstain from the very appearance of evil. You have the prayers of your parents that God would preserve you to his kingdom.

Your friends here are all well.

　　　Your affectionate father,　　　BENJ. TAPPAN,

From Montreal he again wrote to his sister, October 30, 1809. After stating that he, with his partner and one or two other friends, had commenced housekeeping as bachelors, he says:

"But upon the whole I am happier in this sort of life than I was in a boarding-house. We take our turns in the care of the house, and have every thing arranged in the most systematic order. On

Sundays we deviate so much from the custom of the fashionable world in this city, as to attend church *twice;* and in the evening we call our little family together, closing it by reading a sermon. Thus, you see, I am in no danger of losing my good old New England habits."

The young merchants were so successful that they had the means of building a substantial stone warehouse on St. Paul-street, and were, as they fondly hoped, in a way speedily to make money enough to justify them in relinquishing their business in Canada, and returning to the States. The business was a general importing business of British goods, and they prosecuted it with an energy and devotedness that surprised their neighbors.

It was here that he met, for the first time, his future wife, Frances Antill. She was the daughter of Colonel Edward Antill, whose father of the same name came from England while a young man, settled in New Jersey, and married the daughter of Governor Morris of that state. The father of Miss Antill, after graduating at Columbia College, then King's College, pursued his law studies in New York city. In order to perfect himself in the French language, he visited Quebec, where his sister resided, intending to return to New York, fix his abode there, and open a law office. But having formed. the acquaintance of a young French lady, he was so attracted by her beauty that, notwithstanding she was a Roman-catholic, he married her. This was on the 4th of May, 1767. They settled in Montreal.

When hostilities commenced between England and the American colonies, Mr. Antill took the side of the Americans, received a commission of colonel, and joined the army, while his own brother served on the side of the British, with the rank of colonel.

Miss Antill was an orphan. While visiting her friends in Quebec, she frequently heard the two young men from New England ridiculed on account of their strict morality and careful deportment, so much in contrast with the gayety and freedom of the society around her. Her interest was aroused, and her acquaintance with one of them terminated in a life-long attachment. Upon her return to Oriskany, Oneida county, N. Y., the home of her sister and brother-in-law, Colonel and Mrs. Lansing, a correspondence was begun that ended in an engagement, and the parties were married in September, 1810, by the Rev. Dr. Carnahan, afterwards president of Princeton College, New Jersey.

Mr. Tappan embarked for England shortly after his marriage, to purchase goods for his firm in Montreal. In about two months his brother Lewis, of the firm of Tappan & Searle, Boston, joined him. The two brothers, who were engaged in similar pursuits, visited London and several manufacturing towns in England, making their principal abode in Manchester. As leisure afforded, they visited places of interest, seized every opportunity to acquaint themselves with men and things in the land of their fathers, and made purchases of books and prints for their future gratification and improvement. Early

in the ensuing spring, having completed their purchases and forwarded their goods to Liverpool, they
repaired there to ship the goods and embark for
their native land. But as delays of various kinds
occurred, and Arthur was impatient to return to the
United States, he left his business with his brother,
who shipped the goods of both, and embarked for
home a few weeks after.

On Arthur's return to Montreal, notwithstanding
the gloomy state of political affairs between the
United States and England, he did not anticipate
any serious interruption to his mercantile business.
On the contrary, he and his partner in trade anticipated a career of success, so auspiciously begun.

The following letters were written to his sister
Eliza during his residence in Montreal:

"MONTREAL, June 28, 1811. . . . . Although it is
now eleven at night, and I have just finished a hard
day's work at the store, I cannot miss the opportunity by Mr. D—— to inform you of our health.. . . .
I am at the store and constantly hurried from morning till ten and eleven at night."

Writing to his sister of the illness of his wife,
Montreal, March 10, 1812, he says: "The weather
is now fine, and we hope by riding out the fever will
be surmounted. I wish our dear mother was here.
She would be worth a thousand physicians."

Writing to the same, May 20, 1812, after descri-
bing his domestic happiness, and expressing a strong
desire that his sister would visit him, he says: "I
have written lately with considerable anxiety re-

specting the prospect of this country being made the
scene and theatre of war; but my fears are now
very much abated, as you will naturally conclude
from my urging you to visit us."

The affairs between the two countries became
more and more serious, until the Congress of the
United States issued a declaration of war against
Great Britain, in 1812, when an invasion of Canada
by the United States forces was threatened. The
two partners continued in Montreal, attending to
their embarrassed business. They had the mortifi-
cation to witness the United States soldiers, surrendered by General Hull, marched through the streets
of that city amid the derision of the people. As the
war advanced, the Canadian government required
all citizens of the United States living in Canada to
take the oath of allegiance to the king of England,
or to depart from the province. Several who were
engaged in trade at once took the oath, and some
went so far as to exult in the disaster that had
attended the American troops.

Tappan and Sewall refused to take the oath of
allegiance, and were therefore obliged to quit the
province rather summarily, and at a considerable
sacrifice of property. The firm was dissolved, and
the partners sought an asylum among their friends
in the States. Such goods as were not prohibited
by the order of Sir George Provost they brought
away with them. The bonds given to the United
States in this case were afterwards remitted by an
act of Congress. Subsequently they were able, after

great exertions, to take away the residue of their goods, and the bonds given for them were also remitted by the same authority. Still the losses were very severe, and the young merchants were greatly disappointed at having their business prostrated and themselves nearly ruined.

Soon after, he wrote to his sister:

"ALBANY, Sept. 6, 1812.

".... You want to know what my future plans are, and where I intend to fix my residence. I am about as much at a loss to give you a satisfactory reply, as I am to answer the inquiry that is sometimes put to me of, 'Where do you belong?' To this inquiry I generally say, 'I belong *where my wife happens to be at the time.*' My object in coming into the States was principally to look after the debts due to my firm. Had it not been for this, I should not have relinquished the joys of my own fireside to become a wanderer without a place I can call my home. As it is, I can form at present no settled plan. My debtors are very scattered, and they will take up much of my time. . . . . This town is most convenient for me on account of my business, and I may conclude to remove here for a time. I am to leave again to-morrow for Vernon, where I go to receive some more of my goods on their way from Canada. Those I have taken to New York are chiefly sold, and at prices to save me from loss."

After leaving Montreal he returned to Canada for a short time, to try to collect some claims. The firm had dealt largely in blankets for the Indians,

3*

and money was owing to them in several places.
He used afterwards to laugh heartily in relating
that he was arrested about this time as a spy, by a
British soldier, near the Canada line, whom he
allowed to take him to the commandant without
disclosing who he was. The commandant happened
to be an old friend of his, and exclaimed on seeing
him, "Mr. Tappan, how came you here?" The soldier walked away, quite crestfallen.

• His next letter states that he left his wife and
infant at Albany, in good health, where he expects
to reside with his family during the winter; and
adds:

"NEW YORK, Oct. 30, 1812.

"..... Alas! when shall I realize again those
heart-thrilling delights which spring from the possession of a home! When I reflect on the happiness I possessed a few months since in the bosom
of my own little family, where each morning and
evening we united in praising the bounteous Giver
of all our blessings, and felt our happiness increased
by the pleasing exercise, the contrast my present
situation presents spreads a melancholy over my feelings. But though this cruel war has made a sad
breach in my enjoyments, it has left me much to
be grateful for. It is not my disposition to ponder
on misfortunes past, or waste my life in ungrateful
anticipations of future ills. .... Could we view
these little changes as they are designed by Providence to weaken the ties that bind us to earth, they
would have a most salutary effect on our hearts."

IV.

AFTER a few months of restless inactivity, residing at Northampton, Albany and Boston, endeavoring to secure the property of the late firm in Canada, he proposed to his brother Lewis, who was then in the importing business in Boston, to furnish him with a moderate capital, with which he could commence at New York the importation of British drygoods. An agreement was made, and a store hired at No. 162 Pearl-street, the style of the firm being Arthur Tappan & Co.

The business was commenced soon after the treaty of peace with England in 1815. It was conducted successfully the first year; but in 1816 the importations so greatly exceeded the demand, and the country was so flooded with goods imported by American merchants or consigned by English manufacturers, that freshly imported cotton goods from England were sold by the package at thirty or more per cent. less than cost and charges. It was necessary for Arthur Tappan & Co. to sell their goods at any rate, in order to make remittances to their bankers in London, who had come under acceptances for them to the manufacturers. Mr. Tappan, therefore, finding it impossible to sell his goods at satisfactory prices, at private sale, and being anxious to fulfil his engagements abroad, disposed of a large part of them at auction, and remitted the proceeds to England.

To facilitate the sale of the remaining goods, the packages were broken up, and the "jobbing" business was begun, that is, selling by the piece. To do this more advantageously, Mr. Tappan quit the chambers he had occupied, and took another store, No. 120 Pearl-street, Hanover-square, on a lease of ten years, at a rent that appears very inconsiderable at the present day, namely, one thousand dollars per annum, in a situation deemed so eligible at that time. In order to be nearer to his place of business, he moved his residence to Gold-street, near Maiden-lane, a street now occupied solely by stores.

In August, 1817, he dissolved with his brother. The unfortunate result of the importing business had of course essentially lessened his means of prosecuting trade of any kind; yet, without loss of credit, he resolved on persevering, and if possible, building up a profitable establishment on the ruins of the previous one. With admirable courage he battled against adversity, living economically, and working laboriously early and late. For a time he associated with himself one or more clerks as partners; and on dissolving with them, he formed a partnership, in 1826, with Mr. Charles Keeler and Mr. Alfred Edwards, his nephew, the firm being as previously, Arthur Tappan & Co.

After changing from the package to piece sales, he changed also the kind of goods he dealt in. Manchester cotton goods were superseded by India and French goods. They were purchased in part at Boston, on the credit of his elder brother John, who, with his accustomed generosity, loaned both his money and credit. The business proved so successful, that in the course of two or three years the money was all repaid.

The business was a cash business, and the prices but a small percentage over the cost. As the business increased, other merchants in the trade marvelled how it could be carried on advantageously. The fact was, the goods were chiefly bought in packages on a credit of four or six months, and sold by the piece at about the bare cost, the profits being only equivalent to the interest on the amount of the sales until the expiration of the credit. The low prices attracted the attention of purchasers, and neighboring merchants predicted that this new kind of business would soon come to a termination.

One of them assured Mr. Tappan's brother that he was attempting a hazardous, and as he believed, a ruinous business; that he was selling his goods at the cost, and that he would find that the expenses would " eat him up." This was intimated to him; but the shrewd man smiled, kept his own counsel, and persevered. The business rapidly increased, and the small profit on the aggregate sales soon amounted to a large sum. The number of salesmen, few at first, were soon increased, and ere long the silk store of Arthur Tappan became known over the whole country, until the sales amounted to upwards of a million of dollars annually—an amount far short of what is sold at the present day by numerous dealers, but considered at that period extremely large.*

Prosperity did not seduce him into personal or family extravagances, or induce him to hoard riches. On the contrary, it led him to reflect seriously upon his obligations as a STEWARD of the Lord. His wife was already a member of an evangelical church, and her influence undoubtedly had a salutary effect on a husband who always manifested for her a warm attachment. They attended the Presbyterian church in Murray-street, of which Rev. JOHN M. MASON, D. D., was the minister. He was at the time a man of commanding talents, unrivalled eloquence, and extensive influence.

When about thirty years of age, Mr. Tappan united with Dr. Mason's church. He had never forgotten the instructions of pious parents while under their roof, nor the faithful counsel they had given him in their letters in subsequent years. He had been a child of prayer, and the strong faith evinced by his parents, especially by his mother,

---

* It would amuse the millionaires in trade, at the present time, to know what notions respecting trade prevailed half a century ago. A neighbor, Mr. A——, is said to have stepped into the store of the late Stephen Whitney, when the following dialogue took place : Mr. A—— : " What amount of goods do you think Arthur Tappan sold last year?" Mr. W—— : "I do n't know; but they do a large business, and I should not be surprised to learn that their sales amounted to four or five hundred thousand dollars." Mr. A—— : "You are right; their sales last year, it is said, were half a million of dollars." Mr. W—— replied : "Only think of that!"

made his conversion not an unexpected, although it
was a joyful event to her and his other Christian
friends. The mother's fervent prayers were answered.
What encouragement must she have derived from
the fulfilment of the divine promise, to pray for the
conversion of other children and grandchildren!
"The effectual fervent prayer of a righteous man
availeth much."

About this time he had the pleasure of welcoming to the city his youngest sister, with whom he
had corresponded at an earlier period, and for whom
he had much affection. She was married in 1817 to
ALEXANDER PHŒNIX of New York. The brother and
sister both anticipated much happiness as residents
of the same city, and during the brief period it
pleased God to spare her valuable life, the anticipation was fully realized. Her sudden death in 1819,
however, in her twenty-ninth year, blighted these
fond hopes. He found consolation in this bereavement where alone it can be found, in the character
and service of an Almighty helper and supporter.

Dr. Mason took notice of his activity and consecration of property at an early date. On looking at
a subscription paper, soon after Mr. Tappan had
united with his church, as his son Rev. Erskine
Mason afterwards related, he said: "That subscription of Arthur Tappan I regard as the best subscription on the paper, for it carries the heart with it,
and is a large sum in proportion to his ability."
After Dr. Mason's relinquishment of the pastoral
office, he was succeeded by Rev. Dr. Snodgrass,

upon whose ministry Mr. and Mrs. Tappan attended.
As his success in business increased, so did his giving to benevolent objects. It was his prayerful
inquiry: "Lord, what wilt thou have me to do?"
He resolved on consecrating a large portion of his
gains to the cause of the Redeemer, by engaging,
heart and purse, in the benevolent operations of the
day.

It was a marvel to many persons that a man who
appeared to be so enterprising in business, and so
bent on making money, should be so distinguished
for his benevolence; and one intimated that philanthropic deeds and money-making were at war with
each other. "If a man of business is also a philanthropist," said this person, "he is in danger, while
he is laying up treasure in heaven, of losing it on
earth." This was quite plausible; and yet Mr.
Tappan endeavored to unite the seemingly opposite
traits of being benevolent and yet energetic in
business.

He perceived the reason why there are no more
persons of enlarged philanthropy among men of
business, and why those who are benevolently disposed frequently act by fits and starts. He saw the
difficulties and temptations that influence men of this
class, and that too often lead them to vacillate, and
sometimes dissemble or betray a righteous cause.
He was aware also that some merchants who professed anti-slavery sentiments made cowardly com-
pliances in their intercourse with slaveholding customers; but he believed that the principal part of

those who avowed such convictions were made of
"sterner stuff," and maintained their principles even
if adherence to them lessened their gains. He honored such.

In his own case, his open avowal of anti-slavery
sentiments, and his steadfast maintenance of them,
saved him from losses he might, by a contrary
course, have incurred. There were rivals in his line
of business, who urged their claims upon Southern
patronage by alleging that. they were free from the
taint of abolitionism. Some of this class became
engulfed in embarrassment and even ruin on account
of attracting to their stores unprincipled Southern
traders. They thus found, to their disappointment
and dismay, that there is "no friendship in trade."
One or more of these firms that undertook to build
up their fortunes on the predicted ruins of Arthur
Tappan's business, suffered so much and so speedily by the *patronage* of the "Southrons," that they
were the subjects of derision even of men who "sold
their principles with their goods."

An old friend of his, now living, says: "I was
first associated with Arthur Tappan in 1820, in aiding the 'American Sunday-school Union' in establishing schools in the valley of the Mississippi. At
a public meeting in Masonic Hall, he gave five thousand dollars to the object." About the same time,
at the suggestion of Rev. JONAS KING, late missionary to Greece, he forwarded money for the establishment of a scholarship in the "Theological Seminary at Andover," as appears by the following:

UNION. N. J., BELLVILLE P. O., Sept. 15, 1855.

MR. J. L. TAYLOR:

DEAR SIR: I have yours of the 13th inst., and am happy to learn the scholarship established in the Andover Theological Seminary by me, through the intervention of my friend Jonas King, has been instrumental of good. It was given for the purpose of being applied in aid of needy and deserving young men seeking the gospel ministry; and my wish has been, and still is, that the income arising from the gift may continue to be so applied, in the absence of any nomination by me, by the trustees to one or more such students in your seminary as they shall designate.

I am very respectfully your obedient servant,

ARTHUR TAPPAN.

FOR THE NEW YORK OBSERVER.

NOTE FROM DR. JONAS KING.

In your paper I noticed an article with regard to the late Arthur Tappan, which reminded me of an act of benevolence performed by him about forty-five years ago, and known perhaps only by me, or some one who may have examined the books of the Treasurer of the Theological Seminary at Andover.

I took tea with him one evening at the time above mentioned, and in conversation I spoke of the establishment of a scholarship at Andover, which I considered of some importance.

Soon after this I left for Andover, where I was going to spend a year as resident licentiate, and in a few days I received from Mr. Tappan a letter enclosing a check or order from him for the payment of sixteen hundred dollars ($1,600) for the establishment of a scholarship as above mentioned. This I handed over to Mr. Farrar, the then treasurer of the seminary.

I suppose, of course, the money was applied to the object for which it was solicited by me and given by Mr. Tappan.

Yours truly,   JONAS KING.

He became an efficient member of the "American Bible Society," which had been formed in 1816;

subsequently of the "American Tract Society;" and in these and various other ways he aimed to be faithful, as a good steward of the LORD JESUS CHRIST, and to promote the cause of evangelical religion to the extent of his ability. The claims of foreign and domestic missions, of education, and of the poor, were near his heart, and he contributed to them, in labor and money, with cheerfulness and liberality.

From Gold-street he moved his residence to Whitehall-street. Here he lived very pleasantly three or four years, when he moved to No. 19 Broadway. After residing here about an equal time, he purchased the house No. 25 Beach-street, opposite St. John's Park, and took up his abode there. At the opposite side of the park, corner of Varick and Laight streets, was a Presbyterian church, of which Rev. Samuel H. Cox was pastor; and to this church Mr. and Mrs. Tappan transferred their membership. He had for a summer residence a hired house at Bloomingdale, on the bank of the North river, six miles from the City Hall, where his friend Pelatiah Perit afterwards resided. At another season, he occupied, during the summer months, a house on Love-lane, where his former pastor, Dr. Mason, had previously lived. This location was near the Bloomingdale-road, now an extension of Broadway. It was then a rural situation, and considered quite out in the country. During their residence on Love-lane, they attended the Presbyterian church on Bleecker-street, near Broadway; and they ever after felt a warm friendship for the pastor, Rev. Matthias Bruen.*

Writing to his eldest daughter, 30th August, 1826, after speaking of his intention to visit the Catskill mountains with his wife, he says:

".... I enclose a short letter received from your grandfather since you left us. You will see that your cousin Ann has been made the instrument in the hands of God of awakening great attention to religion at the place where Mr. Wilder now resides.† This will be interesting news for you to communicate to Mrs. Sexton, Mr. Wilder's sister. Your grandfather feels exceedingly anxious for his grandchildren, that the last prayers of your departed grandmother may be answered. These prayers, you know, were for the salvation of their precious souls. Since your grandmother's death, several of your cousins have experienced that change of heart which

* Mr. Bruen had a brilliant career as a scholar, philanthropist, and minister of the gospel, but was cut down by a short and distressing illness, September 6, 1829, aged 36 years. He studied with Dr. Mason, was ordained in London, passed six months in Paris, and was employed as a missionary in the city of New York. During his labors he collected the Bleecker-street congregation. The American Home Missionary Society, the Bible, the Sunday-school, the Tract, the Foreign Mission Societies engaged his efforts. He was the corresponding secretary of the General Union for Promoting the Observance of the Christian Sabbath, and died greatly beloved.

† The cousin alluded to was Ann Tappan, afterwards Mrs. Brewster, now deceased, the daughter of Arthur's brother William She was but fifteen years of age when, in Mr. Wilder's family at Ware, Mass., she exerted a happy influence among the young people of the village, during a revival, in leading them to the Saviour.

we are told in the word of God is absolutely necessary to salvation.*

"My beloved daughter, your parents feel a tender solicitude for your soul, and those of our other
dear children. It depends now on yourself whether
you will share in the blessing that your grandmother's last prayers were put up for, and which God
has so evidently shown he is ready to bestow. And
will you not accept the blessing? Shall God wait
to be gracious, and will you reject his offers of
mercy? If you are willing, go to your room and
tell God so, and plead with him that he will make
you still more willing. Plead earnestly, and depend
on it you will not be sent away empty.

"I am your affectionate father,

"A. TAPPAN."

During the most prosperous years of Mr. Tappan's life, he bought what he considered a more
permanent residence for his family. In 1828, he
purchased of Professor S. F. B. Morse, of telegraphic
celebrity, the house in New Haven, in Temple-street,
formerly occupied by the professor's father, Rev. Dr.
Jedediah Morse. There he had a house and garden
that greatly pleased him, and his family enjoyed
advantages they had not hitherto possessed. He
could visit them once a week at least, after the toil
of a week's labor in New York, and find some res-
pite from the turmoil of the mercantile metropolis.

* It is a remarkable fact, that within a year or two after the
death of Mrs. Sarah Tappan, upwards of twenty of her grandchildren were hopefully converted. Many of her grandchildren
had been converted previously.

V.

MR. TAPPAN imputed his success in trade to what was then somewhat of a novelty. "The secret of our success was this," he said. "I had but *one price*, and sold for cash or short credit." But it was also owing to another cause, which his modesty prevented him from stating. This was his RARE INTEGRITY. His customers had the fullest confidence that when they made purchases at his store, they would not be cheated by false weights, or measures, or fugitive colors. Every thing was what it was represented to be. Even those purchasers who disliked his opinions, and also those who professed to hate him and his philanthropic and religious character, highly prized the principles on which he conducted business, especially when they were the parties benefited. Even slaveholding merchants, who were in the constant practice of robbing their poor victims, were more than satisfied with the treatment they received at his hands.*

The confidence felt was so great, that merchants

---

* It was thought at that day, but not now, that it was a heavy and unjustifiable charge to bring against a slaveholder, that he robbed his "servants;" but if they had felt the force of what is said by the apostle James, they might have acknowledged its truthfulness: "Behold, the hire of the laborers who have reaped down your fields, WHICH IS OF YOU KEPT BACK BY FRAUD, crieth: and the cries of them which have reaped are entered into the ears of the Lord of Sabaoth." Jas. 5:4.

who visited the city to make their purchases, would frequently lay aside the goods they wanted, immediately on arriving in the city, with full confidence that if any article fell in price in the market, before they made up their assortment, a reduction would be made with or without their asking it. Merchants from distant places, who could not conveniently come to the city, some of them being unacquainted personally with Mr. Tappan, would send their orders for the goods they wanted—often considerable quantities—with entire confidence that they would be selected with care, and put at the lowest market price, the same as if they had been on the spot. This principle of trade may be in practice now, and probably is in some cases, but it was considered rare at the time, and Mr. Tappan enjoyed a large monopoly of it. The surprise is that it is not universal, as confidence is the life of trade, often supplying the place of a capital, and enabling a merchant to transact business with the best portion of dealers.

It is an old saying, "Honesty is the best policy." John Howe, a highly respected citizen of Boston, who amassed a fortune in the lumber business, used to say, "If there were no principle in the case, I would be honest from policy; it is the surest way to make money."*

The "one price" rule occasioned one day no little merriment in the store. The wife of an American gentleman, who had long resided in London, and

* Grandfather of Colonel Frank E. Howe of New York.

who was herself an American woman, being in
New York, thought it a good opportunity to supply herself with India crapes, then much in vogue.
After inquiring for the best place to make her
purchases she drove to the store of Arthur Tappan & Co., accompanied by her "secretary." She
had not been there long before one of the clerks
came in haste to the desk of one of the partners,
and said, "Will you come, sir, and see a lady who
insists upon having a reduction in the price of the
goods; she will take no denial; is making much disturbance, and insists upon seeing one of the partners." On his approaching, she said, in an excited
manner, "This clerk refuses to sell me these crapes
at the price I offer for them, and I have sent for you
to direct him."

The rule of the store was explained to her, as the
clerk had previously attempted, and the reason of
its adoption was given; but it was all to no purpose; she raised her voice, appeared very angry,
and said: "I came to this shop to lay out considerable money; I want some pieces of these goods for
myself, and some for my friends, Lady A——, the
Duchess B——, Lady C——, etc.; your clerk will
not oblige me, talks about a rule; I never heard of
such a rule in any London shop; there they let me
have goods at my own price. If I can't buy at
prices I think reasonable, I shall not come here to
purchase any more." Finding that neither the airs
she put on, nor her threats had succeeded, she quit
the premises, to the no small amusement of many

of the clerks and customers, who witnessed the scene.

Mr. Tappan felt in after-life, the injury that had resulted from his not pursuing the system he adopted when he commenced the jobbing business in Pearl-street, of selling only for cash, or short notes, as they were called, payable, with interest, at some bank. The general practice of merchants, at that day, the earnest solicitations of his customers, the temptations to sell at greater profits, and the apparent success of the credit system, influenced him to depart, by degrees, from the rule he had established, until his principal sales were made on credit. He conducted this credit business also disadvantageously, compared with neighbors in the same kind of business, for as he had but one price, and they generally had prices suited to the length of the credit given, he could not afford to take the risks of prolonged credits, as others did.

Had he rigidly adhered to the wise rule adopted at an early period, he would have saved himself great anxiety and perplexity, probably acquired in the end more property, and been able thus to extend the sphere of his usefulness by still more liberal benefactions. He saw this, when it was too late, and regretted it, and hoped others might profit by pursuing a different course.*

In the year 1821 Mr. Tappan made himself an honorary director of the "New York Evangelical Missionary Society." He also constituted himself a

* See Appendix 2, for facts in relation to the credit system.

4

member for life of the "Young Men's Missionary
Society of New York" in the same year; and in
1824 a member of the "United Domestic Missiona-
ary Society." In 1826 he made himself a director
for life of the "American Home Missionary Society,"
at its organization. He was also the auditor of the
Society from its beginning till 1839, thirteen years.

In the year 1824 he exerted himself on behalf of
the tract cause, giving his time and money freely.
In February, 1825, he was surprised by a call at his
store before sunrise. It was by Rev. William A.
Hallock from the New England Tract Society, proposing to form a National Tract Society in New
York. Meetings for prayer and consultation were
held. He gave $5,000 for that object, which was soon
increased to $20,000. The site of the present Tract
House, 150 Nassau-street, was bought, the corner-
stone laid May 11th, officers were chosen, he was
elected Chairman of the Finance Committee, and
devoted himself with undying ardor and success to
its best interests, as will further appear in subsequent
pages.

It has been already stated that after the formation of the "American Bible Society" he took a deep
interest in its success. Besides subscribing liberally
to its funds, he made himself and several of his
friends life directors, circulated many copies of the
Scriptures, and gave other substantial proofs of his
attachment to the cause.

In 1825, Mr. Tappan was a member of a committee of the managers "to devise and take meas-

ures to raise by subscription the requisite sum to
pay off the debt remaining due on the building of
the American Bible Society." It seems he declined
the election as a manager in that year on account
of other engagements, but being relieved, in some
measure, of the pressure of business, he was reëlect-
➤ ed in 1828, and accepted the trust. By the record
of the society it appears that on the 23d April, 1829,
a favorite plan of his was brought before the managers for supplying every family in the country with
a copy of the Bible, he having pledged himself that,
provided the board of managers should adopt a
resolution to recommend to the society at its then
approaching anniversary, "to supply every family in
the United States with a Bible, that may be willing
to buy or accept one," and the said resolution should
be adopted by the society, he would contribute
towards its accomplishment, the sum of $5,000.

His proposition appears to have been accepted,
for at the annual meeting of the American Bible
Society, in the following month, on motion of the
Rev. Dr. Milnor, seconded by Dr. Boyd, the following resolution was adopted:

Resolved, This society, with a reliance on Divine aid, will
endeavor to supply all the destitute families in the United
States with the Holy Scriptures, that may be willing to purchase or receive them, within the space of two years, provided
sufficient means be furnished by auxiliaries and benevolent
individuals in season to enable the board of managers to carry
this resolution into effect.

It does not appear that he kept any list of his
numerous gifts to benevolent objects. Neither was

he accustomed to talk about them. If he had seen them paraded in newspapers it would have disturbed him. He delighted in giving to good objects without solicitation, and felt a satisfaction in often anticipating the calls of the "Lord's collectors."

Yet he did not give to every object patronized by good men. The calls of this sort for his charitable consideration were very numerous; these visits sometimes annoying him by their length and unseasonableness.

.Occasionally the manœuvres of persons soliciting his aid called forth his reproofs, as in the case of a distinguished lawyer, who called upon him at his store to solicit a contribution set on foot by a brother, a celebrated doctor of divinity. Mr. Tappan did not seem disposed to comply with the request. The applicant became importunate, and said : "I want your *name* more than your money; be so kind as to head the subscription, and you will not be called upon for the money." Instead of being flattered by such a request, he made the proposer of it feel abashed for having intimated to him such a proposal. His manner, if not his words, said: "Is thy servant a dog, that he should do this thing?"

Among his benefactions were the following : 1. To the AUBURN THEOLOGICAL SEMINARY, New York, as appears by the farewell address to the graduating class of 1865, by Professor HOPKINS, who stated that "Mr. Tappan was the early friend of the seminary, donating it the sum of $15,000," which "at once set its wheels fully in motion, by enabling the trustees to secure the valuable services of its first professor in theology, the late Dr. Richards."

2. To the MILNOR PROFESSORSHIP in Kenyon College, Gambier, Ohio. From statements made incidentally by Bishop CHASE, at different times, it appears that Arthur Tappan of New York, originated the movement by offering $1,000, provided $10,000 should be subscribed. Bishop Chase contributed $1,000, but who made up the balance cannot now be ascertained.

3. THE YALE COLLEGE FUND. Dr. Bacon, in his sermon on the death of Arthur Tappan, says: "And when it appeared that the young men, aided by that society [American Education Society] were hindered from coming to Yale College, because there was at that time no funds, as at other colleges, for the payment of their tuition-bills, he assumed, in 1828, the responsibility of paying for the tuition of all beneficiaries here, till the number should be more than a hundred." Allusion is made to this, in an article in the "New York Observer," of August 16, 1828, as follows:

EXTRAORDINARY MUNIFICENCE.

It is understood that a benevolent individual has offered to pay the tuition, at Yale College, of one hundred indigent pious students, who are looking forward to the gospel ministry. The price of tuition being $33 a year, the offer is equivalent to $3,300 per annum, for four years. In consequence the directors of the Connecticut Branch of the American Education Society issued a circular.

The following note from the president of the college relates to the same subject:

YALE COLLEGE, August 28, 1833.

DEAR SIR: I take particular satisfaction in communicating the enclosed vote of our corporation, and in expressing my personal acknowledgments for the deep interest which you have in the most efficient manner manifested in the promotion of education upon Christian principles, and the important aid which you have given in time of difficulty and danger, to sustain the cause of piety and industry and order in the college.

May the blessing of heaven ever rest upon you, and on your unwearied efforts to advance the interests of truth and righteousness. With affectionate and high regard, your obedient servant,   JEREMIAH DAY.

ARTHUR TAPPAN, ESQ.

The following was the vote alluded to in the above note:

At a meeting of the president and fellows of Yale College, September 20, 1832:

Voted, That the thanks of this board be presented by the president to Arthur Tappan, for the generous provision which he has made for paying the tuition of more than twenty students in the present and preceding graduating classes, during the whole of their collegiate course, amounting in the whole to four thousand and forty-eight dollars.

A true copy of record taken by   JEREMIAH DAY.

4. AMERICAN EDUCATION SOCIETY. He took very great interest in Rev. Mr. Cornelius' efforts on behalf of this society, while he was secretary. He often conferred with him at his house, and had much correspondence with him. From letters to this devoted servant of Christ, written between 1827 and 1830, taken from the files of that society, and kindly furnished by its present secretary, Rev. Increase S. Tarbox, the following extracts are made:

"I have consulted Dr. Spring regarding the individuals named by you as speakers at the anniversary of the Education Society. . . . I hope the sum voted by the Presbyterian Society last evening, will encourage you a little. . . . . The Young Men's Society have their anniversary to night, and hope to get some money. . . . . If, with all your efforts at the east, to provide for the next quarterly payments, you are likely to fail, I hope you will let us know of it through the 'Recorder,' and I will try to get you something more from our society here. If you do not like to publish your necessities to the world, please let me know privately. You know the great interest I take in your labors. May God spare your health and prosper your efforts.

"Yours, very respectfully, and affectionately,

"ARTHUR TAPPAN.

"December 11, 1827."

On the fifth of March, 1828, he writes: " . . . . I perceive by your favor of the 24th ult., that God is trying your faith by obliging you to remain comparatively inactive. I sincerely regret the cause of this suspension of your active efforts, and hope your dear wife will soon be in the enjoyment of perfect health. Perhaps you will not regret having been prevented coming here at this moment, when you learn that money is so exceedingly scarce, and so much distress is consequently felt," etc.

On the 13th of March he refers to his former letter and writes more encouragingly: " . . . . . . It is more painful to me than I have words to express to contemplate any suspension in this and similar efforts when so much is to be done. I am happy to say, that there are indications that the pressure for money is subsiding. It is my present opinion that the first of April will be the most favorable moment for you to be here, and I would recommend that you make arrangements with that view. Still, I am sensible that you will not labor to so great advantage as you might at some other period. Every one will be influenced more or less in their feelings by the recent smart, which a scarcity of money has made all feel, and which will, I fear, have the effect to make people less liberal. The hearts of men are in the hands of Him who has promised to give the heathen to our Saviour for an inheritance; and abundant encouragement has been afforded the past year for us to believe that God is waiting to second and gloriously prosper every effort of his children for the advancement of the Redeemer's kingdom on the earth."

On the 28th of March he writes approvingly of the resolutions to be offered at the meeting in New York, that Mr. Cornelius had forwarded for his examination, and that of another friend. He also alluded to different gentlemen who had been proposed as speakers; to suitable places where the meeting might be held, and adds:

"The Executive Committee of the Presbyterian Education Society is called together .... We have no money in the treasury, and I see no way but borrowing to provide a considerable sum due in April to the beneficiaries under our care. I think we shall rather resort to borrowing than appeal to the public just on the eve (as we hope) of your coming here to present the subject, as any call, however insignificant, would be seized by some as an excuse, when applied to by you. . . .

"I learn with much concern from your letters, that Mrs. Cornelius is still feeble. If you will bring her with you, and leave her with us while you go South and West, Mrs. Tappan and myself will be happy to entertain her, and will do all we can to make her comfortable. What say you to this? Mrs. Tappan joins me in this invitation, and you know we never make empty professions. Cannot you dispose of your children in such a way that Mrs. Cornelius would be at ease about them? . . . I hope you intend to make an effort in this city this spring. Money is still scarce, though I think getting less so. It will be a bad year for merchants generally. This should not slacken, but induce greater efforts. May I suggest an affectionate remembrance to your dear wife? In Christian bonds, yours respectfully."

He writes again, October 24th, 1829: "Our mutual and truly valuable friend, Rev. Mr. Patton, wrote you yesterday, giving you advice of some interesting events that have transpired here. A great effort is evidently making to build up the *General Assembly Education Board*, and there is no little danger in my opinion, of the whole Presbyterian church deserting your society. I think you had better visit us soon, meet our board, and by arranging for some alterations in the constitution of your

4*

society, which appear to be advisable, prevent the
disaffection among our friends, which we are threatened with."

Being at Northampton, Mass., on a visit to his
aged father, he writes, January 20th, 1830, to Mr.
Cornelius, as follows: ".... I write now to recommend to your attention, and through you to your
board, Mr. Robert O. Dwight, now in this town, as
a suitable person to fill the office of treasurer. I
have entire confidence in his integrity, and believe
him fully competent to the business. If the board
shall think fit to appoint him, and he can be persuaded to accept, I will be his bondsman, provided it
is made the duty of the treasurer to deposit in bank
the money of the society, in the name of the society.
I suppose the bondsman would then only take the
risk of the integrity of the treasurer; and it is with
this view, and in the hope of doing a service to the
society, that I offer to be the bondsman."

Being at home in New York, he addressed the
following letter to Mr. Cornelius, which is inserted
at length:

To Mr. CORNELIUS.   NEW YORK, April 12, 1830.

REV. AND DEAR SIR: I have your much esteemed letter
by Rev. Mr. Peters, and have conferred with our brother
Patton on its contents. He is possessed of my views, and I
believe we are of one mind. I feel the importance of the
deliberations of your board at this eventful crisis, and would,
if I possibly could, accompany our delegation. I hope that
my not doing so will not convey the impression that I do not
attach vast importance to your removal to this city. You
know what has been said by a stanch friend to voluntary
associations about a congregational "probe." If you come

here, (let me repeat it,) it must be in *such a manner* as to take away all suspicion that you are not a thorough-going Presbyterian.   By enlarging the branch of the Presbyterian Society, the appearance of "letting down " may be avoided, at the same time the duties of the secretary of the branch will be increased, and those of your successor at Boston lessened.   I do not like the plan you suggest of forming a new society. Any important alterations in our organization will be likely to strengthen and extend the impression among those who wish us ill, that our past plans have not been founded in wisdom. They would take fresh courage from what would be construed into a defeat on our part.   As to permanent funds, we have none now, and we may avoid having any in future, if it is thought best.

I feel that it is asking much of our eastern brethen to propose to them to give you up, but they are accustomed to taking enlarged views of the interests of Zion, and will excuse us for calculating much on their disinterestedness.   I have all the feelings of an eastern man, and but little of the Presbyterian, except the name.   If I know my own heart, I have no *sectarian* or *sectional* feelings.   I wish only for that which shall result in the greatest good.   May God direct your deliberations, and then I know all will be for the best, whether the result is for you to come here or not.   If Providence should so order it as to fix your residence here, you will be welcomed by many, but by none with more sincerity than by Mrs. Tappan and myself.

He wrote to the same, April 29, 1830, of his application to the trustees of the Brick church, in which to hold the expected meeting and adds: "Mrs. Tappan and myself will expect you to come to our house, and we shall be disappointed if you do not. If Dr. Beecher comes with you, please say to him, we shall be happy to accommodate him also.   Dr. Edwards is with us, so that we can promise you some good company."

Both Mr. and Mrs. Tappan, it seems, were not negligent of the apostolic injunctions, "use hospitality," and "be not forgetful to entertain strangers."

On the 19th and 27th of October, 1830, he writes to Dr. Cornelius, (for it seems that some college had affixed D. D. to his honored name,) of his meeting with the executive committee, the appointment of agents, and sundry other matters of the new society, and concludes as follows: ". . . . . I regret that your society is embarrassed in its pecuniary concerns. If I had any voice in your committee, I would urge an entire liquidation of all your permanent funds—scholarship and all. Let all be expended, and by the time this is done, we may hope to see the self-educating system so far perfected as to make very little aid necessary for the young men. The consent of those who have given the money must of course be obtained, but sooner than have the millstone of permanent funds around the neck of the society, I would give back the money, if consent cannot be had to use it."

Dr. Cornelius had a ready wit, that was a valuable aid in his arduous labors, of which the following is a specimen: On a certain occasion, he entered Mr. Tappan's store and asked to see him. As he came in, another partner, who was not then personally acquainted with him, accosted him as a purchaser of goods, informing him that they had just received a large assortment of a particular article that he should be happy to show to him, etc. "Will

you just examine the goods, sir?"   "Why no, not
now," replied Mr. Cornelius, "I have come for the
proceeds."*

Mr. Tappan's letters to Dr. Cornelius are similar
to those he was accustomed to write to the actua-
ries of different benevolent societies from his little
recess near the centre of his store, with his bank
books, bills of purchases, and papers of various kinds
lying about his desk.   While customers doubtless
imagined that the silent person, standing or sitting
there, was wholly engrossed with his financial concerns, his purchases and payments and the oversight
of his large business, the prominent thoughts in his
mind were the sayings of his Master: "The field is
the world"—"Occupy till I come."

He managed in the midst of business, to have
considerable leisure, and it was his habit to have
no spare chair to offer to callers.   When a friend or
stranger honored him with a call, his practice was
to rise and receive him with much economy of
speech, and as no seat was at hand, the person,
whoever he was, soon took his departure from the
taciturn and busy merchant.   There were exceptions to this rule, however, and when one or more
venerable persons waited upon him, with affairs
they deemed very important, he would, if not par-

* Rev. Dr. Elias Cornelius died at Dr. Hawes', in Hartford,
Conn., on Sabbath morning, February 12, 1832, of brain fever,
"brought on probably by excessive care, toil, and labor."   His
age was only 37.   He was indeed a burning and shining light.
The memoir of Dr. Cornelius, by Rev. B. B. Edwards, was published in 1833.

ticularly engaged, have chairs brought for them,
and listen to their story.

Neither did he spend much time in eating and
drinking. A cracker and tumbler of water sufficed
for a luncheon. He ate to live, but did not live to
eat, being always very abstemious, as well from
principle as from regard to his invariable headache.

He took a deep interest in the settlement of
Rev. JOSEPH S. CHRISTMAS, over the Bowery Presbyterian church, in the city of New York, and cherished pleasing anticipations of the usefulness of this
youthful and popular preacher. Mr. Christmas had
been pastor of the American Presbyterian church in
Montreal, and removed to New York in expectation
that a change of climate would be beneficial to his
health. His new charge, however, soon experienced
a sad disappointment, as, after a ministry of only a
few months, he died at the age of 27, having been
seriously ill only three or four days.*

Like the youthful and celebrated Rev. THOMAS

* Mr. Christmas, in early life, had a passion for painting, to
which art he intended to devote his life; but, becoming religious,
he resolved to be occupied in more important and useful toils.
His father was very solicitous that he should be a physician, and
made all the arrangements for his entering upon the study of
physic. The son was constrained by a sense of religious duty to
disappoint the paternal hopes. He studied theology at Princeton,
and in 1824 went to Canada, where he was ordained to the gospel
ministry. Here he labored upwards of three years, when ill
health compelled him to ask a dismission. Soon after, he lost both
of his children, and, in a little time, his wife. "Oh, beware of
the world!" was her counsel. "How deeply am I convinced that
the worldly intercourse of professing Christians is utterly wrong!

SPENCER, of Liverpool, England, whose ministration attracted throngs of delighted hearers, when Mr. Tappan was in that town in 1810 and 1811, and whose sudden death soon after spread a gloom over the country, Mr. Christmas was the ornament and hope of the religious community. His premature death was a severe affliction to Mr. Tappan, and to many other attached friends and co-laborers, who felt the truth of the saying of Job: " *Thou destroyest the hope of man.*"

Mr. Tappan removed his church connection to the Bowery church on the principle of colonization, for of such colonization he was a sincere admirer; and he devoted to the cause of Christ in this destitute portion of the city his whole power.

A member of the church, in speaking of him, says: " My husband and myself both remember him when we were associated in the Bowery church; as 'full of faith and good works,' so that it could be said of him that in imitation of our divine Master and Lord, 'he went about doing good.' A few words from him, were more than volumes from some men, for, I presume, he never said anything that he did not mean."

After the death of Mr. Christmas, the congregation was somewhat divided in their preferences with regard to a successor. Unsuccessful efforts were made to secure the services of a suitable person, and

It cuts out the very heart of piety. Seek not the things which are your own, but things which are Jesus Christ's." This bereavement was perhaps the means of preparing him for heavenly bliss. See Allen's Biographical Dictionary.

at length a compromise resulted in the choice of
Rev. Dr. Woodbridge, of Hadley, Mass. He accepted the call, and performed the duties of pastor
several years. He was a strong-minded man, and
of a positive character, but he did not succeed in
building up the church.

Mr. Tappan, after attending public worship at
the Bowery church about a year, resumed his attendance at Laight-street church, with his family.
Here, as well as elsewhere, he engaged in distribu-
ting religious tracts, exploring the destitute portions
of the city for scholars for the Sunday-school, visiting prisoners, and endeavoring to allure the young
and their parents to church, and setting an example
of Sabbath-day work, congenial to his disposition,
and worthy of imitation.

The Education Society was one in which he took
a deep interest. He exerted himself in behalf of
beneficiaries, to recommend them to the patronage
of the society, and contributed to the fund for their
support. In 1807, he was chosen chairman of the
executive committee of the New York branch of
the "American Education Society." In May, 1831,
he was elected president, and filled that office, and
also that of chairman of the executive committee
until May, 1833, when he sent in his letter of resignation, as appears by the record of the executive
committee: "A letter was received from Mr. Arthur
Tappan, resigning his office of president, owing to
the removal of his residence from the city, without
the bounds of this society. The letter contained a

full expression of his affection for the society, and willingness still to aid its operations."

Rev. Dr. PATTON, who succeeded Dr. Cornelius as corresponding secretary, says, in a letter to the compiler:

"My memories of your brother Arthur Tappan are all pleasant. It was my privilege to work with him in many of the benevolent agencies to which he devoted so exemplarily his time and money. For a series of years, he was the chairman of the executive committee of the society for the education of pious young men for the gospel ministry. He was deeply interested in this cause, and was very punctual in his attendance at the monthly meetings. When the effort was made to have me relinquish my pastoral charge, and take the oversight and executive agency of the society, he promptly offered to pay half the salary for five years, and to make it sure he would give his five notes for $1,000 each, payable yearly. I do not think that his interest in the education of young men for the ministry ever flagged."

He was succeeded in the office of president of the Education Society by Hon. Theodore Frelinghuysen.

In the month of May, 1830, the free church plan was commenced in the city of New York. The success was very great. Six churches were successively formed. Large numbers of persons, who probably would not otherwise have attended public worship, were attracted to these churches;

and many were converted under the ministrations of the pastors, aided as they were by the active exertions of the officers and members. This system accorded with the views of Mr. Tappan, and received his support.

Having possession of Masonic hall, in Broadway, as lessee, he gave the use of it to the First Free church, in 1831, for the unexpired term of the lease, and endorsed the notes of the committee of the church for $5,400. And when it was contemplated to hire the Chatham-street theatre for ten years, to alter it for the use of the Second Free church, under the ministry of Rev. Charles G. Finney, he presided at a meeting of the friends of the enterprise. A subscription was begun, in aid of it, and Mr. Tappan contributed his share of the $8,000 secured.

VI.

EARLY in the year 1828, he invited his brother Lewis to be a second time associated with him in business. They continued partners until the year 1841, when the connection was amicably dissolved. This arrangement relieved him from the pressure of business, and enabled him to devote more time to philanthropic objects and occasional recreation.

Before it took place, however, he conceived the plan of establishing a new daily commercial paper, one that would exert a wholesome moral influence, abstaining particularly from publishing immoral advertisements. He included in the category those relating to spirituous liquors, circuses, and theatres. It was his desire also to demonstrate the feasibility of publishing a daily journal of a better class in every respect than the papers of the day, and especially one that would not infringe upon the Sabbath.

A new paper, styled the *Journal of Commerce,* was commenced, on his sole responsibility, September 1, 1827. It exists at the present day, owned by other proprietors, and with some change in its character. The first editor was William Maxwell, Esq., of Virginia, who had two or more assistants. The business department was conducted by Mr. David Hale, of Massachusetts, who had unlimited discretion with respect to the expenditure of money.

After nearly a year's trial, finding that he had expended upwards of thirty thousand dollars, and that the paper was not answering his expectations, he came to the resolution of abandoning the attempt. His brother then took it off his hands, and with the temporary aid of Mr. Horace Bushnell,* one of the assistant editors, and Mr. Hale, continued the publication, Mr. Maxwell retiring. An announcement was made of the principles upon which the paper would be conducted.†

An association was formed of a few early friends of the enterprise to carry on the paper until a permanent arrangement could be made. The actual property was inventoried, and the estimated value was credited to the new proprietor. The members of the association, of which Arthur Tappan was one, subscribed various sums, liable to be paid, *pro rata*, as the receipts fell short of the expenditures. Meantime, efforts were made to secure the services of a permanent editor, and to remove some misapprehensions existing in the public mind.

The daily press was unfriendly to the plan of starting a new paper, and it was felt that the avowed principles upon which it was to be conducted were a reflection upon the conductors of existing establishments. Many persons, not connected with them, doubted the feasibility of sustaining a daily paper as proposed, and not a few sneered at the attempt to effect a reformation in conducting papers already

---

* Now Rev. Dr. Bushnell, of Hartford, Conn.
† See Appendix 3, for further particulars.

existing. It was said too that the principles upon
which the new journal was ostensibly conducted
were not adhered to; that the business editor and
superintendent, Mr. Hale, did not refrain from labor
on the Sabbath, or the hours deemed sacred in New
York.

In order that the new proprietor could certify from
his own knowledge that, in regard to the Sabbath,
the day was not infringed upon by any work connected with the paper, he made it an invariable
practice to stand by and see the printing office and
editors' office closed at 12 o'clock every Saturday
night, and opened every Sunday night at the same
hour. This was done for four months, while the establishment was under his control. The paper made
its appearance punctually every Monday morning,
as on other days, and no subscriber was known to
complain that its delivery was delayed. The facts
became so generally known that the taunts subsided,
and what had been deemed impossible, was shown
to be a veritable fact.

The *New York Observer*, in noticing the accusations that had been made, put forth a defence of
Mr. Hale, previous to the change of proprietorship,
in an article ending as follows:

" The only *serious* charge which *we* bring against
the *Journal of Commerce* is, that it has not been sufficiently decided, or rather has not gone far enough,
in supporting good morals and exposing vice. That
it has been highly useful in this respect, we admit;
but we think it might have been more so. And

we are happy to state (which we do on the best authority) that such changes will be made at the close of the present year, as shall effectually secure this object. We shall then see whether the papers which now condemn it because it has been no more decisive in these matters, will, or will not, assume the opposite ground. We hope they will not. But as to the past we do not believe it was in the power of man to edit it in such a manner as to moet their approbation."*

After several ineffectual attempts to secure the services of a competent editor, towards the close of the year an agreement was made with Mr. Gerard Hallock and Mr. David Hale, by which they were to be editors and conductors of the paper, and to have two years, if they requested it, to determine whether they would be the purchasers of the establishment at the valuation made at the transfer with the addition of the sums paid by the members of the association. At the end of the time they agreed to become purchasers. The sums advanced by the members of the association, were returned to them, and six thousand dollars, the estimated value before mentioned, were paid to Mr. Arthur Tappan, which reduced his advance for establishing the paper to twenty-five thousand dollars.

The purchase was an advantageous one on the part of Hale and Hallock, as on the foundation laid by the original proprietor, a commercial paper was established of the first class. . The sale was satisfac-

---

* See *New York Observer* of August 23, 1828.

tory to all parties interested. The merchants, who, as proprietors, or members of the association, had devoted considerable time to the object, had secured, as they thought, its accomplishment, and were relieved from further responsibility, while those who succeeded them, by their unwearied diligence and enterprise, secured for themselves and their successors an ample fortune. It would have been very gratifying to Mr. Arthur Tappan, after expending so much in laying the foundation of an establishment that has been so profitable to those who succeeded him, if they had conducted the paper in support of, rather than opposed to, the anti-slavery sentiments he afterwards cherished, and had made it an auxiliary to the great plan of universal emancipation that has, under an overruling Providence, been so signally successful. But he rejoiced in all the good it accomplished.

In the following letter, addressed to his brother, thirty years after his connection with the *Journal of Commerce* had ceased, he gives the views he held at the establishment of the paper and subsequently:

"NEW HAVEN, Dec. 6, 1858.

". . . Mr. S—— has given me a newspaper containing a statement of what is called the origin of the *Journal of Commerce*, etc. As there are, in that publication, several erroneous assertions, I send the paper to you, that they may be corrected in an article addressed to the editors of the Journal, or otherwise.

"First. The fact that Hale and Hallock gave so

many thousands of dollars for the paper is sufficient evidence that it was not run down to so low an ebb as the writer represents.

"Second. The cause of its not succeeding better was not *abolition*, for that subject had not then been broached. It was the theatres, and particularly the indecent dancing there; and the desecration of the Sabbath, and the use of intoxicating drinks, that called the paper into existence. There was also a desire to have newspapers better printed. At that time most of them used ink that blackened the hands on handling them. And if papers were issued on Monday, most of the work was usually done on the Sabbath.

"The fact that the first editor was from Virginia is further proof that the slavery question was not a reason that the paper did not succeed better. We needed, in order to stem the torrent of opposition from other newspapers and their supporters, and from the supporters of theatres, Sabbath breaking and intemperance, an editor, or editors of true *Yankee grit*, who, when they attempt an enterprise that is practicable, always succeed. These were found in Hale and Hallock, from whom I do not desire to detract any of the merit they have so richly earned."

The SABBATH QUESTION, as it was called, attracted the attention of Christians at this time throughout the country. The desecration of the Lord's day was a just occasion of alarm, and Christians of different denominations were considering the subject, with an earnest desire to effect a reformation, especially with reference to the opening of postoffices, the transmission of the mails, and the various ways in which the fourth commandment was openly disobeyed in the community. In these efforts Mr. Tappan took a decided part, as appears by the following extract from the *New York Observer:*

THE SABBATH.

At an adjourned meeting of citizens of New York, held on the evening of April 19, 1828, to promote the better observance of the Sabbath, the undersigned were appointed a committee to make arrangements for a meeting of such delegates as have been or shall be appointed to meet in this city to take into consideration the subject of forming a general society for the promotion of this object. In pursuance of this appointment, we hereby invite a meeting to be held at the American Tract Society's house on Tuesday the sixth of May next, at four o'clock, P. M.

ARTHUR TAPPAN,
JOHN STEARNS,
JOHN NITCHIE,
D. M. REESE,
ELIJAH PIERSON.

A meeting was accordingly held. It was well attended by gentlemen from different parts of the country, and the proceedings were animated and harmonious. A constitution of a new society was formed, called "The General Union for Promoting the Observance of the Christian Sabbath." Article II. stated that "it should consist indiscriminately of the friends of morality and religion, of all denominations, who may choose to combine their influence for the promotion of this interesting object;" and Article III. averred that, "As the weapons of the Christian warfare are not carnal, but spiritual, the

5.

great means employed by this society for effecting their design, shall be the influence of personal example, of moral suasion, with arguments drawn from the oracles of God, from the existing laws of our country, appeals to the consciences and hearts of men, and fervent supplications to the Lord of the Sabbath."

Hon. STEPHEN VAN RENSSELAER was chosen president, Rev. M. BRUEN corresponding secretary, and ARTHUR TAPPAN treasurer, of the society.

At the first anniversary, May, 1829, at the Methodist church in John-street, New York, the corresponding secretary read the annual report of the executive committee, and several important resolutions were offered and adopted. The following gentlemen took part in the proceedings: Jeremiah Evarts, Esq., Rev. Dr. Milnor, Rev. Charles P. McIlvaine, Rev. Dr. Proudfit, Rev. Dr. McAuley, Hon. Charles Marsh, and Rev. Dr. Beecher.*

Dr. Beecher and Mr. Evarts took an active part in promoting the interests of the society. Thirty thousand copies of an able address, written by the former, were published at its commencement and widely circulated. Meetings were held in furtherance of the objects of the society, in various places, and much enthusiasm was evinced for a time in efforts to accomplish the object aimed at.

The subjoined letter was written by Mr. Tappan to his brother, who was on a visit to Boston; Mr. Fre-

---

* Mr. Evarts remarked after the meeting, that it was the ablest speech he had ever heard from Dr. Beecher.

linghuysen disappointed the hopes of the friends of the cause by declining the appointment of the secretaryship of the "General Union," which he did, after deliberate and prayerful consideration, in the belief that he could do more good to the general cause of Christian philanthropy in other spheres.

"NEW YORK, June 4, 1828.

"I have your letter informing me of your doings on the subject of the Sabbath, and have handed it, as you requested, to Mr. Pierson.

"I am sorry to inform you, that Mr. Frelinghuysen has declined. This is a great disappointment to me, as it will be to you. What is to be done? I feel as if Mr. Frelinghuysen should not be despaired of until another effort has been made to obtain him. But this must devolve on your committee. You have done nobly in Boston. I cannot learn that there has been, or is likely to be, a public meeting in Philadelphia. The subject was brought before the general assembly by Dr. Beecher, and resolutions brought in by a committee were adopted. But clergymen returning from Philadelphia heard nothing said about a public meeting.

". . . While I was writing, a clergyman came in, who has been at Mr. Frelinghuysen's house, some days past, and he thinks we may yet succeed in obtaining him. He says Mr. Frelinghuysen is deeply interested in the subject. Probably Dr. Beecher's address has influenced him some. I do not despair of him. . . . . If we engage Mr. Frelinghuysen, there ought to be some way devised for obtaining funds.

Can you get the society at Boston to be responsible for a specific amount?"

Several distinguished persons were solicited to accept the office of general agent, with assurances of a competent salary, but they all declined. Dr. Justin Edwards, being at the time about to resume his labors in the temperance cause, declined the call, and wrote:

"Sabbath-breakers are generally rum-drinkers; and while they continue the use of distilled liquors, it will not be possible to lead them duly to observe the Christian Sabbath. In order, therefore, to accomplish the great object of the General Sabbath Union, as well as that of the Bible Society, the Home and Foreign Missionary societies, and every other benevolent institution, I think it proper for me at present to labor to banish the use of distilled liquors from the earth."

Others concurred in the opinion of Dr. Edwards, and among them the officers of the society, who thought that an interest would not be felt in the specific object while so many persons, including professors of religion, manifested lukewarmness in other departments of Christian obligation. Still they would have persevered had it been in their power to secure the services of a competent person to be the actuary of the enterprise. After very strenuous exertions they failed in obtaining such a one. In a short period, therefore, the society ceased its operations, much to the regret of Mr. Tappan, and those who had been associated with him in the efforts, long pursued, to rescue from desecration the day set apart by the Creator, in the infancy of the race, to promote the well-being of man, as well as his own glory in all ages.

But the labors of those particularly interested in the effort were not wholly ineffectual. The publications that were issued, and the meetings that were held, awakened attention to the subject of Sabbath desecration, and in numerous instances produced salutary reformations. Among other instances of the kind were the following: A postmaster in one of the villages of New York, who at the age of twenty-five had a salary upon which he depended for support, resigned his place because he could not conscientiously keep the postoffice open part of the Lord's day, as was required by the act of Congress. He related this in Mr. Tappan's store.

In one of the religious papers was the following article, headed, "STAGES ON THE SABBATH.—Messrs. Editors: Having recently travelled through the valley of the Connecticut river, I was pleased to learn that a large proprietor of stages in Vermont had come to the resolution not to suffer a single horse owned by him to travel on the Lord's day; and the resolution is put into practice. This proprietor is a member of the Baptist church. He told me he had long felt the impropriety and inconsistency of permitting his horses and stages to travel on the Sabbath, but as he was a mail contractor, he did not know how to avoid it. The measures of the *General Union* had, however, taken hold of his feelings and conscience, and he then easily found a way to avoid the evil, which was to dispose of his contract. Let others go and do likewise."

It is believed that very many instances of a similar character resulted from the attempt made to secure a better observance of the Lord's day. Those most actively engaged in the enterprise, after it was started, were business men; and their own affairs, and their labors in other societies, prevented them from continuing their labors in this society, under the disadvantage of having no able person to fill the office of agent.

The efforts made for the suppression of INTEM-PERANCE early enlisted Mr. Tappan's feelings and co-operation. Especially was he interested in the question of PURE WINE for churches at their communion seasons. Pledges of total abstinence from all intoxicating drinks were made by large portions of the community, especially by church members. An exception was made of wines used on sacramental occasions. The non-abstaining portion of the people were quick to see this, and to use it as an argument against total abstinence. Leading Christian men engaged in the temperance cause saw and acknowledged the inconsistency, and were desirous of providing a substitute for the alcoholic wines universally used at the Lord's Supper.

Mr. Tappan encouraged the publication of facts on the subject, and the employment of temperance lecturers, who advocated the entire disuse of all alcoholic beverages, whether at communion seasons or otherwise. This discussion produced some division among the friends of temperance. Wine is the article, said they, that was used by the Saviour at the institution of the ordinance; it has been used in the churches ever since; and since the pure juice of the grape cannot be had, it is sacrilegious to disuse the commercial wine of the day, or provide a substitute. It was evident, he believed, that two kinds of wine are mentioned in the Scriptures, one fermented, and the other unfermented; that the former is called "a mocker," "the poison of dragons," and the latter, the wine that "such as be faint may drink." This theory explains the passages condemnatory of wine, and those that commend its moderate use.

Some denied that the wines usually sold contained any considerable portion of alcohol. To demonstrate the error of this opinion, Mr. Delavan, a distinguished advocate of total abstinence, caused choice wines from his cellar to be analyzed, and published the result. It was found that alcohol composed more than fifty per cent. of the wines. He therefore caused the bottles to be broken and the contents poured into the street. It was manifest that inferior wines, such as were commonly used, contained a much greater proportion of alcohol, and it was made evident that a large part of the "wine," so called, in general use, including that used by the churches, did not contain any juice of the grape, but was manufactured from the most deleterious articles.

Mr. Tappan, and other out-and-out temperance

men, saw at once that while alcoholic wines were
allowed at communion seasons, an insuperable ob-
stacle existed in extending the reformation among
church members. Those persons who, before or
after uniting with the churches, had been habituated
to a free use of intoxicating drinks, and had been
induced to take the pledge of total abstinence, would,
it was feared, have the appetite for such beverages
rekindled, unless the pledge included wine at the
communion as well as on other occasions.

To meet the difficulty, various suggestions were
made with regard to providing a substitute, and the
subject underwent ample discussion. Mr. Tappan
encouraged a temperance firm, who were in the gro-
cery business, to procure and offer for sale an article
called PURE WINE, warranted to be free from alcohol
and all impure mixtures, and publicly recommended
it. In this way he believed that the example of the
churches would aid rather than frustrate the temperance reform, and prevent its enemies from taunt-
ing church members with using alcoholic wine at
communion seasons while they denounced its use at
other times.

Many churches availed themselves of the opportunity; and the quality of wines used for religious
purposes has since that period been much improved.
Wine-bibbers, however, employed their wit and ridicule with regard to efforts tending to make their
favorite beverages unpopular, and too many members of churches quailed before the opposition. Mr.
Tappan was one of those who believed that ferment-

ed wines were not used by the early Christians. But whether used by them or not, he held that Christians at the present day are bound to abstain from their use, if detrimental to others.

It was not a little annoying to those who assailed Mr. Tappan with their ridicule in consequence of his claiming that the wine created at the marriage festival at Cana must have been unfermented wine, that a .distinguished Jew in New York, during the controversy, stated in his daily paper that unfermented wine was used at the Passover by the Israelites. The editor, MORDECAI MANASSEH NOAH, was deemed good authority, and his testimony corroborated the statements of Mr. Tappan, and aided the friends of "pure wine."

He had the satisfaction to believe that success had attended his efforts, and that intoxicating wines were far less used, after attention had been directed to pure wines, than before, and that consequently the temperance cause, so dear to him, was greatly promoted.

In the "Life and Labors of Justin Edwards, D. D.," page 327, is the following extract of a letter from that eminent servant of Christ to his wife, written while he was engaged in the temperance cause:

"I cannot but hope that in some way the Lord will provide means to extend and perpetuate this work of mercy, till there is not a drunkard on the globe, and not a sober man to make the drunkard's drink. Mr. Arthur Tappan, at the monthly concert, . put in a thousand dollars for foreign missions; and

5*

soon after, at a missionary meeting, subscribed four thousand dollars; about three times as much as all the rest of the people. I expect that he will give me something for temperance."

Mr. Tappan was of course a PROHIBITIONIST. He never encouraged halfway measures in questions of moral reform, and was not of the number that interpreted thus the declaration of the apostle: "I am made all things to all men, that I might by all means save some." He was an *immediatist* also, not as an abolitionist merely, but on all subjects touching the proper restraint and thorough reformation of men; for he believed that there was more energy, consistency, and perseverance, and more probable success in the ultimate attainment of an object, when reformers acted from principle instead of policy, and had for their motto the talismanic injunction: TOUCH NOT, TASTE NOT, HANDLE NOT.

Did he then omit to employ *moral suasion* for the correction of evil and the reclamation of offenders? By no means. He was now, as he had ever been, a zealous advocate of moral suasion; but when the community was ripe for it, he was for using prohibition with incorrigible transgressors. If men could be persuaded to abandon hard drinking, he rejoiced in it; but if they would, in spite of remonstrance and entreaty, become drunkards, he was decidedly for prohibiting the distillation and sale of the article that enabled them to destroy body and soul. It is lawful for a legislature to prohibit the sale of poisons. Intoxicating drinks are poisons, and therefore it is right that they should be prohibited. And when lawmakers understand the subject, and can enact prohibitory laws, it is their duty to enact and enforce them in such a way as best to secure the object. He believed that men have no right to destroy themselves or their neighbors, and so far as prohibitory enactments will prevent such *felo de se*, and such *homicide*, they ought to be enacted.

He had no confidence in the license system, and considered it wrong and wicked, believing that "the traffic in intoxicating beverages is a dishonor to Christian civilization, inimical to the best interests of society, a political wrong of unequalled enormity, subversive of the ordinary objects of government, not capable of being regulated or restrained by any system of license whatever, but imperatively demanding for its suppression effective legal prohibition, both by state and national legislation." Meantime he was in favor of employing moral suasion unceasingly, for all who will yield to it; and legal enactment, to be vigorously enforced, for those who will not be influenced by moral suasion.

Sound policy, he believed, required prohibitory laws against the traffic in intoxicating beverages; but he relied on a higher authority. The Bible is prohibitory on the subject. It is a principle of the Divine government, that designs that are criminal if consummated, must not be meditated or commenced: "Whosoever looketh on a woman to lust after her, hath committed adultery with her already in his heart." Therefore, when it is said, "No

drunkard shall inherit the kingdom of God," we
have the teachings of the Saviour, that a voluntary
act that knowingly leads to drunkenness is, in the
Divine mind, drunkenness itself.

From childhood he had also been opposed to the
use of TOBACCO in all its forms, considering its use
wasteful and injurious, alike to body, intellect, and
soul. His personal cleanliness made him shrink
from one whose breath and apparel, and even countenance, betokened that he was addicted to the use
of the "filthy weed;" and he knew too many whose
stomachs and nervous system had been greatly impaired or irreparably deranged by it. He felt grateful to his parents, whose example had been so effica-
cious in this respect, believing that, with regard to
such a pernicious habit, children of the third and
fourth generation are often the victims of the en-
slavement of their progenitors to this offence against
cleanliness and health. It was a grief to him that
the farmers in his native town had fallen into the
"tobacco mania," and for the sake of making money,
were turning their beautiful fields and meadows into
tobacco patches. He mourned over the fact, also,
that some men, who had been distinguished for their
advocacy of the temperance cause, had, on taking
up the practice of smoking, fallen into the habit of
using intoxicating drinks. He wished to warn those
who had not thus fallen of their danger: "Wherefore, let him that thinketh he standeth, take heed
lest he fall."

Dr. Hosack the elder, in a temperance lecture

delivered in Murray-street church, (Rev. Dr. Mason's,) where Mr. Tappan had attended, in alluding to the use of tobacco, said something like the following: "I warn you against the use of tobacco. It affects injuriously the physical and mental functions. Besides, it leads to intemperance, as there are very few men who use it who content themselves with washing out their throats with cold water." This celebrated physician discarded the opinions of medical men who recommend to their patients the use of tobacco and intoxicating drinks, and founded his own upon the deleterious nature of the articles, their natural effects, and his observation during a long course of practice.

Mr. Tappan's friend, Dr. William Patton, long associated with him in benevolent enterprises in New York, and now a resident of New Haven, Conn., has given his testimony respecting the baneful effects of smoking during his early ministry, and the beneficial results of entire freedom from this habit. It corroborates the opinion of Dr. Hosack fully.*

There are men who will disregard the opinions of physicians and ministers of the gospel, if adverse to their long-indulged habits, although these opinions are founded upon physiological principles, observation, or experience, who will be restrained by the tender and self-denying declaration of the apostle: "Wherefore, if meat make my brother to offend, I will eat no flesh while the world standeth, lest I make my brother to offend."

* See Chicago *Advance* of May 5, 1870.

VII.

It was in the year 1831 that Mr. Tappan became
interested in efforts then making to repress LICEN-
TIOUSNESS in New York. His attention had been
called to the subject previously. When in London
in 1810, he attended one Sunday evening, the religious services at the Magdalen Asylum, then on
the Blackfriars road. The singing was by the inmates, who were screened from observation by a
curtain in front of the choir. Their performance
was so excellent that an American clergyman who
was present, remarked afterwards, "They sang as if
they had never been sinners." It was stated that
large numbers of these "fallen women," had been
restored to their families, friends, and society, and
many of them had continued honorable and correct
in their behavior.

At his visit to Philadelphia, in later years, he
was so much impressed with the importance of
doing something for the prevention of the sin, and
the restoration of those who had wandered from the
path of virtue, that he held conversations with persons who had interested themselves in the subject,
in respect to what had been done, and what was
contemplated. When efforts were made in New
York to correct the evil, he lent the project all the
aid in his power.

Mr. John R. McDowall, a licentiate in the ministry from Princeton, New Jersey, had come to New York in the month of September, 1830, to do what he could for its enlightenment and purification. It was an errand of benevolence, and his first object was to labor as a domestic missionary among the poor, particularly in bringing their children under the influence of Sabbath-school instruction. "While engaged in this way, in the neighborhood of the Five Points, where he was instrumental in establishing a Sunday-school, he was brought under the painful observation of some of the hideous developments of the sin of impurity. . . . . He soon decided that this opened a field which should, under God, be the one for his future labors."*

Mr. Tappan became deeply interested in Mr. McDowall's labors. Having so many young men in his employment, most of whom were separated from their homes in the country, he felt for them much solicitude, and also for other youth in a city so full of temptations. Seeing that efforts were made for their protection and welfare, he stepped forward, with his influence and purse, to aid in this praiseworthy enterprise. He felt compassion also for the wretched women, who had been beguiled and ruined by unprincipled men. The disagreeableness of the subject did not deter him, for he had no love of reputation when it must be kept unsullied by refusing to interfere in a question of this kind, or declining to go into the haunts of vice, and the dens of iniqui-

* See a communication in "The Advocate of Moral Reform," of January 1, 1837, by Stephen Brown, M. D.

ty on an errand of mercy. On the contrary he gloried in all the soiling that attaches to one in such
efforts. To save the tempted, and reform the fallen,
he was willing to explore the recesses of Satan, and
engage in an unpopular enterprise.   -

There existed at the time an association named
the "Female Asylum Society," but on the formation
of the "New York Magdalen Society," in the spring
of 1831, of which Mr. Tappan was the president, the
former society became merged in it.   Mr. McDowall
was elected chaplain to the new society, and began
to publish essays, containing facts and appeals calculated to arouse public attention, and enlist the
sympathies and benefactions of benevolent persons.
He had also a periodical, styled *McDowall's Journal*,
that entered into the subject of this reform with
zeal and fearlessness.   As he prosecuted the work
he secured the countenance of a considerable number of influential ministers and laymen in the city,
and in different parts of the country, whose names
were freely given to his testimonials and circulars,
recommending both him, and the cause of which he
was such an intrepid advocate.

Donations were made for the support of Mr.
McDowall, and in aid of his journal, and other efforts
put forth by individuals in various states, who seemed to feel a deep interest in the subject and in his
self-denying labors.   Parents and guardians in the
country, who had sons and wards in the great city,
so full of attractions and temptations, manifested
much interest in the movement.   Societies were

formed in many towns, also in churches, not only in the city of New York, but in other cities and villages. Some of them were composed of men, others of women. Mothers and sisters hoped to do something consistently with their appropriate spheres of duty, to abate, if not eradicate, an evil so prevalent and so desolating, and to afford protection to sons and brothers so greatly exposed in a large city.

The country appeared to be moved. Public meetings were held, lecturing agents were employed, publications were circulated, and the work seemed to advance prosperously. Mr. McDowall was the leading agent, and his labors diffused through the other agencies an enthusiasm seldom evinced. But when, in June, 1831, the Magdalen Society published their famous report, made up of statistics of the vice in question, gathered chiefly by Mr. McDowall, in his explorations and inquiries, and estimates made of the extent of the prevailing vice, it was received with a burst of indignation and with threats of vengeance. "The city has been slandered," exclaimed the vicious and their quasi allies among certain professing Christians. "This audacious and libellous man must be put down, and the society that has patronized him must be silenced," was the general cry.

The city press, with few exceptions, commented upon the report with severity; some of the religious newspapers censured the agent without stint, and *McDowall's Journal*, in which the report was published, was presented as a nuisance by the grand

jury of New York, the foreman of which was an
elder in a Presbyterian church! The uproar seemed
like a renewal of the scenes at Ephesus, in olden
times.

It may be that Mr. McDowall was not always so
prudent and discreet as he should have been, and
that his zeal and courage were greater than his
judgment. He was also more gifted in searching
out and exposing iniquities than in suggesting remedies. It was a subject of great delicacy and difficulty, it must be confessed, requiring much experience and wisdom in prosecuting it, in gathering and
publishing facts, and applying remedies. The evil
however was notorious, active efforts for its prevention were demanded by the public voice, and yet
too many "experienced, competent men" hung back.
A devotedly pious young man, full of zeal for his
Master, and desirous of doing good, seeing that no
one waged battle with this foe to society, stepped
into the breach, and risked every thing in efforts to
stay an iniquity that threatened the ruin, for time
and eternity, of thousands of the young. He resolved on gathering additional facts and publishing
them, trusting that public sentiment would lead to
the adoption of efficient measures for the restraint
if not suppression of the iniquity. Let not his zeal,
even if it trespassed sometimes on the borders of
indiscretion, be severely censured. There were wiser
men than himself, doubtless, among those who sanctioned his proceedings, but few of them that had his
indomitable courage and perseverance.

The editor of the Portland (Me.) *Christian Mirror*, of December, 1832—considered a conservative paper—justly said: "We have concluded that he [Mr. McDowall] is actuated by disinterested benevolence, if such a thing exists on earth, for we see not what other principle is adequate to sustain him in exemplary labors, reproach, self-denial, and malignant threatenings of violence in such a revolting scene of action."

Mr. McDowall did as well as he could under the trying circumstances in which he was placed. He gathered the moral statistics of crime, and published them under the inspection and endorsement of two physicians, without fear of consequences. This bold assault upon vice was an unpardonable offence in the opinion of all parties interested either in perpetrating or concealing crime. Unjust judges, unprincipled "officers of justice," covetous landlords, hoary and youthful men of dissipated habits, together with all who profited by the wretchedness of lewd men and women, were boisterous in their denunciations of McDowall, who might have said, "The world cannot hate you, but me it hateth, because I testify of it, that the works thereof are evil."

Mr. Tappan saw that Mr. McDowall had come to the city, with a desire, in imitation of his Master, to go about doing good; that he had overcome his natural diffidence, and had gone forward, through evil report and good report, to accomplish a reformation, that has been opposed more than any other by the powers of darkness, and the selfishness and depravity of vicious men. He believed also, that much good had been accomplished, and he desired to stand by him. He did so as long as he could anticipate satisfactory results from his labors.

The position of Mr. Tappan, as president of the society, as one of the committee to prepare and publish the Magdalen report, and as the avowed friend and supporter of Mr. McDowall, exposed him to much unmerited censure. He was threatened with personal violence, his house was supposed to be in danger of being mobbed, and he was denounced, not only by the openly wicked, but by some well-meaning but timid Christian men, as the upholder of a dangerous man, and the patron of a disgraceful cause. The circulation of the report had alarmed all dissolute men, and had unnerved a large majority of the Christian community. The wicked feared exposure, and the opposers of wickedness were apprehensive that reformatory measures had been overdone.

The committee charged with the duty of preparing and publishing the report, made up from the statistics gathered by Mr. McDowall, were Arthur Tappan, Stephen Brown, M. D., and David M. Reese, M. D. All of them were members of churches, and stood well in the denominations to which they belonged. The report was written by Dr. Reese, as he avowed to the compiler, saying, with characteristic complacency, "They say it is the best thing I ever wrote." One can judge of the surprise felt on seeing, in an evening newspaper, a day or

two afterwards, a card to the following effect: "I
am not the author of the Magdalen Report, D. M.
Reese, M. D." On meeting him, soon after, the
inquiry was put, "How came you to publish such a
card, after stating that you were the author of the
report?" The reply was, "They threatened to
tear my house down."

Both Mr. Tappan and Dr. Brown treated the
recreancy as it deserved. Large portions of the
community would, after the denial of Dr. Reese, believe, of course, that one of his associates on the
committee was the author. They were content to
have it so understood, and took no notice of the
denial. Dr. Brown, during the whole turmoil, was
firm as a rock. He was an able physician, a calm,
thoughtful man, "and one that feared God, and
eschewed evil." He believed that he had done
his duty. As a physician he had acquired much
knowledge of the state of things in the city, and he
believed in the truthfulness of the statements made
in the report.

In the course of the year, the society was dissolved. Mr. McDowall thenceforth continued his
labors wholly on his own responsibility. He continued to publish a periodical, circulate moral reform tracts, and preach in the open streets at the
Five Points and the neighborhood, to "publicans
and harlots." He was lampooned, caricatured,
shunned by many, and, at length, reprimanded by
his Presbytery. He saw fit to publish some criti-
cisms respecting the Magdalen Society, which Mr.

Tappan felt called upon to answer, under his own
signature, but in a friendly tone, feeling much esteem for Mr. McDowall, although he did not approve
his whole course.   This answer was in the *New York
Evangelist* of January 26, 1833.

MR. LEAVITT—DEAR SIR : Your correspondent, Rev. Mr.
McDowall, has made some statements respecting the late
Magdalen Society that require explanation.   The assertion
that the efforts of the society were discontinued because of
the opposition of the unprincipled, or for want of funds, is
without foundation.   The true cause was the discouraging
fact that we saw *no* fruits of our labors, and the conviction
on our minds that it was a waste of moral effort ; that the
same amount of effort applied *as a preventive* in the distribution of tracts, the faithful labors of the tract distributors, the
temperance effort, etc., would produce unspeakably greater
results.

The mismanagement of the asylum, mentioned by Mr.
McDowall, admits of explanation.   It may be sufficient now
to say, that while he has stated the truth, he has not stated
the *whole truth*.   When, for instance, he says the females were
allowed to visit the place of their abode, he omits to inform
the reader, that it was a mother who went in care of some
faithful person to try to reclaim a daughter, or a sister to try
to win a sister, and induce her to enter the asylum, etc.
That mistakes occurred, I do not deny, but they were never
sanctioned by the executive committee.   Our by-laws were
good, but they were not in all cases strictly observed by some
members of the committee.   It is not true that we "closed
the asylum, and turned the females into the street ;" and I
am surprised that Mr. McDowall should make the assertion.
The care of the females remaining in the asylum was transferred to a gentleman who had shown a warm interest in
the cause, and who engaged to carry on the effort on his own
responsibility.

I send you a communication from a highly respected
correspondent, which will throw light on the cause of Mag-

dalen reform, and will point out to the friends of the cause the best course for obtaining the desirable end. Your friend,

ARTHUR TAPPAN.

Mr. McDowall made a respectful reply, in which he said, that when the efforts were in a languishing condition Mr. Tappan "resuscitated the concern;" and that "there is no real contradiction in our separate statements." After a career of arduous and ill-requited labor for the good of others, he at length sickened and died in poverty, December 13, 1836, aged 35. His funeral was attended at the Broadway Tabernacle by many friends of humanity. A sermon was preached by Rev. Joshua Leavitt, then editor of the *New York Evangelist*, which was printed in the paper, and also in pamphlet form.

Dr. Brown, whose testimony has already been borne, and who attended him in his last sickness, says: "His persecutions from the wicked, out of the church, gave him very little trouble; but his recent trial by his presbytery, and suspension from the ministry, was a source of great and indescribable anguish of mind. He looked upon it as not only cruel to his feelings, but in a high degree unjust, and of course unrighteous. His nervous system was weakened, his body became prostrate, and he rapidly sunk."

Several societies for the same avowed purpose were formed, but one after another, with but one or two exceptions, were soon relinquished; yet Mr. McDowall's labors were not in vain. It is supposed that the moral reform efforts, since his death, and

continued at the present day, are the result of his
labors. "The path of the just is as the shining
light, that shineth more and more unto the perfect
day."

This subject has been dwelt upon at such length
because it was one in which Mr. Tappan took a
deep interest, and for which he suffered much unde-
served censure. The labor he shared with a few
others, but the expense devolved chiefly upon him.
He believed that if the ministers and laymen who,
at one time, stood by Mr. McDowall, had continued
faithful to the cause; had wisely corrected his mistakes, and continued their confidence, vastly more
good might have been achieved, a noble philanthropist saved from a premature death, and a cause
so eminently entitled to the support of a Christian
community preserved from even temporary defeat.
What was wanted, after gaining the moral statistics,
was a discreet plan of a remedial character, to be
followed out with persevering energy. Still the seed
sown has sprung up and borne fruits of righteousness, and Mr. Tappan never regretted the agency he
had in sowing it. May those who have succeeded,
emulate his example, and the examples of McDowall
and Brown, and be, like them, faithful unto death!

It will come in place here to present some considerations that induced Mr. Tappan to take such a
strong interest in the subject. He knew that the
evil was one of great moment, involving both the
temporal and eternal welfare of men and women,
especially of the young. He believed also that in-

structions and warnings respecting it were very infrequent and indefinite; that parents, school-teachers, and even ministers of the gospel, were very remiss in their instructions on this subject. Books on such themes are rarely consulted and seldom put into the hands of youth, while publications and pictures of a lascivious character are widely diffused by youthful associates and the emissaries of the devil. The consequences are disastrous. These impure publications and pictures are suffered to influence and corrupt the young without any sufficient antidotes. Young persons also, in their academical studies, pore over the lascivious writings of heathen authors without any adequate correctives. They indulge impurities hurtful to body, and mind, and soul, often without knowing the deleterious effects of such transgressions. Having no religious principle, they brave the warning of Scripture, and being destitute of physiological knowledge, they commit " sins of ignorance," unaware of the consequences.

Both nature and revelation teach most important truths on the subject, but on parents and teachers devolves the duty of making suitable applications of such knowledge. Are not parents in duty bound to instruct their children fully on matters of such vital importance, relying upon God to bless their efforts? The aid of the family physician can be had, if necessary, and few young persons but would be alarmed at the lessons he could give, respecting the consequence of yielding to "youthful lusts;" the idiocy, insanity, disfigurement of body, and imbecility of mind, often produced. Children can be taught that the Creator "has not made the body for uncleanness nor indulgence in sensuality."

If parents, by plain teachings from the Bible and other books, or by the instrumentality of the family physician, discharge their duty faithfully, the happiest results may follow. Is it too much to say, no parent has a right to rear a family of children without imparting to them, personally, or by a more competent teacher, every thing necessary to be known respecting one's own body, and the danger of illicit communication with others. Children at an earlier age than is generally supposed, acquire pernicious habits that torment them all their days, and which might be avoided by instructions early and faithfully given. So thought the founders of the New York Magdalen Society, in the efforts to oppose "the vice of vices."

Besides family instruction, Mr. Tappan was fully persuaded that pulpit instructions could be presented with effect, on a subject at once so delicate and important. A minister, contemporary with him, once said: "I can not preach on the seventh commandment." Other clergymen have shirked the duty, while some have performed it effectively, and in an unexceptionable manner. But parental and professional instruction, with the warnings of Scripture, are chiefly to be relied upon; and these, it is believed, will, in most cases, be adequate to accomplish the end designed.

While he considered PREVENTION the chief object

to be aimed at, as it respects the young and inexperienced, he believed that asylums for "fallen women," such as exist at the present time, were worthy of confidence and deserving ample support ; and it is pleasant to be able to state, on the authority of the chaplain of one of these excellent institutions, that within a few years past, there has been a growing interest in the reformation and salvation of the inmates.

He was also in favor of municipal and legislative interposition. Crime must be subject to law, and receive punishment. When city functionaries, faithful legislators and upright magistrates, perform their duty, vice will hide its head, dens of iniquity will be broken up, and a moral purification will take place. But effectual moral efforts will never be made unless the ministry and the church take the lead. Profligate jurors, unprincipled attorneys, and debauched judges, can not be relied upon for the prevention of crime, or the punishment of transgressors. Christians, in and out of city councils, and legislative halls, must coöperate with virtuous magistrates, in reformatory labors.

Mr. Tappan believed that, as "an ounce of prevention is worth a pound of cure," a large proportion of the viciousness of both sexes could be forestalled and prevented by early, faithful, persevering instruction and warning; that on religious instructors rests much of the obligation, but that parents are called in providence to discharge a duty in this respect to their children that cannot be neglected, nor evaded, without great injury to their offspring, and great guilt to themselves. Children, in every department of society, are liable to wrong influences, and corrupt habits, from the destroyer of souls and his emissaries. Pointed instruction, from parents and religious teachers, as well as moral education, will alone, under God, save the young, amid the snares set for them.

He has given a COMMANDMENT, that if fully explained, and set home upon the youthful mind and conscience, with all the needful explanations, such as father and mother can give, and which they are inexcusable if they do not give, may preserve the moral purity of children and youth, and thus save families and society from untold wretchedness. This subject was one upon which Mr. Tappan pondered deeply. He knew that he had the Bible on his side, and he resolved that, with the aid of the God of the Bible, he would do something to awaken the community, and arouse parents and guardians, to the consideration of saving the tempted, and rescuing the fallen.

Those Christians and parents who shrink from such investigations and exposures, and refuse to attack vice in its strongholds, from false delicacy or prudery, have little resemblance to the Master, who did not keep himself aloof from the vicious, or apologize for open and persevering efforts to reclaim them. The ungodly and self-righteous of that day taunted him for such association with the vicious, and they have since that period continued to taunt both men and women who boldly enter the den of

iniquity to snatch its victims from the roaring lions
that seek to devour.

Mr. Tappan received some scratches in his efforts
of this kind, but he considered them in the light of
trophies rather than evidences of defeat. He was
willing to lend his name, give his money, and contribute personal labor to this cause; and to unite
with good men and women in such self-denying
labors. There were some of this class, among his
own and the other sex, as there always has been,
who "despising the shame," like their divine Lord,
esteem it an honor to snatch as brands from the fire,
the unhappy and miserable victims of self-indul-
gence and pollution, and to lend their aid in exposing and bringing to condign punishment flagrant
offenders.

His experience in other labors for the reclamation of the wicked, and the punishment of evil-doers,
had taught him that incipient efforts are often defeated, and that final victory sometimes results from
early discomfitures. In the efforts made for the
recovery of the licentious he knew also that defeat
has often attended philanthropic labors; and it
might be so again. He felt willing, however, to
make renewed efforts with the best agency at hand,
believing that even partial failure in a good cause
was better than inaction when a mighty evil was
to be assailed; and that good seed, prayerfully
sown, would spring up and bear fruit.

VIII.

MR. TAPPAN'S mind had been for a long time directed toward the condition of the people of color, and he spared no pains to gain information both as to the free and the enslaved. In the course of his inquiries he had some correspondence with WILLIAM WILBERFORCE. The *American Colonization Society* was then in the ascendency, and its friends claimed to be, *par excellence*, the friends of the colored race.

Near the close of the year 1816, a meeting was called to assemble in Washington City, to form the society. HENRY CLAY presided. The project originated with slaveholders, although some good men from non-slaveholding states, were associated with them in the scheme. The ostensible object was expressed in the second article of its constitution:

"The object to which its attention is to be *exclusively* directed is to promote and execute a plan for colonizing (with their consent) the free people of color residing in our country, in Africa, or *such other place*, as Congress shall deem most expedient." The object in view, therefore, was the removal of the free negroes to Africa, if Congress so determined; but to any place out of the United States, if it should be deemed preferable by the national legislature.

Mr. Tappan, with many other friends of the

blacks, was induced to give the society a cordial support. When, however, it became known to him that New England rum, powder and shot, and weapons of war were regularly sent to Liberia by the society, and supplied to the colonists, he remonstrated.* And when he saw that slaves were manumitted on condition that they should be sent to Africa, he came to the conclusion that he could no longer aid a society that inflicted such an injury upon the colonists and the natives of Africa, besides trampling upon its own constitution.

The society, by sending to Africa SLAVES who gave no consent to go there, *unless a choice of evils, between expatriation and slavery,* be called a "consent," violated its own constitution, as Mr. Tappan believed; and by sending rum, powder, shot and guns demoralized both colonists and native Africans. Many northern people had been induced to give their confidence, their money, and their prayers under the assurance that the Society was missionary in its design, and would also tend to the extinction of slavery.

As the society proceeded in its operations, the minds of thousands were opened to the design of the leaders in the enterprise. Among them was DANIEL WEBSTER, who, in his palmiest days, in presence of a committee appointed in Boston to report a constitution of a Society to be called the *Massachusetts Colonization Society,* said, "I cannot give my sanction to the object, for I see that it origina-

---

◦ See Appendix 4, for *facts.*

ted in a plan to get rid of the free negroes in order
to render slavery more secure, and I will have nothing more to do with it."*

After the commencement of the anti-slavery agitation the opposition to the Colonization Society
increased. Mr. Tappan was applied to from various
quarters, to know the reason of his withdrawal from
it. On being applied to by the Anti-slavery Society
at Andover, Mass., to give his views respecting the
"American Colonization Society," he replied in a letter, thus introduced by the secretary to the editor
of the Liberator: "Theological Seminary, Andover,
March 29, 1833. Mr. Garrison : In the correspondence of the Anti-slavery Society in this seminary,
the following communication has been received from
a distinguished philanthropist, which it is presumed
will be read with interest by the Christian community."

NEW YORK, March 26, 1833.

MR. LEWIS F. LAINE, SECRETARY OF THE ANTI-SLAVERY SOCIETY IN
    THE THEOLOGICAL SEMINARY AT ANDOVER :

DEAR SIR : Your communication of the 8th inst. has remained till now unanswered, in consequence of a press of
other cares. You ask my opinion of the Colonization Society, and suggest the inquiry whether with its present principles and character, it is worthy of the patronage of the
Christian public ? My engagements do not admit of my
giving an elaborate answer to this inquiry, or explaining at
length my views of the colonization project.

○ This was said in presence of JOHN TAPPAN, and other members of the committee, who after such a declaration, declined
reporting a constitution for an auxiliary society in Massachusetts.
Mr. Webster afterwards made a speech in behalf of the Parent Society at Washington.

When this society was organized, I was one of its warmest friends, and anticipated great good from its influence, both in Christianizing Africa and abolishing slavery in our country. At one time, I had a plan for establishing a line of packets between this city and the colony, and for opening a trade with the interior of Africa. I also offered to pay one thousand dollars to the society, if the one hundred individuals, proposed in the plan of Gerrit Smith, could be found in one year. I mention these things to show how heartily I entered into the scheme.

The first thing that shook my confidence in the society, was the fact that ardent spirits were allowed to be sold at the colony, and, as the agents wrote me from Liberia, in giving the assortment suitable to make up an invoice, were considered indispensable.

I used the little influence I had with the society to obtain a prohibition of the admission of ardent spirits into the colony; with what success may be seen in the fact, that no less than fourteen hundred barrels of the liquid poison have been sold there within a year.

With my feelings somewhat cooled by the knowledge that ardent spirits, tobacco, powder and balls, were leading articles of trade at the colony, I read with some care the arguments of that distinguished and fearless philanthropist, W. L. Garrison, in the *Liberator*, and was soon led to ask myself whether this splendid scheme of benevolence was not a device of Satan, to rivet still closer the fetters of the slaves, and to deepen the prejudice against the free colored people.

I now believe it is, and that it had its origin in the single motive to get rid of the free colored people, that the slaves may be held in greater safety. Good men have been drawn into it, under the delusive idea that it would break the chains of slavery and evangelize Africa; but the day is not far distant, I believe, when the society will be regarded in its true character, and be deserted by every one, who wishes to see a speedy end put to slavery in this land of boasted freedom.

You are at liberty to make what use you please of this

6*

expression of my sentiments. I rejoice to witness the effort that is everywhere making to let the captive go free, and that the number is daily increasing of those who are resolved not to cease their efforts in every lawful way to secure to our colored fellow-citizens equal rights with others.

That your society may be eminently instrumental in dissipating prejudice and pouring light upon the intellect of the millions of our countrymen who are held in bondage, is the earnest prayer of your fellow laborer,

ARTHUR TAPPAN.

The following letter, published in the *New York Evangelist* of June 29, 1833, is a corroboration of the statements made in the preceding letter to Mr. Laine :

MR. LEAVITT—DEAR SIR : The Colonization Society has given a wide circulation to the remarks referred to in the enclosed communication, and I ask as a favor that you will admit to your columns my vindication.

I am truly yours,

A. T.

TO REV. R. R. GURLEY, SECRETARY OF THE AMERICAN COLONIZATION SOCIETY :

In the *African Repository* for May, I observe some remarks accompanying the letter recently addressed by me to the Anti-slavery Society in the theological seminary at Andover. The writer of the remarks makes me say, that because ardent spirits are sold at Liberia, I was led to the belief that the colony was founded in the single motive to perpetuate slavery. I ask if my language will justify this construction ? I certainly drew no such inference *from such premises*, as a re-perusal of my letter will satisfy any candid mind.

The writer of the remarks says, my language would lead to the belief that I had received from the agent of the Colonization Society the statement, "that ardent spirits was an indispensable article of trade at the colony." This inference is correct. It was from Doctor Randall I had that information, as his letter in my possession will show.

It will be incumbent on me to produce my authority for the assertion that "fourteen hundred barrels of ardent spirits have been sold at the colony in one year," when the society has denied the fact, as they doubtless have the means of doing if it is untrue; and when they do deny it, I shall show that *not half the truth has been told*, as I am now enabled to state from more recent information.

It is said I have no authority for the opinion that the Colonization Society "is a device of Satan, and owes its existence to the single motive to perpetuate slavery." I would ask if it is not supposable, that Satan sometimes uses good men to promote his purposes? What else will account for the fact that so many of our best men are now "led captive at his will" in the unrighteous prejudice against the colored man? a prejudice that is to be found in this land of boasted freedom alone, out of the eight hundred millions that people the earth. Yes, let me repeat it, a prejudice that exists in this country alone, against the sentiment of the whole world besides, and which in the face of heaven we dare to allege as a reason why the colored man cannot be elevated in this country. What! Shall eight or nine millions of "pale-faced" human beings, arrogate to themselves the right to trample under foot their fellow-men, because the color of their skin is different, when, too, a vast majority of mankind is on the side of the colored man? I ask then if there is no reason to believe, that such a prejudice comes, not from God, "who made of one blood all the children of men," but from the source I have ascribed to it?

I have no intention to impugn the motives of those great and good men, Finley, Mills, and others, who it is said first conceived the idea of the Colonization Society. But there is abundant evidence, that a similar plan had been in agitation in the Virginia legislature year after year, before these estimable men broached the subject, and we know that when the plan was brought forward by them, it had its chief support from slave-owners, who have never evidenced the purity of their motives by giving freedom to their slaves, a measure one would expect naturally to flow from a sincere desire to benefit the colored men.

Trusting in a sense of justice to obtain for this, admittance into the next *Repository*, I am with great personal esteem, Yours,

ARTHUR TAPPAN.

The demoralizing effects of rum shipped to the coast of Africa have not ceased. Mr. Walker of the Gaboon Mission, states facts that should crimson the faces of all persons who have been instrumental in shipping from this country, and pouring upon the benighted people of that country, this burning lava. His letter "closes with statements which may well cause Christians to respond earnestly to the call for prayer in behalf of a heathen people, cursed and wasted away by the traffic in rum from Christian lands; and for the Christian missionary called to encounter such evils brought in from his own home, and creating a barrier against his success more hopelessly impregnable than all the native paganism, vice, and degradation of that people." Mr. Walker concludes his letter thus :*

But Satan is not to be thus defeated, and where the foot of the white man has never trod, the fiery stream of alcohol rolls and burns, causing waste and anguish and horrors greater than the middle passage ever witnessed. Some people wonder why the coast tribes of Africa waste away and disappear. It is no wonder to one who lives here, with his eyes open, unless he himself has come within the maelstrom. The coast is beleaguered with the hosts of Satan ; and they are bold, persistent, untiring, unscrupulous, unmerciful. If you wish to know some of the concomitants of the rum trade and rum drinking, read Prov. 23.:33. These are our real obstacles. Heathenism is bad, but unmixed it is not impregnable. Nine-tenths of the liquor exported from Liverpool

---

* Missionary Herald, February, 1870, p. 49.

comes to this coast. American traders generally are the same. Pray for us, that there may be found ten righteous men here, and that all the people perish not.

The very facts adduced by friends of the Coloni-zation Society in support of its claims, and particu-larly those that were offered to justify the expatria-tion of the people of color to another land, seemed to Mr. Tappan's mind irresistible to influence him and others, to oppose it. "The prejudice against the negro is so strong that it cannot be overcome; even Christianity cannot overcome it." This, thought he, is a slander against the religion of Jesus. "They never can be elevated here to equal rights, and will ever be unhappy and miserable while they remain among us." This, if true, thought he, is . our fault and not theirs. We are bound to remove obstacles, give the colored man a chance, offer him the right hand of fellowship, do away with oppres-sive enactments and usages, treat him as a fellow-citizen, and fellow-Christian, *here*, in the land of his nativity. Christ died for the colored man as well as for the white man. He is no respecter of persons. He taught that "a certain man"—a poor slave per-haps—fell among thieves, who robbed him, and left him half dead. A true picture of slavery!

And we are told that there came down a certain priest that way, and when he saw him, he passed by on the other side. Likewise a Levite, when he was at the place, came and looked on him, and also pass-ed by on the other side. But a certain Samaritan, when he saw him had compassion on him, bound up his wounds, and took care of him. "Which now of these three, thinkest thou," said our Lord, "was neighbor unto him that fell among thieves?" The answer was, "He that showed mercy on him." Then said Jesus unto him, "Go, and do thou like-wise."

It behooves us, then, thought Mr. Tappan, to act the part of the Samaritan toward the poor colored man, bond and free; bind up his wounds of body and mind, take care of him in his own land, the land of his birth; console, relieve, and administer to his best good here, rather than among strangers, in a distant, heathen land. He saw nothing in the para-ble of the Good Samaritan to justify sending the colored man to Africa, to do him good there.

The Saviour taught that *neighbor* means any one whom we can benefit, by administering to his imme-diate wants; and the dictionary interprets the word to mean "a countryman," a "fellow-being," "one that needs our help." The negro, reasoned Mr. Tappan, is a fellow-countryman, he needs my help, it is for his good, and for the honor of Christianity that assistance be afforded him, here and now; and hating caste, and loving the Saviour, he shall have it so far as it is in my power, with divine aid, to give it.

This subject has been discussed at such length because he was once a zealous supporter of the colo-nization scheme, and abandoned it for wise and good reasons, much to the annoyance of his former asso-ciates, some of whom were never reconciled to the course he felt constrained to take, and seized every opportunity to oppose the anti-slavery cause, in which he heartily engaged when he turned away from the Colonization Society. He believed it to be, not the friend but the foe of the people of color. But he acknowledged that there were individuals who continued to cling to that scheme, and were yet their friends. He deplored their delusion, but resolved on exercising candor, while true to his own matured judgment.

The people of color, from the beginning, had an instinctive dislike to the colonization scheme. This dislike was not prompted by the originators of the anti-slavery reform, as their opposition is dated anterior to the agitation of the slavery question. In January, 1817, a month or two after the formation of the Colonization Society, more than three thousand free people of color assembled in Philadelphia to express their views of the society. At this meeting they unanimously replied to the question, "Are you willing to accept its offers?" with an emphatic NO. They sent forth an address, "To the humane and benevolent inhabitants of the city of Philadelphia," from which the following is an extract:

We have no wish to separate from our present homes for any purpose whatever. Contented with our present situation and condition, we are not desirous of increasing their prosperity but by honest efforts, and by the use of those opportunities for their improvement, which the constitution and the laws allow to all. It is, therefore, with painful solicitude and sorrowing regret, we have seen a plan for colonizing the free people of color of the United States, on the coast of Africa.

We *humbly*, respectfully, and fervently entreat and be-
seech your disapprobation of the plan of colonization now
offered by the "American Society for colonizing the free
people of color of the United States." Here, in the city of
Philadelphia, where the voice of the suffering sons of Africa
was first heard ; where was first commenced the work of abolition, on which Heaven has smiled, for it could have success
only from the great Master ; let not a purpose be assisted
which will stay the cause of the entire abolition of slavery in
the United States, and which may defeat it altogether ; which
proffers to those who do not ask for them, *benefits*, but which
they consider *injuries*, and which must insure to the multitudes, whose prayers can only reach you through us, *misery*,
sufferings, and perpetual slavery.

JAMES FORTEN, CHAIRMAN.

RUSSEL PARROTT, Secretary.

Meetings of people of color were held in most of
the cities and towns in the United States, at that
early period, and it was their united and strenuous
opposition to the expatriation scheme that first
induced WILLIAM LLOYD GARRISON and others to
oppose it.

No wonder that such an appeal, when it became
known to Arthur Tappan, and when he became personally acquainted with the leading men who had
adopted it, touched his keenest sensibilities, and
attached him more strongly to his oppressed fellow-
men. In company with his friend, Mr. Jocelyn, he
visited Philadelphia, and had interviews with Mr.
JAMES FORTEN, and other intelligent and influential
men of color. Their industry, thrift and respectability deeply impressed him, and he fully sympathized with them in their distrust of a society, composed largely of slaveholders, that aimed at their

removal from the land of their birth and affections to a heathen land.

This feeling was intensified as the sentiments of influential colonizationists were promulgated, from time to time. In the Fifteenth Annual Report of the *American · Colonization Society*, the managers say: " *Causes beyond the control of the human will* must prevent their ever rising to equality with the whites." "The managers consider it clear, that causes exist, and are operating, to prevent their improvement and elevation to any considerable extent, as a class, in this country, which are fixed, not only beyond the control of the friends of human-ity, BUT OF ANY HUMAN POWER. Christianity cannot do for them here, what it will do for them in Africa. This is not the fault of the colored man, *nor of the white man*, nor of Christianity; but it is AN ORDINA-TION OF PROVIDENCE, and *no more to be changed than the laws of nature*."

No wonder that abolitionists, the world over, rejected such atrocious sentiments. English philan-thropists, as well as American, uttered their con-demnation of them. "No one," said Judge WILLIAM JAY, "surely need to blush at acknowledging that he has been deceived in the society, since WILBERFORCE placed his name at the head of a protest against it. The following is an extract from this protest: 'We must be understood utterly to repudiate the prin-ciples of the AMERICAN COLONIZATION SOCIETY.'"

It will be in place here to insert a most eloquent appeal on behalf of the much abused people of color,

by one of their own number, the late Rev. PETER
WILLIAMS, rector of St. Philip's church, New York:
"We are natives of this country; we ask only to be
treated *as well* as foreigners. Not a few of our
fathers suffered and bled to purchase its independence. We ask only to be treated as well as those
who fought against it. We have toiled to cultivate
it, and to raise it to its present prosperous condition.
We ask only to share equal privileges with those
who come from distant lands to enjoy the fruits of
our labor."

Mr. Williams, during the mob violence in the
city of New York, was the leading minister of the
gospel among his people, and also a member of the
executive committee of the *American Anti-slavery
Society.* He was required by the bishop of the dio-
cess, Mr. Onderdonk, to renounce his connection
with it. Such a command pained the heart of the
good man, and he would have refused compliance,
but the influences employed were too powerful for
him to withstand. He submitted, and prepared an
apology to be submitted to his anti-slavery friends,
in which, while obeying the order of his spiritual
chief, he expressed his opinions, modestly but firmly,
of the anti-slavery cause. This apology he left with
his ecclesiastical superior, who undertook to alter
it by expunging several sentences, and then causing
it to be published without consulting Mr. Williams!
The aggrieved man of God keenly felt the outrage,
but deemed himself bound by his ordination vows
to submit in silence.

It appears necessary to express such views of the colonization scheme because, even at this day, ignorant black people are persuaded that Africa is their natural home, that they will never have their rights in this country, etc.; and their consent is gained to be shipped off to a distant land, where the advantages for successful labor and education are far inferior to what they are in the United States. And this, when there is such a demand for labor at the South, and colored men of good capacity are elected to the judicial bench, to state legislatures, and even to Congress!

While we write, a report is published in one of the daily papers, of a public meeting on Brooklyn heights, at a church (St. Ann's) on the evening of the Lord's day, in which one of the speakers uses the following language: "In the United States, with ten to one against them, the blacks must ultimately be crushed by and give way before the whites in the great struggle of life." And the audience, in a Christian church, are invited to lend their influence, and contribute their means, and thus to fulfil this unchristian prophecy. The speaker said, that "those who were willing might go to Liberia, where they would become agents in the grand work of civilizing Africa." If thus capable they should by all means be retained in this country to teach the first principles of Christianity to those, who yielding to an unchristian prejudice, would expatriate them. Mr. Tappan contended zealously for the extinction of this prejudice to his dying day, and it is fit that a remonstrance against such a perversion of Christian benevolence should accompany this tribute to his memory.

It is sometimes asked, "Have not the colored people the same right to emigrate to Africa that other persons have to emigrate to any part of the world they choose?" The answer is, certainly they have. Abolitionists, and intelligent free people of color, oppose the Colonization Society because it was directed by slaveholders and their allies, not to benefit the blacks, but to get rid of them, or for the double motive in some cases; and it is a matter of history that very few, if any colonizationists, then or since, have labored for the extinction of slavery.

Slavery being abolished, and the full rights of citizenship secured to the people of color, the question now is, ought or ought not the colonization scheme to be encouraged? As already conceded, colored men have the right to go where they please, and white men have a right to help them to emigrate. All this is allowed. But no individual or society has a moral right to inculcate the impossibility of people of color rising here as well as abroad. Such sentiments are anti-republican and unchristian; particularly when the rights of colored men, to their fullest extent, have been recognized by the Fifteenth Amendment to the Constitution of the United States.

Is it not worthy of the most serious consideration of all truly benevolent and Christian men whether it is consistent with the principles of our

government and of Christianity to encourage the
emigration of any citizen to a foreign land, especially to a heathen land, who is not a person of moral
and Christian principles, and who emigrates to do
good. Mr. Tappan, in his mature life, believed it
was wrong to encourage the emigration of persons
who went from selfish motives, whose principles and
habits were unworthy of imitation, and who themselves needed the restraints of moral and religious
institutions, instead of being models for the imitation of those less favored than themselves. He felt
that encouragement to emigrate should be held out
to those, and those only who desired to go with a
missionary spirit. Was he not right?

Mr. Tappan had no objection, of course, to the
emigration of deserving men of color to Africa,
though he did object strongly to the coercive system, direct or implied; and thought it against the
genius of Christianity to encourage men who were
destitute of religious principles, and especially if
destitute of common morality, in going from a Christian to a heathen or semi-heathen land.

Among those he aided to return to their native
shores was an African named ABDUAL RAHAMAN, a
son of one of the native kings. He had been captured in war by a neighboring tribe; sold by his
captors to slavetraders; and by them brought to
New Orleans. After living a slave at Natchez, Mississippi, forty years, he was recognized by a surgeon in the United States' navy.

The surgeon had been attached to a United

States man-of-war off the coast of Africa, and having gone ashore to hunt, was left by the ship. He lodged one night at the house of Abdual's father, and on seeing the son at Natchez, he made interest with influential persons on his behalf. He was bought of his master with a view to send him to Liberia, as it was thought he could be of great service to the colonists by influencing his countrymen to befriend them.

He came to Boston, where through Mr. Charles Tappan's exertions, a considerable sum was raised in Massachusetts for his benefit. He recommended him to his brother Arthur in New York, who, in conjunction with other friends, paid a large sum to redeem Abdual's wife and children from slavery. The whole family embarked for Liberia, with a number of other emigrants. Abdual died in six weeks after his arrival, and half of the number of emigrants met within the time the same fate.

Abdual Rahaman was a Mohammedan, of Moorish extraction, well educated, tall and dignified in his appearance, and read the Arabic language fluently, and wrote it with elegance. His princely bearing, and intelligence excited much interest, wherever he went, and contributed to increase the indignation felt for the cruel system of slavery.

IX.

AFTER ceasing to feel an interest in the Colonization Society, Mr. Tappan applied himself more than before to the improvement of the people of color in their own country. He inquired into their condition and wants, and took pleasure in aiding them in all ways consistent with their best good. He was especially desirous of promoting their intellectual and moral elevation. To this end he spared no expense of time or money. Whatever plans of usefulness were suggested he investigated, and aided, so far as they appeared judicious.

After purchasing a house in New Haven for a family residence, and being there almost weekly himself, he formed an acquaintance with Rev. Simeon S. Jocelyn, who was minister of a congregation of colored people in that city, and his friendship and intimacy continued with this devoted friend of theirs during his whole life. With him he ascertained the condition of the colored people in New Haven and elsewhere, and they united in devising plans for their benefit.

He learned that a society had been formed at New Haven, called the "African Improvement Society," in which several prominent Christian ladies took a deep interest, and he gladly coöperated with them, and the advisory committee of gentlemen, in carrying forward its plans of usefulness. It was his practice, as opportunity offered, to attend the meetings of the colored people, to counsel them, express his sympathy with them in their trials and privations, and to manifest that he discarded, both in sentiment and practice, the hateful caste feeling that so extensively prevailed in the country, and in no part of it more than in Connecticut. At the same time he aimed to be discreet in his deportment, and thus avoid all reasonable censure. He knew that the prejudice against the colored people was vincible, but at the same time he realized that it was deep-rooted, and must be removed, not by extreme measures, but by their gradual elevation.

Believing fully in the equality of all men in the sight of God, as laid down in the Scriptures, and in the Declaration of Independence, it was his earnest desire to show that he regarded the colored man as a fellow-citizen; and to treat him as he would a white man in the various walks of life. This course of action he believed was consonant with the principles of our republican government, and the precepts of Christ. The contrary course he believed to be cruel as well as dishonorary to Christianity and insulting to the Creator; so contrary to the principles of the gospel that it is a marvel that it any where exists in lands called Christian. It is also so opposite to the spirit of republicanism that foreigners are greatly surprised that it prevails in a country where the doctrine of equality of all men before the law lies at the foundation of the government.

God has made of one blood all men, black and white; and Christ has died for all, and offers salvation to bond and free, Jew and Gentile. He has provided mansions in heaven for all true believers; and shall man, in his egotism and pride, spurn his colored brother, like himself made in the image of God, and invited to a glorious immortality? Especially is it befitting those who think they have been redeemed by the atoning blood of the Saviour to set at naught, or stand apart from those who are made, by the all-wise Father of all, of a different complexion from themselves? Such a prejudice is enough to make angels weep!

He believed also that the total abolition of the caste feeling is for the welfare of the whole community, white and colored. Thus judging he determined to evince by his whole deportment that he despised caste, and was the friend and brother of all men without distinction of complexion or condition. To those who objected to this course, and to all who opposed it, he could say: "Whether it be right in the sight of God to hearken unto you more than unto God, judge ye."

He was fully impressed with the importance of parents so training their children, that they will grow up with kind feelings toward the poor, and especially toward those whose complexions expose them to the insults of coarse-minded and hard-hearted persons. For the harmony of society, and the welfare of the whole people, it seems important that great forbearance should be exercised on the

7

part of the rich toward the poor, and the laboring classes toward each other, irrespective of condition or complexion. It is all-important also that, now the people of color are invested with all the privileges of citizenship, and of course brought into closer affinities, hostilities of every kind should come to an end.

If, as children, they are not allowed to meet in the same week-day and Sabbath schools, and encouraged by parents and teachers to behave kindly to each other, how, as men, will they be able to meet at the polls, sit on juries, attend political meetings, practise at the bar, unite in processions, and mingle with their fellow-men in the various walks of life, on equal terms, as the religion of Jesus, and the laws of the land require?

A convention of people of color was held in Philadelphia in 1831, of delegates from several states, to consult upon the common interest. It was numerously attended, and the proceedings were conducted with much ability. A resolution was adopted that it is expedient to establish a collegiate school, on the manual labor system. Soon after, a committee appointed for the purpose made an appeal to the benevolent, in which they stated the disadvantages under which their sons and daughters were placed, in not being able to gain admission into seminaries of learning, or in mechanical establishments; the strong desire felt for their education, and the necessity that existed for such a school. They also suggested that New Haven, Connecticut, would be a suitable place for its location. Mr. Tappan who had given much attention to the subject, expressed his satisfaction in view of the laudable enterprise, and promised substantial aid, while Mr. Jocelyn and other friends of the colored people coöperated with him in devising a plan for carrying out the desired object.

It was supposed that a favorable impression had been made at New Haven, with regard to the elevation of the people of color, and that the officers of Yale College, and influential citizens would not oppose, but rather aid the project. BENJAMIN LUNDY had been there, and had addressed the members of the Legislature of Connecticut in the statehouse on the importance of educating the blacks, and his address had been very favorably received.* A bookseller in the city had published an edition of a pamphlet by CHARLES STUART, on the beneficent results of emancipation in the West Indies, at the request of Mr. Tappan, and chiefly at his expense, a large part of which had been circulated.† The impression on the public mind seemed to be good.

* This unostentatious and meritorious man died in August, 1839, at Hennepin, Illinois. A western paper said of him, "The pioneer editor of the anti-slavery enterprise has gone to his rest." In General WILSON'S article in the *Atlantic Monthly*, February, 1870, p. 243, commemorative of EDWIN M. STANTON, it is said : "Benjamin Lundy, the early abolitionist, was a frequent visitor at his father's house, and Mr. Stanton once told me that he had often sat upon that devoted philanthropist's knee when a child, and listened to his words."

† A world-wide philanthropist, and outspoken Christian. He was an Englishman by birth, and long a captain in the British East India service, from which, at the period alluded to, he had

Mr. Tappan, therefore, after causing inquiry to be made of some of the professors, and other leading individuals, united with Mr. Jocelyn and other persons friendly to the enterprise in projecting a college or high school, for colored youth. It was believed that some of the professors would give them the benefit of their lectures. It was supposed, also, that young men of color might come from various parts of the country, and from the British Islands, and avail themselves of the opportunity to acquire a solid education. Mr. Tappan purchased several acres of land, in the southerly part of the city, and made arrangements for the erection of a suitable building, and furnishing it with needful supplies, in a way to do honor to the city and country. His heart was full of the subject, and personally and by letters he invited the aid of other friends of the colored people, and urged forward the undertaking with his accustomed zeal and liberality.

To his great regret, and that of his associates, the people of New Haven, became violently agitated in opposition to the plan. Misrepresentations were made of the designs of the founders, fears were expressed that both city and college would suffer injury, if the scheme was prosecuted. "The whole

retired on half pay. During a series of years he lectured on the anti-slavery subject, and other moral reforms, in England and the United States, with disinterested zeal and fearlessness, giving his time and money for the promotion of benevolent enterprises. He died in Canada, at an advanced age, having been promoted to be a major in the British army. He might appropriately have adopted the motto of *Franklin:* "Where liberty dwells, there is my country."

city was filled with confusion." The people had heard of Mr. Tappan's supposed wealth and generosity, of his determination to carry forward favorite plans at all events, and seemed to fear that the city would be overrun with negroes from all parts of the world. There were not wanting persons to inflame the public mind. "A negro college by the side of Yale College!" "The City of Elms disgraced for ever!" "It must not and shall not be!" Such was the popular cry.

Even persons of calm judgment and philanthropic views on most subjects, were carried away by the clamor. They seemed to imagine that the success of the enterprise would be a stain upon the city, injure its business and bring a stigma upon Yale College. A panic seemed to have seized the minds of the people, and it was decided to have a public meeting of the citizens to take into consideration the project of establishing the "odious institution," and expressing their views upon it. Accordingly the mayor of the city summoned a meeting to be held on the 8th of September. There was great excitement. Mr. Jocelyn calmly stated the facts and corrected some of the many misrepresentations. But very few of those supposed to be favorable to the enterprise, came forward in this exigency to sustain it. Mr. Tappan was in New York, and of course not present at the meeting. The opposers of the measure rallied in strong force and were vociferous in opposition. Several of them belonged to the legal profession, and by their inflammatory speeches, added greatly to the excitement.

But there were a few who did not quail before the storm. One of these noble spirits was a native of Virginia,* who had been educated at New Haven, and lifted up his voice in favor of giving colored youth a chance to acquire an education in the "land of steady habits," and with great manliness, as a lover of universal education, avowed his belief in the brotherhood of man according to the Scriptures. A distinguished lawyer,† a native of the city, came to his support, and the support of Mr. Jocelyn, and in a speech of much force defended the right of the friends of the people of color to establish a school for their benefit wherever they chose; repudiated the notion that such a school would be injurious to the city or the college; and lamented the excitement and the opposition to what he deemed a praiseworthy undertaking. But it was all in vain! The following resolution was submitted for adoption, and was passed by nearly a unanimous vote:

Resolved, by the Mayor, Aldermen, Common Council, and freemen of the city of New Haven, in city meeting assembled, that we will *resist* the establishment of the proposed college in this place, by every lawful means.

In view of the unexpected hostility to the measure, Mr. Tappan and its other friends abandoned

---

* Mr. James Donaghe, now a resident of Brooklyn, N. Y.

† Roger S. Baldwin, Esq., afterwards the defender of the "Amistad Africans," Governor of Connecticut, and Senator in Congress, who, from conviction and hereditary proclivities, was ever the friend and advocate of the colored man.

it. They .published in the *New Haven Journal* a
full account of the proceedings, with a remonstrance
against the action of the city meeting, the dishon-
orable caste and pro-slavery subserviency manifested by the leaders of the opposition; and an
appeal to the Christian and honorable feeling that
should exist in the community. They had the satisfaction to know that the appeal met the approbation of not a few in New Haven, and in other parts
of the country. Many persons attributed the opposition of the people of New Haven to the education
of the people of color, to the prevalence of colonization sentiments. It was thought to be against the
policy of colonizationists to favor their elevation in
this country. It was the opinion of Judge Jay,
that "the colonization party in New Haven could
have prevented this high-handed oppression, but
their influence was exerted not for, but *against* the
improvement and elevation of their colored brethren."* However this may be, the prevalence of
caste has been very great, and exists at the present
day, when happily slavery is abolished.

An improved state of feeling, however, commenced soon after the action of the "Common Council and freemen of the city of New Haven." A distinguished professor in Yale College, within a year
or two, publicly expressed sentiments in favor of the
elevation of the colored people, and we have reason
to believe uttered the sentiments of others in the

* See "Miscellaneous Writings on Slavery," by William Jay, p.
32.

faculty of the college and in the city. He said: "It is delightful to see so many of our colored people living in neat and comfortable dwellings furnished in decent taste, and sufficient fulness: thus indicating sobriety, industry, and self-respect—to see their children in clean attire, hastening of a Sabbath morning to the Sunday-school; and other days, with cheerful intelligent faces, seeking the common school."* At a subsequent period, when the "Amistad Africans" were incarcerated in the New Haven jail, many of the inhabitants, including officers of Yale College, did all in their power for the protection and education of the hapless strangers.

The triumph of prejudice and unchristian feeling toward the people of color at New Haven, had, as might have been expected, an unhappy influence in other parts of the state. Miss Prudence Crandall, a member of the Baptist church, had a female boarding-school at Canterbury, Conn. A pious colored young woman applied to her for admission, stating that she wanted to get a little more learning—enough, if possible, to teach colored children. Miss Crandall received her. The parents of the white pupils were displeased, and insisted that the colored pupil should be dismissed. But the inhabitants of Canterbury made the greatest opposition. They were led on by a few distinguished individuals in the place, among whom was a prominent lawyer, who then and afterwards attained to

* See remarks of Professor Silliman, Senior, in "African Repository" of 1832, p. 184.

an unenviable notoriety.* Miss Crandall pondered
the subject, reflecting with pain upon the disabili-
ties to which colored youth throughout the country
were subjected, and, with a disinterestedness and
heroism that entitle her to universal commenda-
tion, determined not to accede to the demand. But
finding that the feeling was very strong against the
admission of colored persons into schools of white
persons, she resolved to open a school *exclusively* for
colored girls. She made the announcement. This
notice, instead of allaying, increased the commotion
in the Canterbury community.

Among those who took part in befriending Miss
Crandall was Rev. SAMUEL J. MAY, son of Col. May,
already mentioned as the gentleman with whom Mr.
Tappan boarded in Boston during his clerkship, (the
worthy son of such a father,) who resided in a neighboring town. The friendship manifested by Mr.
May came to the knowledge of Mr. Tappan, who
was in no wise disheartened by the recent discomfiture at New Haven. On the contrary it inspired
him with new zeal on behalf of the much wronged
people for whose improvement he felt so great a
solicitude. He wrote to Mr. May to encourage and
aid him. Mr. May's narrative is so full and inter-

* Andrew T. Judson, Esq., is the person alluded to. He manifested an exceedingly wrong spirit at the time and afterwards;
but as a judge of the United States district court subsequently,
although not evincing much legal acumen or judicial ability, he
presided during the trial of the "Amistad Africans" in a way to
secure the respect of their friends, while he disappointed the
expectations of his political partisans at the seat of government
and elsewhere.

esting with respect to the part Mr. Tappan took in
the matter, that it is inserted at length, and is honorable not only to Mr. Tappan but to the benevolent narrator:

A TRIBUTE TO THE MEMORY OF ARTHUR TAPPAN.°

BY REV. SAMUEL J. MAY.

SYRACUSE, July 26, 1865.

The tidings of Mr. Tappan's death, just received, have
set my bosom aglow with the feelings of respect and gratitude to him that have long been cherished there. I have
known that most excellent man from my childhood; and
most of my memories of his good deeds are the same that all
must have who have been acquainted with his large and wise
beneficence for the last fifty years and more. But there is
one of his philanthropic acts that would have been known
to none on earth excepting him and myself, unless I had
sometimes privately told of it. And now that he has gone
from us, it is due to his unostentatious charity that this act
should be recorded upon the public memory.

Many of your readers may have heard of *the Canterbury
school for colored girls;* but none of them probably know how
much Mr. Tappan did to uphold that truly Christian enterprise, and defend it against the malignant assaults of its enemies. I wish I had an opportunity to tell you, and all who
love fidelity to principle, how naturally, how providentially
Miss Prudence Crandall was led, in the spring of 1833, to
open her boarding-school to the daughters of colored people,
as well as others; how cruelly she was persecuted, and
shamefully traduced; how patiently she bore her trials; how
courageously she persisted in her endeavor to maintain the
position she knew it was her duty to take; and how fully
she was justified by the decision of the highest tribunal of
the state of Connecticut. But the story is too long to be
recited here. I have taken my pen only to tell you what Mr.
Arthur Tappan did to strengthen the hands and encourage
the heart of that noble woman.

° From the *New York Independent.*

Of course, as I lived in an adjoining town, and there was not a man in Canterbury who would lift a finger in her defence, I could not refuse to proffer Miss Crandall such assistance as I might be able to give. She made me her attorney ; and I went to a town meeting to speak in her behalf, and to suggest such a course as I thought should have been satisfactory to her neighbors, without involving any sacrifice of principle on her part. But they would not hear me. They shut their ears, and rushed upon me with threats of personal violence.

There being no law of the state against which she had offended, her persecutors, by their personal and political influence and intrigue, succeeding in persuading the legislature of Connecticut, then in session, to pass an act making it a penal offence, punishable by fine and imprisonment, for any one in that state keeping a school to take as his or her pupils the children of colored people of other states.

Knowing this law to be unconstitutional as well as immoral, I advised Miss Crandall to disregard it. She did so, was arrested, examined before a justice of the peace, bound over for trial, and committed to jail. Thus I found myself, as her adviser and attorney, involved in a legal conflict with the town of Canterbury that promised to be a protracted one, and would probably be very expensive. But already the affair was noised abroad, and had become the subject of much newspaper comment ; and I had received letters from several of my anti-slavery friends, assuring me of their sympathy, and encouraging me to maintain the ground I had taken.

Better than all, a letter had come to me from Mr. Arthur Tappan, whom I had not then seen for ten years, and from whom I was widely separated by our theological differences— a letter in which he expressed his joy that I had espoused Miss Crandall's cause ; his clear perception of the importance of the principles involved in her case ; his earnest hope that I should not be dismayed by the multitude or the strength of those who had risen, or might rise, up against me ; and added, "But I am aware, sir, that you can ill afford to bear the expenses of the contest you have dared. In this respect I am happily able to help you, and shall consider it a duty and a privilege so to do. I wish you to consider me your banker, assured that I will honor promptly your drafts. Keep your accounts carefully, and let me know whenever you need any money. Spare no necessary expense; employ the best legal counsel; and let this great question be fully tried, not doubting that, under the good providence of a righteous God, the true and the right will ultimately prevail."

Thus supported by one of the wealthiest as well as one of the best men in the land, I assure you I felt equal to what I had undertaken. But I soon found I had not duly estimated the strength, the artifice, or the malignity of my opposers. The Democrats were bitterly hostile, and the Whigs did not venture to show me any favor. The newspapers of the county, and of the adjoining counties, teemed with the grossest misrepresentations, and the vilest insinuations against Miss Crandall, her pupils, and her patrons; but, for the most part, peremptorily refused us any room in their columns to explain our principles and purposes, or to refute the slanders they were circulating. Thus excluded from the audience of the public, I found myself becoming an object of general distrust, and perceived that I was losing my hold upon the confidence of the few who had ventured to give me any support. I kept Mr. Tappan duly informed of every thing that occurred having any important bearing upon the controversy in which he was my strong tower. Especially did I set before him my bad predicament—the disadvantage at which I was contending for the right—inasmuch as my adversaries wielded several newspaper presses incessantly against Miss Crandall's school, and the others would not venture to defend it. I added in one of my letters, "Oh, that I could leave my post long enough to come and spend one hour with you, that I might get the advice from you which I so much need."

On the morning of the third or fourth day afterward, as soon as it was practicable for him to come, the door of my study was opened quietly, and in walked Mr. Tappan. He had left all his then immense business in New York, and hastened to me, that he might the better judge, after a personal survey of the field, what ought to be done. I never grasped a human hand with more joy and gratitude. He sat in conversation with me a couple of hours, and possessed himself of all the information I could give him in the premises. He then rode to Canterbury, six miles from my house in Brooklyn, that he might see Miss Crandall; satisfy himself that she was all that I had represented her to be; and give her renewed assurances that, as far as his sympathy, personal influence, and wealth (which then was very great) could aid her, she should not want help and protection. In about three hours he returned to my study, very much gratified by what he had seen of the Canterbury school, and its devoted teacher. He had also learned still more than I had been able to tell him of the persecutions and annoyances to which that excellent young lady was continually subjected.

After a few minutes, he said to me, in his quiet, subdued manner: "I believe I now fully understand 'the bad predicament' of which you wrote to me in your last. It is even worse than I supposed. You must start a newspaper as soon as possible, that you may disabuse the public mind of the misrepresentations and falsehoods with which it has been filled. Scatter the numbers of your paper broadcast over the community. Get all the subscribers you can, and I will pay all-the expenses you may incur more than the income you receive from subscribers and advertising patrons."

I was elated at the prospect thus opened to me of a speedy deliverance. I informed him that fortunately there was then in town a press with types and other necessaries that had been, a few days before, abandoned by the proprietors of an unsuccessful newspaper. "We must have it," was his prompt but calm reply. "Let us go immediately and secure it." Forthwith we started, walked to the village, found the person who had the disposal of the abandoned printing office, and engaged it for a year. The next week a new paper called *The Unionist* appeared, under the very able editorship of Mr. Charles C. Burleigh. It was conducted with so much spirit and power by him, and afterwards by his brother, Mr. William H. Burleigh, that it rendered us essential service, and helped. no doubt, to make Windham county the

most anti-slavery county of the state of Connecticut. Four
or five different trials were had of the case, which her persecutors attempted to make against Miss Crandall, for the
crime of keeping a boarding school for colored girls. The
first came off before a justice of the peace in Canterbury, in
May, 1833, and resulted in her committal to the jail in Brooklyn. The last she had before the "supreme court of errors "
of the state of Connecticut, at Brooklyn, in the month of
July, 1834, and resulted in her favor. The Hon. William
W. Ellsworth, of Hartford, and the Hon. Calvin Goddard, of
Norwich, were her counsel.* They exerted themselves generously in her behalf, and refused to receive any thing more
than the retaining fee, of $50 each, which I sent them in the
beginning. Nevertheless, the other expenses, the fees of
minor lawyers, the costs of court, etc., added to the expenses
incidental to the establishment of *The Unionist,* amounted in
all to over six hundred dollars, which Mr. Tappan promptly
paid. This is but one of the almost countless acts of generosity which illustrated all the prosperous portion of his life.
It was not by any means the greatest. But you will not
wonder that I remember it with especial thankfulness; nor
refuse a place in your columns, that I may record it to be
remembered and admired by the thousands of your readers.

Mr. Tappan undiscouraged by opposition, devoted his time to other efforts for the improvement
of the colored people. He was one of the originators of the "Phœnix Society," in New York,
formed in 1833, and composed of young people,
chiefly colored young men. The president of the
society was Rev. Christopher Rush, afterwards
bishop in the Zion connection of colored Methodists,
a most estimable man. Rev. Samuel E. Cornish was
the agent of the society, his salary being paid by
Mr. Tappan, who was treasurer, and bore a large
part of the expenses of the library, hall, etc. He

* Henry Strong, Esq., was also associated with them.

was a frequent visitor to the library and teachers' rooms. It was a high gratificatiom to him to assist the young men in their laudable efforts to acquire education, and prepare themselves for usefulness in the community. There was a board of directors composed of both white and colored persons.

The object of the society was to promote the improvement of the colored people in morals, literature, and the mechanic arts. In a circular of the officers it was stated that "the society is made up of no particular sect or party. It is designed to be the goal of the entire colored population, and of their friends, in New York city;" and it was also stated: "It is obvious that no foundation of society can be strong without more virtue, and that the arts which are essential to universal industry, are to be promoted as the means of wealth and domestic comfort. A spirit of improvement is now moving the colored people in various places to secure for themselves and their children advantages which they have heretofore but partially enjoyed."

There were to be "ward societies" in the city, and the aims were so laudable, and were set forth in terms so interesting, that they could not but claim respect.

This society will aim to accomplish the following objects: To visit every family in the ward, and make a register of every colored person in it—their name, sex, age, occupation, if they read, write, and cipher—to invite them, old and young, and of both sexes, to become members of this society, and to make quarterly payments according to their ability—to get the children out to infant, Sabbath, and week schools, and induce the adults also to attend school and church on the Sabbath—to encourage the women to form Dorcas societies to help to clothe poor children of color if they will attend school, the clothes to be loaned, and to be taken away from them if they neglect their schools; and to impress on their parents the importance of having the children punctual and regular in their attendance at school—to establish mental feasts, and also lyceums for speaking and for lectures on the sciences, and to form moral societies—to seek out young men of talents, and good moral character, that they may be assisted to obtain a liberal education—to report to the board all mechanics who are skilful and capable of conducting their trades—to procure places at trades and with respectable farmers for lads of good moral character—giving a preference to those who have learned to read, write, and cipher— and in every way to endeavor to promote the happiness of the people of color, by encouraging them to improve their minds, and to abstain from every vicious and demoralizing practice.

The "mental feasts" alluded to were suggested at New Haven, by Mr. Jocelyn, who says:

Not long after the utility of the "African Improvement Society" was proved, it became evident that not only literary, but moral and religious culture among the colored people was important, and I suggested in the early numbers of the *Liberator*, organizations to be called Mental Feasts. They were introduced in Boston and Philadelphia. Mr. Tappan was interested in them. These meetings were rather social, but compositions, essays, poetry, etc., were read by the authors, (young women as well as young men attending,) and topics of interest were discussed in a familiar way. The refreshments were very simple—a cracker and a glass of water—thus avoiding costly preparations of refreshment, which are adverse to mental improvement.

Mr. Tappan and myself attended one of these meetings in Philadelphia and took much pleasure in it. He was ever not only for the emancipation of the slaves, but for the true elevation of the free people of color. He had no caste feeling, and the colored people wherever he went felt that he was bent on their highest good.   It was natural that these attentions to the moral and intellectual wants of the colored people should have suggested the idea of a high school, or college, particularly as colored youth were excluded from them throughout the country."

In Philadelphia, at that time, Mr. Tappan became acquainted with some of the principal colored people of that city, Messrs. Forten, Gardner, Gloucester, Cassey, etc., men of mark, not only among their own people, but who were entitled to and would have obtained distinction in any society of white persons that appreciated moral worth, and intellectual ability.   Two of them were ministers of the gospel and deserved to be ranked with the most pious and useful pastors of the day.

Mr. Forten was a sailmaker.   He employed a large number of hands, white and colored, and was considered among the most eminent in his calling at that day.   It was said by the secretary of the navy, " Mr. Forten can undertake to rig a seventy-four-gun ship, and not call for any money until the job is done."

It will be thus seen that Mr. Tappan took every opportunity in his power, to acquaint himself with the condition and needs of the colored people, both cultivated and unlettered, and to afford them all the sympathy and aid in his power.   He derived a sweet satisfaction in this work of philanthropy, and felt that it did him good while he was benefiting them. In Mr. Jocelyn he realized that he had a wise adviser, and a true-hearted helper.

The Phœnix Society rented, at first, rooms at the corner of Canal and Mercer streets, where they were favored with a cóurse of lectures by severâl clergymen of the city, on moral, scientific, and historical subjects. Afterwards a hall was hired on West Broadway, which thenceforth was named Phœnix Hall. It became somewhat noted in anti-slavery annals. Here the convention of the delegates of the American Anti-Slavery Society was held. They were of the apostolic number of seventy, and after lecturing in different parts of the free states, they met in New York for consultation and plans of enlarged influence. Here also a flourishing evening school for adult colored persons was established, the teachers being both white and colored.

The Phœnix Society established a high school for colored youth, which was continued two years or more.

X.

IN April, 1830, it came to the knowledge of Mr. Tappan that WILLIAM LLOYD GARRISON had been convicted of a libel, at Baltimore, for publishing, with comments, the fact that a vessel owned by Francis Todd, of Newburyport, Mass., had taken slaves "as freight" to New Orleans; and that he was, under the sentence of the court, lying in jail, for lack of means to pay the fine and costs. Mr. Garrison was personally unknown to Mr. Tappan, but he was an innocent man, suffering in a righteous cause. That was sufficient to arouse the sympathy of Mr. Tappan, and induce him to send relief. He silently paid the fine and costs, and Mr. Garrison, on his way to Boston, called on his deliverer to express his thanks for the unexpected favor bestowed upon him.[*]

His appearance and deportment, at that time, were not likely to be forgotten. His manly form, buoyant spirit, and countenance beaming with conscious rectitude, attracted the attention of all who witnessed his introduction to Mr. Tappan.

---

[*] "After seven weeks of close confinement, Mr. Garrison was liberated by the noble, discrimidating generosity of the late Arthur Tappan, then in the height of his affluence, who, so long as he had wealth, felt that he was an almoner of God's bounty, and gave his money gladly, in many ways, to the relief of suffering humanity." See "Some Recollections of our Anti-slavery Conflict," by Samuel J. May, page 17.

After this interesting interview, Mr. Garrison proceeded to Boston, and in a short time commenced the publication of a weekly paper, *The Liberator*. His object was to expose the conspiracy of the slavocracy against human rights, and the cruel delusive character of the American Colonization Society.

The paper had in Mr. Tappan a warm-hearted and liberal supporter. He subscribed for a large number of copies, to be directed to different individuals, in hopes that it would enlist them in the cause of freedom. It had this effect; and several of the early and devoted friends of emancipation traced their first impressions of the guilt of slaveholding, and the heinousness of the expatriation scheme, to the paper sent to them from some unknown friend of the colored man.

Henceforth the condition of the slaves, as well as the condition of the free people of color became leading objects with him, occupying his thoughts, his reading, his conversation, his correspondence, his benefactions, and his prayers. He witnessed, with great satisfaction, the influence produced on the minds of the true friends of the people of color, bond and free, and he had not the shadow of a doubt of the fulfilment of the declaration: "He that goeth forth and weepeth, bearing precious seed, shall doubtless come again with rejoicing, bringing his sheaves with him."

In a year from the commencement of the *Liberator*, viz., January 1, 1832, was formed *The New*

England Anti-Slavery Society, at Boston, and the fact was welcomed by Mr. Tappan and the little band of abolitionists with joy and thankfulness. Meantime the *Liberator* was increasing in influence. With a view to diffuse more extensively anti-slavery principles and to correct the effects of the Colonization Society, the *Emancipator* was established in the city of New York, March, 1833, under the editorship of Charles W. Denison. Mr. Tappan aided this undertaking.

During this year a pamphlet was published at Haverhill, Mass., entitled "Justice and Expediency; or, Slavery considered with a View to its Rightful and Effectual Remedy, ABOLITION," by John G. Whittier. The esteemed author, who has done so much and so ably, in song and prose, for many years for the cause of equal rights, printed only five hundred copies. He sent one to Arthur Tappan who wrote to the author an encouraging letter, and had five thousand copies printed at his own expense. It was for loaning a copy of this pamphlet to a physician in Washington that Dr. Crandall was imprisoned, until his health was entirely destroyed, in the old city prison at Washington.

William Goodell, in his volume, entitled "Slavery and Anti-Slavery," says: "In 1835, Dr. Reuben Crandall, from the state of New York, was arrested, imprisoned, and tried for his life, in Washington City, for having loaned to a white citizen, at his own request, a pamphlet against slavery."

The facts, reasoning and appeal of this early

discussion of the principles of slavery and colonization by Mr. Whittier, arrested the attention and increased the sympathies of Mr. Tappan. With his characteristic sagacity and generosity, he desired to send it broadcast over the land. In reply to the question, "Why I seek to agitate the subject of slavery?" the author said:

"Let the TRUTH on this subject—undisguised, naked, terrible as it is, stand out before us. Let us no longer seek to cover it; let us no longer strive to forget it; let us no more dare to palliate it. It is better to meet it here with repentance than at the bar of God. The cry of the oppressed—of the millions who have perished among us as the brute perisheth, shut out from the glad tidings of salvation, has gone there before us, to Him who as a father pitieth all his children. Their blood is upon us as a nation; woe unto us if we repent not as a nation in dust and ashes. Woe unto us if we say in our hearts, 'The Lord shall not see, neither shall the God of Jacob regard it. He that planted the ear, shall he not hear? He that formed the eye, shall he not see?'"

The concluding paragraph of this eloquent publication is as follows:

"And when the stain on our own escutcheon shall be seen no more; when the Declaration of our Independence and the practice of our people shall agree; when Truth shall be exalted among us; when Love shall take the place of Wrong; when all the baneful pride and prejudice of caste and color shall

fall for ever; when under one common sun of political Liberty the slaveholding portions of our Republic shall no longer sit, like the Egyptians of old, -
themselves mantled in thick darkness, while all
around them is glowing with the blessed light of
freedom and equality—then, and not till then, shall
it GO WELL FOR AMERICA!"*

Public attention in the .city of New York had
recently been drawn to the slavery question by a
discussion between R. S. Finley and Simeon S.
Jocelyn at Clinton Hall, on the comparative merits
of colonization and immediate emancipation. This
discussion resulted in the adhesion of several persons, who were subsequently numbered among the
supporters of the anti-slavery cause in the city.
They were convinced by the arguments, facts, and
fervent appeals of Mr. Jocelyn, that the Bible and
the claims of humanity required them to abjure the
colonization scheme, and to advocate the recogni-

---

    *   2d, 5th mo., 1870.

MY DEAR FRIEND LEWIS TAPPAN: My pamphlet on Slavery,
"Justice and Expediency," was printed in the early summer of
1833. I only printed five hundred copies. I sent one to thy
brother, and soon received from him a very kind letter. He had*
five thousand copies printed at his expense.

In the very early days of the anti-slavery cause, thy brother's
sympathy and liberality were the main dependence of the zealous
but poor young men who engaged in it. We all remember him
with gratitude. When Garrison was imprisoned, I appealed to
Henry Clay to use his influence with his Baltimore friends in his
behalf, and he wrote me that he intended to have assisted him
through Niles of the Register, but had been "anticipated by Mr.
Tappan."

           Always and truly thy friend,
                    JOHN G. WHITTIER.

tion of their colored brethren, in the land of their birth, to all the privileges of citizens and Christians; in other words, that as "God hath made of one blood all nations of men for to dwell on all the face of the earth, and hath determined. the times before appointed, and the bounds of their habitation," he requires that the rights of the "Americans called Africans"* as equal before the law as well as equal before the gospel, should be recognized here in the land of their nativity, rather than in Africa.

The *New York Evangelist*, conducted for a time by Rev. Samuel Griswold, and afterwards by Rev. Joshua Leavitt, entered into the discussion, and espoused the cause with ability and fearlessness. The *Genius of Temperance*, edited by William Goodell, was already committed to the cause. Mr. Tappan felt a deep interest in these publications. "By coöperation between the Messrs. Tappan and a few others, very large issues of anti-slavery tracts were circulated monthly during the greater part of this year, and sent by mail to clergymen of all denominations, and other prominent men throughout the country. A great amount of important information was thus diffused."†

The abolitionists of the city had made such progress in the diffusion of their sentiments, that they were encouraged in the belief that the time had come to form a society, and thus combine and

---

* The expressive words of Mrs. Child in her "Appeal," published in 1833, a work of great merit, and one that exerted a powerful influence.

† See "Slavery and Anti-Slavery," by Wm. Goodell.

extend their influence. Accordingly, a CALL was
made for a meeting of the friends of immediate
emancipation, to be held at Clinton Hall, on the 2d
day of October, 1833. The notice was published in
the papers of the day, and by showbills put up in
the streets and on public buildings.

Very soon a counter-notice was published in a
similar manner, signed by MANY SOUTHRONS, inviting
a meeting at the same time and place. The object
was evidently to outnumber the friends of freedom
at their own meeting, and crush in the shell the
anti-slavery enterprise. The proprietors of Clinton
Hall, alarmed at the demonstrations made, undertook to annul their agreement. Application was
then made to the lessees of Clinton Hotel, near by,
but in vain. The "Southrons," encouraged by their
Northern sympathizers, seemed to triumph.

But when every hall appeared to be closed
against the abolitionists, it occurred to one of them,
who was a trustee of Chatham-street Chapel, that
the lecture-room of that building afforded sufficient
accommodations for the meeting. Verbal notice
was accordingly given at a late hour of the day,
and as many as could be convened on the emergency, fifty or more in number, assembled at the
appointed hour.

Their opposers, finding Clinton Hall shut against
them also, adjourned to Tammany Hall, in large
numbers, filling the building and the street opposite. The meeting was duly organized, General
Bogardus, United States marshal, in the chair.

8

Resolutions of a denunciatory character were adopted, and inflammatory speeches made by prominent
citizens.   The proceedings were published in the
city papers, along with gratulations for the "security
of the Union!"*   Before separating, they learned
where the abolitionists were assembled, and adjourned the meeting to Chatham-street Chapel by
acclamation and shouts of, "Let us rout them!"
Arrived at the place, the numbers swelled to two
thousand or more.   They found their steps arrested
by the closed iron gates at the entrance of the passage leading to the chapel, the keys of which were
in the hands of the trustee previously alluded to.
Being thus kept at bay, the mob made fruitless
efforts to gain admittance, meantime shouting, "Ten
thousand dollars for Arthur Tappan!"   Several abolitionists were called by name, and loud threats were
uttered.

Within the building the abolitionists were holding their meeting with an order and solemnity befitting the occasion.   It was commenced with prayer
for Divine protection and guidance.   Resolutions
were adopted that it is expedient to form an anti-
slavery society, and that committees be appointed
to report a constitution and board of officers.   On
the reports of committees being received, they were,
after some amendments, severally adopted.   A committee was then appointed to prepare for publica-

* See a valuable work entitled "Slavery and Anti-Slavery," by
WILLIAM GOODELL, who was early associated with Mr. Tappan in
the temperance and anti-slavery cause, and whose writings have
been highly prized by thousands of philanthropists and patriots.

tion the proceedings, and have them inserted in the morning papers of the ensuing day. The meeting was then adjourned, *sine die*.

The keys of the iron gates were now handed to the janitor, with instructions to unlock them, and let the clamorous multitude in while the abolitionists were withdrawing. Mr. Tappan and a few others went to a private door, in the rear of the building, but finding it fastened, they withdrew by another passage a few moments before the infuriated· crowd had burst into the room where they had held the meeting. The mob, seeing that the persons against whom they meditated mischief had escaped,* amused themselves by organizing a mock meeting, forcing a negro man to take the chair, whom they addressed as Arthur Tappan, and requiring him to make a speech. The man made some hesitation, but his audience would take no denial. Summoning, therefore, all his courage, he addressed them after this sort, as it was reported:

"I am called upon to make a speech! You doubtless know that I am a poor, ignorant man, not accustomed to make speeches. But I have heard of the Declaration of Independence, and have read the Bible. The Declaration says all men are created equal, and the Bible says God has made us

---

* It was afterwards made known that one of the mob pursued Mr. Tappan and his friends through the unlighted main hall of the chapel, with a light and a drawn dagger. The janitor of the chapel, who had taken a deep interest in the proceedings, saw the villain as he followed the little band, blew out the light, and took refuge in one, of the slips.

all of one blood. I think, therefore, we are entitled
to good treatment, that it is wrong to hold men in
slavery, and that—" They would hear him no further, but with yells and curses broke up their meeting and dispersed.

The committee appointed to prepare for publication the proceedings of the anti-slavery meeting,
proceeded forthwith to execute the trust. They sat
up to a late hour, and then went to the editorial
rooms of the daily press. At the office of the *Journal of Commerce*, Mr. Hallock, the editor, informed
them that an article was already in type, the pur-
port of which was that the meeting of the abolitionists had been interrupted, and the persons attending it dispersed, without accomplishing their object.
On being made acquainted with the actual facts,
he, from a sense of justice, substituted the official
account of the proceedings for the fictitious statement that had been imposed upon him.

At the office of the *Courier and Enquirer* the
committee learned that the editor, James Watson
Webb, after writing and giving out his editorial,
had gone to his home. The next morning, the public manifested much merriment at the appearance
of the *Courier and Enquirer*. The leader of the editor was couched in language evincing a high degree
of exultation at the supposed defeat of the abolitionists in their attempt to organize an association
to oppose slavery, and reaffirm the doctrines of their
revolutionary forefathers. But when, in the same
paper, was seen the official statement of the success-

ful efforts of the abolitionists in forming the New
York City Anti-Slavery Society, in juxtaposition, as
it were, with the anticipated triumph of their opponents, the "broad grins" of the defeated party mingled with the serene satisfaction expressed by those
on the opposite side of the question.

The heading and leader were as follows:

New York.

☞ PRINCIPLES, NOT MEN. ☜

THURSDAY MORNING, OCTOBER 3, 1833.

GREAT PUBLIC MEETING.
THE AGITATORS DEFEATED!
THE CONSTITUTION TRIUMPHANT!

Some thousands assembled in the vicinity of Clinton Hall
to mark their detestation of any attempt to organize a society
in this city fraught with danger to the Union, and based
upon an open violation of the Constitution of the United
States. Information was there given, however, that the trustees of the Hall, with the single exception of ARTHUR TAP-
PAN, had prohibited any such meeting ; in consequence,
those who had assembled quietly to vote down these disor-
ganizing fanatics, organized and adjourned to Tammany
Hall. Not less than five thousand persons were present.

We rejoice that this opportunity has been presented to
the inhabitants of our city to convince their Southern brethren of their determination not to *countenance*, in any manner,
the interference of TAPPAN, GARRISON, & Co. with their slave
property.

PER CONTRA.

In the same paper, bought in as an advertisement at a late hour in the night, when the editor
was probably asleep, was the official account of the
proceedings at Chatham-street Chapel, as follows:

ANTI-SLAVERY SOCIETY.

At a meeting of the friends of immediate emancipation of slaves in the United States, held at Chatham-street Chapel last evening (Wednesday), at half-past 7 o'clock, JOHN RANKIN was chosen Chairman, and ABRAHAM L. COX, M. D., Secretary.

After an address to the throne of grace, on motion, it was *Resolved,* That it is expedient at this time to form a society for promoting the abolition of slavery.

A committee appointed at a preliminary meeting then offered the draft of a constitution, which was read, and its principles discussed, when the same was unanimously adopted, and was as follows :

CONSTITUTION
OF THE NEW YORK CITY ANTI-SLAVERY SOCIETY.
(Here the Constitution was inserted.)

The Society then went into the choice of Officers, when the following persons were chosen :

OFFICERS OF THE SOCIETY.

ARTHUR TAPPAN, PRESIDENT.
WILLIAM GREEN, Jr., VICE-PRESIDENT.
JOHN RANKIN, TREASURER.
ELIZUR WRIGHT, Jr., COR. SEC.
CHARLES W. DENISON, REC. SEC.
JOSHUA LEAVITT,
ISAAC T. HOPPER,
ABRAHAM L. COX, M. D.,   WITH THE ABOVE,
LEWIS TAPPAN,   MANAGERS.
WILLIAM GOODELL,

After which the meeting was adjourned.

JOHN RANKIN, CHAIRMAN.
ABRAHAM L. COX, Secretary.

The same day, the *Journal of Commerce* came out with a fair statement, ending as follows :

After all, it appears that the immediate emancipationists outgeneralled their opposers ; for while the latter were besieging Clinton Hall, or wasting wind at Tammany Hall, the former were quietly adopting their Constitution at Chatham-street Chapel. They had but just adjourned, we understand, when the din of the invading army, as it approached from Tammany Hall, fell upon their ears; and before the audience was fairly out of the chapel, the flood poured in through the gates as if they would take it by storm. But lo! they were too late; the Anti-Slavery Society had been formed, the Constitution adopted, and the meeting adjourned! So they had nothing to do but go home.

> "The king of France, with eighty thousand men,
> Marched up the hill, and then marched down again."

Shortly afterwards, Mr. Tappan met with a few friends to consider the propriety of issuing a call for an anti-slavery convention, to form a national society. The CALL was published in the anti-slavery newspapers, while letters were addressed to individuals in different parts of the country believed to be interested in the cause, inviting their attendance. The convention met in Philadelphia, December 4, 1833; had a harmonious meeting; adopted the Constitution of the "AMERICAN ANTI-SLAVERY SOCIETY," and a DECLARATION OF SENTIMENTS; and voted that the Society should be located in the City of New York.

ARTHUR TAPPAN was chosen President of the Society. He had neither sought the office nor expected it, but he was elected because, as one of the delegates said, "He will not flinch; you can rely upon him." He did not attend the convention, owing to a press of business, but his heart was much interested in the proceedings, and they had his entire concurrence. The executive committee of the new society had regular meetings, at which Mr. Tappan presided. His yearly subscription in aid of the Society's operations was three thousand dollars, which was in addition to considerable sums paid by him otherwise for the promotion of the cause. He continued its liberal supporter while he had the means. He fully identified himself with the cause so unpopular at its commencement, but destined to have, under the sanction and good providence of God, a glorious success.

During the six or seven years that he was connected with this society, he attended the annual meetings in New York, and presided, it was remarked, with unusual self-control and dignity amid the exciting scenes that often took place, owing to the feverish state of public feeling, and the attempts of the populace to disturb and break up the meetings, urged on as they were by embittered editors of the public press.

The society met with rapid and great success. Its auxiliaries were numerous and efficient; its agents, of whom there were many, lectured throughout the free states; the publications were scattered far and wide; and not a few men and women of culture and influence joined themselves to the ranks of the sect "everywhere spoken against."

THEODORE D. WELD, one of the lecturing agents of the society, had engaged to deliver a course of lectures at one of the towns in Jefferson county, Ohio. Previous to delivering the first, he gave notice to the audience that he had no objection to any one taking notes of what he should say. He observed a young man taking notes, and at the close made

inquiries about him. He was told he was a young
lawyer residing in the place. On reaching his lodgings, the stranger came to his room, introduced himself, and said: "I went to your lecture with the
intention of taking down your argument, and reply-
ing to it at a future time, but you have entirely
swept away the ground of my opposition." It was
predicted by the law partner of this young attorney
that if he lived, his talents would insure him the
office of attorney-general of the United States. The
prediction was fulfilled, and subsequently he actually
held a more important office in the government, that
of Secretary of War, during the tremendous conflict
that resulted in the downfall of slavery, and gave to
the name of EDWIN M. STANTON an enduring place
in the affections of his countrymen, and in the history of his country.*

It cannot be truly denied that some who were
engaged in the enterprise were indiscreet, and sometimes rash, both in language and measures; but it
is believed that, considering the opposition they met
and the false statements uttered respecting their
principles and measures, rarely has any reform been
conducted with more discretion. Still, as is ever
the case when aggressive movements are made for
the correction of public sentiment and the wicked
practices of men, the abolitionists were subject to

* The death of this distinguished patriot, in the early part of
1870, has been a national affliction. He was born at Steubenville,
Ohio, in 1815; was a law partner of SENATOR BENJAMIN TAPPAN;
and just before his lamented death had been appointed as associate justice of the Supreme Court of the United States.

denunciation both from the pulpit and the forum, in the walks of business, in religious and literary assemblies, and to social ostracism of themselves and families.

The publications issued by the society, and the annual reports contained in its newspapers, or published in pamphlet form, can be fearlessly appealed to in justification of the above remarks, while the attacks made upon individuals and the societies with which they were connected, by the pro-slavery press, evince in their spirit and language ample evidence of the falsity of most of the accusations.

The facilities given to slaveholders by obsequious and unprincipled magistrates in the Northern states for the recovery of their slaves, and the not unfrequent kidnapping of free people of color, under the forms of law, were notorious. Abolitionists and their colored friends were on the *qui vive;* but while they secured the freedom of many, they were often baffled by the subtlety or knavery of official persons who seemed to feel it to be an honor to bow the knee to the lords of the slaveocracy.

In illustration of the preceding remark, a case may be stated that occurred under the observation of the compiler. His attention was called by a colored man, who said, "I have just come from Recorder Riker's office, where is a man they are going to send into slavery; do come over as soon as you can." On reaching the office, then in the City Hall, it appeared that a stranger was urgently demanding that the recorder should give up a black man, who was present, whom he alleged was his slave. Several colored persons were there ready to affirm that the person claimed had lived in the city six months or more, and they believed they could prove that he had never been in a Southern state. Apparently yielding to the evidence and pleadings, the recorder at length said: "I will adjourn this hearing until to-morrow at 9 o'clock, A. M., when all parties will attend, and I will do what the law requires."

In anticipation of the hour of adjournment a few minutes, the writer went to the recorder's office, where were assembled the sympathizing friends of the colored man. Addressing the writer, this magistrate, to his astonishment, said: "I have given up that negro to his master, who told me the whole story; I believed every word he said, for he is a perfect gentleman—a perfect gentleman, sir, entitled to entire confidence." "Given him up!" was the reply; "did you not adjourn the hearing, sir, to this morning, and notify all parties to be present?" The recorder replied: "Yes, yes, I think I did, but I learned all the facts from the master; he satisfied me that the man belongs to him; and I believe he is to be relied upon—he is a most gentlemanly man. I believe every word he said."

While this was taking place the slaveholder and the victim of judicial tyranny were on their way to Virginia. The recorder listened rather impatiently to the expostulations offered and turned away from the grieved and disappointed colored persons that thronged his office, to take his seat on the bench of

the criminal court. Such was the administration of
the law in those days, in reference to fugitive slaves,
and those claimed as such! This was the first judicial announcement made that the negro has no
rights that white men are bound to respect. The
poor blacks were trembling with alarm, the remonstrances of their friends were unheeded, and base
acquiescence in the claims of Southern despots
almost universally prevailed throughout the Northern states.

In November, 1835, a meeting of the friends of
human rights was held for the purpose of adopting
measures to ascertain, if possible, the extent to
which the cruel practice of kidnapping men, women,
and children, was carried on in this city, and to aid
such unfortunate persons as may be in danger of
being *reduced to slavery*, in maintaining "their
rights." A committee was chosen, styled the "committee of vigilance," "to protect unoffending, de-
fenceless, and endangered persons of color, by
securing their rights, as far as practicable, and by
obtaining for them, when arrested, under the pretext of being *fugitive slaves*, such protection as the
law will afford."

The first anniversary of the "committee of vigilance" was celebrated on the evening of January 16,
1837, at the Presbyterian church, corner of Thompson and Houston streets, New York, Rev. Theodore
S. Wright, chairman. The exercises continued until
a late hour, while a large audience manifested their
interest by listening with profound attention to the

facts communicated, and to the appeals made, until the close of the meeting.

Rev. John T. Raymond, pastor of a Baptist church in the city, introduced the following resolution:

Resolved, That we commend the vigilance committee to the confidence, coöperation, and prayers of the friends of oppressed humanity.

Mr. Raymond spoke with great feeling on the force of prejudice, and related his own experience in being banished from his native state of Virginia, under a law that forbade free people of color to return after an absence of a year, because he had delivered a speech in New York, in relation to the Wilberforce colony, in Canada. Other addresses were made. The secretary presented to the audience the afflicted wife of PETER JOHN LEE, (a colored man who had been recently kidnapped from Rye, New York, and hurried into hopeless bondage, by the minions of slavery,) and her two fatherless little sons. The audience were deeply affected.*

The above account of the committee of vigilance is here presented because Arthur Tappan, and most other abolitionists, after becoming acquainted with its principles and measures, were greatly interested in them, and because such was the origin of the system of operations afterwards pursued, styled the "UNDERGROUND RAILROAD," which aided not only

* The *New York State Vigilance Committee* was formed fifteen years after; its object being "To assist persons seeking freedom from chattel slavery, and to protect and defend those whose personal liberty may be called in question."

fugitive slaves, long resident in the free states, but their relations and brethren in slave states to escape into Canada. At first, some abolitionists doubted the propriety of such measures, fearing they would not be justified in aiding slaves to escape from their masters: but reflection convinced them that it was right to ignore human enactments which were contrary to the law of God, and that it was not only right to assist men in efforts to obtain their liberty, when unjustly held in bondage, but a DUTY. He was always ready to help the flying fugitive on his way to Canada, or elsewhere, and was active in this benevolent work. It is a sufficient answer to those who pretended that it was wrong to meddle with slaves, or protect them in their flight from bondage, to quote the memorable saying of Lord BROUGHAM: "There is a law above all the enactments of human codes. It is written by the finger of God on the heart of man; and by that law, unchangeable and eternal, while men despise fraud, and loathe rapine, they shall reject with indignation, the wild and guilty fantasy that man can hold property in man."

The agitation of the slavery question in England for many years, in which THOMAS CLARKSON and WILLIAM WILBERFORCE were ably seconded by many coadjutors, and which resulted in an act of emancipation, that passed the British Parliament, and received the royal assent August 28, 1833, quickened the zeal and animated the hopes of the abolitionists in the United States.

The details of the act were adjusted on this basis namely:

1. The entire extinction of slavery, to take place on the 1st of August, 1834.

2. Field laborers, above six years old, to serve as apprentices for six years.

3. Domestics or house servants to serve as apprentices four years.

4. Children under six years, to be free, and children thereafter born to be free.

5. The slaves to pay no part of their redemption money, but a compensation of twenty thousand pounds, sterling, to be paid out of the public treasury, to the planters, *at the close of the apprenticeship.*

In Antigua and Bermuda, the colonial legislatures preferred to dispense with the "apprenticeship system," believing immediate and complete emancipation to be safest. The vexations attending the system in other islands led to its voluntary abandonment, and the entire freedom of the field laborers, on the 1st of August, 1838, two years before the time limited in the statute. The whole number liberated, in the British islands, was about eight hundred thousand.*

The abridgment of the apprenticeship system was due mainly to the efforts of JOSEPH STURGE, one of the most liberal and devoted friends of the slave among the British emancipationists. At his own charge he went to the West Indies in 1837, accompanied by two or three friends, whose expenses he

* See Goodell's "Slavery and Anti-Slavery."

defrayed, investigated the evils of the system, and
published the results. The effect was so great that
it soon led to the abandonment of the system.*

The executive committee of the American Anti-
Slavery Society deemed it so important that the
misrepresentations of the pro-slavery press of the
United States should be corrected by a publication
of facts and testimony ascertained on the spot, that
they deputed James A. Thome and Joseph H. Kim-
ball to proceed to the West Indies to make the investigations, Mr. Tappan contributing a large share of
the expenses.†

Both deputations arrived in the West Indies
near the close of the year 1836. The facts published by them had a remarkable agreement, and carried conviction to the minds of disinterested and
liberty-loving people, throughout the civilized world,
of the safety and advantage of immediate emancipation. American abolitionists were greatly cheered
and encouraged in their labors by the gratifying
intelligence thus spread before the people, and were
sanguine in belief that it would lead speedily to
universal freedom; but slaveholders and their allies
persistently labored to falsify the information, and
counteract its influence.‡

The venerable Thomas Clarkson wrote, for the

* See "The West Indies in 1837; being the Journal of a Visit
to Antigua, etc. By Joseph Sturge and Thomas Harvey."

† See "Emancipation in the West Indies, a Six Months' Tour
in Antigua, etc., in the year 1837, by J. A. Thome and J. H. Kim-
ball."

‡ See Appendix 5, for an interesting statement of Joseph Sturge.

information of Arthur Tappan, and his anti-slavery friends, that he had been informed by a British consul that *fictitious statements* respecting the condition of the emancipated in the West Indies and the condition of the islands, were sent to the United States as warnings to the people not to encourage the abolition of slavery.

While the abolitionists were active and fearless in their efforts to arouse public attention to the atrocities of slavery, the leading people of color were not inactive in labors to diffuse light and intelligence among their people; and to make them worthy of equal privileges wherever they should be secured to them.

They commenced the publication of a journal, edited and conducted by colored men, entitled "The Colored American and Advocate." It was commenced March 4, 1837, with the means contributed by anti-slavery friends, Mr. Tappan giving the largest·sum, and was a neatly printed and well edited paper; the proprietor was Philip A. Bell, and the editor Samuel E. Cornish, both men of color, men of abilities, of much consideration among their people, and respected by all who knew them.

The paper was intended to be the organ of colored Americans. Its columns were filled with excellent selected and original matter. It ably advocated the emancipation of the enslaved, and the elevation of the free colored people; and to this end it urged on the whites the abolition of caste, and on their own people a thorough education. Gifted men, among the people of color in New York and elsewhere, and there were not a few of them, had an opportunity, that was well improved, of addressing their people, and the public at large, in the columns of this excellent paper.

The appearance of this paper was cordially welcomed by Mr. Tappan, whose confidence in the editor was very great; and he believed it an important auxiliary to the cause of emancipation in promoting, on behalf of the people of color, LIBERTY and EDUCATION. It was sustained a year or two, giving abundant evidence of the capability of colored men to sustain a respectable newspaper, and was then discontinued, as were several other anti-slavery papers, during the financial convulsion that occurred throughout the country.

On the third day of December, 1863, a meeting of members of the convention that formed the "American Anti-Slavery Society," was held in Philadelphia, commemorative of that event, to which Mr. Tappan was specially invited. The following letter accompanied the invitation:

BOSTON, November 12, 1863.

DEAR AND VENERATED SIR: Thirty-three years seven months ago I was lying in the cell of the city prison in Baltimore, for the crime of exposing and denouncing certain townsmen of mine, whom I detected in carrying on the domestic slavetrade, between that city and New Orleans. Comparatively unknown at that time, and utterly without means to pay the fine and costs of court that were imposed upon me by a slaveholding judge, I might have died within those prison walls, if your sympathizing and philanthropic heart had not prompted you, unsolicited, to send the needed sum for my redemption. It is not for me to trace the consequences of that deed to the cause of the oppressed since that period; but I desire to assure you that my gratitude to you is as fresh and overflowing as it was when I was delivered from my incarceration, and will ever remain so.

It is now more than a score of years since I had the pleasure of seeing you. Time, of course, has been busy with us both in making his impression upon us, although I am considerably younger than yourself. On the 10th of next month I shall complete my fifty-eighth year. I presume you have numbered fourscore years. May God grant us the inexpressibly happy privilege of witnessing a universal jubilee, a horribly wicked rebellion suppressed, and peace and unity secured from sea to sea, before this "mortal shall have put on immortality." Your ever grateful friend,

WM. LLOYD GARRISON.
ARTHUR TAPPAN, ESQ.

At the meeting Mr. Garrison said: "The first letter I hold in my hand is from one who deserves to be held in honorable and lasting remembrance for his early, devoted, and long-continued service in our cause; I mean the first president of the American Anti-Slavery Society, once the distinguished merchant-philanthropist of the city of New York, ARTHUR TAPPAN; the benefactor to whom I owe my liberation from the Baltimore prison in 1830; and but for whose interposition at that time, in all probability I should never have left that prison, except to be carried out to be buried. I think it is some twenty years since I had the pleasure of looking into his face. But I could do no less than to send him a letter of invitation to be present at this commemorative meeting, renewing my expression of gratitude for all his kindness to me personally, and my admiration for all he had done in the cause of the oppressed; and I was glad to receive this letter in reply."

The letter was read, as follows, by WENDELL PHILLIPS GARRISON, one of the secretaries:

NEW HAVEN, Nov. 17, 1863.

WM. LLOYD GARRISON, ESQ., DEAR SIR: Few events could give me so much pleasure as the receipt of your note of the 12th inst. During the years that have intervened since we last met, I have often recalled the time when we were united in working for the slave, and regretted that any occurrence should have estranged us from each other.

I shall be glad to attend the meeting at Philadelphia, but my advanced age (seventy-eighth year) and growing infirmities may prevent. I am, very truly, your friend,

ARTHUR TAPPAN.

XI.

THE most unfounded charges were brought against the abolitionists, many of them being absurd as well as malicious. They were accused of a design to change the social habits of the community, to mix up people without any regard to distinctions in society, and to enforce associations of persons of education and culture on equal terms with ignorant and degraded persons. Not only an unscrupulous press, but persons moving in refined society gave out, as credible facts of which they were personally cognizant, that it was part of the creed of anti-slavery people, that marriage relations ought to take place between white and colored persons.

It was a singular fact, said a writer, that those who profess belief in strong, instinctive, insurmountable prejudices against color, are the very persons who are most alarmed about amalgamation by intermarriages; as if the two propositions did not obviously destroy each other. It was said that at a town meeting in New Hampshire the question was discussed, whether colored people ought to be admitted into schools upon equal terms with white scholars. One individual arose and treated the subject after the usual manner of those who have thought little about it. "If we cultivate these people," said he, "the first thing we shall know, they

will be marrying our daughters. Such a thing as a
kind social relation between the two races was never
intended by Providence. The colored people are
naturally inferior, and cannot be elevated. It is
impossible for us to exist together in the same community with them on equal terms; you might as
well try to mix oil and water."

Upon this, a plain farmer remarked: "Why, I
thought you said just now that the first thing we
should know they would be marrying our darters.
Now, if they wont mix any better than ile and water,
what are you afraid on?"

At the same meeting, a person observed that he
had no objection to colored people's being educated,
but they might get up schools for themselves. It
was his opinion that white folks had better let the
niggers alone. An elderly man arose, and asked the
following question: "When the angel of the Lord
commanded Philip to enter the chariot of the Ethio-
pian, and explain to him the Scriptures, what if
Philip had answered, 'I think, Lord, it is best for
white people to let the niggers alone'?"

These anecdotes illustrate the kind of dialogues
that were carried on in those days on the part of
the opponents and friends of emancipation. It appears almost incredible at the present day, that
stories respecting the social intercourse of leading
abolitionists with people of color should have the
currency they did during the heated controversy.
Persons in the higher walks of society, at that time,
did not scruple to repeat the slanders, sometimes

vouching for their truthfulness from their own knowledge!

The anti-republican and unchristian feeling of
caste, though much abated, has not yet been discarded, either by the cultivated or ignorant members of society. Abolitionists merely proclaimed
anew the doctrine maintained by the founders of
the republic, that all men have equal natural rights,
and are entitled to life, liberty, and happiness. It
follows, of course, that black men have the same
rights as white men; the right to acquire knowledge,
engage in pursuits of their own selection, and ele-
vate themselves in the intellectual and moral scale,
without molestation. Is it not an obvious sequence
that, as citizens of the same country, and as children of the same family of which God is the Father, they ought to be treated irrespective of complexion?

Mr. Tappan, and those associated with him, contended against the cruel and heartless usages of
society that oppressed and degraded the people of
color. They were excluded from the public schools,
academies and colleges, they were forced to sit in
"negro pews" in houses of public worship, often
obliged to partake of the bread and wine at the
Lord's supper after they had been served to the
white communicants, and denied the privilege of
obtaining instruction in theological seminaries to
qualify them to preach the gospel. They were refused seats in omnibuses and cars. They were compelled to remain on the decks of steamboats, while

other passengers were taking repose in cabins and staterooms. They were excluded from places of public amusement. They were forbidden the privilege of voting, and in all manner of ways maltreated, often by persons of less education and refinement than themselves. They were shut out from the jury seats even when their own people were on trial, and thus a fundamental principle of law and equity was ignored that a man has a right to be tried by his peers.

The whole community, with few exceptions, took part against them. Law-makers, magistrates, schoolmasters, ministers of the gospel, sextons, and hodcarriers seemed to conspire to browbeat persons of color, as unworthy to "live, move, and have a being" with themselves, or to pass by them with frigid indifference to their just claims.

The blindness as well as prejudice of the community, at that day, is illustrated by an anecdote told by Frederick Douglass. He attended public worship, and was directed to a "negro-pew" in an elevated corner of the gallery. The Lord's supper was celebrated. The preacher invited all the white brothers and sisters to come forward and partake of the elements; and when they had thus partaken, he looked up to the negro pew, and with outstretched arms exclaimed, "We now invite our colored friends to come down and partake of this holy feast, for the Lord is no respecter of persons!"

There were even then a few ministers who abhorred the caste feeling so generally prevailing, and

who did not hesitate to trample upon the usage as
a desecration of the house of God, and an abomination among Christian people.   Among these was
Dr. John M. Mason of the Murray-street church in
the city of New York.   He had invited a young
slave girl, Katy, afterwards the well-known and
highly respected Mrs. Catharine Ferguson, to unite
with his church.   He knew the hostile feeling that
prevailed at the time among certain prominent
members of his church, and was determined to
show his disapprobation of it.   Accordingly, when
he saw the timid girl standing afar off, near the end
of the broad isle, he went from the communion table, took her by the hand, and as he led her to a
seat near the Lord's table, he said aloud :

"For ye are all the children of God by faith in
Christ Jesus.   For as many of you as have been
baptized into Christ, have put on Christ.   There is
neither Jew nor Greek, there is neither bond nor
free, there is neither male nor female ; for ye are all
one in Christ Jesus."*

On another similar occasion, as the colored
members of the church were slowly coming down
stairs from the gallery to take the back seats, one
of the elders spoke to Dr. Mason across the com-

* Mrs. Ferguson had the privilege and the honor of establishing the first Sunday-school ever formed in the city of New York ;
and during her life she took from the almshouse and elsewhere,
at different times, forty children, white and black, supporting
them until they were of sufficient age to go into service, and then.
placing them in families to be reared for usefulness.   See tract
published by the Boston Tract Society.

munion table, saying, "Don't let the black people partake until the white members have got through." The doctor said, "Well, well;" and then addressing the colored communicants, he said, "Come this way, take seats here." He placed them in front of the table, and helped them to the bread and wine before it was passed to the other members of the church. ·

Anti-slavery men refused to be a party to all unrighteous conduct, set their faces against caste usages, and denounced them. For doing this they were slandered and maligned. On one occasion, Mr. Tappan finding the Rev. Samuel E. Cornish, a colored member of the First Presbytery of New York, of which the Rev. Dr. Spring was a member, standing on the steps of the Laight-street church, Rev. Dr. Cox's, invited him to take a seat in his pew. No little excitement was the result. The devotions of the congregation were much disturbed.

The services being over, one or more of the elders or trustees called upon the offending member of the church, remonstrated with him on the gross impropriety he had committed, and requested him in terms very like threatening not to repeat the offence. ·

Mr. Cornish was a mulatto, neat in his person, gentlemanly in his deportment, a well-educated man, a good preacher, and both he and Mr. Tappan had been managers of the American Bible Society. All this did not protect them from insult and annoyance in a house consecrated to the worship of

God on the part of those who professed to be his worshippers.

Dr. Cox, in view of the angry feelings prevailing in his congregation towards Mr. Tappan, attempted in his weekly lecture to set the matter right. He warned his people not to indulge these inhuman prejudices, and said that they might well inquire how white the Asiatics were, or how white must the complexion of the Saviour be, were he now on earth, in order for us to tolerate his person or endure his presence.

One of the daily papers, the *Courier and Enquirer*, came out with a violent attack upon Dr. Cox for his utterances to his own people, accusing him of having stated that the Saviour was a colored man, etc. Dr. Cox vindicated himself in another morning paper, the *Journal of Commerce*,* and gave a suitable answer to the aspersions. "How great and anti-philosophical, as well as anti-Christian," said he, " the prejudice of us Americans against our colored brethren ; that such a sentiment, ... guardedly applied to the complexion of Jesus Christ, should rouse the angry feelings of many . . . . whose blindness mistakes for piety the antipathy which despises the Creator in his creatures !" But for his vindication of Mr. Tappan, his espousal of the anti-slavery cause, and his controversy with the *Courier and Enquirer*, he was remembered afterwards by that paper and the mob, when his house and person were threatened and assailed.

* See *New York Evangelist* of June 21, 1834.

It so happened that a fellow-townsman of Mr.
Cornish, one of his own playmates in Virginia, a
man of a skin rather darker than his own, mixed at
the time and after with the "bulls and bears" of
Wall-street on equal terms. And why? Because
he had shaved his head, put on a wig, had considerable property, was an astute financier, and called
himself a Brazilian!

Mr. Tappan recognized among the colored inhabitants many excellent persons—scholars, artists, worthy members of society and of the church. They
were entitled to, but did not enjoy the privileges
and amenities of society. They were cramped in
their laudable efforts and aspirations by an insane
and heartless prejudice, as unmanly and preposterous as it was unchristian. The fact that so many
of the proscribed class stood up against the unjust
opprobrium, and by their industry, attainments, and
good conduct, had made their way to competence
and affluence and usefulness in spite of opposition,
was evidence sufficient of their inherent capabilities
and perseverance in the race of life.

Included in the number of the estimable colored
men contemporary with Mr. Tappan, was the Rev.
Theodore Sedgwick Wright, pastor of the church in
Frankfort-street, New York. He had his theological education at Princeton, N. J., and was highly
esteemed by his instructors, among whom was the
venerated Dr. Alexander. And yet, while attending
as a spectator, the annual meeting of the "Literary
Society of the Alumni" of Nassau Hall, having pre-

viously been a member, his unassuming deportment and evangelical piety did not screen him from rude and disgraceful treatment by some of the students in the chapel. His only fault was having a skin not colored like their own.

It was in Mr. Wright's church that a distinguished lawyer of New Orleans, recently deceased, Alfred Hennen, Esq., who was also an elder in the Presbyterian church of which Mr. Wright was a minister, on witnessing for the first time a commodious and well-lighted church belonging to colored people, a congregation of well-dressed and respectable persons, an organ and a choir of excellent singers, and an educated preacher, exclaimed, " This is a new and interesting scene to me, and I shall never forget it." The minister, unconscious that he was present, supplicated for slaveholders, for the country, and for the church, in a way that touched the feelings of Mr. Hennen, and called forth his warm encomiums.

He afterwards said to the friend who had accompanied him: " At your house to-day you convinced me that all the doctrines of the abolitionists are correct and unanswerable, except that of immediate emancipation, and I promised that if satisfied of the correctness of that doctrine, I would liberate my slaves forthwith. I am now satisfied on that point, and am resolved no longer to retain the relation I hold to slavery. You will soon hear from me, and, meantime, I wish you to give me copies of your principal publications, that I may take them to

New Orleans and show them to my friends." His request was complied with; but except a casual expression of remembrance in a letter to a mutual friend six months afterwards, he was not heard from again. For aught that was known, his convictions subsided, his promise was forgotten, and he remained a slaveholder until the proclamation of President Lincoln.

Mr. Tappan did not claim any peculiar merit for being free from the caste feeling that so generally prevailed. In childhood he had been taught to respect worthy colored persons. From one of them he had been the recipient of many kindnesses when quite young. Near the residence of his parents lived a colored woman, who had once been a slave in the family of a daughter of President Edwards, the mother of President Dwight of Yale College. She was kind to children, had a motherly watchfulness over them, and sometimes screened them from harsh treatment. Arthur was often at the house, with his hoop or sled, playing with the grandchildren of Madam Dwight, and many kind words and bits of cake did he and the other children receive from LILL, as she was called. At one time, when the little ones had wandered a mile or two from home, she went, near the close of day, in search of them, and brought them back.

Her memory was ever precious in his recollection, and next to their mothers, he and the other children thought her the best friend in the world. This pious and tender-hearted woman, Sylvia, lived during two generations in the Dwight family. She was an exemplary member of the church, and her remains repose in the central part of the village burying-ground, having a headstone at the grave, with an inscription commemorative of her excellent character. Her kindness to Arthur, and the affectionate regard he had for her, doubtless laid the foundation for the interest he ever after took in people of color. Dear old "Lill!" The subject of this narrative never looked, it may be, upon a colored face without thinking of you as a friend of Jesus, and as an inheritor of a glorious immortality.

It was during the year 1834 and afterwards that Mr. Tappan, accompanied by his long tried and devoted friend Mr. Jocelyn, who had moved to New York, was accustomed on Sabbath mornings to explore the streets in the ward where the poor people of color chiefly dwelt, visit them in their different rooms, inquire into their wants, administer relief, give them useful advice, invite them to Sabbath-schools, often praying with them. "He had," said one, " a deep sense of the worth of the soul, and the importance of efforts for the salvation of men."

An anecdote of an interesting character has been related by a merchant who was accustomed to purchase goods of Arthur Tappan, showing the hard feelings cherished towards him by unthinking and prejudiced persons, and how they were overcome by the Christian conduct of the abused man. This merchant said he was travelling in a public conveyance, and heard one of the passengers violently abusing Mr. Tappan. He replied, "I was formerly of the same opinion with yourself, and believed that man as much of a hypocrite as you do; but I ascertained that he was a humble Christian, and a praying, godly man. Once, while purchasing goods of him, I noticed a poor woman who came to solicit charity, and I heard him promise to call and see her. I had the curiosity, when he left the store, to follow him. I saw him enter the lowly dwelling, and listened at the door to inquiries he made, the prayer he offered, and his offer of pecuniary assistance. Now, as long as I live, I will never speak evil of that man again, nor hear him abused, without lifting up my voice in his behalf, for I know him to be a true philanthropist and a man of God."

It was seldom that he wrote any thing in defence or in explanation of his course on the anti-slavery or other reforms, but the following letter, addressed to a nephew residing in a foreign land, acquires an interest from its being an authentic exposition of his own feelings and views during several trying periods of his life.

TO A. F. STODDARD, ESQ., OF GLASGOW, SCOTLAND.

NEW HAVEN, Aug. 27, 1863.

MY DEAR NEPHEW : I have this day received yours of the 8th inst. Before this reaches you, the tidings of the death of my dear wife will doubtless have reached you. The event has made a great inroad on my happiness, but I will not murmur, but be thankful that she was spared to me fifty-three years; and now my aspiration is that we may soon be reunited where sorrow is unknown.

Respecting my early experience in the anti-slavery cause, I have time now to give you but a brief history. When it commenced, the news soon reached the South, and a large hotel was speedily filled with young Southerners, sons of "the chivalry," who came on to employ the southern argument, the bowie-knife and the pistol, to arrest our proceedings. By employing a young man to go to the same hotel to board, I found out their plans, and took the necessary precautions to elude them. My family was at the time living in this city, and I lodged in a building where rooms were let without board, and very near where the Southerners were congregated. Learning that they had fixed on the night for attacking me, and had provided tar to give me a coat of it on the coming *Sabbath* night, I, with a friend, left the city and spent the day up the North river. By changing my place of lodgings I again frustrated their attempt to get me.

It was our first object to get an anti-slavery society formed, and a time and place were agreed on. When the time came, we discovered that the enemy were on our track, and we went as privately as possible to another place; but by the time we were fairly at work, our enemies were upon us, and we hastily finished by adopting a constitution and appointing the officers, and escaped by the rear entrance while the mob were forcing the front door.

The only overt act of mine in the way of amalgamation, that I remember, was my giving a seat in my pew in Dr. Cox's church to a *clergyman* who, as I entered the church, was humbly waiting at the door for some one to invite him in, though he lived in the city, had a congregation (colored) of his own, and was but slightly tinged with the despised color, and I may add, was highly respected as a colored man; yet so great was the offence I committed, that the occupants of one or more neighboring pews withdrew from the society, and a great ferment was occasioned.

Though I advocated the sentiment that as Christians we were bound to treat the colored people without respect to color, yet I felt that great prudence was requisite to bring about the desired change in public feeling on the subject; and therefore, though I would willingly, so far as my own

9*

feelings were concerned, have *publicly* associated with a well educated and refined colored person, male or female, I felt that their best good would be promoted by my refraining from doing so till the public mind and conscience were more enlightened on the subject. If, therefore, you should know of any one's charging me with any gross assault on the fastidiousness of the age, when I became the avowed friend of the colored man, you may set it down to the score of ignorance or malignant falsehood. As to the assertion, that I understand is made against me on your side of the ocean, that I or any other one of my family have ever put arms into the hands of colored men or women in New York or anywhere else, it is without the slightest foundation. If the publication of what I have stated will be of any use in correcting public sentiment with you, please to use it.

With kind regards to your family, I am affectionately

Your uncle,

ARTHUR TAPPAN.

XII.

EXTENSIVE manifestations of mob violence were commenced in the summer of 1834, in the city of New York, and for two years or more prevailed in other cities and villages in different parts of the country. They were instigated by a servile press, and aided by unscrupulous politicians, who found in the apathy of a large majority of the people, opportunity to work upon the passions of the masses, in attempts to stifle free inquiry and free speech on the subject of American slavery.

Arrangements had been made by the executive committee of the American Anti-slavery Society to have a public meeting on the fourth of July, in Chatham-street chapel, to celebrate the anniversary of American Independence. It was thought to be a fitting occasion to speak of the rights of man, and to advocate universal freedom on a day consecrated by our forefathers to the maintenance of the unalienable rights of "life, liberty, and the pursuit of happiness," intended to be secured to themselves, their descendants, and all the inhabitants of the land, then and thereafter, to all generations.

DAVID PAUL BROWN, Esq., an eminent lawyer of Philadelphia, who had for many years been the friend and legal adviser of the people of color, bond and free, was invited to deliver an oration. A hymn was written for the occasion by JOHN GREEN-

LEAF WHITTIER, to be sung by a select choir, concluding in these words:

> "And grant, O Father! that the time
> Of earth's deliverance may be near,
> When every land and tongue and clime
> The message of thy love shall hear—
>
> "When smitten as with fire from heaven,
> The captive's chain shall sink in dust;
> And to his *fettered soul* be given
> THE GLORIOUS FREEDOM OF THE JUST!"

The Declaration of Independence, and the declaration of sentiments adopted by the society at its
formation, were also to be read.

A large audience was convened; a solemn address was offered to the Throne of Grace, the Declaration of Independence was read, but when the
declaration of sentiments was commenced, it became
manifest that hundreds of young men who sat near
the doors had determined if possible to prevent its
being heard. At length, however, the reader's voice
and perseverance triumphed over the noisy demonstrations. When the orator of the day, however,
had uttered but a sentence or two the exclamations
were so loud, and the derisive cheers so boisterous,
that, after several attempts to proceed, he felt
obliged to desist, and the meeting came to an abrupt termination, amid the hurrahs of the rioters.

On the following Monday, July 7, an article appeared in the *Courier and Enquirer*, a daily paper
edited by James Watson Webb, ridiculing Mr.
Brown's attempt to deliver his oration, and throw-

ing obloquy upon the abolitionists, while it misrepresented their sentiments. No one could fail to understand the animus of the concluding paragraph: "However much we may regret such irregularities as those at Chatham-street chapel, it must be borne in mind that it is the Tappanists who produce them."

The evening of the 7th had been selected by the people of color to celebrate their anniversary, and listen to an oration on American independence by one of their own number, Mr. Hughes. THE NEW YORK SACRED MUSIC SOCIETY, had a lease of the chapel for every Monday and Thursday evening. As they were not to use it for the evening of the 7th, an arrangement had been made by which the colored people could have possession on that evening. One of the officers of the society, Dr. Rockwell, who had not been apprized of the fact, on passing by and seeing the building lighted up, stepped in to see the reason of it. Supposing, as was stated, that leave had been given to the colored people to use the room in violation of the agreement with the society, he was highly incensed, and commanded the speaker, who was in the midst of his oration, to desist, and ordered the audience to disperse.

The officers of the meeting not being disposed to obey the order, Dr. Rockwell and some members of the society, who had come there ignorant of the arrangements by which the colored people were in possession of the room for that evening, proceeded to remove the occupants of the platform by force. Resistance was made and the blacks overpowered the whites. A portion of the furniture was destroyed during the melee.

The *Courier and Enquirer* of July 8, seized the occasion to defame the colored people and the abolitionists, and to stir up the populace to vengeance against them. The editor, under the heading of " *Negro Riot*," said :

Another of those disgraceful negro outrages, with which our city has been afflicted for some days, and with which we shall continue to be annoyed, until Arthur Tappan and his troop of incendiaries shall be put down by the strong arm of the law, occurred last night, at that common focus of pollution, Chatham-street chapel. During the afternoon of Monday, July 7, a black fellow, named Hughes, was to deliver an oration on the subject of American Independence, to a congregation of blackamoors at Chatham-street chapel. THE NEW YORK SACRED MUSIC SOCIETY have a lease of the building for Monday and Thursday evening of each week, and had assembled as usual for the purpose of practice, when to their utter astonishment they found the orchestra filled up with negroes and negresses. The Vice-president and members of the Sacred Music Society, after the blacks had commenced their proceeding, insisted upon their right to the room, etc.

The riot at the chapel last evening was a riot commenced and carried on by the negroes themselves. The white citizens present were there with no disposition to disturb the blacks. It was the Sacred Music Society alone that interfered, as they were fully justified in doing : and when they mildly insisted on their clear rights they were beaten—yes, beaten, fellow-citizens, by the bludgeons of an infuriated and an *encouraged* negro mob ! How much longer are we to submit ? In the name of the country, in the name of heaven, how much more are we to bear from Arthur Tappan's mad impertinence ?

Such was the perversion of facts, and such the
too successful efforts made to stir up the populace
to take vengeance against the despised people of
color and their anti-slavery friends. The editor of
the *New York Evening Post*, of the 8th of July, remarked: "The story is told in the morning journals,
in very inflammatory language, and the whole blame
is cast upon the negroes; yet it seems to us, from
those very statements themselves, that, as usual,
there have been faults on both sides, and more
especially on the side of the whites."

In another editorial in the *Courier and Enquirer*
of Wednesday, July 9, headed "The Fanatics," it
was said:

A meeting was held at Clinton Hall last night for the purpose, we believe, of again discussing the question of immediate abolition. . . . There were about fifty negroes, male and
female, present, and about twice that number of white people. Learning that there is to be another meeting to-night
at Chatham-street chapel, we caution the colored people of
this city against it. No one who saw the temper which per-
vaded last night can doubt that if the blacks continue to
allow themselves to be made the tools of a few blind zealots,
the consequences to them will be most serious.

The above inflammable article seems to have
been a sheer fabrication, as none of the prominent
people of color, or abolitionists, heard of any such
meeting.

In the *Courier and Enquirer* of Thursday, July
10, was an account of the proceedings of the mob
under the head of "Disturbances in the City." The
paper states that a considerable crowd collected in
front of the entrance to the chapel, (the gates of

which were closed,) and remained for some time in silence, as if waiting to learn the result. "No indications of a meeting, however, were apparent," said the editor; but, in the same paper, he afterwards said, "it seems that a meeting was held; the mayor appeared accompanied by the district attorney and some police officers, and the meeting hastily adjourned."

The only meeting held, it is believed, was that of the rioters, who were in search of the law-abiding abolitionists, and the peaceable people of color, determined on creating a disturbance in compliance with the insidious intimations given by the profligate paper alluded to. As they fled from the chapel there was a cry of "To the Bowery! to the Bowery!" but a portion of the assemblage proceeded to the house of Lewis Tappan, No. 40 Rose-street. The *Courier and Enquirer*, well versed in the art of suppressing facts, or fabricating them, disposed of this attack by simply saying, "We learn that a brickbat was thrown into one of the windows; but no other injury was then done."

A portion of the rioters repaired to the Bowery theatre, to be revenged on one of the actors who, it was reported, had used some "disrespectful expressions towards the American people." A body of watchmen with their clubs came down the Bowery, and about the same number shortly after from the park. The theatre was closed, and a few persons collected in the rear, on Elizabeth-street, and broke some windows.

About half past nine o'clock, a bell was rung, and a cry arose of " Away to Arthur Tappan's!" A great number then proceeded to the house of Lewis Tappan, his wife and children being at the time · with him at Harlem. They broke open the door, smashed the blinds and windows, the looking-glasses, crockeryware, and threw the furniture into the street. The mob next lighted a fire and fed it with the beds and bedding taken from the house.

Mr. Arthur Tappan, being in the city, went to the house of his brother, muffled up so as not to be recognized, mixed with the rioters, and afterwards repaired, with Mr. Jocelyn, to the office of the mayor, whom they persuaded to send to the house a posse of the police, to disperse the mob. This was attended with some success. He heard one of the officers inquire, " Who is that man?" and on being told, the officer said, "I shall not be able to protect him if it is known that he is here." The name was being called on every side, with curses. "He had better leave," said the officer. At this time an alarm of fire was ordered to be sounded, which brought the engines to the spot, and order was finally restored at this place.

Hon. SCHUYLER COLFAX, now Vice-President of the United States, being then a boy and living in New York, his native city, had the curiosity, with thousands of other persons, to visit the scene of mob violence the next day, relates that the impressions he then received against the "institution of slavery" had an abiding influence. The sacrifice of property, in the loss of furniture and the damage to the house, was a small sacrifice upon the altar of freedom, especially when it made such an impression on one who has since become both an ornament and a blessing to his country.*

A feverish state prevailed throughout the city on Thursday, and it was evident that the rioters had greatly increased in numbers, in strength, and in intentions of mischief. Indications were very apparent that they intended to attack Mr. Tappan's store, in Pearl-street, Hanover square. Numbers of persons were prowling about, and some ventured to throw stones and break some of the windows. By the advice of the mayor the store was defended, night and day, with firearms, the clerks and several men engaged for the emergency at all times ready to use them if occasion required. Mr. Tappan was at the store day and night, overseeing and directing all the movements for the defence of the property. He directed that no violence should be offered to the assailants, unless they obtained entrance by breaking in the doors and windows.

The editor of the *Commercial Advertiser* stated that Assistant Alderman Johnson, one of the counsel of Rev. Dr. Janeway, owner of Chatham-street chapel, had called upon him and requested the insertion of the following CARD: "The owners of the Chatham-street chapel have been assured by the lessee" (Mr. William Green) "*that no meeting on the subject of slavery shall be hereafter held in the building.*

* See Appendix 6, for Mr. Colfax's letter.

The chapel will be closed *this evening*, until Sunday next, and then opened only for public worship."

On Thursday night, July 10th, an attack was made on the store. Almost every pane of glass at the front end of the store was broken, but the perpetrators of the mischief feared to proceed farther, being apprised that a large force from within would open fire upon them if they persisted in their designs. The next day the windows and doors on the front of the store were barricaded, and at night a number of men, as before, armed with muskets, stood prepared for any onset that might be made.

Large crowds of people had been through the day constantly passing back and forward in the vicinity of the house of Lewis Tappan. At night the number of persons assembled there became immense, and they branched off into different directions. Some gathered about the gate of the Chatham-street chapel, but finding it was not open they soon left the spot. Others proceeded to the church of Rev. Dr. Cox, at the corner of Laight and Varick streets, and others to his dwelling house on Charlton near McDougal-street. In both places, before the watch arrived, they broke a few windows, but the timely interference of the police, and a small detachment of cavalry and infantry that came to their aid by command of the mayor, prevented farther injury.

The mob also visited the houses of John Rankin, William Green, Rev. H. G. Ludlow, and the office of McDowall's Journal. The churches and schools of

the colored people were also marked out for the
vengeance of the infuriated multitude.

On Friday afternoon, July 11th, the mayor issued
a proclamation, which was posted in every part of
the city, requiring and ·commanding all good citizens to unite in aid of the civil authorities, to put an
end to these disreputable occurrences. Major-Gene-
ral Morton issued an order, directing the several
brigades of his division to be on their respective
parade grounds at 4 o'clock, P. M., on Saturday the
12th, to assist the civil authorities in putting down
the rioters. The military and civil forces assembled
from time to time the ensuing week. At the same
time the whole body of the city police were put in
requisition, and a large force of military, consisting
of cavalry and infantry, amounting, it was said, to a
division of troops, was ordered out, and the next
day stationed at the arsenal, to be ready in case
their interference should be required.

The "respectable" portion of the community,
that had, thus far, looked on with indifference, or a
willingness to see the hated band of abolitionists punished to a certain extent by popular violence, began
to be alarmed for the safety of their own property,
it being reported that the mob intended to make
some demonstrations in Wall-street, where the moneyed institutions of the city were principally situated.
The persons interested were at length aroused to
stimulate and sustain the magistracy in efforts to
suppress disorder and defend the rights of the citizens, abolitionists included. And ere long the su-

premacy of the laws was amply maintained by the
military force under arms, prepared to sally forth at
short notice, to suppress crime, and guard the public peace. Meantime the riotous acts were continued, the law-breaking individuals, justly supposing,
it may be, that the imbecile mayor only meant a
feint by issuing the proclamation and summoning a
military force, as while exhorting the people to
abstain from breaking the laws, he had seen fit to
allude to the doctrines and measures of the abolitionists, as the acts of " a few misguided individuals," in a way not calculated to allay popular ferment.

On this night, Dr. Cox's church was again attacked, and the windows demolished. The Presbyterian church on Spring-street, of which Rev. H. G.
Ludlow was pastor, was assailed by the mob, who
very deliberately prepared themselves for a regular
attack upon this edifice. They placed a barricade
of carts and wagons across the street, in order to
prevent the military and authorities from interfering
with the designs of the multitude, and then commenced a fire of stones and missiles at the church.
By such means the doors and windows were smashed, and the crowd made a rush for the interior.
The building was instantly filled to overflowing, the
organ, pulpit and pews demolished, and the infuriated mob were in the act of tearing down the galle-
ries, when a troop of cavalry arrived and put an end
to their proceedings, after the rioters had been for
a long time undisputed masters. The mob then

passed up Laurens-street, to the house of the pastor, whose family had retired. Here they broke in the windows and doors. A company of military appeared, formed in line, and the mob speedily quit the place.

On their way down the city they broke some of the windows in the colored church, corner of Leonard and Church streets. They also materially injured the colored church in Centre-street, near Anthony. The windows were broken, and the interior much damaged. The house of the minister, adjoining, Rev. Mr. Williams, shared no better fate. For one or two hours the mob were left undisputed masters of the ground. Four or five houses, occupied by colored persons, in Mulberry-street, were completely despoiled. A colored barber, named Davis, in Orange-street, whose property to the amount of several hundred dollars was destroyed, fired four musket shots at the assailants, and wounded one man.

The attacks of the mob, consisting of two to three thousand persons, in the neighborhood of the Five Points, were directed to all the houses known to be occupied by blacks. A dozen or more in Orange, Mulberry, Elm, and Centre streets, occupied by colored people, were more or less injured, the roofs torn from several, and the furniture they contained was either burned or broken to pieces. Among them was the "Mutual Relief Society Hall," in Orange-street. The house of a colored man in Leonard-street was forced open, and robbed of $192 in specie, four watches, and other articles. Other acts of wanton barbarity committed in the neighborhood, were reported in the newspapers.

While the watchmen and peace officers were engaged in quelling this mob, a third mob, amounting to some thousands, gathered in front of Arthur Tappan's store in Pearl-street, and threatened demolition to that establishment. To accomplish their purpose the more readily, the crowd had caused a load of stones to be dumped near the store and had supplied themselves with brickbats from the ruins of a recent fire in Pearl-street, which they might have used with effect, had not Justice Lowndes, accompanied by a company of watchmen, appeared just as the attack began, when, after a few minutes, there was not a rioter to be seen.

At two o'clock on Saturday morning the rioters had generally dispersed, though the police and military were still on duty. The depredations, it was evident, were not committed by the same persons, but by different bodies. The tranquillity was undisturbed during Saturday and Sunday.

On Saturday, July 12th, a handbill was posted in different parts of the city, as follows:

AMERICAN ANTI-SLAVERY SOCIETY—DISCLAIMER.

The undersigned, in behalf of the executive committee of the "American Anti-Slavery Society," and of other leading friends of the cause, now absent from the city, beg the attention of their fellow-citizens to the following DISCLAIMER:

1. We entirely disclaim any desire to promote or encourage intermarriages between white and colored persons.

2. We disclaim, and utterly disapprove, the language of a

handbill recently circulated in this city, the tendency of
which is thought to be to excite resistance to the laws. Our
principle is, that even hard laws are to be submitted to by all
men, until they can by peaceable means be altered.

3. We disclaim, as we have already done, any intention to
dissolve the Union, or to violate the constitution and laws of
the country; or to ask of Congress any act transcending their
constitutional powers; which the abolition of slavery by
Congress, in any state, would plainly do.

ARTHUR TAPPAN,
JOHN RANKIN.

On the 17th July, several members of the executive committee of the American Anti-Slavery Society addressed a letter to Mayor Lawrence, in which
they presented a statement of facts, showing that
they had neither done nor designed anything inconsistent with their duty as patriots, as Christians, as
friends of the Union, and of the peace and prosperity of the city. The letter concludes as follows:

Having thus expressed our principles, and disclaimed a
few of the numerous charges promulgated against us, we do
not wish to trouble you, or the Common Council, with more
detailed expositions, not being conscious that we ought to
recant or relinquish any principle or measure we have adopted, and being willing as free American citizens, to live and
die by the constitution of our society, and the declaration of
the National Anti-Slavery Convention.

We herewith transmit to you a copy of each of the publications issued by the society since its formation, and have
the honor to be

Your fellow-citizens, respectfully,

ARTHUR TAPPAN,
JOHN RANKIN,
E. WRIGHT, JR.,
JOSHUA LEAVITT,
WILLIAM GOODELL,
LEWIS TAPPAN,

NEW YORK, July 17, 1834.   SAMUEL E. CORNISH.

" The communication was treated with great contempt by the Board of Aldermen, although a perfectly respectful document," said the *Evening Post*.

It is manifest that an effectual stop could have been put to the riotous proceedings had the public authorities been prompt and efficient in using the police force. Their culpable apathy was notorious. The maddened rioters, intoxicated with success, and believing that the magistracy of the city winked at the tumult, were prepared to molest the moneyed interests of the city, including the property of some of these magistrates. Then, and not till then, was the majesty of the law displayed; and the riot quickly subsided.

The editor of the *Courier and Enquirer*, above all other editors of the daily press, had employed his utmost skill to inflame the public mind and bring about the discomfiture of the anti-slavery party. On Friday, July 11th, he said: "It is time for the reputation of the city and perhaps for the welfare of themselves, that these abolitionists and amalgamators should know the ground on which they stand. Now we tell them, that when they openly and publicly promulgate doctrines which outrage public feelings they have no right to demand protection from the people they thus insult."

This was said, while in the same paper, the editor professed that it was "a painful task" to record the mischief he himself had instigated. "Deeply indeed," he says, "is the state of things to be deplored." Again, in his paper of July 14th, he

10

stated: "On the whole, we trust the immediate abolitionists and amalgamators will now see in the proceedings of the last few days, sufficient proof that the people of New York have determined to prevent the propagation among them of their wicked and absurd doctrines, much less 'to permit the practice of them. If we have been instrumental in producing this desirable state of public feeling, we take pride in it. Let our political opponents make the most of the avowal. New York will henceforth not permit the ears of her people to be polluted by tenets that degrade Christianity, are an insult to common sense, and threaten the greatest disasters to the inhabitants of many of our sister states."

He goes on to say: "The indications of public indignation which have been exhibited against this church [Dr. Cox's] have induced six of the trustees to call upon us with a request that we would state to the public that' of the nine trustees who represent the congregation only *one* approves of the doctrines and opinions of Dr. Cox, and not one-fortieth of his congregation coincide with him on the subject of immediate abolition."

During all this period, Mr. Tappan was enabled to retain his accustomed composure and firmness, carrying on his large business as usual, bent on discharging his duty fearlessly, as a citizen and Christian, let the consequences to himself be what they might. He put his trust, not in an arm of flesh, but in that BEING who causeth the wrath of man to praise him, while the remainder he restrains.

The New York papers, with only one or two exceptions, had denounced the abolitionists, and continued to misrepresent them. The *Courier and Enquirer*, edited by James Watson Webb, was the most virulent, and the *Commercial Advertiser*, edited by William L. Stone, the most unscrupulous, if possible, while the *New York Times*, the *Journal of Commerce*, the *New York Evening Star*, the *New York Mercantile Advertiser*, the *Truth Teller*, and *New York Observer*, followed in the train, misrepresenting and abusing the abolitionists and the people of color.

Better things were expected of the *American*, edited by Charles King, whose family had professed to espouse the cause of freedom, but even he could now say: "The grand jury have their duty to perform at the present exigency, and one of the first we hold to be, to indict Dr. Cox, Mr. Tappan, and their associates as PUBLIC NUISANCES. We are credibly informed, that among our most respectable citizens there is testimony enough in relation to their share in the present shameful proceedings, to sustain a bill against them."

Posterity will be surprised that the editor of the *New York Observer*, a professed evangelical paper, should have published the following: "It is said that abolitionists agitate the subject of slavery in a way that endangers the safety of the South and the Union of the States. This is true. It is true that some of the most conspicuous of the abolitionists are wild and reckless incendiaries, and if they should succeed in infusing their spirit into the mass

of the population at the North, civil war would be
excited in the South, and there would be an end at
once to our happy union."

While the city press generally, including one or
more of the religious journals, was in violent opposition to the abolitionists, the *New York Evening
Post*, a democratic political paper, edited by WILL-
IAM LEGGETT, who was not at the time an abolitionist, came out manfully in opposition to the riots, and
to the quasi support given to them by the daily and
weekly press, and in vindication of the colored people, and their friends.   He said: "The fury of de-
mons seems to have entered into the breasts of our
misguided populace.   Like those ferocious animals
which, having once tasted blood, are seized with an
insatiable thirst for gore, they have had an appetite
awakened for outrage, which nothing but the most
extended and indiscriminate destruction seems capable of appeasing.   The cabin of the poor negro, and
the temple dedicated to the service of the living
God, are alike the objects of their blind fury.   The
rights of private and public property, the obligations of law, the authority of its ministers, and even
the power of the military, are all equally spurned
by these audacious sons of riot and disorder."

The progress this intrepid and distinguished
man afterwards made in anti-slavery principles is
shown in a letter he addressed to a friend:

AYLEMERE, NEW ROCHELLE, N. Y., October 24, 1838.

What I am most afraid of is, that some of my friends, in
their too earnest zeal, [referring to the Congressional election

of 1838, when Mr. Leggett was a candidate in the nominating committee,] will place me in a false position before the public on the slavery subject. I am an abolitionist. I hate slavery in all its forms, degrees, and influences; and I deem myself bound by the highest moral and political obligations, not to let that sentiment of hate lie dormant and smouldering in my own breast, but to give it free vent, and let it blaze forth that it may kindle equal ardor through the whole sphere of my influence. I would not have this fact disguised or mystified, for any office the people have it in their power to give. Rather, a thousand times rather, would I again meet the denunciations of Tammany hall, and be stigmatized with all the foul epithets with which the anti-abolition vocabulary abounds, than recant or deny one tittle of my creed. Abolition is, in my sense, a necessary and a glorious part of democracy; and I hold the right and the duty to discuss the subject of slavery, and to expose its hideous evils in all its bearings, moral, social, and political, as of infinitely higher moment than to carry fifty sub-treasury bills.

. . . And here let me add, I would not, if I could, have my name disjoined from abolitionism. To be an abolitionist, is to be an "incendiary" now. . . . The stream of public opinion now sets against us; but it is about to turn, and the regurgitation will be tremendous. Proud in that day may well be the man who can float in triumph on the first refluent wave, swept onward by the deluge which he himself, in advance of his fellows, had largely shared in occasioning. Such be my fate! and, living or dead, it will, in some measure, be mine. I have written my name in ineffaceable letters on the abolition record, and whether the reward ultimately come in the shape of honors to the living man, or a tribute to the memory of a departed one, I would not forfeit my right to it for as many offices as ——— has in his gift, if each of them was greater than his own.[o]

The following statement is furnished by Rev. S. S. Jocelyn:

The address of Mayor Lawrence, after the night of the

* See 2d vol., pp. 335, "Life and Writings of Wm. Leggett."

mob, breaking your furniture and burning part of it in the
street before the house, was posted all about the city. Though
it called upon the citizens to preserve law and order, it rather
inflamed the populace by its reference to the "misguided
abolitionists," who, it was intimated, had uttered inflammatory
sentiments, and were guilty of reprehensible conduct. Those
were indeed days of darkness. Satanic power seemed to prevail, reminding one of the hour of darkness at the time of
the betrayal and crucifixion of Christ. Men's faces gathered
blackness. Mr. Arthur Tappan, and others of our number,
were looked upon as public enemies, seeking to annihilate
all the valuable interests of the nation, all the (so called)
sacred rights of the Southern States, and the commerce of
the city.

I recollect the fearful night when the mob in great force
threatened to break into Mr. Tappan's store, and destroy
both property and life. I was in the store part of the time,
and also mingled with the crowd, and heard the mutterings.
"These Tappans, Arthur and Lewis, are always making
trouble; they tried to get up Sunday mail laws; now they
are engaged in abolition acts; *it is time they were stopped.*"
It was noised about that there was a sufficient provision of
arms and men in the store, and that Mr. Tappan intended to
use them in defence of his property and rights. This did
more to keep the peace than all the police or military forces
outside. The clerks in Mr. Tappan's employ, and several
friends who volunteered their services, were in the store, fully
armed, and ready to stand by the life and property of the
assailed.

During all this time Mr. Tappan was as firm as man
could be. He moved about quietly and coolly, giving directions, animating his friends by his bearing and words.
While he placed all due reliance upon the force organized in
the store, he evidently looked up to the God of the oppressed as his chief defender. On Saturday the bank directors,
and the principal merchants, began to be apprehensive for
the safety of their own treasures and goods. The mob had
become more and more emboldened and reckless, seeking
not only to wreak their vengeance upon obnoxious individu-

als, but to plunder the banks. Moneyed men were exceedingly frightened at the apparent strength and violence of the
mob, and the possible results of the storm that was raging,
upon which they had hitherto looked with unconcern.

Some of the friends of Mr. Tappan's family, who did not
sympathize with him in his anti-slavery opinions, were apprehensive that his life was in danger; they recalled to his recollection that rewards were offered for his head, and that it
was said, a vessel was prepared to take him South. To allay
their fears he promised to spend the ensuing Lord's day in
the country, and accordingly he left with me Saturday afternoon for Poughkeepsie. We stopped at the City hotel,
attended church, and returned to New York Monday
morning.

Mr. Tappan's family lived at this time at New Haven, and
he had lodgings at the house in Cedar-street where I boarded.
On our return from Poughkeepsie we found soldiers stationed
in our rooms. We were told that during Saturday night
men were seen lurking about the house, and their conversation was heard by some of the inmates. They seemed to be
concocting mischief, and at length agreed upon a time to
come again and seize Mr. Tappan. They came, but on seeing soldiers about, guarding the premises, they went away.
On the Sabbath also parties were seen hovering about; but
fearing, as it seemed, the armed force, no violence was
attempted. Mr. Tappan went to his store on Monday as
usual, and continued to do so daily, with the calmness becoming the great benevolent and Christian principles that animated him, filling his soul, and banishing all fears of consequences.

At one time I had a room contiguous to his at a boarding-
house, and there was a door between them. He often invited me into his apartment, where we sat and sometimes
prayed together. The childlike simplicity and deep reverence of his prayers were peculiar. I saw him occasionally
also in his house. His tenderness and courtesy in domestic
life were very happy. Both he and·Mrs. Tappan sympathized with and aided me in my labors among the colored
people. I always had a most welcome reception from them,

and all their family. His influence was highly spiritual, and blessed to his family and those intimate friends, who best knew how to appreciate his excellent traits of character.

The brevity and explicitness of his style of conversation were in harmony with his mode of speaking, either as a presiding officer of a public meeting, or a chairman of a committee, though when perfectly released from care, he could be for a time fluent, and no stranger to humor, enjoying a stroke of pleasant wit, especially if it had a good moral element.

The Church of Christ, with all its defects, was dear to him, and hence his fidelity to it in endeavoring to remove its blemishes, especially the giant sin of slavery and the sin of caste, which was so exceeding great at the North. God, who heard his prayers, permitted him as well as ourselves to see the day of deliverance to the slave and the nation, and to witness a great change for the better, in the churches on these subjects. Formerly, instead of regard for anti-slavery efforts, many of them exhibited decided opposition. A great change for the better, but still how slow the abolition of caste! I have often witnessed his sensibility when conversing upon the wrongs and sufferings of others, and remember well his deep emotion, even shedding tears, on hearing statements of the Christian Commission during the civil war.

XIII.

MR. TAPPAN took great interest in the election of
Rev. Dr. Lyman Beecher of Boston to be the senior
professor of Lane Seminary, near Cincinnati. It
was owing to him chiefly that the appointment took
place. For many years he had been desirous of
promoting education at the West, especially of
young men for the Christian ministry in the valley
of the Mississippi. It was therefore with peculiar
gratification that he had induced a man of such
eminent qualifications to assume the oversight of
this theological school. His satisfaction was much
increased when he learned that a large number of
the students of Oneida Institute, in the state of
New York, had decided to resort to Lane Seminary
to prosecute their studies. He encouraged the
trustees in the enterprise, and held out to them
expectations of liberal pecuniary aid.

While the students were pursuing their studies
with energy and success, and interesting themselves
in the great topics of the day, preparatory to entering upon the duties and responsibilities of life, the
anti-slavery cause, among other questions, came up
for discussion. The students had already formed
societies for different objects, such as, for Inquiry
on Missions, for Mutual Improvement, a Bible Society, a Foreign Mission Society, a Colonization Socie-

10*

ty, and a society for Miscellaneous Discussion.
These societies had been formed without the for-
mality of asking permission either of the faculty or
the trustees. *Neither body took any exception to them.*
When the students saw fit to add to the number an
Anti-Slavery Society they submitted to Dr. Beecher,
at his request, the preamble and constitution. He
expressed his entire approbation of their spirit and
sentiments.

The anti-slavery and the colonization questions
had become exciting ones throughout the whole
country, and the students deemed it to be their duty
thoroughly to examine them, in view of their bearing upon their future responsibilities as ministers of
the gospel. The condition of the colored people in
the neighborhood, many of whom had escaped from
bondage in the adjacent states, added to the interest
felt in these questions.

The trustees became alarmed, fearing a loss of
interest in the seminary, a loss of funds, and a loss
of students. The professors, though generally sympathizing with the students, shared to some extent
the apprehensions of the trustees, and were unwilling to oppose them. They advised the students not
to discuss either the anti-slavery or the colonization
question, as the subjects were exciting, and the discussion of them would be likely to excite opposition
in the neighborhood, and might result in serious
differences among the students themselves. A committee of students waited on the faculty, and expressed to them their confidence, that they could

discuss grave moral questions, of deep public interest, without quarrelling among themselves; they
also stated that they should feel it their duty to
go forward in the discussion, if it was not prohibited. They were assured that no prohibition was
intended. The discussion therefore proceeded, and
was conducted with almost entire unanimity.

The trustees soon expressed a determination to
prevent all further discussion of the comparative
merits of the policy of the Colonization Society,
and the doctrine of immediate emancipation, either
in the recitation rooms, the rooms of the students,
or at the public table; although no objection had
previously been made to the free discussion of
any subject whatever. During the vacation that
followed, in the absence of a majority of the professors, this purpose was framed into a law, or rule,
of the seminary, and obedience to it required from
all.

The trustees laid down the doctrine that "no
associations or societies ought to be allowed in the
seminary, except such as have for their immediate
object, improvement in the prescribed course of
studies." This was followed by an *order* in these
words: "Ordered that the students be required to
discontinue those societies [the Anti-slavery and
Colonization societies] in the seminary."

When this arbitrary order of the trustees was
passed, Dr. Beecher was on a journey to New England, in the interest of Lane Seminary. In the
hearing of thousands, at Boston, New York, and

other places, he had spoken of the students in high terms. "They are," he said, "a set of noble men, whom I would not at a venture exchange for any others." Professor Stowe also "had vindicated the character of the students, asserted their diligence in study, their respectful demeanor towards the faculty, their obedience to law, and their Christian deportment."

On his return to the West, and while in New York, Dr. Beecher invited several prominent abolitionists to meet him and Rev. Dr. Skinner, at the Tract House, on subjects growing out of the recent discussions at Lane Seminary. Accordingly, Arthur Tappan, John Rankin, S. S. Jocelyn, S. E. Cornish, and several others attended. Dr. Beecher stated that he had conferred with leading men, in Boston and elsewhere, with respect to the difficulties between the trustees and the students, and he had invited the present meeting to see if the discordance between anti-slavery men and colonizationists could not be harmonized. He said that he did not think the differences were so great that this could not be effected without material sacrifices of opinion and feeling. Both parties, he added, believed slavery to be an evil, and both desired its removal, if it could be effected peacefully and on righteous principles.

Dr. Skinner also expressed a hope that contention would cease, and that Christian men, who aimed to promote the welfare of the colored race, would no longer be at variance on subjects of so much importance, and which involved the peace of the country and the world.

They were replied to by Mr. Tappan, and other friends of the anti-slavery cause present. They stated the principles and aims of the two societies, and the measures that had been pursued by them, showing that both in principle and conduct, they were diverse and in direct opposition. One of them considered slaveholding a crime against man and a sin against God; that the government had been founded on the doctrine of the equality of man before the law; that Christianity inculcated love to our fellow-men, and discarded prejudice, alienation, and tyranny in all their forms; that this country was the birthplace and home of the colored man, bond and free, and that here he should be allowed his freedom, his civil and religious rights; that coercing him, directly or indirectly, to leave the country was inhuman and unchristian; and that genuine love to the people of color would best be manifested in administering to their comfort and welfare on their native soil.

Colonizationists, on the other hand, while professing to send to Liberia only those who went with their own consent, offered, in fact, to the colored people, merely a choice between two evils, and choosing either, instead of being a benefit to them, was opposed no less to humanity than to the constitution of the Colonization Society itself. The society had its origin, and main support in prejudice against color; this caste feeling was strengthened by it;

sending to Africa ignorant slaves, emancipated for
the special purpose, and a degraded portion of the
free people of color, did not tend to the civilization
and elevation of themselves, or the people of that
country. Intemperance and war were both fostered
by sending rum and guns with the expatriated people; and the existence of the Colonization Society
was a hinderance to the prevalence of anti-slavery
sentiments. The discussions were earnest but mu-
tually respectful and kind. The two reverend gentlemen were assured that all they had said had been
attentively considered and weighed, but it did not
remove objections to the Colonization Society, or
lessen attachment to the anti-slavery cause.

Dr. Beecher expressed very great surprise and
disappointment. Being pressed on the subject of
the recent course of the trustees of Lane Seminary,
in forbidding discussions on the slavery question, he
in the most emphatic manner declared that their
action did not meet his approbation, as he believed
in the absolute right of the students to confer
together and discuss the subject of slavery and
colonization. He also said he would never consent
to the suppression of such discussion in the Seminary.

The meeting was closed by a most appropriate
and fervent prayer, offered by the colored brother,
Mr. Cornish, suggested, as was felt, by the Holy
Spirit. He alluded with deep pathos, to the wrongs
inflicted upon his people, to the wicked prejudice
and sufferings under which they groaned, to the
gratitude they felt in hope of deliverance through

friends raised up to plead and defend their cause, to the injurious influence of other schemes in creating hostility to the country and to Christianity, and he implored the benediction of the Almighty upon the advocates of his people, then present, and all of similar heart and mind throughout the land. Mr. Tappan and the other brethren felt greatly strengthened and refreshed by such an utterance. It seemed as if the whole body of the people of color was pleading at the Throne of Grace.

Dr. Beecher returned to Lane Seminary. He found that the trustees were resolute, the faculty fearful and undecided, and the students determined and unyielding, repudiating the doctrine laid down by the trustees, and the "order" based upon it. Dr. Beecher said the "order" could not be repealed at present, and advised the students to remain in expectation that it might ere long be disregarded. They replied that their self-respect and future usefulness would not allow of their obedience to the "order," or of their remaining members of a seminary, one of whose laws they should be constrained to violate. In what they had already done, they had violated no law of the seminary, they had made no failure in their duty as students; and in view of the assurance that the law or rule would not be repealed, they asked and received honorable dismissions to any seminary they might desire to unite with, and withdrew from Lane Seminary, publishing a "Statement of Reasons," to which fifty-one students attached their signatures.

It is an admirable production, both in temper and argument, and concludes as follows:

"Finally, we would respectfully remind the trustees, that even though students of a theological seminary, we should be treated as men—that men, destined for the service of the world, need, above all things in such an age an this, the pure and impartial, the disinterested and magnanimous, the uncompromising and fearless—in combination with the gentle and tender spirit and example of Christ; not parleying with wrong, but calling it to repentance; not flattering the proud, but pleading the cause of the poor. And we record the hope that the glorious stand taken upon the subject of discussion, and up to the close of the last session, maintained by the institution may be early resumed, that so the triumph of expediency over right may soon terminate, and Lane Seminary be again restored to the glory of its beginning.

"CINCINNATI, Dec. 15, 1834."

Dr. Beecher regretted the decision of the students, but he did not exercise the wisdom and firmness that the exigency required. He might have thrown himself into the breach, and said to the trustees: "I have never had such an opportunity; I cannot be separated from such 'noble men;' you must repeal the 'order,' or I shall feel constrained to put myself at the head of these students and lead them elsewhere." Had he done this, he might have saved the seminary from the loss of such a band of moral heroes, and gained to himself a reputation beyond any thing that he had previously acquired.

But, on the contrary, he acquiesced in the arbitrary rule of the trustees. A truly noble and fearless man in many respects, the opposition that prevailed at the seminary and throughout the country seemed to overcome him. Born to be a leader, under some circumstances, this eminent man failed at this time in an essential attribute of leadership of moral and religious enterprises. He had previously avowed in his lectures at the seminary, as was understood, that true wisdom consists in advocating a cause *only so far as the community will sustain the reformer.* Is this Christian philosophy? Does it accord with the conduct of the prophet Daniel, or that of the martyrs and confessors of ancient times? Is it possible that the glorified spirit of BEECHER now approves such a sentiment?

Mr. Tappan, though he anticipated good results from the decision of the students, was greatly disappointed at the course taken by the trustees and the faculty. He had induced Dr. Beecher to leave a field of usefulness in Boston, to assume a post deemed second to none other in its prospective usefulness; he had promised to endow a professorship, or what was equal to it; he placed a high value upon the students who had repaired to the institution to place themselves under the theological and ethical teachings of "a master in Israel;" and his bright anticipations were, for the moment, eclipsed. But good often proceeds from seeming evil. Providence had provided an asylum for the students, who had also met with a grievous disappointment; and the patron and the students soon rejoiced together.

It was natural that Mr. Tappan should feel grieved that one on whom he had so greatly relied, one with such rich endowments, with such zeal, eloquence, and influence, one who had so "earnestly contended for the faith which was once delivered unto the saints," should, when all these qualifications seemed gifts of God to be called into exercise at such a crisis, have been restrained by his view of expediency, overlooking, as would seem, the example of those who said: "We ought to obey God rather than men."

He the more regretted it because it seemed to be the settled policy of his clerical friend, with regard to moral reforms, as will appear from the following statement. At a time subsequent to the departure of the students from Lane Seminary, Dr. Beecher called at the store of Mr. Tappan, where he was remonstrated with for the course he had taken at that institution. He justified it, and said, "The anti-slavery doctrines, if true, ought not to be pushed to such an extremity." He was respectfully asked, "If, doctor, when you preached your sermons on intemperance, many years since, you had known all the principles connected with the temperance reform that you now know, would you not have divulged and enforced them at the time?" He replied, "I would not have done it."

Mr. Tappan, believing that what is right is the highest expediency, considered that a golden opportunity had been lost by this venerable man to achieve increased influence and more extensive usefulness. In view of the history of Lane Seminary and Oberlin College impartial men will decide. The following letter from THEODORE D. WELD, who was one of the students of Lane Seminary, gives interesting facts in relation to the exodus of the students, besides his estimate of Mr. Tappan's character:

HYDE PARK, Mass., Jan. 1, 1870.

. . . . I cherish the memory of Arthur Tappan with deep reverence, and garner it among my most precious things. So simple in all his tastes and habits, so quiet and modest, yet so firm, independent, and conscientious, that nothing could swerve him from the right—so careful and deliberate in forming conclusions, yet instant and indomitable in executing. Economical in spending, yet always bountiful in giving. So faithful and true, so scrupulously just in all things. Never seeking his own; of few words, each straight to the point, and that a *deed*, and how often a great one; so earnest in daring for the weak against the strong. The *race* has a right to know more of one of its great benefactors; and I rejoice that it is about to get through you some part of its due.

You asked me what I know about Arthur Tappan's promise to Mr. Vail of $10,000 for Lane Seminary. I find that I cannot recall the details with sufficient accuracy to set the whole matter right, and therefore had best not attempt it. I had the facts from Mr. Vail, and from your brother, and distinctly recall the fact that to *me*, it seemed perfectly clear that, under the circumstances, your brother was fully justified in taking the course that he did.*

* A former professor writes: "All I know in respect to Mr. Arthur Tappan's subscription to the funds of Lane Seminary, is

You asked me to state what I know of his gifts to the colored schools of Cincinnati. When the anti-slavery students of Lane Seminary established evening-schools for the adults, and day-schools for the children of the three thousand colored of Cincinnati, your brother wrote to me, saying in substance, "Draw on me for whatever is necessary for the schools, teachers, househire, books, etc."

As the students were occupied with their studies and recitations in the daytime, it was necessary for them to get others to teach the day-schools, and as none but earnest abolitionists would teach negroes gratuitously, or were fit for the work, your brother paid the travelling expenses to Cincinnati of a number of young ladies from central New York, and of others from Northern Ohio for that purpose. The young ladies declined all compensation for teaching, and your brother paid their board.

The amount that he advanced for the use of the schools, I have now no means of stating. As soon as Mr. Tappan heard that the trustees of Lane Seminary had passed a law dissolving the Anti-slavery Society, and prohibiting anti-slavery discussions, and that the students, finding that the faculty would enforce the action of the trustees, were preparing to withdraw to a neighboring village, he wrote to me enclosing a draft for a thousand dollars, to be expended in hiring a building where they might room, in buying such books as they might need, and in paying for their board, etc. The letter also empowered me to draw on him at sight for whatever they might need in addition, during the autumn and

what was repeatedly stated, and I believe published, that it amounted to ten thousand dollars. It was said that he proposed to secure it, but Mr. Vail, the agent, regarded this as unnecessary; and that it was not paid simply because he became unable to do so in consequence of his financial embarrassments. Mr. John Tappan states: "Brother Arthur subscribed, I think, fifteen thousand dollars, and was the originator of Dr. Beecher's going to Lane Seminary. He failed before he was called upon for payment, after Dr. Beecher had left. I afterwards paid half of the amount, viz. $7,500, and referred Dr. Beecher to friends and connections for the rest of it."

winter, or until some permanent provision for completing
their course might be made. He also requested that all who
decided to return to their friends, or to go to other institutions, and were in need of funds, should be provided with
whatever was requisite. As I entered the Anti-slavery lecturing field in Ohio soon after, I do not know what other
amounts were forwarded by your brother to help classmates
in their Anti-slavery Patmos at Cumminsville.

Heartily sorry that I cannot help you, my dear long time
friend, in your labor of love, and with ever vivid memories
of our associate labors in the blessed old cause—*old* yet for
ever *new*,   I am ever faithfully yours,

LEWIS TAPPAN.   THEODORE D. WELD.

Mr. Tappan, notwithstanding his agency in
bringing about the removal of Dr. Beecher from
Boston to Cincinnati, and his grief at separating
from one whose character and services he had held
in high estimation, and from whose labors at Lane
Seminary he had anticipated large results, felt compelled to take the part of the students. He furnished many of them with means of reaching other
institutions, or of prosecuting a winter's study in a
neighboring village. A large number of them made
arrangements to repair to Oberlin Seminary, Ohio,
having received satisfactory assurances that no attempt would be made there to prevent free discussion, or oppose the resolution of the students to
repudiate caste, and treat the colored people, in the
seminary and out of it, as equal with themselves
before the law and the gospel. He resolved to
afford them all the aid in his power in building up
at that place, a school of the prophets. He prevailed on the Rev. Charles G. Finney to succeed

Dr. Beecher, as the spiritual guide and instructor of the students. With the twelve thousand dollars he contributed, a spacious brick building was erected at Oberlin, which in honor of him, the trustees named "Tappan Hall."*

He promised additional aid, but his adverse circumstances prevented the fulfilment of his intentions. This was a source of extreme regret to him, as well as the officers and students. Providence, however, raised up other benefactors, and a collegiate as well as theological department was organized. The number of students increased from year to year, able and self-denying instructors were secured, multitudes of young persons of both sexes received instruction, revivals of religion occurred every year, and the history of the institution shows clearly that the Holy Spirit guided the founders, and has made it a name and a praise in the whole land.

At the "breaking up" at Lane Seminary, and while Mr. Finney was preaching at the Broadway Tabernacle in the city of New York, he was solicited to go to Oberlin. He has narrated the facts in a letter to the compiler as follows:

ARTHUR TAPPAN proposed that I should go West long enough to get the students into the ministry; and he offered to pay all the bills. He was very earnest in this request, but I did not see how I could leave New York, as I felt great reluctance to leave the Tabernacle, and told him that I did not see my way clear unless sufficient funds should be guaranteed. . . . Messrs. J. J. Shepherd and Asa Mahan came to New York to persuade me to go to Oberlin, as professor of

---

° See Appendix 7, for resolutions on decease of Mr. Tappan.

theology. The proposal met the view of Arthur and Lewis Tappan. . . . . The brethren in New York offered to endow professorships if I would spend half of each year in Oberlin. I offered to go on two conditions : 1, that the trustees should never interfere with the internal regulations of the school, and 2, that we should be allowed to receive on equal footing colored students. . . . . The trustees had a great struggle to overcome their prejudices. The brethren in New York agreed in an hour or two to endow eight professorships.

Brother Arthur Tappan's heart was as large as all New York, and I might say as large as the world. He was a small man in stature, but he had a mighty heart. . . . . When I laid the case thus before him he said : "Brother Finney, my income, I will tell *you* on this occasion, averages about a hundred thousand dollars a year. Now if you will go to Oberlin, take hold of the work, and go on and see that the buildings are put up, and a library and every thing provided, I will pledge myself to give my entire income, except what I want to provide for my family, till you are beyond pecuniary want." Having perfect confidence in brother Tappan, I said, "That will do ; thus far the difficulties are out of the way."

Mr. Finney further states :

It was agreed between myself and my church that I should spend my winters in New York, and my summers at Oberlin. . . . . When this was arranged I took my family to Oberlin ; the students of Lane Seminary came and the trustees put up barracks or shanties, in which they were lodged. Students soon flocked here. I was authorized to get a large tent. . . . a hundred feet in diameter. There was a streamer at the top, on which was written in large characters, "HOLINESS TO THE LORD." The text was of great service. Arthur Tappan said : "I want the institution to be known. Collect what money you can, and spread the knowledge of your enterprise through your agencies as far as you can. I do not want you to spread an abolition flag, but carry out your design of receiving colored students upon the same conditions that you do white students ; and see that the work be not taken out of the hands of the faculty, and spoiled by the trustees, as was the case at Lane Seminary. Just let it be known that you thus receive students, and work your own way on, the best you can. Go and put up your building as fast as possible, and for whatever deficiency of funds there may be, after making efforts through your agents, you may draw on me, and I will honor your drafts to the extent of my income from year to year."

I came on the ground with this understanding; but it was further understood between brother Tappan and myself, that his pledge should not be made known to the trustees, lest they should fail to make due efforts as he desired, not merely to collect funds, but to make the wants and objects of the institution known throughout the land. . . . . We pushed on. The location was bad, and it cost thousands of dollars to overcome obstacles. . . .

By the commercial crash of 1837, brother Tappan and nearly all the men who had subscribed the funds for the support of the faculty were prostrated. We were without funds for the support of the faculty, and fifty thousand dollars in debt, without any prospect that we could see of obtaining funds from the friends of the college in this country. Brother Tappan wrote to me at this time, acknowledging the promise he had made me, and expressing the deepest regret that he was wholly unable to fulfil his pledge. Our necessities were then great and to human view it seemed as if the college must be a failure. We had to resort to new subscriptions.

Mr. Finney, in relating afterwards the difficulties with Hudson College and Mr. Coe, said: "Arthur Tappan wrote to put me on my guard against going to Hudson. I found his prediction verified and declined going to Hudson."*

At the time the students were meditating upon the subject of repairing to Oberlin, the views of the trustees and faculty were not settled on the subject

* See Appendix 8, for letter from Mr. Finney.

of receiving colored students, and treating them as equal in all respects with white students. Though they were Christians considerably in advance of the prevailing sentiment of the churches, they had not wholly renounced the hateful prejudice against the people of color that so generally prevailed in the country and in the churches. The Lane Seminary students were fully aware of this, and determined not to go to Oberlin until both free discussion and the 'right treatment of colored students were fully secured.

The subject so enlisted the feelings of the pious inhabitants of Oberlin, that earnest and persevering prayer was offered, especially by a band of godly women. The result was an acquiescence if not entire harmony of views in the board of trustees, and the adoption of a resolution that students should be received and treated irrespective of color. It was also decided that in the boarding-houses and . elsewhere, no observances should be allowed that infringed upon this rule. CASTE has found no asylum or toleration at Oberlin since that day.

Mr. Tappan made no effort to have the seminary an abolition institution, in such a sense as to exclude differences of opinion and free discussion. He had no desire to force conformity to the principles or rules of the majority; but he did insist as a condition of receiving his patronage, that students should be admitted irrespective of color, that entire freedom should be allowed on the anti-slavery question, and that a high order of religious instruction should be

11

given, especially in favor of revivals of religion. He would be tolerant, but never submit to the "gagging" principle. It was not his nature, and it was abhorrent to his principles.

The experiment of having youth of both sexes taught in the same institution had also his entire approbation, and its great success at Oberlin pleased him to the end of his days. Had his prosperity continued, Oberlin would have had no more liberal patron. He loved the self-denying professors for their sound principles, firm adherence to them, and rejoiced with them in the success of their labors and in the evidences of Divine favor in answer to their prayers, and the prayers of others.

XIV.

THE mob spirit that was intended to put an end to the anti-slavery agitation seemed to extend and increase it. Its abettors might have foreseen this, had they not been blinded by passion. Neither philanthropy nor religion can be put down by such excesses. Daniel Webster, in his celebrated speech at Niblo's Garden, New York, in adverting to the anti-slavery agitation, advertised his hearers that it was in vain to contend against the religious sentiment of a people. And a doctor of the law, of ancient times, proclaimed the same truth: "Ye men of Israel, take heed to yourselves what ye intend to do as touching these men...... Refrain from these men, and let them alone; for if this counsel or this work be of men, it will come to naught; but if it be of God, ye cannot overthrow it, lest haply ye be found even to fight against God."

The slaveholders at the South and their Northern allies exerted themselves to put an extinguisher upon the flame that was diffusing its light over the whole land. Ruffianism for the time seemed to have the ascendency. "Southrons," as they proudly called themselves, attempted to overawe all at the South who had or were suspected to have anti-slavery proclivities; while personally, or by their Northern allies, they stirred up violence at the North. Northern merchants and politicians vied with their

Southern correspondents and coadjutors in efforts to put a stop to inquiries and discussions that brought the "institution" into suspicion and hatred.

A gentleman of New York, who owned a store in Charleston, S. C., received a letter from that city, as follows: "If you are seen going into Tappan's, Rankin's,* or any abolitionist's, vengeance will be poured out on your now flourishing establishment in Charleston. By order of the Select Committee."

A record made in the private journal of a member of the anti-slavery committee, of September 21, 1835, says: "There is a rumor that *one hundred thousand dollars* are offered for Arthur Tappan and Lewis Tappan, to be delivered in some slave state, and that two pilot-boats are in the harbor from the South." In the *New Orleans Bee* was the following notice: "Fifty dollars reward for Arthur. He may be known by being in the habit of preaching among slaves." This was probably meant as a pasquinade, to satirize rumors of large rewards being actually offered. It was believed, however, that rewards of considerable sums were offered, and that plans were on foot for the abduction of Mr. Tappan.

Several of his friends called at his store to inquire into the matter, and asked if he was not alarmed. They were assured that he had great composure; that he did not think any attempt

---

* The late John Rankin, Esq., merchant of New York, who was the first treasurer of the American Anti-Slavery Society, and who for many years contributed to its funds $1,200 per annum. He was a steadfast friend of the cause, and died in 1869, in the eightieth year of his age.

would be made to carry him off; that fear was useless; and he trusted in God.

Not long after, a report was in circulation that
was believed, that a pilot-boat was in the harbor of
New York, from Savannah, Ga., and fears were
expressed by several citizens that possibly, and not
improbably, a plan was on foot to kidnap some of
the abolitionists. It was evident that the slaveholders and their Northern allies intended at least
to frighten them. To an inquiry, "Are the members
of the anti-slavery committee alarmed?" the answer
was, "Not at all. They hold their meetings at the
anti-slavery office regularly, transact the business
on hand, and have no intention to cease their operations."

The daily press, with some exceptions, instead
of attempting to allay popular ferment, lent its aid
in denouncing the abolitionists and encouraging the
violence of Southern men. Meantime efforts were
made by "Northern merchants with Southern principles" to injure Mr. Tappan's business, by persuading Southern merchants not to purchase his
goods, and to combine their influence to break him
down.

Intelligence soon reached the city that great
excitement prevailed at Charleston, S. C. A mob
had robbed the postoffice of that city of a quantity
of anti-slavery publications, July 29, 1835, and
burned them in the street, together with effigies of
Dr. Samuel H. Cox, William Lloyd Garrison, and
Arthur Tappan. The news stirred up sympathizers

in New York, who renewed their reproaches against the abolitionists, and there were apprehensions on the part of many people of mob violence. It was alleged, contrary to the fact, that the abolitionists had sent large quantities of their publications to Charleston, with "incendiary" pictures, to be distributed to the slaves. Mr. Tappan suggested to the committee the propriety of issuing a calm and resolute statement of facts, to allay the excitement at the North, occasioned by the false representations on the subject. Accordingly, an address To THE PUBLIC, written by Judge Jay, was published in pamphlet form and in the religious newspapers, and widely circulated. It set forth the distinguishing sentiments of the anti-slavery party, and explicitly disclaimed the charges so industriously made against it, concluding as follows:

"Such, fellow-citizens, are our principles. Are they unworthy of republicans and Christians? Or are they in truth so atrocious, that, in order to prevent their diffusion, you are yourselves willing to surrender at the dictation of others the inviolable privilege of free discussion, the very birthright of Americans? Will you, in order that the administrations of slavery may be concealed from public view, and that the capital of your republic may continue to be, as it now is, under the sanction of Congress, the great slavemart of the American continent, consent that the general government, in acknowledged defiance of the Constitution and laws, shall appoint, throughout the length and breadth of

your land, ten thousand censors of the press, each
of whom shall have the right to inspect every document you may commit to the postoffice, and to suppress every pamphlet and newspaper, whether religious or political, which in his sovereign pleasure
he may adjudge to contain an incendiary article?
Surely we need not remind you that if you submit
to such an encroachment on your liberties, the days
of our republic are numbered, and that although
abolitionists may be the first, they will not be the
last victims offered at the shrine of arbitrary power.

"ARTHUR TAPPAN, President.
"JOHN RANKIN, Treasurer.
"WILLIAM JAY, Sec. For. Cor.
"ELIZUR WRIGHT, Jr., Sec. Dom. Cor.
"ABRAHAM L. COX, M. D., Rec. Sec.
"LEWIS TAPPAN,
"JOSHUA LEAVITT,
"SAMUEL E. CORNISH,
"SIMEON S. JOCELYN,
"THEODORE S. WRIGHT.
"New York, Sept. 3, 1835."

This year was distinguished, in the anti-slavery
annals, more than any previous year, for the furor
that possessed the public mind against the hated
friends of freedom.   They were grossly insulted,
their meetings were broken up, they were misrepresented and slandered, some of them suffered
personal injury, and a reign of terror prevailed in
many parts of the country.

At the present day few persons have a true idea
of the insults heaped upon prominent abolitionists
thirty-five years since; even those who were con-

temporary with them have but a faint recollection
of the numberless annoyances to which the anti-
slavery people were subject. Continually watched;
their names opprobriously alluded to in the daily
press, and sometimes placed upon the bulletins of
newspaper offices; misrepresentations of all sorts in
the mouths of the community; caricatures and pas-
quinades at every newspaper stand; followed not
unfrequently by droves of boys even from places of
public resort to their own doors; their families insulted by passers-by; their children shunned at
school; significant gestures of intended violence
made by strangers as they were passed in the
streets; objects of real or affected aversion or terror as they had occasion to call at hotels or private
dwellings; sometimes hissed as they passed the
exchange and other places of public resort, and as
they attempted to take a part in meetings; indeco-
rously treated in assemblies of professing Christians; their principles and measures distorted and
falsified, they were considered and treated as dis-
turbers of the public peace, and as outlaws in the
community.

Is it asked, What manifestations did Mr. Tappan
exhibit under such provocations? He preserved his
equanimity, steadily pursued his accustomed avoca-
tions, attended regularly the anti-slavery meetings,
and looked into the future with a serene and confident trust that good would be evoked out of seeming
evil, that the Almighty would protect the victims of
oppression and prejudice and their friends, and fulfil

the believing prayer of the psalmist: "Surely the wrath of man shall praise Thee; the remainder of wrath shalt thou restrain."

At Nashville, Tenn., Amos Dresser, an amiable and pious young man, who went from Ohio to sell books, to enable him to pursue his theological studies, was seized by some of the citizens, under the false charge of circulating incendiary publications, arraigned before a tumultuous assembly in the court-house, and sentenced to be publicly whipped. The punishment was inflicted in the public square in the presence of a large assembly of people, the leading men in the place standing by and directing the proceedings.

A convention of anti-slavery men from different parts of the state of New York, to form a state anti-slavery society, assembled at Utica, and while peaceably attending to the business in hand, in one of the churches of the place, were assailed by a mob of several hundreds of ruffians, headed by Samuel Beardsley, a member of Congress, chairman of a committee of twenty-five leading citizens appointed at a meeting in the court-house. At Boston, the same day, a meeting of anti-slavery women was broken up, and William Lloyd Garrison was dragged through the streets by an infuriated mob, at the peril of his life. The mob was said to have included men of "property and standing."

At Brooklyn, N. Y., the residence of Mr. Tappan, threats of violence had been repeatedly made, and considerable apprehension was felt by his

11*

friends that they might be carried into execution.
Mr. GEORGE HALL, who was at the time mayor, determined to exert his influence and authority to protect him, and save the place from the disgrace of
an unlawful uproar. Though not at that time an
abolitionist, he valued the rights of peaceful citizens
and the reputation of the city.

Being apprised that on a certain night an attempt might be made to seize Mr. Tappan, he made
arrangements with the commandant of the Navy-
yard to have in readiness the marine force, to act,
should their aid be required. He then stationed a
relay of men from Mr. Tappan's residence to the
Navy-yard, at convenient distances, to convey his
messages to the officer in command, while he walked
back and forth before the house, unattended, during
a great part of the night. This fact, so honorable
to that unostentatious, but fearless magistrate, he
never communicated to Mr. Tappan, who little
thought that, while he was seeking repose upon his
pillow, such a vigilant and brave man was volunta-
rily performing the office of sentinel in front of his
house.

Mr. Leggett, as editor of the *Evening Post*, and
as editor of the *Plaindealer* subsequently, boldly
advocated the rights of man, including the negro
and the abolitionist, in opposition to his political
party and a servile press, and within a year or two
became, as might have been expected, an avowed
abolitionist. In an article in the *Evening Post*, of
August 26, 1835, headed "REWARD FOR ARTHUR

TAPPAN," he spoke of the wild fanaticism that prevailed at the South. "How else," he exclaimed, "could such a paper as the *Charleston Patriot* advert, with tacit approbation, to the statement that a purse of twenty thousand dollars had been made up in New Orleans, as a reward for the audacious miscreant who should dare to kidnap Arthur Tappan, and deliver him on the levee in that city. . . . . Is the *Charleston Patriot* so blinded by the peculiar circumstances in which the South is placed, as not to perceive that the proposed abduction of Arthur Tappan, even if consummated by his murder, as doubtless is the object, would necessarily have a widely different effect from that of suppressing the Abolition Association, or in any wise diminishing its zeal and ardor?"

He spoke as became a true patriot, in suitable terms, of the extraordinary conduct of the Postmaster-General, Amos Kendall, in virtually sanctioning the rifling and destruction of the mails by postmasters, in defiance of their oaths of office and of the rights of their fellow-citizens throughout the United States. In alluding to the letter of Mr. Tappan and his associates to the mayor of New York, he said:

"We have here, in the subjoined official address, signed with the names of men whom we believe too upright to lie, and who certainly have shown that they are not afraid to speak the truth, an exposition of the creed and practice of the Anti-Slavery Society. We have already said that, in our judgment, the matters contained in this document, with a single exception, deserve a cordial approval. . . . . We approve of the strenuous assertion of the right of free discussion, and, moreover, we admire the heroism which cannot be driven from its ground by the maniac and unsparing opposition which the abolitionists have encountered."

This heroic political writer rendered great service to the cause of freedom, and Mr. Tappan and his associates held him in high esteem during his brief career. In one of his articles he quoted some lines ascribed to Philip Van Artavelde, saying, "This is the sort of character we emulate." They are applicable to him, and we think also to the subject of this narrative.

> "All my life long
> I have beheld with most respect the man
> Who knew himself, and knew the ways before him,
> And from amongst them chose considerately,
> With a clear foresight, not a blindfold courage ;
> And having chosen, with a steadfast mind
> Pursued his purposes."⊗

* Mr. William Leggett died in New York, May 24, 1839. A collection of his political writings was published the same year, in two volumes, 12mo, selected and arranged with a Preface by Theodore Sedgwick, Jr., and copyright secured by William Cullen Bryant.

XV.

His eldest daughter has, during the preparation of this sketch, sent some reminiscences of her father, that will interest his grandchildren if not others; and they are introduced here as they relate in part to matters of a prior date, but are not specially connected with any thing that follows. It is perhaps needless to say, that they were not penned with any special reference to publication, but rather to be interwoven, if it was thought best, in the narrative. They will also be interesting to children, who dwell upon incidents relating to the early life of their parents, that may not be esteemed of much value to other persons. This daughter says:

"My mother was a professing Christian several years before she married my father. Some of her friends objected to her marrying him, because he was at that time inclined to Unitarianism. He . attended the Scotch church in Montreal, where she worshipped, and there first saw her. He after a time sought an introduction to her from a mutual friend.

"When they temporarily resided in Boston in 1814, previous to their removal to New York, my mother went with him to hear Dr. Channing on Sabbath mornings, and to the Old South church in the afternoon. In this way she knew what he heard, and they conversed about it at home. Her influence was blessed to him, and when they moved to New York in 1815, father took a pew in Dr. John M. Mason's church, and before long he became a member.

"I recollect when father began extemporaneous family prayer, which he kept up through his long life. Before prayer, he used to read in 'Scott's Bible,' the text and Practical Observations. On Sundays, my brother and myself learned a few verses from the Psalms, for which father rewarded us with a sixpenny piece, to be dropped into a missionary box, the contents of which were for the support of two children in India, named for us. He believed that we should thus learn early to take an interest in missions. It was his habit to distribute tracts and Bibles among the seamen, Sunday mornings, before the church service.

"About the year 1819, my parents moved from Gold-street to Whitehall-street, near the Battery. This was a delightful home. Every day when the weather permitted, we spent hours in that, then, pleasant park, under the old trees, or picking up shells and seaweed on the beach at low tide. Father sometimes hired a boat and men to row it, and took us all to Staten Island, or Hoboken, where we wandered in the wild path by the river, or rested under the trees on the lawn in front of the old inn, the only house I remember there.

"Whitehall and State streets, and the Battery, were very different then from what they are at the present time. The Battery was kept in nice order, and was a place of daily resort for the families in the neighborhood, both parents, children and nurses. State-street, especially, was full of elegant houses overlooking the Battery and harbor, and a beautiful street. There was much social and friendly visiting between the neighbors.

"When we were young children, we saw but little of father except on Sunday and holidays, as he was so much absorbed in business. But he supplied us with books, such as could be had at that time, 'Manners and Customs of Different Nations,' 'Life of Columbus,' 'Parents' Assistant,' by Miss Edgeworth, 'Bingley's Biography of Animals' in several volumes;'Pilgrim's Progress,' and 'Tokens for Children,' for Sundays.

"When we were old enough to go to school, we sat up evenings with father and mother, listened to his reading aloud, usually some history, or he would hear us recite our lessons for next day at school. During their whole married life our parents were accustomed to play a game of chess evenings. They did so but a year before mother died, with as much interest as of old. We played draughts, the only game besides chess, we were allowed, and father taught us both games.

"While we lived on Whitehall-street, father gratified our desire to have a garden and flowers. He had beds made in the brick paved backyard, and took my brother and myself one morning early to Grant Thorburn's greenhouse in the old Friends'

Meetinghouse, and filled the basket with annuals ready to transplant. He set them out and watched their blooming, and watered them with as much pleasure as his children.

"Afterwards we lived at No. 14 Broadway, opposite the Bowling Green. Here we resided about four years. From there we moved in April, 1816, to No. 20 Beach-street, on the south side of St. John's Park. On the opposite side of the park was Dr. Cox's church, which we attended. Here he lived during a large part of his tumultuous anti-slavery life, when he was every where spoken evil of. Before he became so unpopular, his house was open to ministers, delegates of societies, and missionaries. My dear mother was always ready for them, with generous hospitality, and believed that their prayers would bring down a blessing on the family. Messrs. Temple and Cornelius were there for weeks. Bishop Chase of Ohio, Dr. N. W. Taylor, and Dr. Beecher were there while the New Haven Seminary was being organized, raising funds for it. Dr. Cornelius met them there. They were a genial trio. They seemed to love the children, and noticed them affectionately. Dr. Taylor, I recollect, used to draw pictures of horses and dogs, to amuse the little ones. He was very winning in his ways with them, and we all loved to have him visit us. As observers we children had no reason to conclude that Christian ministers were an unhappy class of men, but on the contrary, the happiest and most cheerful. Mother was delighted to have them together, and Dr. Cox, and Rev. Mr. Ludlow, were often at the table to meet her guests.

"Dr. Cox was our pastor until my father thought it his duty to help the Bowery church, and attend on the ministry of Rev. Mr. Christmas. We, however, often attended Dr. Cox's church with my mother, as she could not always go so far as the Bowery, where we went about a year, and then all returned to Dr. Cox's. He was very much beloved by us all, and a frequent and welcome visitor. He seldom came without teaching us some facts in history, wishing us to take notes with pencil and paper. He often repeated from his stores of memory, pages from Cowper, Scott, and other poets. He also taught us from the Bible, making religion attractive to us. Three of my sisters and myself were members of his church.

"In 1828, father bought a house in Temple-street, New Haven, next to Dr. Taylor's. It had a large garden. He had the grounds and greenhouse filled with rare and lovely plants, shrubs, and choice fruit. The house in New York was kept open, and he came up to New Haven every Saturday, and returned on Monday, now and then giving himself a longer vacation of a week or two. This was before the day of railroads, when New Haven was comparatively a quiet and rural city. Father enjoyed his house there, as we all did; the new friends, the drives and excursions about the city, by land and water, the garden and flowers, and the rest he found from his busy New York life.

"In August 1831, God took home our dear little sister Mary Lansing, eight years of age; a lovely, gentle child, and tenderly mourned by us all. Our brother Arthur died while we were at Love Lane, New York, one year old, a beloved little one.

"It was during these happy New Haven summers, that feeling ran high against father on account of the part he took against slavery. Some who had been warm friends, grew cold, and shook their heads at him as a fanatic. He felt this keenly, but it did not deter him from doing what he felt was his duty to God and man.

"I was at home in 1835, in New Haven, I think, when one evening about ten o'clock, shouts and loud cries were heard in the street before the house, and we feared violence, but the mob were content with abusive language, and the throwing of stones against the house. The next evening we watched with great anxiety, but were unmolested. Judge Jonas Platt was making us a visit at the time. These were days of fearful anxiety for mother. Father was in New York. She could not prevail on him to leave.

"Mother told me that when she was a little girl, she saw an old slave whipped by his master. She, with some other children were playing together on a back piazza of a house near the Battery in New York. The boys were making chips and litter, which the old man had to sweep up, and he asked them to try and be more careful. They complained of him, and the master came out with a horsewhip,

and whipped him. Mother said the old slave never
uttered a word, but the tears ran down his cheeks;
and, said mother, 'I wept too.' It made a deep
impression upon her and early enlisted her sympathy for the slaves.

"While father was sitting with me, a freed slave
came into the parlor to attend to the fire. He had
escaped from Norfolk, Va., hid himself in the woods,
and came North with a Union officer, as his servant. He had been in several battles with him,
and nursed him when wounded. I told father his
story. He rose at once and went to Gordon, took
his hand, and said, 'I am pleased to see you; for
thirty-five years I have worked for this day; study
hard, and learn all you can; you can then rise and
be any thing you choose.' Gordon stood looking
into father's face, quiet, pleased, and gratified. I
never saw any one so anxious to learn to read as he
was; it was a pleasure to teach him. He carried
his book in his pocket, and studied it every spare
minute.

"My mother's mother, it appears, was a Roman-
ist. She was buried in St. Paul's churchyard, New
York, and General and Mrs. Hamilton were mother's sponsors in baptism, which looks as if she
became an Episcopalian, which agrees with what
my mother told me, as I remember.

"When mother expressed fears to have him return to New York, he smiled and said, 'Trust in God.'
He evidently felt 'In God have I put my trust; I
not will be afraid what man can do unto me.'

Threats of assassination did not daunt him. From day to day, for months, mother did not know what news the mail might bring concerning him. God spared him to see the slaves set free, and opposing friends then congratulated him.

"Previous to residing in New Haven, we had always spent most of the summer months out of New York city; sometimes we went with mother to Oriskany, N. Y., to revisit the old house where my parents were married, then and now the residence of her dear brother and sister Lansing. In front of their house was a green lawn shaded with old trees, while a small river skirted the place. Uncle and aunt were delighted to welcome mother and her children, and it was always a happy time.

"We spent weeks often during the summer at Paterson, N. J., among mother's friends, Mr. Colt's family. One of them, who was then, and still is, a real missionary, writes to me, 'Some forty or more years since, your father used to send my mother, who is now ninety years old, boxes of books, Bibles, and tracts, to distribute among the Sunday and infant scholars, and in the neighboring villages. She remembers that in one instance a person was so much impressed with the truth contained in a tract, that she thinks was given by him, as to change his course of life altogether, and establish a 'Tract Society' among his acquaintances.

"Father took us also in summer, to Northampton, to visit his parents. I recollect his father and mother with pleasure. They were very kind to the

children. At one time we saw Polly there, who
had lived with my grandparents and their daughter, Mrs. Pierce, forty years. She told us that she
used to take care of father when he was young, and
she amused us children by telling us anecdotes of
his childhood. Once, when she was ill, he would get
up in the night and go to the pump to get water
for her in his little tin cup, to allay her feverish
thirst.

"On one of these visits to Northampton, father
took grandfather, mother, and myself in his carriage to Amherst College, to call on President
Humphrey. During the call, Dr. Humphrey sent
for a number of Greek students to come to the
parlor to speak with father, who had helped them
in getting an education. He had a tender affection
for both of his parents, and used to keep their
engraved likenesses in his portfolio, and when he
opened it to write, he would lay them out before
him, even in his counting-room, so strong and constant was his love for them.

"My father enjoyed getting away from business
and cares into the country. He liked to take his
'carryall,' with old Syphax, the good horse, noted
for his great size and perfect form; and our two
saddle horses, and with mother and two children, set
off for a long excursion. These journeys were full
of pleasure. Often father and one of his children
would set off early in the morning, and ride on
horseback ten miles before breakfast. He made
several journeys in this way with his wife and chil-

dren. He seemed to grow young and light-hearted, and throw off care; and such excursions prepared him to return to the city and his varied duties.

"Mother, at our request, would tell us of her early years. At the age of two, she was left an orphan. Her father, when he was dying, committed her to the care of General and Mrs. Alexander Hamilton. When Gen. Hamilton was Secretary of the Treasury, and Gen. Washington, President of the United States, they lived opposite to each other in Philadelphia, and the children of the two families were together every day. Mrs. Washington took the Custis children, and Angelica Hamilton, and Fanny Antill, (my mother,) in her carriage to dancing-school twice a week. She stayed with them through the lesson and brought them home.

"Mother remembered Gen. Washington once sitting on a sofa in the room where the children were playing, and laying aside his newspaper, to watch them, and smile and encourage them to continue their frolic. Once, on a reception evening, when the drawing-room in his house was filled with ladies and gentlemen, talking and laughing, and the children were amusing themselves in a corner, there was a sudden great stillness—and mother looked up with surprise and awe, and saw Gen. Washington coming through the folding doors.

"From the time mother was twelve years old, until she was married, she resided with her sister, Mrs. Lansing, who, with her husband, filled well the place of the tenderest father and mother to her.

They had four children, who were near her own age.   -

"Father liked to tell us of his first meeting mother in church. They sat opposite each other in a square pew. He said he was attracted by her bright black eyes, and cheerful and animated expression. She was naturally bright and cheerful, generous and unselfish. It was her constant aim to make a happy home for her husband and children—a home where friends were ever welcome, and the poor and sorrowful found help and comfort. When father was absent, and there was not any guest to officiate, mother always led in prayer at family worship."

XVI.

SOUTHERN merchants had become shy of trading with New York abolitionists, and were in many
cases deterred from purchasing, as before, of a man
so obnoxious as Arthur Tappan. Some of them
bought with fictitious names, and many employed
other ways to circumvent their customers and the
public in their places of residence. It was a fortunate circumstance that the Southern trade fell off,
as many New York merchants who solicited that
trade, some of them going so far as to proclaim
that they were not abolitionists, found by woful experience, on the failure of their Southern debtors,
that in selling their principles with their goods they
had made a great mistake.

The most strenuous efforts were made by slaveholders to injure the business, and molest in all
imaginable ways, those who professed anti-slavery
principles; and insults of various kinds were resorted to by many of them. Letters were often received
by the friends of freedom of an insulting description; sometimes enclosing a small specimen of tar
and feathers, one enclosing the ear of a negro, and
most of them written profanely and obscenely. Rewards were offered for the abduction, or heads of
leading abolitionists. Fifty thousands dollars had
been offered for the head of Arthur Tappan. On

being informed of it he pleasantly remarked: "If that sum is placed in the New York Bank, I may possibly think of giving myself up."

Southern attorneys having collecting business for the firm, would relinquish the prosecution of claims. But some of them were too high-minded to do so. A certain attorney, belonging to the state of Georgia, who had solicited business of the firm, and who had received from them a note for collection, after commencing a suit, abandoned it, and wrote that he could no longer act for them on account of Mr. Tappan's avowed hostility to slavery. Hearing of a high-minded lawyer from that state who was at the head of the Georgia delegation in Congress, (Colonel FOSTER,) the circumstances were stated to him and his advice asked in the premises. He magnanimously replied: "I will undertake the transaction of any business you may have in my state; send an order to the attorney to transfer the business to my law-firm, and it will be faithfully attended to." But few were known to act so nobly.

The anniversaries of the American Anti-slavery Society were well attended. The places of meeting were filled by those who took a deep interest in the movement, by many who were attracted by curiosity, and by not a few who resorted to them from malicious motives, seeking for an opportunity to create a riot. Of course the meetings were exciting. Now and then a newspaper would give its readers a fair account of the proceedings, the principles avowed, the sentiments of the speakers, and the resolutions adopted; but generally the whole was caricatured, either wittily or malignantly. Politicians decried the agitators as those who alienated southern electors from their parties; merchants were incensed because they feared trade would be diverted from the city to other places; ministers of the gospel stood aloof lest their ecclesiastical associations should be interfered with, their churches agitated, and sinners remain unconverted! Meantime the populace were stirred up occasionally to deeds of violence by a pro-slavery press, and the corrupt sentiment of persons of influence in the community.

It was a great grief to Mr. Tappan that the benevolent societies, in which he had taken so deep an interest, shrunk from the avowal of principles so dear as he believed to the Saviour; so much in harmony with the Constitution of the country, and so conducive to the public weal. It grieved him also that so many men with whom he had formerly associated in benevolent and Christian enterprises, with some of whom he had gone to the house of God in company, and who in other respects, were men of principle and active piety, should ignore a cause of so much importance, one so conducive to strengthen all the precious institutions of the country, and raise the nation to a higher elevation as a moral and Christian people. Some merchants with whom he had been accustomed to act in benevolent societies, while avowing their hostility to slavery, were guilty of conduct that he could not help reprobating. When they had occasion to sue their delinquent customers in the slave states, and slaves were levied upon as the property of their masters, such New York merchants, would sanction the proceedings, and sometimes attempt to justify them. But few, it is believed, gave directions in advance that "slave property" should never be taken in satisfaction of judgments, and in cases where it was levied upon, without the knowledge of the creditors, that it should be at once relinquished.

He mourned over this state of things in secret, and spread his complaints before a just and holy God, who had promised to vindicate the cause of the oppressed, to make the wrath of man praise him, and to sustain all good causes and those who advocate them. As a Christian he bore his part in church meetings, and though seldom addressing them would, as occasion required, utter his thoughts, praying for the slave, for his deluded master, for the peace of the church, the good order of society, and the extension of pure and undefiled religion, at home and abroad. Such prayers, especially when the *slave* was mentioned, the sin of the nation in regard to slavery confessed, and the judgments of God upon a guilty people alluded to, were unacceptable, even in a lecture-room, at church meetings; and displeasure was often manifested by professors of religion, who, if they did not hate the principles of abolition, and all who adopted them and resolutely carried them into practice, hated the introduction of them into religious assemblies, especially in prayer meetings, conceiving that the harmony of such meetings should not be disturbed by introducing, either in exhortations or prayers, "disputed topics."

On one occasion, at a monthly concert of prayer, in the First Presbyterian church in Brooklyn, Mr. Tappan, being called upon to offer prayer, on his introducing into it the subject of the poor slave, there were such manifestations of disapprobation, on the part of a portion of the audience, that he felt the interruption and was induced quietly to take his seat. Boasts were afterwards made that he had been "scraped down." But it is believed that the pastor, and the best persons present, disapproved of the indecorum.

Strenuous efforts were made by many conservative men to induce Mr. Tappan to relinquish anti-slavery agitation. Leading men, presidents of banks and insurance companies and others, took great pains to persuade him of the inutility of his efforts, and the efforts of those affiliating with him, to accomplish the object they had in view. He was entreated to forbear, out of regard to his own reputation and safety, for the sake of his family, his friends, and especially for his own credit's sake that was in imminent jeopardy. He was assured, that many of the directors of banks declared they would not discount his paper, or the paper of any merchant having his name upon it. They conjured him, therefore, by all these considerations, to cease the advocacy of the anti-slavery cause; at least to be more quiet, to resign his office as president of the

American Anti-slavery Society, or to ·publish some
disclaimer, something at any rate that would pacify
the public, restore tranquillity, and preserve his
credit with the moneyed institutions. He was assured that such a procedure would even increase his
reputation in the community! He listened to what
was said, but gave no assurance that he should alter
his course.

A deputation was soon sent to him in behalf of
leading men connected with moneyed institutions,
and he was renewedly appealed to, and the considerations before urged were reiterated with such others as were deemed available. When it was said to
him, "Should any disaster occur to you, it would be
felt by your creditors, whom you are bound to protect, and whose interests connected with your credit,
you have no right to injure," he seemed much impressed. He felt more for his creditors than for
himself. But he said nothing. His mind seemed
to be deeply engaged in thought. It was evident
that he felt a peculiar responsibility, not only to his
creditors, his partners, his family, but to his clients,
the poor slaves, and above all to his God. At length
he spoke, and with great seriousness and emphasis,
said: "You demand that I shall cease my anti-
slavery labors, give up my connection with the Anti-
slavery Society, or make some apology or recanta-
tion—I WILL BE HUNG FIRST!"

A merchant who knew him well, said with reference to his strong convictions of duty, his conscientious regard for the right, and the strength of his

religious principles, "That man has the spirit of a martyr!"

Governors of states in their messages to legislatures joined in the hue and cry against those who they seemed to think were "turning the world upside down," and even the President of the United States did not think it beneath his high office, openly to assail and denounce the abolitionists. And at a crisis, when the public mind was much inflamed against their principles and measures; and when, from political motives or mercenary considerations, men did not refrain from unfounded misrepresentations and calumnies against those who were simply engaged in recommending to the observance of the people the sentiments advanced by the founders of our government, and the precepts of Christ. President JACKSON in his message to Congress seized the opportunity to increase the odium attached to the abolitionists, and to join in the cry for the destruction of their enterprise. The executive committee deemed it a fit occasion to enter a SOLEMN PROTEST against the denunciations of the President. It was from the pen of one of their number, William Jay, who had cast in his lot with the "sect everywhere spoken against," and was never, before or afterwards, known to swerve from the cause indicated by an enlightened conscience. The protest, headed by Arthur Tappan, was widely circulated. The points were as follows:

First: Because in rendering that judgment officially, you assumed a power not belonging to your office.

Secondly: We protest against the *publicity* you have given to your accusation.

Thirdly: We protest against your condemnation of us *unheard.*

Fourthly: We protest against the *vagueness* of your charges.

Fifthly: We protest against your charges, because they are *untrue.*

And the protest concludes in these words:

We have addressed you, sir, on this occasion, with republican plainness, and Christian sincerity; but with no desire to derogate from the respect that is due to you, or wantonly to give you pain.   To repel your charges, and to disabuse the public, was a duty we owed to ourselves, to our children, and above all to the great and holy cause in which we are engaged.   That cause we believe is approved by our Maker ; and while we retain this belief, it is our intention, trusting to His direction and protection, to persevere in our endeavors to impress upon the minds and hearts of our countrymen the sinfulness of claiming property in human beings, and the duty and wisdom of immediately relinquishing it,

When convinced that our endeavors are wrong, we shall abandon them, but such conviction must be produced by other arguments than vituperation, popular violence, or penal enactments.

NEW YORK, Dec. 26, 1835.

XVII.

On the night of December 16, 1835, a disastrous
fire took place in New York. It swept over a district of fifty or more acres, the oldest part of the
city, where were the stores and warehouses of the
principal merchants. It was a cold night, the mer-
cury standing at zero, and the wind boisterous. A
multitude of stores, dwelling-houses, and some public buildings were destroyed. Strenuous exertions
were made by the fire department and the citizens
to stay the progress of the flames, and to preserve
the property endangered, but it seemed in vain.
The hydrants and hose were frozen, so that it was
almost impossible to obtain water, and the people
were put to their wit's end, and almost despaired of
arresting the conflagration. No one who witnessed
the devouring flames will ever forget the scene.

The Dutch Reformed Church in Garden-street,
and the Exchange building in Wall-street, were
burnt. The fire left nearly all the buildings in the
"burnt district," as it was called, a mass of brick,
stone, and iron. The streets were obliterated, and
it was not easy for the owners or occupants of buildings to identify the lots upon which they had stood.
The number of buildings destroyed was estimated
at six hundred and forty-eight, and the personal
property consumed amounted to over fifteen millions of dollars. The fire commenced at a quarter

to nine o'clock on Wednesday evening, and burned
until twelve o'clock on Thursday. It was stated
afterwards that the ruins were burning for five
months.

Mr. Tappan's store was not far from the building where the fire commenced, No. 127 Pearl-street,
and on the opposite side of the street. But the
flames were driven across the street, and caught the
buildings as if they had been tinder. As his store
was of granite, and unusually well built, it was
hoped that it might be saved, and stay the progress
of the fire in that direction.

It so happened that the executive committee of
the American Anti-Slavery Society were in session at
their rooms in Nassau street, about half a mile from
Hanover-square, where Mr. Tappan's store was sit-
nated. Most of the members of the committee
accompanied Mr. Tappan to the place, when the
alarm was given, and arrived on the ground to see
that the flames were devouring the adjacent store.
One of the partners, and several friends, among
them a considerable number of colored men, were
already in the store, removing the goods.

They were at first thrown into a pile in the centre of the square, together with goods taken from
other stores in the neighborhood; but the progress
of the flames was so rapid that it was feared the
goods thus deposited might be consumed, as they
afterwards were, and Mr. Tappan therefore directed
that the remaining goods should be taken from the
rear to a friend's store in the neighborhood. Had

it not been that his store extended to the street in
the rear, very few of the goods could have been saved.
All hands were thus engaged until the flames burst
into the store, and several persevered until they
were driven away by the scorching heat. In a
short time the store, and a considerable part of the
goods, were destroyed, the walls standing for a time
and then falling, as had the walls of the other buildings over which the fire had passed.

As the flames swept on, in the direction of the
store where the goods saved had been deposited, it
was thought best to remove them a second time. A
vacant store, remote from the fire, No. 25 Beaver-
street, was hired, to which the goods were removed.
Thus about two-thirds of the stock was saved, and
the other third was either burned, stolen, or trampled under foot in the streets. But it was ascertained, the next day, that about twenty thousand
dollars' worth of the goods thus twice moved, belonged to neighbors. They were, of course, restored
to those who could identify them, and this was the
prevailing rule with all who had been so fortunate
as to save their own goods, or the goods of others.

A much larger amount of goods might have been
saved by their owners, if, amid such bewilderment,
they, and the people who volunteered their services,
had not been somewhat under the dominion of a
panic, that for the time almost deprived them of
their judgment. For example, a person aiding in
the removal of Mr. Tappan's goods, was very carefully unscrewing a timepiece, of the value of about

fifteen or twenty dollars, when he was called off and a parcel of costly goods was thrown into his arms of the value of at least a thousand dollars.

In the store was a fireproof closet, as it was supposed, and in the closet an iron safe, in which was kept the valuable papers of the firm, among them half a million dollars in value of notes receivable. A short consultation was held by the partners, to determine whether the contents of the iron safe should be removed. They all believed that the fire could not invade them, but prudence seemed to urge their removal. The notes were accordingly removed to the dwelling-house of one of the partners; and very fortunately, as it was found afterwards that all the papers left in the iron safe were so charred as to be almost worthless.

A good providence was apparent in the above, and also in the fact that the colored friends drawn to the store by grateful feelings towards Mr. Tappan, worked all night with a will, and were instrumental in saving a large amount of property. "The hand of Providence," says one of the former clerks, "was also put forth in other respects. On the morning of the day when the fire took place, a large quantity of India silk goods was received, and the porter was directed to hoist them to one of the lofts, but he neglected to do it, a thing very unusual; and thus the whole, being in the basement, were saved. Another circumstance occurred: A large invoice of French goods had been purchased, and all but two packages had been sold the after-

noon preceding the fire, and delivered to the purchaser beyond the limits of the burnt district. It
was proposed to delay the delivery of the goods to
the next day, but the clerk remained until it was
dark to see the goods sent away."

After a night of great anxiety and personal labor,
the partners assembled at breakfast at an early
hour with some of the principal clerks. The question was put, "What is to be done next?" The
response came from Mr. Arthur Tappan, "Rebuild
immediately." A clerk was despatched to Samuel
Thompson, the experienced builder of the burnt
store, and in an hour or two a contract was made to
erect a new store on the site of the old one "with all
possible despatch." A notice was then inserted in
the papers of the day, as follows:

ARTHUR TAPPAN & CO. acknowledge with grati-
tude the efficient exertions of their friends and fellow-citizens in saving (by the blessing of God) the largest portion of
their goods, all their books of account, and most of their
papers. They give notice that they have taken the new and
commodious warehouse, No. 25 Beaver-street, into which
their goods are moved, and where they will be arranged in
a short time; and where they will be happy to see their
friends and customers, until their store in Pearl-street shall
be rebuilt, for which they have made arrangements.

The effect of such a CARD was precisely what was
anticipated. It greatly encouraged other merchants
and owners of real estate, to bear up bravely, in a
season of despondency; to rebuild, and not a few
of them expressed their thanks for the prompt and
encouraging notice. Great activity prevailed in the

mercantile community in "repairing damages," and making preparations to recommence business at the old stands. Instead of real estate falling in value, it seemed to rise. A. Tappan & Co. were offered a hundred thousand dollars for their lot, with only the brick and stone remaining upon it.

The firm had, as they supposed, fully insured their stock of goods, but in consequence of the failure of several insurance offices, and the inability of others to pay the full amounts insured, resulting from losses by the fire, they found, on settling, that they had lost forty thousand dollars. This amount would have been much larger had not part of the insurance been effected in other places. The mob spirit that had prevailed in New York had led the firm to insure somewhat largely in Boston, and other cities in New England.

A new store was erected, early in the ensuing year, of granite from the same quarry in the state of Maine as the former store, and in the most substantial manner, several thousand dollars being expended for iron shutters, and other fastenings, to secure the property against loss by mobs, should they again occur. Other buildings were speedily erected, more convenient and substantial than the old ones, and ere long, as if by magic, the whole "burnt district" was covered by new and substantial stores, dwellings, and public buildings. A new impulse was given to trade, and with crippled means, but indomitable courage, merchants seemed to outvie each other in extending their sales.

A man somewhat noted for his wickedness, but who had been religiously educated, accosted one of the firm of A. Tappan & Co., and said : "I admire the spirit of your concern. You soar above all the sufferers by the fire. You put your trust in God." But there were those who indulged in very different language, cursing the abolitionists and blaspheming God. Some of them expressed joy that the fire had not spared the store of Arthur Tappan, as it at one time *threatened* to do, while others lamented that he had suffered less than most of his neighbors. And there were not wanting men, even Christian professors, who openly said, "He is now deprived of the means of extensive mischief." He might have said, as did one of old, "They that sit in the gate speak against me; and I was the song of the drunkards."

Hundreds of thieves, it was said, were arrested after the fire, and taken to the police office, but not one of them a man of color! Several persons called at the new place of business, after the fire, for compensation for services said to have been rendered on that memorable night, but not a colored person preferred any claim. Doubtless they felt that they had worked for a benefactor.

It was a man of color, who, by his thoughtfulness and bravery, arrested the fire, in one direction, as it threatened to extend to Broadway, and possibly to the North river. Thomas Downing lived in Broad-street near Wall-street, and perceiving that the flames were fast extending from the ruins of the church already mentioned, in Garden-street, (now Exchange-place,) and might sweep away his premises and hundreds of other buildings, set his wits to work to devise some method of arresting the fire. Finding in a shed in the rear of the burned church edifice some barrels filled with vinegar, he went to his house, brought pails, knocked in the heads of the barrels, bailed out the vinegar, and as fast as the flames caught the fence, dashed it on until the fire was subdued at the place, and a large amount of property saved. For this heroic act Mr. Downing received the thanks of the merchants.

A financial crisis was approaching. The expansion of trade much beyond the actual wants of the country, the extensive credits given by merchants, the failure of Southern traders to fulfil their engagements, added to the severe losses by the fire, and other causes, were rapidly bringing on general bankruptcy, a calamity greater, perhaps, than the fire itself. Although Mr. Tappan had aimed to be prudent, selling for cash to a greater extent than most firms in the street, yet he began to feel the effects of the prevailing system of over-trading and long credits. All his resources, of capital and credit, were required to sustain his own business; but several firms, that had been accustomed to receive aid from him, were now in straitened circumstances, and appealed to him, to sustain them. He did afford them much assistance, probably more than a prudent regard for self-preservation justified.

Money became more and more scarce, the banks could only extend partial relief, and the discount on

business paper sold in Wall-street was very great.
Under these circumstances, appeals for loans were
made to the United States Bank, located in Philadelphia, by numerous merchants. Not all of them
could furnish adequate security, and the applications of many were rejected. Firm after firm suspended, or became publicly insolvent. Great con-
sternation prevailed in the mercantile community.

Mr. Tappan made an appeal to Mr. Biddle,
president of the United States Bank, and who was
then considered a Napoleon (the first) in finance.
His brother went to Philadelphia, and urged on
Mr. Biddle the importance of sustaining the firm,
and suggested that any disastrous occurrence to it
might involve the stoppage of several others. The
sum of one hundred and fifty thousand dollars was
obtained on A. Tappan & Co.'s note, endorsed by
the firm with which they interchanged endorsements.
This substantial relief appeared to be sufficient, not
only to keep the credit of Mr. Tappan's firm good,
but to enable him to supply the necessities of smaller
concerns depending upon him.

The financial condition of the country, however,
not improving, and the debtors of Arthur Tappan
& Co. failing, in all quarters, to fulfil their engagements, the firm was put to great straits. They were
under the necessity of making another appeal to the
United States Bank, but it was in vain. The president said it was with the utmost reluctance he felt
obliged to deny the second application of so respectable a house, but the resources of the bank, and the

claims of other parties, absolutely forbade compliance. On his brother's return from Philadelphia, Mr. A. Tappan was at his desk anxiously waiting to hear the result of the application.

When he saw his brother, he asked, " What success?" The reply was, " We cannot obtain the money." " What then is to be done?" " Nothing, I suppose, but to suspend payment," was the obvious reply. He bore the disappointment like a man who had done all he could to avert a calamity, and when it came, resigned himself to the will of God. He felt deeply the necessity of adding to the general distrust, of delaying the payment of his debts to those who needed the money, of disappointing the hopes of parties that leaned upon him, of not continuing the stated sums he had engaged to pay for the support of benevolent objects, and the other contributions he was wont to make.

He calmly and resolutely set about making needful arrangements to make the blow fall as lightly as possible upon others, doing all he could for the benefit of his creditors, and to retrieve, if possible, his defeat. The suspension was publicly announced in May, 1837, and occasioned much sympathy on the part of many. After taking a full survey of his position and means, he, with the full concurrence of his partners, made a proposition to the creditors of the firm, to give new notes for existing ones, payable in six, twelve, and eighteen months, with interest. The whole amount of indebtedness was eleven hundred thousand dollars.

It was not an easy thing to fulfil this new engagement, as the credit of the firm was greatly impaired, and a necessity laid upon them to purchase largely for cash. Added to this was the fact that a few of the creditors, who had refused " signing off," had to be paid in full, at earlier periods than those who had readily acceded to the proposition, unmindful that, in the uncertainties of trade, they might be under the necessity of some time asking a similar favor of their creditors. The creditors generally complied with the terms proposed, with full reliance that they were the best that could prudently be offered. Within the time the whole amount of indebtedness, with the accruing interest, was paid, together with a million and a half dollars for the purchase of new goods. The scarcity of money during the time bore heavily upon debtors, and Mr. Tappan had to pay tens of thousands of dollars for extra interest, to enable him to meet the notes given on retiring the previous notes.

The result was deemed very creditable to his financial skill and laborious exertions. It raised him still higher in public estimation as an honorable merchant. He afterwards said, " The cause of our suspension was having a very heavy stock of goods at a time of great general financial embarrassment."

XVIII.

MR. SETH B. HUNT, who was one of Mr. Tappan's clerks for several years, has furnished the following narrative, which may serve as an agreeable episode :

At 122 Pearl-street, New York, June, 1830, I first saw Mr. Arthur Tappan. He was sitting at his little desk in the middle of the warehouse. I wanted a clerkship. He wanted an older person as salesman. He said I was too young. I told him that difficulty would daily grow less. He smiled, and engaged me at $150 per annum.

January 1, 1831, I found my account credited at the rate of $450 per annum. I concluded he had made a mistake, and put down a 4 instead of a 1. I drew his attention to it, and he laughed, and said if I was satisfied he was.

About that time, McDowall made his report about the Magdalen Asylum. It created a great excitement, and brought on Mr. Tappan and those who signed the report, great odium. Some of his friends backed out of it, and left him to bear the reproach and *pay the bills*. This he did—made no fuss about it, nor complained to any one, so far as I know.

. . . . I do n't quite remember the date, but the New York City Anti-Slavery Society was formed in the old Chatham-street Chapel, and before the conclusion of the ceremonies a great noise was heard outside. The mob was attempting to batter down the iron gate on Chatham-street. It did not give way, but when it was unlocked in rushed the mob like madmen.

At the conclusion of the short meeting, we all ran out a back way. I went back into the chapel to see the mob break every chandelier, lamp, bench, and every other article *break-able*. They put a big black man in the pulpit, and in pure derision held him there, while he was addressed as chairman, and while the *smashing* was going on—hooting, screaming,

groaning, crowing, yelling; so began the New York Anti-
Slavery Society!

Soon after came what are called the Abolition mobs. Mr.
Arthur Tappan's store, 122 Pearl-street, was one of the principal objects. His business was suspended, the oldest clerks
were put on guard; thirty-six stand of arms were bought at
Hinton's, in Broadway, and five hundred ball cartridges.
This looked like business. For several nights and days we
were behind the closed doors to defend Mr. Tappan's property. The mob, one afternoon, battered the front door with
an awning-post. Every window above the first story was
broken by stones, there being no shutters above the first
story.

Some thirty or forty of us were ready behind the door,
Mr. Arthur Tappan himself in command. Every moment
we expected the door to give way. "Steady, boys," says Mr.
Tappan. "Fire *low*. Shoot them in the legs, then they
can't run !"

Mr. Cornelius W. Lawrence was mayor of the city at the
time, and refused to send relief. Mr. Tappan was perfectly
calm and composed. He certainly was as *brave* a man as I
ever saw.

In after years I lived in Brooklyn his next-door neighbor,
and so modest was he that he never alluded to these stirring
scenes. Nothing seemed to annoy him more than to talk
about himself.

He had an innate modesty as delicate as a girl's. When
he entered a prayer-meeting, he usually sat down with the
colored people near the door. He was not a ready speaker,
nor what some would call *gifted* in prayer. But the simple
earnestness of his petitions, his deep humility and reverence
before God, never failed to make a lasting impression.

Mr. Tappan made no pretence to superior mental endowments, but his moral nature was permeated by a sense of justice. He had in every respect an exalted virtue. No one
could be much with him and not *feel* this to be true. His
personal purity no one would question. I have seen him get
irritated at some trifle, and yet when the providence of God
had stopped his business and seemed to have ruined him in

that respect, he was the most cheerful of any one of us. Rarely did he indulge in jokes, but on that occasion he was in the mood of it, and got off not a few of them.

In regard to his Christian character, he appeared to be fully impressed with the great truths of Revelation, and daily doing his duty under its awful sanctions. The simplicity of his faith, the purity of his life, the steadiness and constancy of his pious efforts, the unquestioning obedience with which he walked forward in the path of duty, reminded one of a primitive Christian believer; and the charm of it all was, that when he had so done his duty and achieved a great act, he seemed totally unconscious of it himself.

In 1833 or '4, he boarded with Mrs. Eleanor Woods, 21 Broadway. I also boarded there. He had one set of keys to the store; I had a duplicate set. It grew to be a strife which would be at the store earliest to open it. One morning I went at six or half-past. Opening the door, I found Mr. Tappan sitting on a case of goods, behind the door. He smiled, and informed me he had got up, as it was light, and had, without looking at his watch, come down, supposing it was day; but on looking, he found it only half-past two o'clock—a bright moonlight! He then tried to relock the door, but could not. The fact was, there was a certain spring you had to press with your finger to lock the door, and having never locked it, he was unacquainted with it. The watchman finding him there and the door open, and not able to lock his own store, threatened to take him to the police station. But neither of them being able to lock or otherwise secure the door, there was no alternative but for him to sit patiently behind the door and watch the watchman, and the watchman to watch him. In the evening I often had occasion to go to his room. His open Bible showed what book was his delight.

After he retired, and towards the close of his life, some of those who had been his clerks offered, if he needed, to buy for him an annuity. He sent word that "the voyage was nearly over, the provisions on board just about sufficient to last out the voyage; more were not needed." Noble words of an heroic spirit!

The indictment against Socrates was, that he brought into contempt the religion of the country and corrupted the youth of Athens. A majority of his eleven judges voted to convict him of these charges, and cóndemned him to drink the hemlock. In the delay of his execution, friends offered to send him away to avoid death. Socrates declined their generous offers. He well knew how utterly *false* were both the charges on which he was condemned, and calmly accepted his fate, trusting that even Athens would do justice to his memory. So with Mr. Arthur Tappan. The opinions and approval of his fellow-men he valued. Kind actions or words also deeply affected him ; but the voice of his conscience ever produced on his part a ready obedience. His life was pure ; his example influential for good ; his memory blessed.

NEW YORK, Nov. 27, 1869. SETH B. HUNT.

At a later date Mr. Hunt writes:

At one time my firm purchased a large lot of children's handkerchiefs at auction. Among them were those on the subjects of temperance, Sunday-schools, and abolition of slavery. The latter were particularly striking—a negro kneeling and chained, with the motto,

"AM I NOT A MAN AND A BROTHER?"

Some of these were sold by the package and shipped South. The store of the purchaser was taken possession of by the vigilance committee, and of course a great stir was made about the affair in the papers.

The next season after that, I saw a tall gentleman, blue coat, metal buttons, standing at the door looking in. I bade him good morning, and asked him to walk in. He declined, and said he believed we employed " nigger " clerks to wait on people. I assured him such was not the case, and he appeared greatly surprised. I asked him again to come in, and gradually he had got inside the door. Then turning very seriously to me, he said, " Before I consent to look at your goods, you must tell me if you *be really* an abolitionist." "Well," said I, with equal seriousness and concern, "before I consent to show you any goods, I must ask you *one* question ; are you, or are you not, a close-communion Baptist?"

"What has that got to do with your showing me your goods?" "Exactly as much as your asking me if we are abolitionists, before you consent to look at our goods."

This illustrates the feelings which animated a majority of dealers from the South. How high this feeling ran, even in New York, will be illustrated by the following anecdote : I boarded at the Merchants' Hotel, in Broad-street, kept by a man named Thurston, at the time of the riots. After breakfast, one morning, Mr. Thurston told me he wished I would find another boarding-place. I asked the reason, or if I had done any thing amiss. He said, "No; but the other boarders declared they would not have a clerk of that d——d abolitionist, Arthur Tappan, in the house." So he sent up to the top of the house for my trunk. I paid my bill, and went to board at 21 Broadway, with that godly and noble woman, Mrs. Woods.

I took a kind of boy's oath against slavery, and whatever I have since done or left undone, that oath has been fulfilled. I came, when a lad, from Vermont, thinking little, and at the time caring less, on the subject ; and yet here I was turned out of a hotel for being a clerk to an abolitionist ! In less than a week from that time, "Jim," the colored waiter, and I helped one slave to run off to Canada.

Mr. Arthur Tappan was sometimes rather ungracious in small affairs, but always noble in important matters ; for instance, in the end of 1835, I failed to arrange terms to stay with the firm of Arthur Tappan & Co., and parted with Mr. Tappan, as I thought, coolly. He certainly was not over-courteous when we parted. I feared I had in some way offended him. What was my surprise, one day, soon after my leaving him, when he stood at my desk, looking earnestly at me, and said, "I thought you might need a bank endorser, and I came to say that we would go on your paper for twenty-five thousand dollars." Before I recovered from my surprise or had time to thank him, he was half way out of the store. The custom then was for merchants to *exchange* paper to use in bank. I had no occasion to avail myself of the offer, but it illustrates one trait of his character. His motto seemed to be,

"DEEDS, NOT WORDS."

XIX.

THE anti-slavery cause was steadily advancing.
Cradled in storms, opposed in its infancy and youth
by political and ecclesiastical bodies, it now, in vigorous manhood, asserted its uncompromising principles, maintained its ground, and pressed forward
with energy and hope, trusting that, under the blessing of a God of freedom and righteousness, it would
attain to a glorious consummation. Some questions
arose among abolitionists concerning the treatment
due to colored people by their professed friends, in
the social circle and the walks of business; and
respecting the obligation of keeping the cause free
from entanglement with other mooted questions;
and with reference to agitating the public mind with
the political relations of the subject.

The discussions of these questions, with the
vehemence natural to those who were, *par excellence*,
the friends and exponents of free discussion, made
the enemies of the anti-slavery cause exult with
anticipations of the speedy dissolution of the association for the deliverance of the slave. But these
hopes of the conservative, time-serving, and fearful
portions of the community were not destined to be
fulfilled. The seed of freedom, widely sown by
indefatigable agents, had struck deep root, and was
to spring up and bear abundant fruit. The sentiment of the renowned champion of freedom, MIL-

TON, was to have fresh corroboration: "Though all the winds of doctrine be let loose to play upon the earth, so TRUTH be in the field, we do injuriously to doubt her strength. Let her and falsehood grapple. Who ever knew truth put to the worse by a free and open encounter?"

The executive committee of the American Anti-Slavery Society issued new publications; they published an address to auxiliary societies, congratulating them upon the success of the cause, urging them to renewed efforts, and advising to an increased supply of means to carry on the work. Articles favoring emancipation were inserted in the daily papers; and in various other ways the cause was urged forward with zeal and energy. No one felt a deeper interest in these measures than ARTHUR TAPPAN. His purse, his prayers, his time, his influence were consecrated to the cause; he never doubted its eventual success; and he gloried in the opportunity offered him of being one of its leaders. He, in common with all his fellow-laborers, rejoiced in the emancipation of the slaves in the British West Indies, eight hundred thousand in number, and in the tidings borne to these shores by so many witnesses of the success that had attended that great act of freedom, both as it respected the good conduct of the emancipated and the acquiescence of the principal part of the planters.

The news from the West Indies greatly exhilarated the friends of the colored man in this country, as it added weight to the arguments in favor of the

13

safety as well as righteousness of immediate emancipation on the soil.

A disastrous event in this our land showed them
that men who would be true to the sacred cause of
immediatism, must, here as well as in other lands,
wage this holy war at the risk of their lives, and
sometimes at the sacrifice of life. The intelligence
of the death of ELIJAH P. LOVEJOY, of Alton, Ill.,
November 7, 1837, murdered by a pro-slavery mob,
filled the hearts of his friends with grief, and the
friends of liberty with horror. A public meeting
was held at Broadway Tabernacle on the occasion,
a funeral discourse was pronounced, and at a
special meeting of the executive committee of the
society appropriate resolutions were adopted and
widely published. They recommended to all the
auxiliary and other anti-slavery societies, and all
friends of immediate emancipation, to hold solemn
public meetings on the 22d of December, to com-
memorate in a suitable manner the martyrdom of
Mr. Lovejoy; enjoined it upon all agents of the
society to make new and more vigorous efforts to
enlighten the minds of the community respecting
the doctrines and measures of the society, to secure
funds for the increase of agents and the multiplica-
tion of publications; called upon ministers and others who had hitherto declined a public advocacy of
the cause, now to stand forth and plead for the suffering and the dumb; and directed that fifty thousand copies of the monthly newspaper, entitled
HUMAN RIGHTS, be published, in mourning, contain-

ing a biographical sketch of Mr. Lovejoy, the efforts
made by him in the cause of freedom and other
moral reforms, a history of the mob, etc., with an
appeal to the American people and the civilized
world. These resolutions were signed by ARTHUR
TAPPAN, chairman, and sent forth on the wings of
the wind.

There were abundant reasons for earnest activity, in this as well as in other parts of the country;
for while the abolitionists were all alive in promul-
gating their sentiments, and maintaining them at
whatever cost, the friends and allies of the slave
power were also alert and outspoken; men "who
whet their tongue like a sword, and bend their bows
to shoot their arrows, even bitter words; . . . .
they commune of laying snares privily; they say,
Who shall see them?" In a bow-window in the
most public street in the city of New York were
exhibited Bowie knives, with the inscription on the
blade, DEATH TO ABOLITION. These weapons of
assassination were, it was said, manufactured in
England. If this were so, it was evident that they
were intended and ordered for the American market; and the fact that about the same time a manu-
facturer in the neighboring town of Newark, N. J.,
fabricated similar instruments, with the same motto,
demonstrated the animus of opponents, while the
measure was to the threatened party a vain terror.

Men in high places continued, though less numerously than heretofore, to misrepresent and malign
the men whose only offence was the assertion and

defence of right principles; and leading clergymen made strong efforts to suppress the agitation that prevailed; while Recorder RIKER spoke of the danger of "*turning loose*" two millions of slaves. Amid all the agitation, the abolitionists seemed to be the only sane portion of the community.

By-and-by, more favorable changes took place in public sentiment. Monthly concerts of prayer for the enslaved were observed in many places, and anti-slavery societies were formed in a large number of churches. The anniversaries of anti-slavery societies were more largely attended, and statesmen began to feel the importance of guiding rightly the awakened consciences of the people. The effect of these measures was soon apparent in the community, as the following anecdote evinces:

At a village in the state of New York, where at one time there had been but two abolitionists, one a Presbyterian and the other a Methodist, and only a meetinghouse of each denomination, the two resolved on having an anti-slavery lecture. Being unable to procure a suitable place, they advertised that, on such a day and hour, a lecturer would deliver an address *at such place as might be offered.* The day arrived, and the lecturer came. "Where is the meeting to be held?" inquired he. "We do not know," replied the brethren, "no place has been offered us yet." At this moment they heard the Methodist bell strike, and a few seconds after the Presbyterian bell. Both houses were opened, and as the Presbyterian meetinghouse was the largest, the meeting was held there, and the whole village turned out to hear the lecturer.

Another gratifying evidence of a change in sentiment favorable to the anti-slavery cause, was the fact that business men, who had imagined that the world was coming to an end, if the abolition heresy prevailed, were convalescent and nearly restored to their right minds. Before the great fire in 1835, Arthur Tappan & Co. were obliged to insure their stock of goods partly in Boston, because the best New York insurance companies could not take all that was wanted; but this year the Boston companies equalized their premiums on New York risks with the officers in the latter city. To the question, "Why did you not do so before?" the answer was, "The difference was for *abolition risk.*" Thus it appeared *that* risk was then considered at an end.

The annual meeting of the Anti-Slavery Society, May, 1838, was the largest that had ever been convened. Arthur Tappan presided. The services continued about four hours. Letters were read from several distinguished persons, and among others, one from the Hon. JOHN QUINCY ADAMS. He said : "It will not therefore be in my power to attend the meeting of the Anti-Slavery Society, but my best wishes will be with them, that their institution may be blessed with the smile and approbation of Heaven for the promotion of the general cause of human liberty, and for the extermination from the face of the earth of the doctrine fit to have issued from the head of Caligula or the heart of Nero, that *bondage* is the appropriate corner-stone to the *temple of freedom*."

Other statesmen have been, by fits and starts, outspoken in denunciation of slavery, but who have not, like Mr. Adams, been the constant advocates of human freedom. Miss Martineau, in her "Retrospect of Western Travel," in mentioning President MADISON, whom she visited, says: "He observed that the whole Bible is against slavery; but that the clergy do not preach this, and the people do not see it."

It may be pertinently inquired why a statesman who uttered the above sentiments, and who long previously avowed them in the convention that adopted the constitution of his country, continued to uphold slavery by his own example, and left to his heirs a hundred or more persons in bondage, to be sold, as their necessities might require, at the auction block. With regard to his remark about the "clergy," the charge might have proceeded more appropriately from other lips. The fact is, both statesmen and clergymen, prophets and priests, smothered their convictions, thus bringing to mind the declaration of ancient times: "A wonderful and horrible thing is committed in the land; the prophets prophesy falsely, and the priests bear rule by their means; and my people love to have it so: and what will ye do in the end thereof?"

The revulsion in Mr. Tappan's mercantile affairs had given him poignant grief in many respects, as will naturally be supposed. But it was not so much on his own account as for others that this grief was intensified. Submitting without a murmur to the decree of an overruling Providence, he could not but be grieved that the suspension of his mercantile firm necessarily deprived other firms of the support he had cheerfully given them in his prosperity; that it increased the load under which his solvent creditors were weighed down; that it obliged him to postpone or relinquish the aid he had encouraged benevolent and religious institutions to expect from him; that it curtailed his expenditures for charitable objects, and especially for the anti-slavery cause. Still, with resolute courage and hopeful effort, he buckled on the harness anew, relying upon his industry, perseverance, integrity, the good will of the community, and above all, the sustaining grace of God.

His business appeared to be gaining success, and there was a prospect of recovering the prosperity he had previously enjoyed. Others saw this as well as himself, and efforts were made to draw him into speculations of various kinds, some of them having connection with mercantile business. He listened to one or more of the schemes that were projected by men of considerable experience, but after full consideration, resolved not to engage in any other business than that he had so long pursued, for the present at least. Besides, his confidence in institutions that had formerly interested him was considerably lessened. " I do not," he said, " see the use of money as formerly. If I give it to a literary institution it may be perverted. Holiness is wanted more than money or men. Oberlin seems to be doing some good, and also the Oneida Institute."

In the course of eighteen months, the renewed notes, given after his suspension, for eleven hundred thousand dollars, were, as already said, all paid, though to effect this object the interest, with the sacrifices to raise money, amounted to more than a hundred thousand dollars. But his business was apparently prosperous, and continued so, while the sales were for cash or notes on a short time. He had made great efforts to continue his business on its former scale. To this end unusual risks were taken, particularly in selling goods on credit to a dangerous extent. Northern customers were very slack in payments, while those at the South paid little or nothing. So great was the distress at the South, that a lawyer in Alabama wrote to a merchant in New York: "There is at this time no money in circulation here. A thousand dollars' worth of good real property, will not at this time [in 1840] command seventy-five dollars in cash."

A fatal mistake was also made by Mr. Tappan in yielding his consent to the proposition of a friend, to be concerned in real estate operations, and making himself responsible for the result. Business too suddenly fell off, money became very scarce, three per cent. a month being paid for interest, and failures taking place every day. Another suspension seemed inevitable; but in order to avoid it, the firm took up its paper by paying half the amount in cash, and giving new notes for the other half. Notwithstanding these efforts, the perplexities of business increased, until he felt compelled to retire from the firm, his brother having previously dissolved his connection with it, to engage in another pursuit, at a time when the affairs of the copartnership seemed prosperous. Mr. Arthur Tappan went into bankruptcy, surrendered up all his property, and lost all but his honor. To use his own words: "We did a prosperous business, and paid up the whole, with interest, within the eighteen months stipulated. The second interruption to the business was because *I* was unable to meet *my* engagements for land purchases made by Mr. P——, with my responsibility, and I only of our firm failed. The business went on under a new firm, and the debts of the firm were, with some extensions, all paid with interest." He submitted to the misfortune with cheerful resignation, surrendered all his property to the marshal of the district, took his watch from his pocket and sent it to the marshal to be sold with his furniture, went into the service of his former partners, and continued housekeeping on a scale suited to his altered circumstances.

A merchant in New York, who had long known him in his days of prosperity, but had not sympathized with him in his anti-slavery enterprise, said: "If Arthur Tappan will allow his name to be put up on my store, and sit in an arm-chair in my counting room, I will pay him $3,000 a year."

Besides a consciousness that he was acting as

became an honorable merchant, and a Christian, he set an example worthy of imitation by other merchants involved in bankruptcy, avoiding "the appearance of evil" and having a conscience void of offence. He did not, of course, pretend to excuse himself for entering upon such a speculative project. He aimed to benefit a friend, who had not been fortunate in his own business, relied upon this friend's judgment rather than his own in the speculation, and was probably influenced also by a desire to retrieve some of his own losses. It was an error, but, being in, he made the best of it. His advances, though not sufficient to discharge the obligations, were equal to the sum his creditors had paid for the property.

Among other sympathizing friends of Mr. Tappan, was the world-renowned philanthropist JOSEPH STURGE of England, who, in his visits to New York, had been greatly interested in his public character, and felt for him a strong friendship.

In Mr. Sturge's work, entitled "A Visit to the United States in 1841," he states:

I had much pleasure and satisfaction in my intercourse here with several individuals distinguished in the anti-slavery cause, some of whom I met in 1837, during a short visit to New York on my way to the West Indies. Among them ought particularly to be mentioned the brothers ARTHUR and LEWIS TAPPAN. The former was elected president of the American Anti-slavery Society on its formation, and remained at its head until the division, which took place last year; when he became president of the American and Foreign Anti-slavery Society. His name is not more a byword of reproach, than a watchword of alarm throughout the slave states, and the slaveholders have repeatedly set a high price upon his head by advertisement in the public papers. In the just estimation of the pro-slavery party, ARTHUR TAPPAN is ABOLITION personified; and truly the cause needs not to be ashamed of its representative, for a more deservedly honored and estimable character it would be difficult to find. In personal deportment he is unobtrusive and silent; his sterling qualities are veiled by reserve, and are in themselves such as make the least show—clearness and judgment, prudence and great decision.

He is the head of an extensive mercantile establishment, and the high estimation in which he is held by his fellow-citizens, notwithstanding the unpopularity of his views on slavery, is the result of a long and undeviating career of public spirit and private integrity, and of an uninterrupted succession of acts of benevolence. During a series of years of commercial prosperity, his revenues have been distributed with an unsparing hand through the various channels which promised benefit to his fellow-creatures; and in this respect his gifts, though large and frequent, are probably exceeded in usefulness by the influence of his example as a man and a Christian.*

The same friend expressed his deep concern at the subsequent losses of Arthur Tappan, as was indicated in a letter to his brother dated—

BIRMINGHAM, ENG., 9mo. 17, 1842.

MY DEAR FRIEND: .... The ways of God are not as our ways, nor are his thoughts as our thoughts. In his fatherly corrections he often sees meet to try us most closely upon those points which we think most hard to bear, and to teach us there is such a thing as an unlawful desire for lawful things; and perhaps thy noble and generous-hearted brother, who wished only for wealth to enable him to lessen the sum of human misery, may be permitted to see that neither his happiness nor his usefulness would have been promoted had his desires in this respect been granted.

* See Appendix 5, for statement respecting Jamaica.

I hope and believe that the Divine blessing will accompany him to his retirement, and should his day of active labor be nearly closed, may he be permitted the assurance that his day's work has kept pace with the day, and that to him who feels that, through the boundless mercy of a crucified Redeemer, he has a well-grounded hope that he shall safely enter that city "whose walls are salvation, and whose gates are praise," it matters little whether he be actually employed or belong to those of whom it is said—

"They also serve who only stand and wait."

Please remember me affectionately to him.

XX.

AT the seventh annual meeting of the American Anti-slavery Society, May, 1840, a division of the body took place. Causes had been in operation some time that weakened the bonds which held the members of the society together, and they at last culminated in a rupture that left each portion to pursue the course it deemed necessary to secure ultimate triumph over a common enemy. But as we are not writing a history of the anti-slavery enterprise, no attempt will be made to state, at length, the causes of the division.

The editor of the *Philanthropist* said: "It is unnecessary to enter into an explanation of these causes, but they may be ranged under the general heads of non-resistance—woman's rights—denunciation of the clergy—personal ambition—unavoidable sectarian affinities and prejudices."* To which may be added different views of the Constitution of the United States, as it respects the support or non-support given by it to slavery—also of the declaration of sentiment that accompanied the constitution of the Anti-slavery Society with respect to political action.

Neither portion had, at the time of separation, any idea of favoring any political party, although

* See *Philanthropist* of June 16, 1840.

the minority of those taking part in the proceedings
at this annual meeting claimed that political action
in some form was authorized by the convention that
formed the National Anti-slavery Society, as appears
by the following clause in the declaration of sentiment: "There are at the present time the highest
obligations resting upon the people of the free states
to remove slavery by moral and *political* action as
prescribed in the constitution of the United States."

In accordance with this principle, the executive
committee of the society had adopted the following
resolution :

OFFICE OF THE AMERICAN ANTI-SLAVERY SOCIETY, }
143 Nassau-street, New York,
October 30, 1838.

At a special meeting of the executive committee of the
American Anti-slavery Society it was unanimously

Resolved, That this Committee, concurring in the sentiment universally expressed by abolitionists throughout the
country, that *political preferences* are to be sacrificed to the
interests of *humanity*, are of opinion that the reply of Mr.
Bradish entitles him to the cordial support of abolitionists at
the approaching election, and that on the other hand the re-
plies of Mr. Seward and Governor Marcy show that the cause
of human rights has nothing to expect from the election of
either of them, and hence every vote which is given to either
will be an injury to that cause.

Resolved, That the friends of humanity throughout this
state be earnestly requested to withhold their votes from
Messrs. Seward and Marcy, and every other candidate who
answers to the same effect or neglects to answer at all.

Published by order of the committee.
ARTHUR TAPPAN, CHAIRMAN,
E. WRIGHT, JR., Rec. Sec., pro tem.

This was as far as the society felt prepared to go
at that time. In a year or two, a step or two was

made in advance. In the *National Intelligencer* is a letter stating: "There are abolitionists belonging to both of the above named societies, who are in favor of independent anti-slavery nominations. . . Neither of the societies, as such, favors the plan of a distinct abolition political party. The new society, although it recognizes the rightful existence of human government, will carefully abstain from all the machinery of party political arrangements in effecting its object, and does not require a pledge to vote, as a condition of membership, yet will urge on all the duty of exercising political power in behalf of the slave. It will employ means which are of a moral, religious, and pacific character."*

The whole number attending this annual meeting was, as appeared by the recorded votes, 1,008, and in a test vote the numbers stood 557 against 451. The minority claimed that the majority was swelled by the attendance of a large number of persons, especially women, who came from a single state, with the avowed purpose of controlling the votes of those who had been accustomed to attend the annual meetings. And this claim appeared to be correct as of those attending the meeting no less than 464 were from the state of Massachusetts.

One of the first items of business at the meeting was to choose a business committee. The acting president, FRANCIS JACKSON, nominated a woman on this committee, associated with eleven men. This was objected to, but a majority constituted as already

* See *National Intelligencer* of June 1, 1840.

stated, supported the nomination. Several nominated to serve on the committee, declined serving, in
consequence of the act of the majority. They stated that the innovation seemed to them repugnant to
the constitution of the society—that it was throwing
a fire-brand into anti-slavery meetings—that it was
contrary to the usages of the civilized world—and
that it tended to destroy the efficiency of woman's
anti-slavery action.

But, although the Anti-slavery Society split on
the test vote mentioned, the question of "woman's
rights" was not the only matter of difference, as
has been already intimated. It was thought that
the time had come for a separation, and a new
organization. A preliminary meeting was held to
consider the subject, and after prayerful consideration, it was unanimously resolved that it was best
to separate from the old society, and organize a new
association. A general meeting was notified, and
numerously attended. About three hundred members of the old society enrolled their names, and
organized a convention, which held its sessions during three days.

A new society was formed, named the AMERICAN
AND FOREIGN ANTI-SLAVERY SOCIETY. As its constitution contemplated enlarged action with reference to
the slave-trade, especially co-ordinate with the British and Foreign Anti-slavery Society, the new association introduced the word "foreign" in its desig-
nation.

Whatever may have been thought by the abolitionists, or their opponents, at the time of the separation, of the anti-slavery body it will be conceded now, it is believed, that the cause was greatly promoted by that measure. Like the division of Christians into different denominations, the combined action being an increase of zeal and efficiency, the division of the abolitionists probably called out increased activity and liberality.

ARTHUR TAPPAN was chosen president of the new society, and also chairman of the executive committee, after having declined a re-election as head of the old society, over which he had presided since its formation. He preferred associating with those in whose views he sympathized, although cherishing feelings of regard for many of his former associates. An address "to the friends of the anti-slavery cause throughout the United States and the world," issued by the executive committee and bearing his signature, was widely published. It stated the ground of disagreement in the anti-slavery ranks, gave a history of the proceedings before and after the rupture, and stated the principles that would govern the new society. It ended as follows :

The committee earnestly request the prayers of Christian abolitionists, that they may have wisdom from above, profitable to direct, and they invite all their fellow-citizens who pity the enslaved, who desire to promote the best interests of the slaveholder, who love their country, who respect the rights of man, and reverence the laws of God, to unite with the society in the great work of bringing about the extinction of the slave trade, and slavery, in this land and throughout the world.

ARTHUR TAPPAN, PRESIDENT.

S. W. BENEDICT, Rec. Sec.

Among the members of the old society who were not present to take part in the discussion and vote that led to the separation were the writers of the following letters :

Judge WILLIAM JAY, one of the vice-presidents of the new Society, in a letter to the recording secretary of the old society, dated June 8, 1840, said : "Persuaded as I am that the society under its present control is exerting an influence adverse to domestic order and happiness, inconsistent with the precepts of the gospel, and exceedingly injurious to the anti-slavery cause, I deem it my duty to request you to erase my name from the roll of its members."

JOHN J. WHITTIER, in a letter to Rev. Joshua Leavitt, of June 6, 1840, said : "The anti-slavery host has been severed in twain. The thing which I have greatly feared has come upon us. The original cause of the difficulty—a disposition to engraft foreign questions upon the simple stock of imme- diate emancipation, I early discovered, and labored to the extent of my ability to counteract. . . . But the separation has taken place ; and I can now only hope that both parties will go forward, each in its own way, steadily and without turning aside to assail each other, to promote the great and good cause to which they stand pledged before the world."

An official organ of the new society was com- menced, styled the *American and Foreign Anti-sla- very Reporter*. This publication, together with the published annual reports, exhibit the doings of the society under Mr. Tappan's presidency. During the thirteen or more years he acted in that capacity, he presided at the meetings of the executive com- mittee, and at the annual meetings, contributed to the funds according to his ability, and labored ear- nestly to promote the efficient action of the society.

About this time a considerable number of aboli-

tionists of both societies, chiefly, however, of those
favorable to the new society, united in forming the
"LIBERTY PARTY," an anti-slavery political organization, and put in nomination their own candidates.
Some hesitated, who, at length, voted with their former associates. Others declined voting at all. Not
a few continued to vote with the parties to which
they had long been attached, and some strenuously
opposed the Liberty party. Mr. Garrison and his
adherents were of the latter class. Mr. Tappan,
most of the active promoters of the new society, and
friends of the old committee, went for the Liberty
party.

The *National Era,* a weekly paper, was established at the city of Washington, by the American
and Foreign Anti-slavery Society, under the editorial care of Dr. Gamaliel L. Bailey, former editor of
the *Philanthropist* at Cincinnati, January 7, 1847.
It was sustained by the society until it was firmly
established, when it was sold to the editor without
loss to the Society. By him it was conducted, wisely and courteously, with much advantage to the
cause of emancipation, until his lamented decease.

The paper had a large circulation throughout
the country; and together with the social weekly
gatherings at the house of the editor, gained the
good will of members of Congress of different views
with regard to slavery, and gave a respectability to
abolitionism in the eyes of the nation. Mr. Tappan
was a true friend of the editor, who had his confidence and support. The present Chief Justice

CHASE was the personal friend of Dr. Bailey, advised and otherwise aided him for a series of years, and was the means of introducing the paper to many distinguished persons.

Mr. Tappan, also aided in an attempt to establish another paper in Washington, called "Der National Demokrat," edited by Mr. Frederick Schmidt. It was to be printed in the German language, and to be circulated among the large and increasing portion of the inhabitants who speak or read that language. The Germans who emigrate to this country have, as is well known, democratic tendencies, and on arriving here very often affiliate with the democracy of this country, wholly unsuspicious that the name DEMOCRAT does not always indicate the political character of those who bear it. To undeceive his deluded countrymen was the object of the editor, and it was a grief to Mr. Tappan and other friends that unpropitious events prevented the success of the paper. Other instrumentalities have been happily the means of gaining the attention of a considerable portion of the German population to the true character of American democracy as theorized and practised by political demagogues.

Within this period, viz., September 3, 1846, the AMERICAN MISSIONARY ASSOCIATION was formed from four associations that had previously existed, in all which he took a deep interest. These were the "Amistad Committee," the "Union Missionary Society," the "Western Evangelical Missionary Society," and the "Committee for the West India

Missions." These societies were largely composed of members of the anti-slavery societies, and when merged in the new association formed an anti-sla-. very body that carried on the work of emancipation as well as the work of missions. Mr. Tappan had been a member of the "Union Missionary Society," aud now became chairman of the executive committee of the "American Missionary Association."

The FUGITIVE SLAVE BILL, enacted by the Congress of the United States in 1850, and which astounded all true patriots and Christians by its atrocious provisions, was a source of very great grief to Mr. Tappan. He regretted the apostasy of the renowned Daniel Webster, the subserviency of Millard Fillmore, the time-serving conduct of other political men in and out of Congress, but especially did he mourn over the inconsistency and folly of professing Christians, including a considerable number of preachers of different denominations, who attempted to justify the obnoxious bill from the Bible. His regret at such evidences of dereliction on the part of ministers and church-members did not, however, lead him to abandon the church, defame the clergy, or cease to uphold, so far as he could, by his constant attendance and means, the institutions of the gospel. He hoped and expected that the delusion would ere long pass away, and that recreant divines and church-members would regain the confidence of consistent Christians and the favor of God.

For himself, he made up his mind, deliberately

and in the fear of God, to disobey the requirements of the Fugitive Slave Bill.* Clerical expounders of Scripture united with politicians in inculcating the duty of obeying the law. But he spurned the slavish doctrine. "I will submit to the penalty, if need be, but will not obey." Such was his feeling and his determination, and he would have gone to the stake rather than act otherwise. The iron had entered the soul of every intelligent colored person throughout the country, and it had by sympathy entered the soul of Arthur Tappan.

The annual meeting of the American and Foreign Anti-Slavery Society, May, 1850, was a memorable one. A short time previous, the Fugitive Slave Bill had passed both houses of Congress, and been approved by President Fillmore, "a Northern man with Southern principles." And what excited the virtuous indignation of the friends of liberty beyond all this, Daniel Webster had, in the Senate, espoused the cause of the slaveholders in his speech in defence of the bill. The influence of Mr. Webster, though his moral sense had been evidently ebbing for some time, was so great that a considerable portion of the people, especially the aristocratic part, took open ground as supporters of the iniquitous measure. On the other hand, the anti-slavery

---

* In the days of British oppression, when the Parliament had enacted an arbitrary and unconstitutional bill, Mr. Tappan's maternal grandfather was one of the Bostonians who refused to call it a LAW, and it was styled the BOSTON PORT BILL. By that name it was universally called by the revolutionary patriots, and by the same it will go down on the page of history.

party, now become numerous and powerful, resolutely asserted the unconstitutionality of the bill,
and their determination to disobey it, "sink or
swim."

Under these circumstances the society held its
tenth annual meeting, in the Broadway Tabernacle,
which was entirely filled. Addresses were made by
WILLIAM JAY, SAMUEL LEWIS, and HENRY WARD
BEECHER, full of patriotic feeling. The corresponding secretary, as usual, presented an abstract of the
annual report, and read a set of resolutions. When
he commenced reading the one relating to Mr. Webster, it became evident that there were present many
"sons of Belial," who were resolved on making a
disturbance. The resolution included two verses
from a trenchant poem by Whittier, entitled "*Icha-
bod*." The whole resolution was as follows:

Resolved, That DANIEL WEBSTER, by his disregard of early
professions, his treachery to humanity and freedom, and his
servility to the slave power, has forfeited the respect and
confidence of his constituents and country.

> "Of all we loved and honored, naught
>   Save power remains—
> A fallen angel's pride of thought
>   Still strong in chains.

> "All else is gone; from those great eyes
>   The soul has fled:
> When faith is lost, when honor dies,
>   The man is dead!"

Amid vociferous noise and interruptions, it took
some time to read the resolution; but after several
attempts the reader at length succeeded, and the
vast audience received it with acclamation.

At the next anniversary, held also in the Broadway Tabernacle, May 6, 1851, the chair was occupied by Mr. Tappan, the ninety-fourth psalm was read by Rev. Dr. Lansing, a fervent prayer was offered by Rev. Charles W. Gardner, a colored brother of Philadelphia, an abstract of the annual report was read by the corresponding secretary, the acceptance of which was moved by Rev. Samuel E. Cornish. The addresses were by Rev. Henry Ward Beecher, Rev. Dr. Willis of Canada, and Rev. C. G. Finney. A set of resolutions was read, and enthusiastically adopted.

Mr. Beecher was the principal speaker. At this time, and previously, most of the ministers had kept away from anti-slavery platforms, especially in the large cities. Mr. Beecher, who had recently been settled over the Congregational church in Brooklyn, N. Y., did not hesitate to throw his influence in favor of the anti-slavery question, and thereby gained a hold on the affections and respect of the progressive portion of the community that he has never lost. At this meeting an amusing scene occurred. While Mr. Beecher was making his eloquent address, a young man in the "rioters' corner" of the gallery interrupted him with some outburst that excited a general laugh. Mr. Beecher asked, "Where did you come from, pray?" The youth exclaimed, "I am from up the river." Mr. Beecher, with ready wit, said with a gesture indicating what was in his mind, "*Sing-Sing?*" The laugh and cheers were now directed against the young man, who screamed out,

"No; I am from the South." The reply was, "I thought so." At this Mr. Beecher was loudly cheered, and resumed his speech, while the audience were perfectly quiet, except that at a frequent burst of eloquence they rapturously applauded.

Despite of Congressional bills, framed in opposition to the law of God and the claims of humanity, and the arguments offered in some religious journals, Mr. Tappan was the early and persevering friend and helper of fugitive slaves. He aided them with his purse, advice, and sympathy; and when he learned that the objects of his benefactions had safely reached the Canadian provinces, he did not attempt to conceal his exultation. It has even been said that he, or one bearing his name, owned a horse somewhere near the Susquehannah river, that was often mounted by fugitives, while under the guidance of the north star and a superintending Providence they sped their flight to the land of freedom.

The last public anniversary that Mr. Tappan was able to attend, was held at the Broadway Tabernacle, May 11, 1853. He presided both at the public meeting and the business meeting of the society the ensuing day. Rev. A. N. Freeman, pastor of the Siloam (colored) Presbyterian church in Brooklyn, read selections from the Scriptures and offered prayer; and a resolution suited to the times was read and adopted. An able and interesting address was made by FREDERICK DOUGLASS. He said in conclusion: "It is not in the power of human law to

14

make men entirely forget that the slave is a man.
The freemen of the North can never be brought to
look with the same feelings upon a man escaping
from his claimants as upon a horse running from
its owner. The slave is a man, and no slave. Now,
sir, I had more to say on the encouraging aspects of
the times, but the time fails me. I will only say, in
conclusion, greater is He that is for us than they
that are against us; and though labor and peril
beset the anti-slavery movements, so sure as a God
of mercy and justice is enthroned above all created
things, so sure will that cause gloriously triumph."
(Great applause.)

The deeply lamented President LINCOLN, in after
years, had his heart lacerated in view of the recreancy of men of professed religious principles, some
of them doubtless good but mistaken men, who opposed the emancipation of the slaves, and strengthened the hands of the oppressor. He who is " a
God of knowledge," and by whom actions are
weighed, witnessed throughout the anti-slavery contest the enormous mistakes and even guilt of ministers of the gospel, elders and deacons of churches,
officers of ecclesiastical bodies, editors of religious
newspapers, and leading laymen in the churches and
on committees of benevolent and religious societies,
putting themselves in the scales with slaveholders
to weigh down the poor slaves and their advocates.

At a cabinet meeting immediately after the battle of Antietam, and just prior to the issue of the
September proclamation, says Chief-justice CHASE,

the President remarked: "I made a solemn vow before God, that if General Lee was driven back from Pennsylvania, I would crown the result by the declaration of freedom to the slaves." When informed that certain ministers would not vote for his reëlection to the presidency, he drew forth a pocket New Testament, and said, "These men well know that I am for freedom in the territories, freedom everywhere, as free as the Constitution and laws will permit, and that my opponents are for slavery. They know this; and yet, with this book in their hands, in the light of which human bondage cannot live a moment, they are going to vote against me. I do not understand it at all."

On the same authority it is stated that President Lincoln said with a trembling voice, and his cheek wet with tears: "I know there is a God, and that he hates injustice and slavery. . . . I know that I am right, because I know that liberty is right, for Christ teaches it, and Christ is God. I have told them that a house divided against itself cannot stand; and Christ and reason say the same, and they will find it so. Douglass did n't care whether slavery was voted up or down; but God cares, and humanity cares, and I care, and with God's help I shall not fail. I may not see the end; but it will come, and I shall be vindicated; and these men will find that they have not used their Bibles right."

"Does it not appear strange," said President Lincoln, "that men can ignore the moral aspect of this contest? A revelation could not make it plainer to me than that slavery or the government must be destroyed. The future would be something awful, as I look at it, but for this rock on which I stand, (alluding to the New Testament which he still held in his hand,) especially with a knowledge of how these ministers are going to vote. It seems as if God had borne with this thing (slavery) until the very teachers of religion had come to defend it from the Bible, and to claim for it a divine character and sanction; and now the cup of iniquity is full, and the vials of wrath will be poured out."*

It is true that all who thus voted, or threw their influence on the side of the oppressor, did not believe in the divine right of slaveholding; but those in the catalogue who did not go to this extent threw their weight nevertheless in the scale of oppression against freedom. "He that is not with me is against me."

         * F. B. Carpenter, in the *Indianapolis Journal*.

XXI.

THE formation of the AMERICAN MISSIONARY ASSO-
CIATION, in 1846, has been already alluded to. It
was at first the ally of the American and Foreign
Anti-slavery Society, and when events seemed to
render the active exertions of that society no longer
necessary, it became its natural successor. Arthur
Tappan was elected one of the vice-presidents, was
also a member of the executive committee, continuing in the office to the end of his days. During
all this time he felt a deep interest in its affairs, and
contributed to its funds according to his ability..
He had also participated in the doings of most of
the associations that preceded it, and which at its
formation were merged in it. A brief sketch of
them will not be here inappropriate.

1. The AMISTAD COMMITTEE. This committee,
consisting of S. S. Jocelyn, Joshua Leavitt, and
Lewis Tappan, were appointed at a meeting of
the friends of liberty, September, 1839, to procure
legal counsel for the defence of forty or more native
Africans, who had been seized the preceding month
by the United States authorities, on a charge of
piracy and murder on the high seas, and bound
over for trial at the United States circuit court at
Hartford, Conn.

The facts were these: Ruiz and Montez, two
planters on the island of Cuba, had purchased these
newly arrived Africans, and were taking them, coast-

wise, in a Spanish schooner called L'Amistad, to their plantations, when Cinque the leader and his countrymen rose upon the Spaniards, killed the captain and the cook, took possession of the vessel and ordered Ruiz & Co. to steer for Africa. In the daytime they did so, but at night changed the course of the vessel. By-and-by the United States coast was reached, and Lieut. Gedney, of the United States navy, in command of the brig Washington, captured the party, at the east end of Long Island. The committee employed counsel, made an appeal for funds, and earnestly contended for the freedom of the Africans, in the district and circuit courts, for nearly two years; and on a final hearing before the supreme court of the United States, obtained a decree liberating the Africans, notwithstanding the efforts made by the Spanish minister, aided by the United States authorities, to procure their delivery to the Spanish claimants. The counsel for the Africans were Messrs. SEDGWICK, STAPLES, BALDWIN, and the ex-president JOHN QUINCY ADAMS.

The Africans had been instructed at New Haven and Farmington, Conn., and the survivors, on being released, were sent to Africa, accompanied by two missionaries, with a view to establishing a mission near the west coast. The Mendi mission, as it was called, was subsequently taken in charge by the American Missionary Association, and is still under its care.

2. The UNION MISSIONARY SOCIETY. This was formed at Hartford, Conn., August 18, 1841, by a

convention, to consider the subject of MISSIONS TO AFRICA, being chiefly people of color, from the states of Massachusetts, Rhode Island, Connecticut, New York, and Pennsylvania, including five of the Amistad Africans. The *Amistad Committee* soon afterwards became merged in this society.

3. The WESTERN EVANGELICAL MISSIONARY SOCIETY. This society was formed in 1843, by the Western Reserve Association of Ohio. Its primary object was to prosecute missionary operations among the western Indians. It proposed to be in correspondence with the *Union Missionary Society*. The society established a mission among the Ojibwa (or Chippewa) Indians in Minnesota Territory, which they sustained till 1848, when it was merged in the American Missionary Association.

4. COMMITTEE FOR WEST INDIA MISSIONS. A mission was commenced among the emancipated people of Jamaica. Five Congregational ministers sailed from New York, in the fall of 1839, to join this mission, four of them with their wives. They went to Jamaica, in the expectation of receiving a plain support from the ex-slaves. Being disappointed in this, they appealed to the churches in the United States for aid. Eleven individuals were appointed a committee on behalf of the mission, of whom WILLIAM JACKSON, was chairman. The committee issued a letter-sheet, from time to time, in which were published letters from the missionaries, etc. The American Missionary Association being formed, the committee accepted a proposition from the exec-

utive committee of the new society to take charge of the mission.

The origin of the AMERICAN MISSIONARY ASSOCIATION was as follows: Early in 1846, a call was issued for a convention of friends of BIBLE MISSIONS, at Syracuse, N. Y. An address prepared by Rev. AMOS A. PHELPS,* of precious memory, was read, in which he spoke of the position of the *American Board of Commissioners for Foreign Missions*, with regard to slavery, idolatry, polygamy, and caste. A committee was appointed to call a more general convention to consider the topics above mentioned. This convention was held at Albany, September, 1846. Brethren attended from six or more states. Rev. J. H. PAYNE of Illinois, presided. Two days and one evening were occupied in a free and harmonious discussion. A constitution of a new society was formed, officers were chosen, an able address to the Christian public, written by William Goodell, was prepared, and the four associations already described, were soon after incorporated into the new society. Hon. WILLIAM JACKSON of Massachusetts, was elected president, George Whipple of Ohio, corresponding secretary, and Lewis Tappan, treasurer. The executive committee were located in the city of New York. The *American Missionary*, a monthly paper, took the place of the paper entitled, the *Union Missionary*, and afterwards, in addition to the paper, a monthly maga-

* He died at Roxbury, Mass., July 30, 1847, greatly lamented by those who appreciated his character and services.

zine of the same name and contents was issued, and both continue to this day.*

The *Amistad Committee*, before being merged in the American Missionary Association, proposed to the American Board for Foreign Missions, to relinquish all claim to their partially civilized and Christianized clients, and the unexpended funds in their hands, the privilege of conveying them to their native shores, and establishing a new mission in western Africa, to be in their hands, *provided assurance was given that it should be an anti-slavery mission*, but the Board, by its secretary, Dr. Anderson, declined this overture. It was made in good faith, and as the funds had been contributed by persons of anti-slavery sentiments of all denominations, the committee felt obligated, from that consideration, as well as from principle, to make the tender with that condition.

The duty of seizing such a favorable opportunity to establish a new mission in Africa, appeared to be imperative, though the *Amistad Committee*, and the founders of the American Missionary Association who had but little experience in missionary affairs, shrank from the responsibility, and would gladly have waived all claim to a prosecution of the new enterprise, could it have been otherwise effected on satisfactory terms. As it could not be, they undertook the work and the care of the West India mission with a reliance upon Divine aid.

* See Appendix 9, for records of the American Missionary Association in view of the decease of Mr. Tappan.

It was not an agreeable thing for those who loved and honored the American Board, to appear to be in opposition to it, nor to be arrayed in anywise against the American Home Missionary Society, the American Tract Society, or any other benevolent institution. The American Missionary Association sprang into existence as "a living protest against what was considered the complicity of the above societies with slavery." "Our American Christianity and our American slavery met, on the fields occupied by them, face to face, and the former was vanquished by the latter. The gospel, as proclaimed by them did not appear to be a match for slavery, and the church, as represented by them, seemed to have succumbed under the dreadful pressure of this dominant iniquity."

Arthur Tappan, who had contributed so generously, and labored so earnestly to advance the welfare of these benevolent institutions, was exceedingly grieved at this reluctance to oppose, in all constitutional and legitimate ways, the "accursed system of slavery," to use an expression of William Wilberforce. Mr Tappan talked against the complicity, he wrote against it, influenced others to remonstrate against it, and frequently made it a subject of prayer.

Some one prevailed on Mr. Tappan to write in favor of making or of accepting overtures for a union of the missionary bodies. Objections were suggested, and in reply, he wrote as follows to the compiler:

NEW HAVEN, Nov. 2, 1857.

Thanking you for taking the trouble to write me at so much length, your views respecting the amalgamation of the missionary societies, I made the suggestion as one to be considered maturely and with much prayer for divine direction. Providence is hedging up our way by withholding from us the coöperation of suitable men to sustain and carry forward the enterprise, and we appear to be making no progress in enlisting the churches in our favor; or in bringing them to our views respecting fellowshipping slaveholders and slaveholding churches. What can we expect from the almost universal church in this country, that, even in the free states, grinds the face of the colored people with the denial of every or nearly every political and religious, civil and social privilege ? Even here, in orthodox Connecticut, they are driven to associate in separate churches, separate schools, and to lie in separate *burying-grounds*, and are ignored in all their civil rights as citizens, except that of paying taxes to support magistrates whom they have no hand in choosing; and a poor privilege this ! If there is a better state of feeling towards them in Ohio, it may be better to transfer to that state the location of the main society, and have agencies at the East. . . . .

I am well pleased with the position given me in the Board of the American Missionary Association.*

In the following letter he speaks out the sentiments burning within him, respecting the cruelty of CASTE in our own land, and the backwardness of Christians in reproving what the excellent missionary, PERKINS justly denominated "OUR COUNTRY'S SIN."

NEW HAVEN, Nov. 11, 1857.

. . . . I have seen and conversed with our hearty friend Townsend. He thinks there is yet but very little chance of our getting any of the ministers here to favor our society. His time is entirely engrossed by his bank, but his feelings

---

* Alluding to his appointment as a Vice-president.

are all alive for the slave. I fear there are but few kindred spirits here. He says Thompson succeeded here in getting access to, and interesting many in this city, and would do well again at a proper time. There is now so much distress in the large towns as to make it comparatively an unfavorable field of effort for getting money, but it is a good time to sow the seed for future reaping, as the evenings are long, and people have leisure to hear and read.

I wish we could get some one to write extensively for the papers and other periodicals, in a Deacon Giles or Beecher style, and with a heart profoundly and vividly alive to the great sin of our land, in the free states—I mean the sin that pervades not only the world, but the church, the sin of prejudice against color, the SIN that few professing Christians are without, and the odiousness of which in the sight of God, will flash upon such Christians, when they shall meet their colored brethren at the bar of Christ. If such a writer can be found and engaged in the work, I will give one hundred dollars towards the expenses incurred, and would give much more, if I had it to give. Will you look out for the right pen for the purpose? Whether male or female is immaterial.

It was a constant grief to him that the American Board of Commissioners for Foreign Missions gave a *quasi* support to American slavery in several respects, and especially by withholding their judgment upon the national transgression, when they had, in former years, expressed their disapprobation of other moral transgressions. Although he desired to be cautious in pronouncing an opinion unfavorable to the Christian character of all slaveholders he felt that they should not be recognized as Christians in good and regular standing while they held that relation.

He maintained also that while slaveholders were

admitted to churches by missionaries in our own country, unreproved by Missionary Boards, it would be difficult to attain to much success in foreign lands, as intelligent men in heathen countries must see that slaveholding was contrary to the spirit of the Gospel. The following extract from one of his letters expresses his views on the subject:

NEW HAVEN, January 15, 1858.

. . . . I learn from Boston that no new instructions have been given to the missionaries of the Choctaw and Cherokee missions, who write that 'no slaveholders are admitted to their churches, or have been for a long period, nor have any been excommunicated *who gave evidence of Christian character !*'

. . . . I shall not be able to get a public meeting in behalf of our society (the American Missionary Association) at present, and what is done here must be by private solicitation. If a good agent can be found to canvass this city, I will pay his expenses while here. My recommendation, with that of others I could get, would effect more than my personal applications, for to most I am not personally known, and I have not health and time for a thorough work. My headache troubles me much.

The opposition to the American Tract Executive Committee is working well here, and as the same principle is involved, this will help the missionary cause. Their secretary (American Tract Society) will not be admitted to the churches, nor is he countenanced by the ministers.

In the subjoined letter he alluded to the remarkable success of a domestic missionary, in the conversion of a number of persons in Brooklyn, N. Y., as related at a prayer meeting in the Plymouth Church. It also alludes to the interest he felt in the controversy in the American Tract Society, between those who favored the publication of tracts on the sinfulness of slavery, and those who objected to it. Had he visited New York at the time, his old friends in the Society would have seen four brothers, all friends of the tract cause, and some of them devoted and liberal supporters of the Society, standing up at the public meeting in the church in Lafayette place, to oppose the action of the Society on the slavery question, as they felt bound to do by their allegiance to Christ:

NEW HAVEN, May 3, 1858.

. . . . Your account of the conversion is very wonderful. That "plain man," the teacher of the Bible-class, must have a rare tact for the work. . . . . I send you a printed letter to the secretaries of the American Tract Society. It is the one that was prepared some time since, and in which I referred in my letters to you. I have sent about one hundred and fifty of them to individuals, Life Members and Life Directors . . . . and have about the same number prepared with single wrappers and postoffice stamps, for which I have failed to get names of good men and true. If you can use them, and will write to me *immediately*, I will send them to you by express.

If you think I can be of service in New York, in preparing for the conflict with the Tract Society, will you say so, and I will put on my harness and go down at once. . . . . If this separation is effected by the withdrawal of the South, we shall soon find these timid abolitionists on the ground we now occupy, while we should be shooting ahead.

Mr. EVARTS, secretary of the "American Board of Commissioners for Foreign Missions," had taken open and decided ground against the action of the state of Georgia, and the Federal government, in the removal of the Indians, saying: "We are not bound to conceal our opinion; on the contrary, we are bound to declare it plainly, at least once." He said also, "We do not think we can stand acquitted before God, or posterity, unless we bear a testimony against this course of proceedings." Noble words! worthy of that enlightened, independent, Christian reformer.

Foreign missionaries had frequently written home that CASTE and SLAVERY, as they existed in this country, were powerful obstructions to the conversion of the heathen. And yet with seeming indifference, the Board refused to bear its testimony against caste and slavery in their own country, and considered those members of the Board intermeddlers, who persisted in asking that the rule applied to the tormentors of the Indians, should be applied to the tormentors of Americans called Africans.

The "American Home Missionary Society," composed also of wise and good men, as it respected most subjects, persevered for a long time, in sustaining missionaries in slave states who preached an emasculated gospel, without disciplining slaveholders or pronouncing an opinion against slavery.

The "American Bible Society," after authorizing the publication, on the platform of the "British and Foreign Bible Society," in London, that all the families in the United States who were willing to receive a copy of the Scriptures, had been supplied with a copy of the Bible, made no decided efforts to reach a sixth part of the inhabitants, in the persons of the slaves, but on the contrary, seemed to ignore their existence.

The "American Tract Society," after issuing tracts on the evils of Intemperance, Licentiousness, and Sabbath-breaking, and even Dancing, utterly refused to bear its testimony against a system that included all these practices, with a hundred fold additional atrocities.

The American Board, the oldest, the wealthiest, and the most influential of the benevolent societies of the country, did not only refrain from giving expression of hostility to slavery; it seemed to countenance it in various ways.

He did not expect or wish to have these societies become anti-slavery societies, still he desired, and he thought he had good reasons for the desire that these, founded in a great measure by New England men on gospel principles, and sustained by their donations and prayers, should bear a decided TESTIMONY against the sin of the country—American slavery. He hoped that the influential men connected with these societies, when they saw many of their old associates contending against a giant evil, would aid the arduous effort by their sympathy at least, and bring the powerful influence of these societies in like manner to aid the cause of freedom.

Arthur Tappan had been a liberal supporter of these institutions; he had devoted the best years of his life and his ample means to sustain them; they had enjoyed his coöperation and prayers, and the aid of many excellent men who were associated with him in the arduous work of opposing human bondage. But notwithstanding the reiterated entreaties and remonstrances of these Christian abolitionists, who had been among the original founders and long-tried friends of these societies, these institutions remained dumb and paralyzed before the American Moloch!

Mr. Tappan was fully aware of the excuses alleged for this silence and apparent apathy. He knew also of the violent opposition of a large portion of their friends to the anti-slavery cause, and that they said that the abolitionist body was largely composed of irreligious men, some of them of infidel sentiments; that their publications were couched in harsh language; that the lecturers were intemperate in their speeches; that the measures of the society set public opinion at defiance. These allegations were notoriously untrue, as it regarded a major part of the advocates of the anti-slavery reform, and with reference to the rest of them were much exaggerated. And it is worthy of remark that when the division took place, and a portion of the abolitionists, under Mr. Tappan's lead, drew off and formed a separate society, endeavoring to adopt such language and such measures as Christian men could not reasonably object to, those who had been loudest in their opposition, and most offended with what they termed the unchristian spirit of the abolitionists, kept aloof as well from the American and Foreign Anti-slavery Society of which Mr. Tappan was president, as they did from that of the American Anti-slavery Society of which Mr. Garrison was the head.

It was said, also, in excuse, that the Scriptures nowhere condemned slaveholding in express terms, and that the Old Testament particularly authorized it, or at least winked at it; that the Constitution of the United States guaranteed slavery; and that the founders of our government had made a compromise with the South that the people of the North, for all time, were bound to respect.

It was in vain that Mr. Tappan and his coadjutors, referred to the Constitution of the Anti-slavery Society, to its declaration of sentiments of contemporary date, to its publications from the beginning of the controversy. It was in vain that they asserted the Christian character of a majority of the founders and supporters of the society, to the accordance of its principles and measures with the Bible and the national constitution; to the obligation resting upon Christian men and Christian institutions to take the lead in efforts for moral reform, to make continued aggressive movements against national as well as individual sins, according to the example of Christ and his early followers.

In May, 1852, an effort was made by the executive committee of the American and Foreign Anti-slavery Society to arouse the attention of anti-slavery people to the great interests at stake. "An address to the Anti-slavery Christians of the United States" was prepared and extensively circulated. Politicians by the enactment of the Fugitive Slave-bill and other measures hostile to civil liberty, had moved the literary, business, and ecclesiastical portions of the community to unusual hostility to the progress of the anti-slavery reform. It had been artfully promulgated that the reformers were hostile to the constitution of the country, and that their measures tended to the injury of all classes, and the subversion of the government. A large portion of the people seemed to be stupefied and hopeless in view of the downward career of the nation, the prevalence of a pro-slavery sentiment, and the corrupt influence of men in power, aided by thousands of timid, conservative interested men, in all the various professions and ramifications of society.

It was necessary to alarm and call forth men of principle, and induce them to stand up manfully for their own rights, and the liberties of the people. The objects of the society were frankly and forcibly stated, and the friends of righteousness, justice, and mercy were besought to enroll their names among its members, and to contribute liberally to sustain its measures. This address was signed by forty-two prominent abolitionists, among whom were the following persons, since deceased: David Thurston, Samuel Fessenden, Titus Hutchinson, Samuel Osgood, John Pierpont, Bancroft Fowler, William Jay, John Rankin, Arthur Tappan, C. D. Cleveland, Charles Avery, T. B. Hudson, Joshua R. Giddings, Charles Durkee.

It is believed that this effort of Mr. Tappan, and the other friends of the cause, did much to awaken the sleeping energies of the people, induce them to oppose erroneous doctrine, and stimulate them to renewed action on behalf of civil and religious liberty.

The words of the Earl of Carlisle (Lord Morpeth) in his speech at the anniversary of the British and Foreign School Society, are pertinent to this subject: "Now I look upon it to be the mission—the true, obvious, and permanent mission, both of all individual men and of all corporate bodies, to wage incessant war against those evils which still disturb and desolate our globe. To do so is the real vocation of Christian men and the supreme glory of Christian churches."

These matters are now referred to by way of explanation, and for the justification of Mr. Tappan in the course pursued by him in the contest he felt himself bound to wage against what he considered the injurious policy of men of influence and Christian profession, with many of whom he had labored in the cause of religion and philanthropy. He felt especially aggrieved at the refusal of the "American Tract Society" to bear its testimony against American slavery, and to issue tracts on the sinfulness of slaveholding.

He deemed the excuse offered, that "our constitution requires us to circulate only publications calculated to receive the approbation of all evangelical Christians," wholly insufficient and evasive. That clause he believed, referred to "doctrines," and not to "practices." *All* evangelical Christians did not accept the sentiments contained in the publications of the society on other moral delinquencies, yet the committee on publications, composed of men of various denominations, had concurred in their issues. Why, then, thought this old evangelical friend of the Tract Society, should it not publish tracts on our country's peculiar sin. He thought the course pursued was unworthy of the society, corrupting in its influence, and dishonoring to Christianity: and it is believed that this will be the judgment of posterity.

Is it asked what are the advantages of bringing up at this time, the errors, or even culpable negligences, of institutions that are so dear to the hearts of Christians, so beneficial in their general conduct, and so worthy of the patronage of the churches? Is it not best to let by-gones be by-gones? The answer is, it seems due to the memory of Mr. Tappan to present his views of the delinquencies of these societies, and his efforts in opposition to the evils complained of. No one who knew him can doubt the sincerity and strength of his convictions on the subject. They continued to the end of his earthly career. And any attempt to portray his character would be incomplete that did not recognize his feelings and exertions, during successive years, to withstand what was evil and injurious, and to strive for what was true, and excellent, and imperious, in this regard.

Mr. Tappan did not deny that the officers of the American Board and the directors of the other benevolent societies in this country were good men; but he conscientiously believed that, in not giving their testimony against slavery, they made a great mistake, and when the iniquitous system was abolished the Christian people of the country saw and lamented the fatal error. Considering the vast influence of the Board, he believed that by refraining from all sanction of slavery, and openly avowing opposition to it, the most beneficial results might be expected; that other benevolent societies would imitate the example; that the eyes of the people would be opened to see its atrocities; that legislative bodies would be on the side of freedom; that the church would take action in opposition to the sin; and thus the judgment of God upon a guilty nation be averted.

That such men should have made so grievous a mistake was, he thought, a lesson to the church that should be deeply pondered, not only for humiliation, but for caution. Other evils exist, other conflicts are to be waged, and the church will be called upon to buckle on its armor, and fight the good fight of faith. Chattel slavery is abolished, but the idolatry of riches, the anti-Christian feeling of caste, and the oppression of the poor still exist. Mammon has many worshippers in the church; and multitudes now, as heretofore, profess godliness, and yet "bind heavy burdens and grievous to be borne, and lay them on men's shoulders, but they themselves will not move them with one of their fingers."

Should not the church and posterity have the benefit of the lesson taught by the delinquency of influential men in their individual and associated positions? And should not the facts in the case be put *on record* that the benefit may be secured to those who follow? When an individual in private life makes a mistake, or commits a wrong, if he repents, we should forgive him, and let it pass into oblivion. But is not the case different when the mistake occurs on the part of officers of societies in their official capacity, and on the part of these societies themselves?

Mr. Tappan, in his remonstrances and censures, had in view the good of those who will be the successors of the good but erring men, whose conduct he could not justify or excuse. He was persuaded that as slavery was abolished, men would see more clearly the mistakes made by those who had opposed the anti-slavery movement. He knew that persons at the head of benevolent institutions, like men at the head of colleges and other literary and ecclesiastical bodies, are always in danger of being over-cautious, timid, conservative; and he desired to make every suitable allowance for such tendencies, while he did not cease to lament that golden opportunities had not been seized to discharge high and important duties to the church and to the great Head of the church, to the down-trodden and oppressed countrymen in chains.

Mr. Tappan rejoiced that slaveholding had come to an end, but he lamented that the spirit of slaveholding was still abroad in the community, and that it existed in the church. The eagerness of men to accumulate and hoard money to require services for inadequate compensation, to lord it over the dependent and poor, to widen the distance between the laboring and affluent portions of the community, and to establish unchristian and anti-republican aristocracies in society and in the church, were evidences, he thought, that the animus of slavery still existed.

He deprecated the fact that so many compass sea and land to make and hoard gain, and that members of churches often vie with the ungodly in such efforts; that clerks and sewing women were paid as little as possible, while their employers were getting immensely rich. In view of the common assertion that the law of competition created this state of things he believed that if rich men felt right, they would see to it that all in their employ received ample payment for their services; that the wages of the employé should be somewhat in proportion to the success of the employer, and would be, if the slaveholders' spirit did not still prevail.

Against this worldly and selfish spirit he thought all good men should combine; that especially professing Christians, churches, ecclesiastical bodies, and benevolent societies should bear an unequivocal and decided TESTIMONY until slaveholding, in spirit as well as in practice, should cease. To effect this, he judged that the mistakes and delinquencies of the past should be confessed and repented of, and that the remembrance of them should serve as beacons for direction and security in time to come.

Meantime he rejoiced in the termination of the

self-imposed silence of institutions he ever loved, on
the slavery question, and which had forfeited his
confidence by a non-compliance with what he thought
an obvious, and imperative duty, and which his
allegiance to Christ forbade him to sanction.   He
thought he saw the dawn of better things, in several
respects, and it was the language of his lips and his
heart, PRAISE THE LORD.

XXII.

A MEETING of Mr. Tappan's brothers and sisters was held June 1, 1848, in their native town, and continued about a week. At some inconvenience, owing to distance and other impediments, they had resolved to meet for once, at least, to hold affectionate converse, and to view the interesting scenes of their childhood and youth. Most of them were accompanied by their companions.

Rooms were taken at the Mansion House hotel, where they had a parlor and a table to themselves. Northampton never appeared to better advantage. The weather was delightful. All were in good health and spirits. Much of the time was spent indoors, being occupied in social chat, in reviews of individual and family histories, in grateful recollections. But the weather, the roads, the scenery, the views, the fields, the gardens, the rivers, invited to explorations abroad, and all felt young again.

It is true that the village had greatly changed, and in some respects evidently for the better; there were many new and more tasteful dwellings, an increased number of shops and stores, and more evidences of general thrift. The old meeting-house, the court-house, and school-house, had given place to more spacious and elegant edifices. Instead of one church that accommodated all the inhabitants, there were now five or more, of nearly as many denominations. The inhabitants, now treble in number, seemed also much changed. Formerly these brothers and sisters knew everybody, but now, in their own native town, they seemed almost among strangers. It was only in the ancient burying-ground, where so many familiar names were seen, that they really appeared to be at home.

But the trees were there, especially the venerable and umbrageous elms, the glory of the place ; as were the meadows and the mountains, that gave such a beauty and magnificence to the town and the surrounding country. These unfading scenes brought to mind the familiar and appropriate lines often repeated in youthful days :

> "Sweet Auburn! loveliest village of the plain,
>   Where health and plenty cheered the laboring swain,
>   Where smiling spring its earliest visit paid,
>   And parting summer's lingering blooms delayed.
>   Dear lovely bower of innocence and ease,
>   Seats of my youth, when every sport could please,
>   How often have I loitered o'er thy green,
>   Where humble happiness endeared each scene! "

The brothers and sisters made a visit to the graves of their parents and youngest sister. Here they mingled their tears and rejoicings, while they recounted the various incidents of family history. All dwelt, with sincere congratulations and thanksgivings, upon the characters of their deceased parents. The eldest brother made a short address,

in which he expressed the thought that the example
of the parents had influenced their children in attachment to each other during their whole lives.
At such a place, with such surroundings, with such
reminiscences, and such anticipations, how natural
and appropriate the ejaculation: "Let me die the
death of the righteous, and let my last end be like
his!"

The six brothers took a survey of the old play-
grounds, and the rivers and woods, and thought of
the times when they bathed, and skated, slid down
hill, played ball, trundled hoop, and gathered nuts.
They also visited the old lot and orchard where in
their boyhood they had "picked apples" and "made
hay." While here they thought of the old spring, how
the water once slaked their thirst, and all expressed
a desire to taste it again. Once it would have been
easy enough; "every one could have bowed down
upon his knees to drink." In the dilemma the oldest said to the youngest, as in olden times, "Run and
get a cup." It was soon brought, and never did
pure cold water taste better.

On the Lord's day the brothers and sisters repaired to the house of worship, some to the old
Congregational church, where their parents worshipped, and some to the Edwards church, an off-
shoot of the old church. How changed from earlier
times! Formerly instead of being seated as now,
each family in their own slip, the occupants were
seated by the selectmen. A list was annually prepared by "the fathers of the town," of all the house-

holders, single men and women, and youth of both
sexes, and they were assigned to their places according to some rule, suggested by the tax-lists, or the
social standing of the parties.

The heads of families were arranged in the old
square pews on the lower floor; the widows, single
women, and old bachelors were put here and there,
wherever there were vacancies; the old people occupied the pews nearest the pulpit; and the little
children had seats in the aisles, and on the pulpit
stairs. The deacons sat together on a seat beneath
the pulpit, facing the congregation. One of them,
it is recollected, who was looking forward to be a
minister, employed the time in taking down the sermon, while another, who was very deaf, stood by
the minister, with his trumpet at his ear. The seat-
ing did not always give satisfaction. There was
aristocratic feeling and pride in those days as there
is at present. Some thought they were not seated
in the best pews or with people of their choice, and
the selectmen were accused of favoritism or injustice. Now and then a dissatisfied person would
stay from meeting awhile until resentment cooled
off.

In the gallery the singers filled the first tier of
seats. All the young people who had good voices
were expected to sit with the singers. There was
no *quartette* or organ in those days, and the bass
viol, haut-boy, and violin, were relied upon as
accompaniments. The singing-master, with his
pitch-pipe, and his *fa, sol, la, mi*, led off, while, *for-*

tissimo! the well-drilled choir did their best. It was singing never to be forgotten!

On both sides of the gallery were pews, in which the principal young men and young women were seated, separately, while the youngsters, and those belonging to no particular family, sat on long seats. In winter, as the house was not heated by a furnace or stoves, there was usually no little noise among the urchins, and some of larger growth, in attempts to keep warm by shuffling and stamping, while their seniors, in the pews below, kept up a slam-bang, at the close of the prayers, it being the custom for the whole congregation to stand during those services, raise the seats and let them fall at the close.

Foot stoves were often used in winter, and they were brought in sleighs, and carried into their parents' pews by the younger members of the family. The minister, in extreme weather, would preach in his great coat, and sometimes with his hands in mittens. Notwithstanding all these peculiarities it was a pleasant sight to see the inhabitants of so large a town, gathered in one place for public worship. There were very few absentees in those days, and a large portion of the houses were closed during public service.

The town seemed to the brothers and sisters to be full of strangers. Formerly, at their separate visits to the place, they recognized almost every one, and when death had removed parents the children were known by family resemblance; but now the faces of a large proportion of the inhabitants were unknown to the brothers and sisters. The inquiry was suggested, "Your fathers, where are they?" A few old acquaintances stopped to shake hands after the services were over, and several called at the hotel to express their satisfaction at seeing so many of the family.

It appeared to the people of the town quite a rare sight to see nine children of one family, native born, whose ages ranged from sixty to seventy-seven, the average being about seventy, whose fortunes had been so various, all meeting in health and harmony to visit their native place, the scenes of their youth, and the graves of their parents. And it was exceedingly gratifying to the brothers and sisters to take by the hand those who bore the names of honored predecessors, and who were not unworthy of their ancestry.

The visit seemed short, but extremely gratifying. Nothing unpleasant occurred to mar the joyful intercourse, excepting an accident to the eldest sister that deprived the rest of her society for some days. Each day the Scriptures were read, and prayer offered. No intoxicating beverages were drank, nor was the "filthy weed" used by any one. With cordial embraces the brothers and sisters at length separated to return to their different families and dwellings, thankful for the opportunity with which a kind Providence had indulged them of thus meeting, and with increased love to each other.

"Home of our childhood! how affection clings
And hovers round thee with her seraph wings!
Dearer thy hills, though clad in autumn brown,
Than fairest summits which the cedars crown!
Sweeter the fragrance of thy summer breeze,
Than all Arabia breathes along the seas!
The stranger's gale wafts home the exile's sigh,
For the heart's temple is its own blue sky!"

THE MERCANTILE AGENCY. 345

XXIII.

In the year 1849, Mr. Tappan purchased a moiety of the establishment called the MERCANTILE AGENCY, an institution that had been founded, as an individual enterprise, to obtain and record, for the benefit of merchants who patronized it, the standing of merchants throughout the country, for the use of those who might sell to them on credit. This business gave him moderate employment, enabled him to support his family, and furnished the means of contributing to charitable objects. He was successful in the prosecution of this business, and the profits enabled him to pay the purchase money, and buy an estate on the banks of the Passaic river, in New Jersey, where his family resided, and from which he came to the city daily. The years thus spent were, in many respects, among the most pleasant of his life.

The following extract is from a letter to his daughter, Mrs. M——.

CHESTNUT GROVE, N. J., Jan. 1, 1855.

".... I wish you a happy new year. My headache of the worst type has again recurred, and I am kept at home to-day by it. Dr. W—— has prescribed some medicine, and I have consented, at your mother's request, to take it, though I have but little faith in it. I am determined to let the doctor make a few experiments, and to give him all the credit if it does me any good. . . . .

I feel that we have much to be grateful for to our Heavenly Parent, for giving us such affectionate children and

15*

grandchildren. My earnest prayer is that our happiness, begun here, may be consummated in heaven, with our children and grandchildren. With much love to all,

Your affectionate father,

ARTHUR TAPPAN.

He had contracted to leave the concern of the Mercantile Agency at the end of five years, and he did so, but not without a vexatious suit with his partner, who claimed that he had been paid more than his share of the profits. An arbitration was agreed upon, which resulted in an award in his favor of twelve thousand dollars. In reply to the communication made to him of the decision of the referees, he wrote to his brother, as follows:

Your letter of the 22d of November, has been received. I am, as you anticipated, disappointed, but as the result is not as good as my *hopes*, so it is not as bad as my fears. I am thankful for what I get, and feel much indebted for it to your great effort in my behalf, without which I should probably have got nothing. My chief regret arises from my diminished ability to contribute to religious and benevolent objects; but I will do what I can, and this I trust will meet Divine acceptance, though it will not be equally grateful to my feelings.

After the discontinuance of the co-partnership, he continued to reside at Belleville, N. J.; and here finding that the care of his garden, of which he was very fond, did not give him sufficient occupation, he entered into the iron business, in Newark, a few miles from his residence, and rode daily to that place and back, managing the office business of the concern. It proved an unfortunate undertaking. An abused, perhaps a misplaced confidence in the representations that had been made to him resulted in the loss of a large sum that went, not to the support of the business, but to the payment of old debts of his partner. He had much trouble and vexation in contending against the claims of persons who had obtained the obligations of the firm for the individual prior engagements of his associate in business.

On closing up the business, he sold his estate in New Jersey, and repaired to New Haven, where, with property belonging to his wife, he purchased a house near his former residence. Here, in society congenial to himself and family, after an absence of eighteen years, he took up his abode for the remainder of his earthly career.

He would have been pleased had a wider field been opened to him of useful activity, and if he had possessed the means to do good as in earlier parts of his life. Inaction had always been irksome to him, and it was a new experience to be restricted in his charities, having realized so long that "it is more blessed to give than to receive."

In the following extracts from his letters to his brother, he alludes to his wife with affectionate solicitude:

CLARENDON SPRINGS, Vt., August 7, 1857.

. . . . My stay here is prolonged by the evident though slow improvement of my wife's health. She has still but very little appetite, and I want to see a more radical change in this respect. I had an interview with Judge K—— of this state. . . . . I asked him how extensively the clergy of this state are of the opinion that slaveholding is a sin *per se.* He replied, "They are, I think, very generally of that sentiment." It occurs to me that this makes it important that the American Missionary Association should roll up the ball in Vermont, then east and south, until the church is thoroughly indoctrinated. Now when a revival spirit so extensively prevails in the community, it is a favorable time for the effort. If the *Vermont Chronicle* could be made use of, and other good agencies employed, you and I may yet see slavery receive its death-blow.

He occupied himself in reading, correspondence, social intercourse, visits to the poor, the distribution of tracts, daily visits to the reading-room, and occasional excursions to other places. The people of color were not forgotten by him. With many colored persons he often conversed, affording those in want a helping hand. During the war he also visited the United States' soldiers at the encampment in the south part of the city, and where some of them were sick.

While thus gliding down the stream of life, not unmindful of the life to come, he was soon impressively reminded of the lesson often taught to him and others, that there is no defence against sickness and bereavement; that this world is not our home, or the place of unmixed enjoyment; that, in the language of Scripture, we have here "no continuing city," but are "strangers and pilgrims on the earth."

It pleased their heavenly Father to come very near to Mr. and Mrs. Tappan, by a bereaving providence, taking from them and her family, a darling child, one in whom their fondest hopes rested, and who was the ornament of her home, and the circle and church with which she was connected. Mrs. FRANCES ANTILL SEYMOUR, wife of John F. Seymour, Esq., of Utica, N. Y., died September 5, 1860.

Her parents were warmly attached to this affectionate daughter, and her fond father was accustomed to call her the "morning star." She had been peculiarly and tenderly beloved by him. Pleasing in person, attractive in her manners and disposition, with a heart full of kindness, she was greatly beloved by her numerous friends.

The grandparents had keenly felt the death of a sweet and endeared daughter of Mr. and Mrs. Seymour, and this reiterated bereavement pierced them to the heart; but the character of the child, and the piety of the mother, and above all, the firm trust they had in divine Providence, made them resigned to the separation for a time from those so near and dear to them.

The following letter of Mrs. Tappan to her eldest daughter, then residing in one of the Eastern states, evinces her maternal solicitude and tender affection, as well as her patriotic sentiments, during the national struggle then in progress:

NEW HAVEN, July 22, 1861.

MY DEAR DAUGHTER: I am sorry you have been disappointed in not seeing your son as soon as you expected. If he comes here first, I will try to take good care of him. The young folks are expecting fine times this week, I believe.

There was a great battle, yesterday, Sunday, between the rebels and the government troops. We cannot rely upon all that is said, but we pray that the *righteous* cause may prevail. . . . . Bring to mind the honesty, candor, uprightness, moral and religious principle of ABRAHAM LINCOLN. . . . .

The knowing ones think the South are perfectly aware, that if they cannot destroy the Union, slavery is *doomed;* and so far as we can judge they are in rather a sad predicament. Let us hope for the best, that slavery will be abolished, and the slaves sing for joy. Oh how their *friends* will sing praises to their and our God when the yoke is broken. Then the husband can claim and hold his wife, and the wife her husband, and the children their own parents. Oh, happy, happy day !

I have lately read for the third time, I think, of the emancipation of the slaves in Antigua. How affecting ! Instead of carousing and doing all manner of evil on that day of days to them, they dressed themselves and went to the house of God to pray and praise for the mercy manifested towards them. . . . .

You have been told of your brother's approach to Washington. I do aim to commend him to the protection and tender mercy of our God. My love to my dear granddaughter.   I am, as ever, your own mother,

FRANCES TAPPAN.

Mr. Tappan wrote, July 18, 1861: "My son's wife writes me on the 12th inst. that her husband was just starting to join the army at Washington. If slavery is to be abolished by the war, I think it is to last some years, and that the North as well as the South must be humbled by it."

They soon heard of the death of their only son in one of the Western states, after a lingering illness. Mrs. Tappan's health was affected by this bereavement, and the various vicissitudes of life, though she was sustained by a Christian hope, and the sympathies of her family, and the circle of her friends. Her husband had ever been warmly at-

tached to her, and amidst all the scenes of a busy
life, in prosperity and adversity, in joy and sorrow,
had been attentive, solicitous, and devoted.   It
might be truly said: "The heart of her husband
doth safely trust in her."

On the twenty-first day of July, 1863, he was
parted from his beloved companion. She had gradually declined in health, and after acute sufferings,
was happily released by the messenger of death.
For fifty-three years they had been in the marriage
relation, and his attachment to her seemed to increase with increasing years.   In a letter written to
a beloved niece shortly before her dismissal, she
said: "I will send you a photograph of your uncle,
not great, but good; a kinder and more devoted
husband no woman was ever blessed with; a *bride*
could scarcely receive more devotion and tenderness
than I am daily and hourly receiving."

Her remains were consigned to the grave, in the
family lot of the cemetery, where a headstone was
placed commemorative of her, a space being left to
insert the name, etc., of her partner in life, whenever it should please God to summon him away.

The following was published in the *Independent*,
September, 1863, said to be written by Mrs. Tappan's esteemed friend, Prof. Thacher, of Yale College:

OBITUARY.

Mrs. FRANCES ANTILL TAPPAN, wife of Arthur Tappan,
Esq., for many years an eminent merchant in this city, died
at her home in New Haven, Conn., on the 21st of July last.
Her grandfather, Edward Antill, Esq., a native of New York,

was the son of Edward Antill of Richmond, in the county of
Surrey, England, who was sent as a bearer of despatches
from the home government to the New World, and remaining, became a resident of this city.   His son Edward married the daughter of Governor Morris of New Jersey, and
resided in Piscataway, in that state, where his son, Edward,
the father of Mrs. Tappan, was born in the year 1742.   The
last named Edward Antill was educated at King's (now
Columbia) College, where he was graduated in the year 1762.
He subsequently spent some time in Montreal, Canada,
where he married a lady of French descent.   When the war
broke out between the colonies and Great Britain, he was
called to a colonelcy in the revolutionary army, and became
the intimate associate of some of the most eminent of Washington's subordinates in the council and in the field.

Mrs. Tappan was born May 4, 1785, in Brooklyn, Long
Island.   During the early years of her childhood she was
brought familiarly into the society in which Washington
spent much of his time, and was herself the playmate of
Mrs. Washington's grandchildren; but after the marriage of
her sister with Col. Lansing of Albany, she was withdrawn
to more retired scenes.   She was educated in the family of
this tenderly-loved sister, of whose gentle kindness she
retained the liveliest recollections to the end of her days.

When she was visiting some of her relatives in Montreal,
more than fifty years ago, she became acquainted with Mr.
Arthur Tappan, whom she soon after married, and returned
with him to New York.   From that time her history of
course has been that of her husband.   She sympathized with
him in all his love for the oppressed and all his efforts to
call attention to their degraded condition.   Indeed she shed
tears for the slave long before she became acquainted with
the man who was for many years honored with the abuse of
those who thought more of successful trade than of humanity.   Throughout his years of prosperity she was his loving
and busy co-worker in acts of varied charity and benevolence.   She evinced her love to her divine Master by imita-
ting humbly his life of love to others.   Her hand was open
to the needy, and her door was open to those to whom she

could give a cup of cold water in the name of a disciple. She was given to hospitality.

Nor did adversity work any change in this spirit of gentle love. There remained only the sweet graces of a heavenly soul, that was permitted still to dwell on the earth, that even in weakness it might give strength to those who seemed stronger than she. She was the light of the dwelling. She was the guide of the household.

There were years of suffering which she was called to endure, and her delicate frame was attenuated and bowed under it. But the expression that remains in the memory of survivors is the bright though gentle expression of the kindliest, sweetest love. Death called away a daughter who, had she lived to old age, would only have repeated all that was loveliest in the mother, and soon after, it took from her an only son ; but though her heart was swelled with sorrow, she was still serene—her faith looked up.

With her final sickness came an entire deliverance from the fear of death—nay, she longed for death, saying, "For so he giveth his beloved sleep." She desired her friends to pray that she "might have perfect resignation to the will of God." And amid all her sufferings she found support and consolation in those "faithful sayings" of the divine word, which from generation to generation ever give strength to the souls of God's saints. The Lord was her Shepherd. The Lord was merciful and gracious, slow to anger, and plenteous in mercy. She took delight in these assurances, and in having them read to her. In the strength of them she passed through the valley of the shadow of death, fearing no evil.

It was a great pleasure to Mrs. Tappan to return to New Haven, as she did some years since, that she might there spend the evening of her life among the friends whom she had learned to love, when, in earlier years she had resorted thither for the education of her children. Dr. Taylor and Prof. Goodrich were there to welcome her return. But age and its infirmities, which soon removed them, has now borne her away to follow them to a more blessed home, to the company of the saints and the presence of the Lord, the Lamb.

To a niece a few weeks after the death of his wife, Mr. Tappan wrote the following reply to her letter of condolence:

NEW HAVEN, Sept. 3, '63.

MY DEAR NIECE: It was very kind in you to send me so sweet an expression of your sympathy in my deep affliction. It is hard parting with those we love after a brief acquaintance, but how much more so when our affection for them has been cemented by the most tender and sacred intercourse of over fifty years. I feel that the separation will be brief, and I have much to be thankful for in having loving children with me to share my grief and administer to my comfort.

We have just had a short, but very pleasant visit from your parents on their return home in, as they thought, improved health. I would gladly have detained them longer, but could not.

Your religious reflections are very precious and find a response in my own experience. "The Lord is indeed good, and his tender mercies are over all his works," as I know by precious experience. Praying that you may have largely a similar experience, I am, very affectionately, your uncle,

ARTHUR TAPPAN.

The following is from a letter dated

NEW HAVEN, Oct. 14, '63.

DEAR BROTHER : I have received a letter from Mr. Whipple wishing me to preside at the annual meeting at Hopkinton, Mass., and I have replied to him that my family is so situated as to make it difficult for me to leave home, were I otherwise disposed. . . . Your affectionate

ARTHUR.

He attended the meeting and presided during part of the proceedings, but it was evident that he was much enfeebled.

XXIV.

SOON after his return to New Haven, to spend the remainder of his days, he united with the Centre Congregational church in that city, then under the pastoral care of Rev. LEONARD BACON, D. D., and had much satisfaction in attending the regular week-day religious meetings, in that parish, as his health permitted. He also greatly prized the friendship and pastoral attention of Dr. Bacon. In former times he had differed from him on the colonization and anti-slavery questions, but he was not a man to break the chain of friendship in consequence of differences of opinion. He flattered himself also that the views of his pastor were, in the course of events, more and more assimulated to those he had long cherished.

He also took much delight in religious reading, especially in daily "searching the Scriptures." He felt that his health was gradually giving way, that it became him to be watchful and prayerful in view of the transition that awaited him, and he kept in remembrance the words of Moses the man of God: "The days of our years are threescore and ten; and if by reason of strength they be fourscore years, yet is there strength, labor, and sorrow; for it is soon cut off, and we fly away." Although he felt diffident about his Christian state, and thought much of his shortcomings, yet he had a firm reliance upon the mercy of God through the atoning sacrifice of the Lord Jesus Christ. He was not afraid to die. The death of his beloved companion of half a century, had lessened his desire to live, while his infirmities were loosening his hold on life. He felt that he had no claim to heaven on account of any services he had rendered either to God or his fellow-men. His self-abnegation in the sight of God was remarkable, and no one ever listened to his prayers without being impressed with the belief that he who offered them was exceedingly humble before his Maker. If asked about his hope of salvation, he might have said, as is reported of the aged Rev. Dr. Emmons, " I see nothing in my life that merits eternal blessedness, and I often think I may after all, be a castaway." Perceiving the astonishment depicted in the countenance of his friend, the interrogator, he beckoned him back as unwilling that he should go away under a wrong impression, and feebly said: " If I knew another man who was just like myself, I should have much hope of him!"

Several letters of a miscellaneous character, to his brother in New York, will now be inserted, according to their dates:

NEW HAVEN, May 15, 1857.

. . . . I see by the paper that you were not present at the Abolition public-meeting, and fear you are still unwell. As I have not much to do here, if I can aid you at the missionary rooms or otherwise, let me know, and I will cheerfully do so.

NEW HAVEN, Oct. 20, 1857.

I *have* been *accused* of making a speech in public, but it is not quite true, the occasion was the visit to this city of about 700 East Hamptoners, mostly my friend Williston's employés, who was also present. They came in twelve cars on an excursion, and after they had been welcomed by the mayor and one or two others, I was urged to say something, which I did briefly. I suppose my name was put into the newspaper from a false notion that it would add something to the effect, and not because I said anything to any purpose. I shall probably never be so (mis)represented again.

NEW HAVEN, March 12, 1859.

I have yours of the 11th inst., and learn from it, for the first time, that you have been unwell. Why have you allowed me to be kept in ignorance of that which so nearly concerns my happiness? and why have you not taken me at my word and sent for me to aid you at the missionary rooms? You do not now say how well you are, and whether you are able to be out. If you are still confined at home, do let me know, and come to your assistance.

He had a due appreciation of the talents and fearlessness of the distinguished minister mentioned in the annexed note, nor did he much heed the accusation of his enemies, as they were ready to exclaim: "Thou art beside thyself; much learning doth make thee mad."

NEW HAVEN, Nov. 28, 1859.

. . . . Dr. Cheever's sermon in Friday's *Tribune*, is a capital one, and will I think do great good. I wish it may be read by every doughface professing *Christian* in our land.

NEW HAVEN, January 12, 1861.

. . . Rev. H. T. C—— writes me that there will be a convention of the Christian friends of the church Anti-slavery Society soon in New York, and asks for a communication from me *to be read upon the occasion.* Has this measure your approbation? Regarding, as I do, the present agitation in our country as the answer of God to the prayers of the friends of the slave for their deliverance, I think our policy should be to stand still and wait for His manifestations before we make any further movement. The anti-slavery cause is evidently gaining ground with politicians in the free states, and they are doing a good work for us at Washington. I fear that anything we may do now will excite their fear of being identified with us and slacken their zeal. I therefore hope that the proposed convention will be postponed.

In February, 1861, he writes as follows:

I regret to see the falling off of receipts from the American Missionary Association. The prospect of the curtailment of receipts from —— obliges me to husband my means, or I would send you more. As it is I can hardly restrain my inclination to do so, and feel that I am wanting in faith in the kind providence that has hitherto so bountifully provided for me and mine. If there is suffering with our missionaries for the money due them, I think it should be so stated in the American Missionary, and for one I will respond to it if I have to give my last dollar; for this is a debt that ought to be paid, if it takes the last cent from those who sent them forth.

Again he says:

I see by the last *American Missionary* that the society is doing at St. Louis among the colored people similar labor to that of the Christian Commission among our wounded soldiers. We have recently had a public meeting here of the Christian Commission, and nothing has so much moved the sympathies of our active Christians.

The hope of being instrumental in saving the souls of those who are periling their lives for our country is calculated to draw liberal contributions from those who appreciate the value of the soul, if any thing can, and nothing will give so much credit to our society as the fact that we are doing a similar or rather the same work among the colored soldiers.

NEW HAVEN, April 26, 1861.

. . . . I regret to learn that the receipts of the American Missionary Association are so small. Is there not a large amount of bequests not yet used? particularly of that at Pittsburgh? I fear others as well as myself are so impressed, if it is not so, and that your receipts are affected by it. Would it not be well to publish an explanation for the satisfaction of the friends of the association? In consequence of our national difficulties, my receipts are cut off *entirely* for the time being, and till peace dawns upon us, I have got to husband what I have and deny myself the great pleasure of giving freely. . . .

I fear we shall have a protracted war, and it is difficult to predict what the result will be. If there were a *thorough* anti-slavery feeling pervading the free states, I would hope that the slave states might be conquered and the slave be set free, but we are yet too pro-slavery for this, and I fear are to share more deeply, for our share in the national sin, the just judgments of heaven.

. . . . You have I suppose seen the statement that Gen. Butler offered to recapture some runaway slaves in Maryland. Enclosed is the expression of the righteous indignation of our friend Townsend at such heartless treachery to liberty. I can hardly believe it true, and hope to see it contradicted. I would have made the journey to New York to have witnessed the humiliation of the *Journal of Commerce.* I learn that the editor told a New Haven gentleman that it was a bitter pill.

He took a warm interest in the movements of the "American Missionary Association" with reference to the freedmen. Its appeals for funds for the establishment of schools among them, for the building of school-houses, the employment of teachers, and the success attending such appeals and outlays, contributed much to his enjoyment during his last days. He contributed according to his ability for the promotion of the object; also to the "Sanitary Commission," and the "Christian Commission" the objects of which were precious in his estimation. His interest in these benevolent enterprises and in all matters connected with the terrible conflict in which the nation was involved, were apparent in his conversation, letters, and prayers.

NEW HAVEN, May 20, 1861.

I thank you for your long letter of the 13th, and the official document, which I now return. I am glad it was sent to Butler, though from his reply, he seems to be justified.

I am much taken with the suggestion of our Mendi missionaries to have an establishment at Sherbro Island to promote the cultivation of cotton in that part of Africa. What do your committee think of it? Why not have a company formed at once for the purpose, with a sufficient capital to carry it out? Let colored men be interested, and as they become qualified, take the whole management and ownership if they choose. It would I think, aid very much in promoting civilization and might be a source of great profit to those engaged in it. There should be a good store opened there and a vessel or vessels to send the cotton to market— owned by the concern. I would engage in the undertaking myself if younger, and even now, if better men cannot be found for it. Let me know what you think of it. I hope the South will *insist* on "their rights" till slavery is abolished. It is our only hope of getting rid of slavery. There can be no permanent peace till slavery is abolished. Dr. Tyng acts nobly.

NEW HAVEN, June 26, 1861.

I am glad you are now so well accommodated as to the office. I wish I had a few thousands to help you to keep the wheels in motion. "The Lord reigns, and his ways are not as our ways." It may be the time for us to stand and behold the wonderful workings of His providence.

NEW HAVEN, Oct. 31, 1861.

. . . . We were much gratified with our attendance at the anniversary, and think it was admirably *managed* and sustained in *all* its parts. I hope soon to see it *photographed* in print, and doubt not it will do the society much good, if well presented. If the whole church could have been present to hear the speeches it would have been advanced a whole gen-. eration in its progress millennium-ward.

NEW HAVEN, Aug. 1, 1862.

. . . . I am sorry you are a sufferer from headache. This is an old complaint of mine, and I have rarely a day's freedom from it, and yet have never allowed it to debar me from the duties of life, though it has often curtailed its pleasures.

NEW HAVEN, Jan. 31, 1863.

I acquiesce in your wish in respect to the donation in your hands, but would prefer *not* to have the recipient know whence it comes. Should the war last over a year or two longer, I have the prospect of having my ability to contribute to objects of benevolence much abridged, as my future resources are chiefly in Virginia, where it will I suppose be difficult to operate while the war lasts.

April 18, 1863.

Death is fast weakening our ties to this world and admonishing us that the time of our departure also is at hand. Let us, my dear brother, keep our lamps trimmed and burning, while we do with our might whatever our hands find to do in advancing the cause of righteousness on the earth.

FROM A LETTER TO HIS ELDEST DAUGHTER.

NEW HAVEN, Oct. 3, 1863.

You have brought me so much in your debt by your two long and valued letters that I despair of extricating myself, but I know you will value tidings from the paternal roof even though brief and otherwise not very interesting. . . . Let us, my dear daughter, look to our heavenly Father for a continuance of the kind care we have hitherto experienced, and with grateful hearts submit without repining to the trials of life, and may they serve to weaken our hold on time and ripen us for the enjoyments of heaven. With much love to F—— and L——, your affectionate father,

ARTHUR TAPPAN.

16

XXV.

He loved to resort to the cemetery, where reposes the dust of so many of his valued friends, and the friends of God and man. Especially was he drawn to the grave of his beloved wife, the centre of his earthly affections while sojourning in this vale of tears, and the object of his meditations in the bright world to which he had so good reason to believe she had departed. He would ruminate also upon the place by her side, where he expected soon to rest. This was not, however, a gloomy reflection, for he knew in whom he believed, and anticipated with some satisfaction the time when he should be united to his wife, his departed children, his parents, the friends with whom he had been associated in benevolent enterprises, those for whom he had labored so much, and "to the general assembly and church of the first-born, which are written in heaven, and to God the Judge of all, and the spirits of just men made perfect; and to Jesus the Mediator of the new covenant."

He loved his surviving children and grand-children, and other relations; he took much interest in passing events, and especially in the great conflict in which the country was involved. On the triumph of our forces depended the liberties of the slave, and the welfare of the nation. He looked forward with confident expectation, to the time when the Southern Confederacy would be broken up, the enslaved set free, and the triumph of free institutions complete and glorious. His confidence was founded, not so much in the prowess of our arms, splendid as they were, as in the righteousness of our cause, and the promises of the Almighty. He knew full well that the North had been wickedly in a political league with the South in oppressing the man of color, and by its connivances, apologies, state and national enactments, its preaching, its literature, its fellowship with slaveholders, in church and state, and in benevolent and ecclesiastical associations without rebuke.

He believed that the free states were guilty, in the sight of heaven and earth, for their alliance with the slave states in political and religious affiliations, and deserved the punishment inflicted upon them in the loss of life and treasure. He believed also that God, in his retributive justice, had brought desolation and destruction upon the South for its flagitious cruelty to the colored man. Still, he anticipated that order would be brought out of confusion, that liberation would be given to the slave, and that peace and prosperity would revisit the land, in fulfilment of the prediction: "Surely the wrath of man shall praise thee; and the remainder of wrath shalt thou restrain."

The following letters, addressed to his eldest daughter, who then resided in a distant state, evince the deep interest he took in her welfare, and that of her fatherless children. They are inserted without abridgment, as a specimen of the affection he manifested towards them in their trials, as well as the pleasant retrospect he took of the scenes of his earlier life:

NEW HAVEN, October 9, 1863.

I have acknowledged your last letter to me, but I fear I failed to express sufficiently how much pleasure your letters give me. I assure you I prize them highly, and shall be glad to have them often, and only regret that I am able to make you no better return in the same way. You must find your happiness increased by having your sister with you. I hope you may both derive great benefit from the waters, as I doubt not you will from the pleasant company usually met with at Saratoga.

I have spent much pleasant time there, with your mother, in days gone by, and have witnessed a wonderful improvement in her health in a short time. Once I took her there and to Lake George, when so feeble that she was scarcely able to sit on a horse. At first, I got her on a gentle one, and only walked him a short distance, increasing the distance and the quality of the animal each day. The second week we went on horseback to Lake George, being two days on the way. There we spent another week, riding, and sailing on that beautiful lake, and then her health was so much better, that we rode the eighteen miles to Saratoga without alighting, and the next day left for home, her health being quite restored. I hope you and dear K—— may be equally favored, as your mother was, in the attainment of the blessing of health, without which all other temporal blessings seem of little value.

E—— is now my housekeeper, and we get along very pleasantly. I am sorry you have cause for so much anxiety on W——'s account, and rejoice with you that he has in Alfred E——'s family such kind friends near him.

With much love to yourself, Fanny, Lizzy, and to dear Catharine,   Your father,

ARTHUR TAPPAN.

NEW HAVEN, Oct. 27, 1863.

I must write you a few lines to thank you for your long and good letter of the 22d. I am glad to learn that your health continues to improve, and that you have the prospect of a comfortable winter with your dear children in the American Babylon. Last week I was from home about four days, attending the anniversary of the American Missionary Association at Hopkinton, Mass. We had a very interesting meeting. As I was within twenty or thirty miles of Boston, I was strongly inclined to accompany brother Lewis and his wife there, and make a short visit to brothers John and Charles, but was deterred by regard to Eliza's loneliness at home.

I think you have the promise of a very happy winter, and I rejoice at it, and I hope that your spiritual blessings will be also greatly multiplied.

I rejoice to learn from you that K—— appears to be pretty well, and is likely to return home with improved health. You must have had a very pleasant time together.

E—— and I get along very pleasantly. She takes to housekeeping with a zest, and everything goes on well. I was absent when F——'s birthday anniversary occurred, but learn she had a little party to celebrate it, H—— being the beau in general.

I feel that we have all great cause for gratitude to our Heavenly Parent for his unnumbered blessings, and I am truly thankful to him that so many of my dear children and grandchildren have hearts to appreciate his goodness. Oh, how much it would add to my happiness to be able to feel that *all* of them were in good earnest, seeking the salvation of their souls.

With much love to K—— and to F—— and L——,

Your affectionate father,

ARTHUR TAPPAN.

NEW HAVEN, Dec. 9, 1863.

You remind me through E—— that I am in your debt. Now as I love to be "in debt" to my children when I think they love me, you furnish me with a reason for *not* writing. But I will not take advantage from it, and would gladly fill a sheet if I had topics that would interest you. You must remember that you are in the London of our country, where every great interest centres, and the air teems with news from the four quarters of the world.

My life is a very quiet one. Home is precious to me, for here every thing reminds me of the dear departed, whose image is ever present to me. E—— is ever busy in endeavoring to make home pleasant, and succeeds very well. I enjoy reading, and have just finished Irving's Washington, four volumes large octavo, borrowed of our kind neighbor Goodrich. I have read it now for the first time, and with great interest. It is written in a style worthy of the theme, and has much that was new to me. I hope to have much interesting reading from our neighbor, who kindly offers his books to us. Continue, my dear C——, to enliven my loneliness by telling me all that interests you, and do not delay writing because I am in your debt, for I love to be so to my dear children.

My rheumatism is somewhat abated. I walk with perfect ease, and rest well at night. My appetite is good, and I am very well except the pain in my spine and hips when sitting or stooping.

With much love to each one, your father,

ARTHUR TAPPAN.

The following were addressed to his brother, the compiler:

NEW HAVEN, Dec. 22, 1863.

It is a great satisfaction to me, and must also be to all who have been your and my co-workers for the slave, to see the change that is going on. I have felt from the beginning of the war that God had taken our cause in hand, and would work it out in his own time and manner. We may stand still and witness his glorious manifestations.

In the following letter he refers to some extracts from the Scriptures received from an elder brother, and to the reply of the celebrated Dr. Abernethy of London to a person who had applied to him to know if he could cure the rheumatism:

NEW HAVEN, July 25, 1864.

.... I want them or a copy in my portfolio, to be a constant monitor and quickener in my pilgrimage. I retain no copy, and will thank you for one, or the original. . . .

I am satisfied you are correct, that there is no cure for the rheumatism but "patience and flannel." I have tried, I believe, every other prescribed remedy, and am no better, and now look for relief only from warm weather. As an aggravation, I have the cramp in one of my legs most of the night, and find no effectual remedy. Can you tell me of one ? I am thankful my health was spared to me while my dear wife was with me. A kind Providence so ordered it, and is now, I think, preparing me to follow her.

·Ever vigilant to notice and condemn

"The oppressor's wrong, the proud man's contumely,"

he wrote the annexed letter to the same, to call attention to the report of a glaring instance of villany perpetrated upon a friend of the slave in a distant state, published in the *New York Tribune:*

NEW HAVEN, July 22, 1864.

You have or will doubtless read the account in to-day's *Tribune.* I think that this and similar developments of the fiendish character of slavery should at this time be spread broadcast over the free states. We are in danger of having a peace with the South which will leave the hydra-headed monster alive again to curse our country. My object in writing to you now is to inquire what you and I can do towards averting so great a calamity. No time is to be lost. Will you give it your immediate attention, that we may, if possible, avert the evil, and have the satisfaction to reflect that we have done our duty ? If money is wanted, I will do what I can, and try to influence others. Do you know, and if not, will you ascertain how Mr. F—— is situated pecuniarily ? The hearts of thousands will be open to secure him the comforts he has been so long deprived of. Give me his residence if you can.

Work was his element; not that he loved it for the emolument it often brings, but for its own sake, "the labor itself being a pleasure," and because he could aid others in their chosen employments. In the *American Missionary Association* he felt a peculiar interest. It had his pecuniary offerings to as great an extent as his means afforded, and it had his best wishes, amd above all else, his prayers. He desired to contribute in addition his personal labors in furtherance of its objects. His ambition was not to occupy a position, but to contribute substantial help, and he would therefore have been willing, if the opportunity occurred, to fill any station, however subordinate, that would give him plenty of work in a good cause. Surrounded as he was in his chosen retreat with an affectionate family, and with cultivated and refined society, he often felt, not ennui, but dissatisfaction that he could labor so little in the cause of reforms. He seemed to think slightly of past labors, and panted, as it were, to engage in new moral conflicts, forgetting that his powers of body and mind were enfeebled by advanced life.

He was continually watching for opportunities to help the officers of the association, whenever they were providentially absent from the missionary rooms, or disabled by illness. We have had evidence of this in his frequent letters to the treasurer, and he gave many other proofs of his desire to be useful in a cause he loved so well. Besides, he knew that exercising his faculties strengthened them.

This year several of his former clerks addressed a letter to him that gave him much gratification :

NEW YORK, Thanksgiving Day, Nov. 24, 1864.

To ARTHUR TAPPAN, ESQ.:

VENERABLE FRIEND : The question of the abolition of slavery, we think, has been virtually decided in the recent presidential election, and the cause of justice has triumphed. Slavery on this continent is to die. We who subscribe to this letter were formerly clerks in your employment, and we beg leave to offer you our hearty congratulations.

We bear witness to your fidelity to the great cause of human freedom, years ago, when it cost much to be faithful. You put reputation, time, talents, money, all you had at stake for this cause. Your store was mobbed, and attempts were made to injure your business; your former friends forsook you ; but you did not flinch.

Your heroic example deeply impressed the minds of the young men by whom you were surrounded, the most of whom have emulated your example, and now remain faithful to the good cause.

Now, in the evening of your days, you behold almost accomplished the liberation of the slaves ; and we sincerely trust that the kind Providence which has watched over you hitherto may grant in his mercy, that when your eyes close on the scene of your labor in this world, you may have the joy to know that not one slave remains to be freed on the American continent, and when you open them in that better and brighter world you may receive the plaudit of, "Well done, good and faithful servant."

SETH B. HUNT,	THEODORE M'NAMEE,
HENRY C. BOWEN,	REUBEN TOWNE,
W. E. WHITING,	WALTER P. DOE,
ANTHONY LANE,	EDWIN WILLCOX,
CHARLES DURFEE,	HEZEKIAH D. SHARPE.

He made the following reply :

NEW HAVEN, Dec. 5, 1864,

SETH B. HUNT, ESQ.

DEAR SIR : I have the communication from yourself and other esteemed friends, whom I recognize as once in my

16*

employ, and for whom I entertain a lively regard. Thanks
to a kind Providence, my warfare against slavery was unmin-
gled with self-interest, and that I have a prospect, although
in my seventy-ninth year, of living to see the hydra-headed
monster expelled from our beloved country.

From the tenor of the paper you have sent me, I am led
to infer that all the signers sympathize with me in the hope
of a blessed eternity. This adds in my estimation greatly to
its value. I shall be happy to renew my acquaintance, should
Providence at any time throw either yourself or the other
signers in my way. . . . .

Please let the other signers read this, and to each I send
my kind regards.

Very truly yours,

ARTHUR TAPPAN.

Mr. Theodore D. Weld, some time before Mr.
Tappan's decease, returned several letters he had
in past years received from him; and in an accompanying note to one of his daughters expressed a
wish that a memoir might be written of his life. In
his letter Mr. Weld says:

You may well say of your father that his life will speak
for him. It has and does, and ever will. Such integrity,
conscientious fidelity, and true independence; such simple,
unwavering directness in duty; such sincerity, exact truth,
absence of all self-seeking; a benevolence most prodigal in
its outlay, yet wholly unostentatious; a moral courage that
withheld no jot of utterance or action through fear of obloquy, and yet ever quiet and undefiant; with a sense of justice so quick and intense, that it seemed equally a principle
and a passion.

The preëminent traits of your father's character so impressed me during the years of our mutual coöperation, that
I have ever since felt as though the world would be robbed
of its own, if not furnished with a record of his life by some
one who knew him best and can adequately appreciate his
worth.

XXVI.

THE war, its causes, and its probable results occupied much of his thoughts. He was fond of peace, and much as he hated slavery he had never desired that the slaves should gain their freedom by the effusion of blood. The Anti-Slavery Society, at its formation, in 1833, inserted in its constitution a clause to this effect : "But this society will never, in any way, countenance the oppressed in vindicating their rights by resorting to physical force."

Its founders were men of peace, and they believed in the potency of moral suasion, relying also upon both the promises and warnings of the Almighty Ruler of nations. They believed that prejudice would wear away; that the beneficial workings of emancipation in the West Indies would open the eyes of our slaveholders to see the unprofitableness of slave compared with free labor; that Congress would ere long abolish slavery in the District of Columbia; that as slavery was rapidly disappearing under other governments, their example would influence our own to carry out the evident expectations of the founders of our government; and that self-interest, wiser counsels, political considerations, and other motives would ere long lead to the abolition of American slavery.

There were sagacious men, among the theoretical and practical abolitionists who thought differently.

The former, in view of the character of Southern
men, and the diffusion of intelligence among the
slaves, thought, if they did not desire it, that
"powder and ball" were the only arguments that
would be effectual with the slaveocrats of the Southern states. The latter included those who, while
acknowledging the influence of moral suasion, believed that the retributive justice of God required
the condign punishment of slaveholders. They
reasoned thus: The Almighty has never permitted
nations to trample upon the rights of mankind without inflicting upon them severe chastisements. Both
sacred and profane history bear evidence of this.
Now, as nations are punished in *this* world for their
evil doings, while men in their *individual* character
are judged in the future, it is certain that a nation
persisting in transgression will meet with Divine
chastisement. This being the case the vials of
God's wrath will surely be poured out upon a people
like slaveholding America.

Among the wise and good men who embraced
the anti-slavery doctrines, and believed in the duty
of moral suasion while they expected the judgment
of God upon our guilty nation, was Rev. Dr. John
Black of Pennsylvania. In answer to the question
put to him, thirty years or more, since, "What will
be the result of slaveholding in the United States?"
he unhesitatingly replied, "I believe that it will end
in blood; God's retributive justice seems to require
it." But probably neither Thomas Jefferson nor
John Black ever imagined that the North would

suffer equally with the South in the overthrow of slavery. The late war had not been long waged, however, before abolitionists generally, Christian and unchristian, recognized the arm of Divine Justice wielding the avenging sword for the punishment of a NATION, North and South, that had so long, as slaveholders, or the abettors of slaveholding, trampled upon human rights, defying the arrows of the Almighty.

The early abolitionists, including the founders of the Republic and those who established the more recent anti-slavery societies, believed that argument and persuasion, and the progress of peaceful events, would lead to the discontinuance of human bondage in this land. Like Melancthon, who, when a young man, had such confidence in the power of truth, that he exultantly said to his elder and more experienced brother, Martin Luther, "Let me go abroad, proclaiming the glorious doctrine of the Reformation, and in six months all Germany will embrace it," so they anticipated the speedy triumph of freedom. The sagacious reformer did not like to extinguish the hopes or dampen the courage of his youthful associate and therefore replied, "Go, my brother, and see what you can do." It is said, that within a year, the amiable and disappointed Melancthon returned. "What success have you had?" inquired Doctor Luther. "Ah," said he, "I found old Adam too strong for young Melancthon!"

Such was the experience of the abolitionists. The slaveholders, with few exceptions, were deaf to their arguments and expostulations; a large majority of the merchants, manufacturers, and various tribes of business men throughout the country, believed that emancipation would bring ruin, instead of prosperity; politicians, including the newspaper interest, derided; ministers of the gospel, so called, not only at the South but at the North, attempted to justify slaveholding from the Scriptures, at least apologizing for the system, if not defending it.

Thus the deluded people put their fingers in their ears, and rushed forward. The God of the oppressed, wearied with the obstinacy of the nation, commiserating the sufferings of the enslaved, His patience and long-suffering exhausted, permitted a civil war, such as no previous age had ever witnessed. And while the scales of justice were for a long time held in poise, and doubts were felt as to the possibility of subduing the rebellion, the administration, perceiving that all was lost unless slavery was abolished, proclaimed liberty to the four millions in bondage. They did not at first design to abolish the iniquitous system, but did it at length to save the government. It was not, therefore, an act of humanity so much as of political necessity.

When the determination of President LINCOLN and his cabinet became known there was a general acquiescence. Abolitionists, as well as others, applauded the act, and were willing to accomplish the object in view, at whatever cost. God seemed to look with pity upon a reformed, if not a penitent people, and gave peace to the country.

No man, it is believed, felt greater interest in public affairs at this eventful period, than did Mr. Tappan. From a journal kept by his eldest daughter the following extracts are made:

From his quiet home in New Haven, father watched the great events of the war, and with special interest every indication that freedom would be proclaimed to the slave. He walked to the reading-room and the postoffice every morning, and had always a *Tribune* or *Times*, to read aloud at home; and his comments were always interesting. When word came of the election of ABRAHAM LINCOLN as President of the United States, he said, with a trembling voice, "Let us thank God." At family worship, that morning, he prayed as usual for our country, and thanked God that he had not deserted us on account of our sins. He prayed that we might now have men in office, who would fear God, walk humbly before him, and do justly. He prayed that the country might be no longer a hissing and a byword among the nations, but a model nation to all the world; that through us Christ's kingdom might be advanced throughout the earth.

JULY, 1862. Opinions are very diverse about the generalship of the war. We asked father what he thought on the subject. "Strategy, strategy," said he, "that is all we can say, when we don't want to condemn; all this delay is helping the Southerners, giving them time to raise troops and strengthen themselves." But he added, "The best way is, not to condemn, but to wait patiently, and trust in Providence. I firmly believe that God will put an end to slavery by this war. He is the Great General." "But, father," said we, "think of the thousands of young men, who are dying of fever in the swamps and camps, who have not the satisfaction of feeling that they are dying for their country." He replied: "They give their example of being loyal men, willing to fight and die for their country. If I were a young man," (this he said very earnestly,) "I WOULD WILLINGLY LAY DOWN MY LIFE IF I COULD HELP FREE MY COUNTRY FROM SLAVERY; better lose half the men in it, than not have slavery abolished."

One of us said : "Father, when you began to work to have the slaves freed, you did n't expect to live to see it ?" He said: "No," and pointing up to the sky, he added: "It was like looking up there, to see where heaven is—it seemed so far off, but it was there."

After the proclamation of emancipation, a friend said to him, "Mr. Tappan, you have lived to see a great day." He replied with emphasis : "Yes, I am satisfied now." But later he expressed fears that the colored people would not get the right of suffrage; and he grieved over every account he read of their wrongs and ill-treatment.

One of us said to him, "How heart-rending are those accounts from our imprisoned soldiers." He replied: "Yes, they are horrible, but God allows this to show to the world the hideousness of slavery. It will be printed and go down to the latest generation, to show what slavery can do. It was a great power, and needed a great revolution to break it up, such as man, without God's help, could not bring about." And he said to us: "We shall not probably have much more time to meet in this world; in five years I shall be of the age when my father died, and most of his family also ;" and then he brought out a genealogical chart, with the names of his ancestors in order, several generations back, a long list, most of them having died with a good hope in Christ.

APRIL, 1865. After the murder of President Lincoln, one of us said to father, "What a calamity has come upon us." His reply was, "I don't know that it will be a calamity, but it is a horrible thing that has been done. God will overrule it for the good of our country. He has our country in hand, and will bring it out all right. He saw that we needed this. Lincoln would have been willing to die, could he have seen that it was best for the country. This is the fruit of slavery. It was a kind Providence that his death was so easy. He probably died without pain."

When in the meridian of his days, he made what he thought might be his last Will and Testament. The writer of this narrative, to whom it was shown, well remembers some of its provisions.   He, at that time, was considered a rich man, and believed himself that his means were quite ample.   His bequests and legacies were such as a Christian should make. The provision for his family and for the education of his children, was amply sufficient, but the largest part of his wealth was given to benevolent objects.

That will became of no value, when he found by experience that riches certainly make themselves wings and "fly away as an eagle toward heaven."

During the last year of his life he had some correspondence with his brother and former partner about making a will, and he seemed at the time to relinquish the idea.   He possessed but little property in addition to the house and lot left by their mother, at her decease, to two of his daughters, and believed that his other children would have sufficient property of their own.   What he had he concluded to bequeath to them.   It would seem that at the date he supposed himself to be worth more than he actually was.*

In June, 1865, he addressed the following letter to his brother in Brooklyn:

NEW HAVEN, June 8, '65.

DEAR BROTHER LEWIS : It is quite time that I acknowledged yours of the 22d ult.   I am again in good health thanks to a kind Providence.   Yesterday we were highly gratified by a very unexpected visit from Brother John and his invaluable wife.   He sent on his baggage and thus, relieved of all

---

* The will is dated May 31, 1865, and the executors named were Rev. Chauncey Goodrich, Henry D. White, Esq., and William L. Kingsley, Esq.

care, was able to make us a visit of several hours, leaving in the evening train, expecting to sleep in Boston. I was highly pleased at so unexpected a visit from one so dear to me, and to whom I owe, under Providence, all I am and have been for this world.* I was glad to find his health better than I had supposed it was, and that it cost him less effort to walk. I think he is likely to live some years yet and wish I could see more of him than I can expect to.

I feel that my travelling days are over, and that if I see my brothers it must be at my own home, where they and theirs will be always welcome. But we shall soon, I trust, be gathered in heaven where precious re-unions await us.

What is to be the future of our country is known only to the Most High, but I have from the beginning of the war felt that God would overrule all the seeming evils of it to his glory, and the ultimate good of our nation and the world. With much love to your loved ones at home,

Your affectionate brother,   ARTHUR.

New Haven, July 6, 1865.

Dear Brother : I have yours of the 4th, and thank you for your kind attention to my business, which, as you say truly, under like circumstances it will ever give me pleasure to reciprocate.

I agree with you in rejoicing to see the day of universal freedom in our country, and feel ready to say now, "Lord, let thy servant depart in peace, for I have seen the Divine blessing resting on the efforts of thy servants for the poor slaves."

With much love,   A. TAPPAN,

Mr. Lewis Tappan, Brooklyn, N. Y.

To his brother in Boston he wrote the following, not long before his death, supposed to be the last letter written by him:

---

* His brother John, to whom this letter was shown, protests against this affectionate exaggeration of what he has done for his brother Arthur, and supposes that he only alludes to pecuniary matters, as his moral and religious training was principally by his sainted mother, to whom, under God, all the children are so largely indebted.

NEW HAVEN, July 12, 1865.

DEAR CHARLES: I thank you for your invitation to visit you. At present I have no expectation of leaving home this summer. My health is very good, and I am very happy with my children; but indeed I feel that my travelling days are over.

I am glad that you have a daughter too, to love you, and care for you, in your old age. Our dear children will soon know us no more in this life, and it will be a source of happiness to them, when we are gone, to be able to reflect that they did all they could to make our last days happy. In the mean time we must repay their love to us now in every possible way. With love to your daughter,

Your affectionate brother, ARTHUR.

MR. CHARLES TAPPAN, Boston.

The following is the conclusion of his eldest daughter's narrative:

MAY 3. Father has had a serious illness, from a heavy cold, with fever, and has kept his bed several days. He said to us: "This sickness reminds me I shall not be long here. We must love each other; before long we shall arrive, I hope, at a good port, where we shall not be separated any more. It will be a good one if we choose to have it so. For ever with the Lord, we hope."

He was attacked with a bowel complaint and fever on the 15th of July, 1865, and from the first his brain sympathized, and his mind wandered at intervals. He repeated part of the hymn his mother taught him, "When all thy mercies, O my God." He suffered but little pain, and it required much persuasion to keep him in bed. On Friday he could not swallow, but his lips were moistened. On Saturday he was conscious, when roused and spoken to. An hour before his death—Sabbath morning—he looked upward, and an indescribable expression of awe came over him, as if he saw glories hidden to us. Thus he passed peacefully to his eternal rest.

Another daughter, Mrs. M——, has furnished the following memoranda during the progress of this

narrative. The paper was not written for publication, but for hints to the compiler, who does not
like to abridge it essentially or withhold it, as the
incidents, like the lights and shades of a picture,
however minute in themselves, are necessary to give
a faithful portraiture of the deceased. His children
have submitted the papers they have severally written to the discretion of the compiler, and he desires
to show their affectionate attachment to their father,
and to use their pencil sketches to illustrate more
fully his domestic character. Mrs. M—— says:

I wish something might be said of father's love for sister
Fanny Seymour, and of her beautiful religious character,
that won his love. He used to call her the "Morning Star."
Has uncle spoken of father's fearlessness at the time the mob
attacked his house in Rose-street, and how he went among
them disguised in some way? I have heard him say that
some invisible power seemed to hold them back, and prevent
them from doing what they appear to have designed. Also
of his going to the wharf at ten o'clock at night, to wait for
the New Haven boat, at the time a vessel was said to be waiting in the harbor for him, after a price had been offered for
his head?

Father was very plain in his taste; he disliked jewelry
and other ornaments for mere show. He also disapproved
of wearing mourning apparel, and for this reason among
others, because the poor often run in debt to obtain it.

He had no fears of death; so he told my mother-in-law
during her last sickness. She said, "I wish I could feel as
he does." He replied, "I could go at once joyfully, if summoned."

He preferred home and my mother's society to that of any
company. He would say, "I ought never to have been married, for my headaches make me so unsocial and unable to
add to the happiness of my family."

Father's feelings were so strong for the home missionaries,

that when I returned from our society and read to him the letters brought from them, telling of their privations and needs, he would express so much for them, and desire so to help them more than he could afford to do, that I at last desisted from letting him know their appeals. So of old Mr. Butler, a colored man who worked for us at times. He insisted upon giving to this worthy old man his drawers and other flannel that he needed for his own use. Also of an old colored man who was blind, and a beggar on the streets of New Haven. My father would never pass him without giving him money; and it was the same when the poor blind man followed him to the door.

In his last sickness he was ill only one week. I had the privilege of spending the last evening with him that he was down stairs. He was very cheerful, and went to bed as well as usual apparently, so that we were surprised the next morning that he did not rise. Dr. Charles L. Ives was called in, but father's symptoms did not give way under his treatment. On Wednesday, just before sunset, he took up the New York *Tribune*, deliberately put on his glasses, which were lying by him on the bed, and turned to a short article in fine print about some colored persons. He asked me to let him read it aloud. I expressed some anxiety at seeing him reading a newspaper in his weak state, as he was unable to sit up in bed; so he read the article to himself.

As I was reading to him, he said, with his usual thoughtfulness, "Don't read any longer; as the light is fading, you will strain your eyes." This was Wednesday, at or near six o'clock, and he died on the following Sabbath, at 7 o'clock, A. M. Uncle Lewis came to see him on Friday afternoon. I remember his saying to father, "I hope the Saviour's arms are underneath you, and that he will support you." Father bowed his head, as it was the only reply he could make; but his bow and manner were such—so solemn and significant—that I felt sure he understood just what his situation was. It was as if he had said : "I know that I am going to die, and I feel ready to go, if it be the will of God."

The next morning he seemed very comfortable, and expressed much pleasure respecting the kind attentions of Mr.

Brown, who took care of him through the night. But afterwards, Mr. Brown told me, he had refused any further nourishment. Immediately I prepared some light food, and going to the side of the bed, endeavored very gently to arouse him from the lethargy into which he had fallen.

As I said, "Father, you will take it from me ; you know me ?" at once his whole face lighted up with such a look of affection as I shall never forget. He moved his lips several times quickly, as if he would express his feelings, but he could not speak. It was the last recognition.

On Sunday morning early Mr. Brown told me that my father could not live more than an hour or two. I sent at once for my kind friend, almost brother, Rev. Chauncey Goodrich, and he remained with us until all was over. I had drawn near to father to speak to him, hoping he would recognize me. His eyes were open, and it seemed as if he were gazing intently on some scene before him, unconscious of all about him, and looking into the far-off land. Never before had I been so impressed with the majesty of death.

The funeral took place on the 25th of July, 1865, at the late residence of the deceased, No. 84 Wall-street, New Haven. It was commencement week, and therefore several friends of the family, who had come to attend the exercises in Yale College, had the opportunity to unite with the neighbors and friends in attending the funeral. Among those present were the venerable ex-President DAY, then in his ninety-second year, and Rev. Dr. Massie, of England. A considerable number of colored persons also attended, to pay their respects to the memory of one who for forty years had been the friend and advocate of their people.

All the arrangements were made with the simplicity the deceased had always approved. His countenance did not indicate that the king of terrors had been near to trouble him. On the contrary, it might have been said by one who did not know what had occurred: "He is not dead, but sleepeth." One who had known him for many years, on viewing the calm and expressive countenance, said to a friend: "Look at that mouth and chin; what a determined will!" But there was also an expression of peace and triumph.

Rev. Dr. BACON conducted the funeral services, and on the ensuing Sabbath preached a funeral discourse.

Professor Chauncey Goodrich had charge of the funeral.

The following gentlemen officiated as pall-bearers: Rev. S. S. Jocelyn, Amos Townsend, William E. Whiting, William Johnson, Henry White, Esq., Professor James M. Hoppin, Professor Thomas H. Thacher, and Rev. F. L. Cardozo.*

The procession moved to the cemetery, where the remains were deposited in a grave by the side of his beloved wife, who had died two years previously.

° See Appendix 14.

† Mr. Cardozo is a native of Charleston, S. C., and at the time was pastor of the colored Congregational church in New Haven. He has since been secretary of state for South Carolina.

XXVII.

IN these pages the peculiar traits of Mr. Tappan's character have been incidentally mentioned, but it is reserved for the closing chapter to make a more full portraiture. This will not be attempted solely from the recollection of the compiler. The remembrances of others who knew him in private and public life, will supply deficiencies, and qualify any exaggerations affection may have suggested.

The object has been to present a truthful picture, not only in testimony of a beloved relative, but in honor of a man of God, who, according to his ability and opportunities, consulted the best interests of his fellow-men and the kingdom of the Lord Jesus Christ, in all his labors and offerings.

He never thought of himself more highly than he ought to think, or sought to win public favor by deeds of benevolence. Conscious of his imperfections, and lamenting them, he cast himself upon Divine mercy for forgiveness. Let us view him then in several aspects, as he was known in domestic life and among his fellow-men.

His *truthfulness*. His mother's remark, when he was leaving his parents' roof for the perils and temptations of a city life, will be recollected: "I never knew him tell a lie." During his whole career, it was the testimony of others, both friends and opponents, that his veracity was unquestionable. No falsehood was ever fastened upon him, or imputed to him, by any one worthy of the slightest confidence. Not only so, but equivocation or evasion were foreign to his character. He desired to obey the Great Teacher: "Let your communication be Yea, yea; Nay, nay; for whatsoever is more than these cometh of evil."

This trait, or rather principle, led him to have but one price for his goods; and when he went into the market as a purchaser, which he usually did in the earlier years of his business, if he found that a merchant had two prices, he would turn away and leave his store.

He was solicitous also to have his clerks scrupulously refrain from all exaggerated statements respecting the quality of goods. One of them has recently said: "Soon after I went into Mr. Tappan's employment he observed to me, 'One thing that I wish to impress upon your mind as a salesman is, never, under any circumstances, recommend an article of merchandise for any more than its actual value, so that those who buy of you can have the fullest confidence in your representations.'" It has been said of some one that his word was as much relied on as if he always felt that he was under the solemnity of an oath to speak the truth. The same might truly be said of Arthur Tappan.

His *integrity*. No man ever justly accused him of wronging any one of a cent. The numerous clerks in his employ, and the large number of persons with whom he dealt, were witnesses of this.

17

He would not soil his hands, nor inflict a wound upon his conscience, by unjust gains. If he had, peradventure, taken anything from any man wrongfully, he would rather restore to him fourfold.

The clerk alluded to above, says: "I recollect numerous instances, while the anti-slavery excitement continued, of persons living in the Southern states, who came to our store to purchase goods, remarking: 'I do not come here to buy goods because I like you. I detest your principles, but I believe that Mr. Tappan is an honest man, and will deal fairly with me. That is the only reason for my coming to his store.'" This clerk adds: "As I was about terminating my engagement, and going into business, Mr. Tappan took me aside, and said: 'Never deceive any one; tell the exact truth to everybody; it is the surest way to prosper.'"

Another clerk has remarked: "I inquired of a gentleman what he thought of Mr. Tappan, and he replied: 'He is a man of generous impulses, of great probity, and cannot be turned from a principle any sooner than you can turn the East from the West. He is always courteous and kind, in his treatment of others, though he may differ from them in opinion. I have found him so, though I am an owner of slaves, while he is an abolitionist.'"

After his suspension, in 1837, the largest number of his creditors received his assurances that he had stopped payment from sheer necessity, that if he had gone on longer it would have been at the sacrifice of their property as well as his own, and that in asking for an extension he named the shortest time possible; and they believed him when he said, "Have patience with me, and I will pay thee all." At, or before the time stipulated, he did pay all, with interest, at a sacrifice of tens of thousands of dollars in extra interest. He thought it only common honesty to pay his debts, as promptly as he could, meantime living prudently, in order to avoid the appearance of evil.

His *industry.* Throughout his whole life he was a busy man. No one ever saw him idle. And he labored as diligently for others, whether individuals or societies, as he did for himself. When necessity required it, he was up early and late, setting a good example to those in his employ, and fulfilling the direction, "Be diligent in business."

His *perseverance.* This was a remarkable trait in his character. It seemed that nothing could discourage him. It was evinced when he lost nearly, if not quite all he possessed in Canada, by the war with England, in 1812, and his commencing business in New York, as soon as the conflict was ended; by his change of business from British to India goods, and from the credit to the cash business when his importations had been attended with such heavy losses in 1816; by his contract with a builder to erect a new store, the day succeeding the disastrous fire of 1835; and by numberless facts connected with his history during his long and eventful life. He had confidence in a Superior power, to bless lawful enterprise, but he believed also that

"God helps those who help themselves," and therefore, relying upon Divine aid, he was no sooner
defeated in one enterprise than he entered upon
another, nothing doubting.

His views of *stewardship.* He never forgot his
accountability, as a steward of the Lord. It never
entered his mind that his gains were his own. He
loved business, he was pleased with prosperity, he
delighted in handling goods and money, he was
gratified with domestic comforts and surrounded
his family with them, yet he ever felt that he was
after all but a STEWARD; that what he had, or could
lawfully gain, was not his, but belonged to his
Master; that he had no right to expend his goods
in luxurious living, in vain show, or waste them in
any way; that he had no right to lavish them upon
himself or family; that he was to give an account
of the deeds done in the body, at the GREAT ASSIZE.
He therefore aimed to be, both from a sense of
duty and from inclination, a "faithful and wise
steward."

His *religion.* As a Christian he was devoid of
ostentation and pretence. With a firm belief in the
evangelical faith, he relied upon the mercy of God
through the atoning sacrifice of the Saviour, dis-
carding all thoughts of his good deeds as meriting
reward in another life, although he firmly believed
that as evidences of piety they were essential.

He had much humility and reverence. This was
evinced in his prayers and deportment. He was
regular in family devotions, and in attendance on

public worship; and it is believed that he was constant in the devotions of the closet. A friend, who knew him intimately, observed that his prayers were remarkable for their childlike simplicity and tenderness. He daily perused the Scriptures and meditated upon them. Every one associated with him believed that he had communion with God and endeavored to lead a holy life.

Another clerk brings to recollection the fact that "on the third floor of the store was a small room, carpeted, that we called the BETHEL, where any one connected with the establishment could retire, for devotion, if he wished." It was used in this way by many connected with the store, especially during revivals of religion that prevailed in 1831, and subsequently.

The *unselfishness* that ever distinguished him is worthy of special remembrance, as constituting an element of his religious character. He felt that all he had, his time and money, his energy and his influence, belonged not to him, but to the Lord, to be used in promoting his glory, and the good of mankind. This was the PIVOT on which his actions turned. It constituted his governing principle, and led to that active and diffusive benevolence, that shone so brightly during his whole career. What better evidence could there be of his possessing genuine piety? A man whose aim it is to be benevolent, as the mainspring of his character, from Christian motives, and who is unselfish in his feelings and actions, though he may have imperfections, must have the spirit of Jesus Christ, and be accepted of him.

He did not see that it was his duty to withdraw himself from attending public worship because his minister and a majority of his fellow-members in the church refused to come out decidedly in opposition to slavery, and other enormities. Neither did he presume to censure those who could not conscientiously continue in such connections. "Who art thou that judgest another man's servant? To his own master he standeth or falleth." At the same time, when he saw how ministers of the gospel, and members of their churches treated the great moral questions of the day, the people of color, and the advocates of unpopular causes, he could not but think them greatly deficient in duty and culpable in the sight of God and man.

His attendance on public worship and meetings of the church was constant. He sometimes felt that the minister was timid and vacillating, that most of the church members lacked sympathy with him, and some were violent in opposition, that the poor colored brethren were obliged to sit apart from their white brothers and sisters, in their Father's house, still he held on, earnestly hoping and praying for a better state of things. In this he was not disappointed, for he lived to see the commencement of a beneficial change, both in sentiment and practice.*

* It was marvellous that a "Christian" assembly should ever have overlooked the injunction of the Apostle James: "My brethren, have not the faith of our Lord Jesus Christ, the Lord of glory, with respect of persons. For if there come unto your as-

He did not fear death, and when the summons came, it found him ready to depart. Though he did not have strength to bear much testimony in his dying hours, he yet left a deep conviction on the minds of those around him, that he leaned on an Almighty arm, and knew in whom he had believed. Dying testimony is valuable, but, after all, the life is the thing. He was diffident of his own piety, but no one ever questioned that he was a child of God and an inheritor of the promises.

He was taciturn, somewhat severe in manner, occasionally rigid, sometimes abrupt and impatient, but had within a kind heart. What was said of another might have been applied to him: "His sternness is all outside; he is like one of the pears we often see, rather tough in the skin, but if you cut into it, you will find it quite sweet and juicy." He was also rather undemonstrative. All this may be allowed; but those who knew him most, knew that his peculiarities arose, not altogether from natural disposition, but chiefly from a daily headache. This was not an occasional trouble, as he probably never passed a day without feeling more or less pain in his head. No business or recreation enabled him to throw it off. It was chronic, and literally his thorn in the flesh.

Persons who saw him in the busy scenes of mer-

sembly" a rich man and a poor man, "and ye have respect to him that weareth the gay clothing, and say unto him, Sit thou here in a good place, and say to the poor, Stand thou there, or sit here under my footstool, are ye not then partial in yourselves, and are become judges of evil thoughts, ' etc.

cantile life, or among strangers, or who witnessed his self-possession and gravity when presiding at public meetings, would hardly believe that a person under such self-control and firmness, could evince so much tenderness of heart as he not unfrequently manifested, both in domestic life, and among the poor and afflicted. Notwithstanding the infirmity alluded to, he could be, when free from harassing cares, anxiety, and the absorption occasioned by a press of business, affable, and even playful, manifesting an affectionate concern for those around him. It was remarked that if he hurt the feelings of any one, by undue severity, he was quick to express regret. This he would do even to children, and sometimes with tears in his eyes.

There were other traits in his character worthy of notice. He was neat and simple in dress; a lover of simplicity in everything; unusually abstemious in eating and drinking; frugal,yet hospitable. He was noted for punctuality in keeping all his engagements; strict in adherence to rules; avoiding circumlocution, and never practising it, or liking it in others; never in a flurry, however multifarious, perplexing, or pressing was the business in hand.

It was true that he seldom joked, and was not pleased with being made the subject of joking; that he sometimes appeared unsocial; that now and then he was the victim of misplaced confidence in trusting to the professions of men rather than to evidences of their religious and moral principles; that he was not free from errors of judgment with refer-

ence to business and other matters. These things,
so far as they were faults, he lamented, and strove
against them. If any one thinks he was too exact-
ing or strict, it should be remembered that he was
always more severe with himself than with his fellow-men.

His moral courage was well-known, and on more
than one occasion he gave evidence that he possessed uncommon physical courage. It was owing to
his unselfishness, his love of the right, and his trust
in a superior power. He was scrupulous in discharging all the duties he owed to society as a citizen and a neighbor. One who knew him well in
these relations has said: "He was a man of great
worth of character, of great efficiency and great per-
sistency, and has left his mark on the age in which
he lived."

Already has it been stated that he was more
severe toward himself than toward others. This
trait in connection with his remarkable self-possession on all occasions, and his consideration for those
in his employment, was shown about the time he
suspended payment, in 1837, when all his faculties
were intensely exerted in efforts to raise money to
meet his engagements. One of the youngest clerks,
who had been sent to the bank to deposit a sum of
money to meet the payments of the day, returned
just before the close of bank hours, and said, "I
have been robbed!" It was ascertained that some
adroit rogue had contrived, while the lad was waiting for his turn in the bank, to withdraw from the

deposit-book, part of the money, viz., thirty-five
hundred dollars. Great as the disappointment was
to lose such a sum, at such a time, Mr. Tappan
preserved his equanimity. He listened to the young
clerk's story, and was silent, probably thinking that
it had been injudicious to intrust so young a person with a large sum of money. The clerk was
continued in his place unrebuked, although after
this excused from making deposits of money.

Another instance that was trying to a merchant
making extraordinary efforts to preserve his credit,
at a time when money was difficult to be procured
at even two or three per cent. a month, was in this
wise: for mutual convenience he had exchanged
notes, amounting to twenty thousand dollars, with
a neighboring merchant, who had solicited the favor,
to be discounted at the bank. Both notes fell due
the same day, and each party was, of course, to
take up his own paper. Mr. Tappan paid his note,
and learned, to his surprise and disappointment,
that the other note had not been paid, so that the
next day he was obliged to pay it himself. The
neighbor with whom he had exchanged notes, and
who was the endorser, had relied upon the promisor,
a merchant of another city, to pay the note at the
bank, and in default of his doing so, found himself
unable to do it. Mr. Tappan's own payments were
daily so large that it required, as he thought, his
utmost exertion to meet them; but he managed to
pay this additional sum also, at considerable sacrifice, but without a tremor, or a word of censure.

There is an anecdote connected with the maker of the above note, that deserves record, as an illustration of the character of an upright merchant, and his opposite. The person who signed the note and had transferred it to the merchant who exchanged it for Mr. Tappan's note, had boasted of of making him his model, both as a merchant and a Christian. He lived in a very humble way, dressed with quaker-like simplicity, and gave away many pious books. "The Lord has prospered Arthur Tappan," he said, "and if I do as he did, He will doubtless prosper me also." Not succeeding as he anticipated, he became tired, entered into speculations, moved into a stylish house, threw off his plain attire, and united with a fashionable church. After a time he professed to be unable to meet his engagements, but continued to live in his usual style.

Mr. Tappan's neighbor, whose name was on the note, and who acted honorably in the case, said, "I am able to pay half of that note, and can do no more; you can collect the other half of the other party." On being applied to, this person asserted that he was utterly unable to pay; that if he were sued it would do no good, and only injure him and his family. His attorney corroborated this statement. The suit was suspended, once and again, and renewed because of the positive assurance of Mr. Tappan's attorney that the refusal to pay, and the denial of having property, was all a pretence. At length, judgment was obtained, an execution issued, real estate levied upon and advertised by the sheriff. Even then, and up to the hour of sale, the debtor and his attorney persisted in declaring that the suit was a cruel and heartless measure, and would not yield any thing. But at the last moment, the debtor paid the amount, with interest and costs. He is not the only man who has supposed "that gain is godliness."

Mr. Tappan took much pleasure in aiding unpopular causes; the more unpopular they were the more they secured his patronage, provided they were deserving. His natural inclination led him to this course of action, and having, by one or more acts of this nature, jeoparded his reputation, he felt willing, after an illustrious example, to make himself "of no reputation," drawing a proper distinction between *character*—what a man is—and *reputation*—what men say he is. It was his desire to have an irreproachable character in the sight of God, but for reputation, in the light of the above definition, he had no especial regard. In fact, he believed that a desire to preserve a good reputation often leads to a dereliction of duty, making cowards of men who might otherwise achieve great things for humanity; and that the loss of reputation was often the means of extensive usefulness, leading to an abnegation of one's self in the prosecution of noble deeds.

There was another trait in his character that deserves notice. In giving to good objects he studied to do it in a way to call forth the benefactions of others, and in this way he could say, "Lord, thy pound hath gained ten pounds." But he was never known to make a subscription with the calculation that the condition on which it was made would defeat the object in view, and thus gain to himself the credit of a generous act, while it cost him nothing. If the object was a deserving one, he took pleasure in affording it all the aid he consistently could, but having some knowledge of human nature, and its workings even in good men, he considered its tendencies, and acted in such matters with reference to them.

No man was more indifferent to applause than himself, in consequence of any subscription he made to a meritorious object, though he was not generally studious to conceal his benefactions, especially when his example might operate to stimulate others. At the same time he refrained from all publication of his gifts, direct or indirect, and in his private character, was not disobedient to the injunction, "When thou doest alms, let not thy left hand know what thy right hand doeth." And the satisfaction derived from a consciousness of having done right, was a sufficient and never failing reward, both for the amount expended and the time employed; verifying the remark of a distinguished preacher: "There is no person in the world that so uniformly takes his pay as he goes along, as he who does good at the expense of his own comfort and convenience."*

If he had hoarded money, instead of using it as

* Rev. Henry Ward Beecher.

it was earned, he might have amassed great wealth. But he had no ambition of the kind; through divine grace he laid up treasure in heaven by constant offices of benevolence on earth. Had he acted otherwise, no one in the city probably had a better opportunity than he to become a rich man. He considered it more blessed to give than to receive and hoard, and experienced the truth of the Christion paradox, constantly giving to good objects is constantly receiving. He relied on the Divine promise, that those who seek first the kingdom of God, who consecrate themselves and their gains and time for the advancement of the Redeemer's cause and the good of mankind, shall have the life that now is, and that which is to come.

According to the above statements ARTHUR TAPPAN was a happy man, happy in regard to this life, and happy in view of a glorious immortality—his constitutional infirmities, his buffetings, notwithstanding. Like his divine Lord and Master, he "endured the cross, despising the shame," striving manfully and bravely for the right. He has thus left to his family a priceless inheritance—a good name; and is, we doubt not, in a better world: "*There the wicked cease from troubling, and the weary are at rest. . . . Yea, saith the Spirit, that they may rest from their labors; and their works do follow them.*"

ADDENDA.

THE following letter was received by his daughter, some months after her father's death, from William Lloyd Garrison.

BOSTON, January 25, 1866.

MY DEAR MISS TAPPAN: Your very kind letter enclosing a photograph of your revered father, gives me inexpressible pleasure. This likeness better reveals his features to my recollection than the one he had the kindness to send me, though that is highly prized. Be assured I shall carefully preserve them both in my collection of portraits of friends, the most cherished and beloved—not merely because he was my liberator from the Baltimore prison in 1830, and among my earliest coadjutors in the then persecuted but now triumphant cause of the down-trodden slave, but for his Christian graces and virtues, making his character illustrious and proving his love for God by his love for man without regard to complexion, race, or clime.

He was the embodiment of integrity and justice, of world-wide philanthropy and genuine piety, of true modesty and utter self-abnegation. He had a solid understanding, a great conscience, and a warm heart. No man was ever more faithful to his convictions of duty, lead where it might, through the flood or through the fire.

At all times "ready to be offered" in the service of God, and the cause of suffering humanity, he was serene in the midst of fiery trials and imminent perils, being crucified to "that fear of man which bringeth a snare," and having his life "hid with Christ in God."

There are many forms of martyrdom besides being literally burnt to ashes, requiring as much courage and fortitude, and as great a heart and will, as the stake. Some of the most trying of these he had to confront for a long period in the rabid pro-slavery city of New York, but who ever knew him to shrink from the cross? He could neither be appalled by mob violence nor seduced by worldly interest. As a merchant naturally desiring customers, and a wide market, and having an immense business at stake, he had the most powerful temptation to avoid an espousal of so unpopular a cause as that of abolition, but in the spirit of his Master, he said, "Get thee behind me, Satan." Though not so conspicuously identified with the anti-slavery struggle for some years past as formerly, his interest in it never lessened; and now that the nation has decreed universal emancipation, I doubt not that he is cognizant of the glorious event, and with the liberated millions rendering praise and thanksgiving to God.

Where or what I should have been without his benevolent interposition to release me from my Baltimore imprisonment, it is in vain for me to conjecture. My deep indebtedness I shall never forget.

Your much obliged friend,

WM. LLOYD GARRISON.

The following letters were addressed to the compiler:

FROM HON. GERRIT SMITH.

PETERBORO', January 27, 1870.

MY DEAR FRIEND: . . . It gratifies me to learn that you are sketching the life of your brother Arthur. I held him in very high esteem. He was, in my view, a remarkably earnest, sincere, solemn and holy man. . . . I had but few interviews with him. Once, when breakfasting at his house, we conversed on the subject of caste. I can never forget the deep feeling he disclosed. He said that repentance on the part of those who indulge this wicked spirit, would wet their cheeks with "scalding tears." How often have I recalled those words, "scalding tears!" . . .

Here and there, a man like Bartlet of Massachusetts, had given largely to some one object, but Arthur Tappan was the first man among us to make large gifts to various objects. No other man in the land made a use of money, at once so sacred and so generous. With affectionate regard,

I remain your friend,

GERRIT SMITH.

LEWIS TAPPAN, ESQ.

FROM AMOS TOWNSEND, ESQ.

NEW HAVEN, Nov. 15, 1869.

MY DEAR BROTHER : . . . About the "new cemetery" of which you speak, and the colored people, I am unable to inform you, but the cemetery in Grove-street where the remains of your brother now rest, has witnessed the change to which you refer. Originally the colored people were assigned a position on the extreme western side of the ground. In the avengings of time and of blindfolded justice, this spot has been surrounded by the graves of the rich, the great and the noble, and their humble gravestones are encompassed by the costly and splendid monuments of the honored dead of the superior race.

So "the first shall be last, and the last shall be first." If we, in our time, seek to be on the side of right and truth, and of Christ and humanity, we cannot but be safe, and bide our time ; but if we proudly seek preëminence over the poor and the despised little ones of God, his righteous providence will avenge their cause, and we, or our memories, will be at the bottom.

Heartily wishing you grace, mercy and peace from God our Father, and the Lord Jesus Christ,

Yours in Christian fraternity,

AMOS TOWNSEND.

LEWIS TAPPAN, ESQ.

FROM A NIECE OF ARTHUR TAPPAN.

My recollections of Uncle Arthur in my childhood are of a grave character. I was often at his house to play with his children, but he was absent all day, and often returned with a headache. I remember, that we were then told to be very still, and that I would stand silently looking at him, awed by a sense of his suffering, as he sat upright on the sofa, with his handkerchief thrown over his head.

Afterwards, I remember a brief visit that we had from him at our summer retreat in 1835, in a village in Connecticut. He was travelling *incog.* from New Haven to New York. It was a very tender visit. A price was set upon his head by those at a distance who little knew what a man and a Christian he was, and daily threats and attempts were made against the life of my dear father whom he came to see.

I remember, not more than a year or two after this, undertaking to raise a sum of money for the relief of a deserving woman. Wearied and somewhat discouraged by partial success, I ventured to address a note to Uncle Arthur, asking a donation for this object. I did this reluctantly, because I knew how intensely occupied he was, and how many similar applications he was constantly receiving. I was agreeably surprised by the promptness of his reply and the generous sum that he enclosed, not only, but by the warm interest that he expressed in my little undertaking. From that time I felt that my Uncle Arthur had a very tender as well as a very large heart.

In the summer of 1847, he was not as well as usual, and I was one of a group of younger relatives who accompanied him to the seashore, hoping that the change would benefit him. Those were days of enjoyment to him. He left all care behind, and gave himself up to that delight in nature which only one of her true children could have. He seemed like a lovely happy child, and one at least of that group felt drawn to him by ties of more than ordinary sweetness ever afterwards.

It was at this time that he spoke of his life-long attraction to agricultural pursuits, and to life in the country, and mentioned a walk that he took on Roxbury neck, one fine morning in his early manhood, and the decision that he then reluctantly made, as he stood and looked at the beautiful hills and fields in one direction, and at the city in another, to return to the latter and continue in business there. "I went," said he, "contrary to my instincts. I always feel, when so free from headache as I have been on this journey, that I should have escaped a great deal of suffering if I had decided that morning for agricultural pursuits."

My latest remembrance of Uncle Arthur, aside from his occasional letters, is his last visit to us on his return from Washington in 1864. I said to him, "I suppose you and Uncle C—— called to see Mr. Lincoln?" "No," was the characteristic reply, "we were too obscure men to take any of the time that belonged to the nation."

I thought that, in singleness of motive and humility, he was a brother spirit to Abraham Lincoln, and that it would have been refreshing to the latter to have taken the hand of Arthur Tappan; but I did not reply. I was too deeply impressed by the beautiful unconsciousness of the speaker.

BY REV. WILLIAM H. HALLOCK, D. D.

The following was published in the "*American Messenger*," soon after the decease of Mr. Tappan, and afterwards as a tract, No. 677, in the series of the publications of the American Tract Society.

ARTHUR TAPPAN.

On one act of this merchant prince turned the Tract operations of this country. Near the close of 1824, the Tract Societies at New York and Boston were negotiating for the formation of a truly national institution, in which all the tract societies of the country might be united, when Arthur Tappan at New York sent word to William A. Hallock, then Assistant Secretary of the Society at Boston, that if he would visit New York, and money was wanting, it should be forthcoming. The visit was made, and after many prayerful consultations of Christian brethren, Mr. Tappan one evening, at his own house, said to Mr. Hallock, "What do you want? what kind of a building? how large must it be?" "That must depend on the extent of the Society's operations," was the reply; "we might have the printing in the fourth story, the binding in the third, the general depositary in the second, a store in the first to accommodate New York, and the rest of the first story and the basement might be rented to pay the debt, if any was incurred." "Well. I have determined to give $5,000 to it," was the immediate response. Within a few hours three other men, Moses Allen, now Treasurer, Richard T. Haines, Chairman of the Finance Committee, and W. W. Chester, gave $5,000 more; $20,000 was was raised, and soon increased to $25,000; the present site of the Tract House in Nassau-street was purchased; the na-

tional Society was unanimously organized by delegates from
tract societies in all parts of the country ; the building was
erected ; and the work entered on and prosecuted with an
energy and success rarely equalled. For eleven years Mr.
Tappan was Chairman of the Finance Committee, and gave
the Society not only his continued liberal contributions, but
his wise practical counsels and untiring and efficient personal
labors. His heart was with the destitute and perishing ; he
was an active tract distributer, adding charities for the body
to food for the soul ; calling in active Christian coöperation,
and superintending and encouraging the labors of many. In
a meeting of gentlemen in the Tract House to raise funds
for supplying the destitutions of the great West, Mr. Tappan very characteristically said, "I want to give two tracts
to every family in the valley of the Mississippi, so that none
shall be passed by. I will give $1,000 for this object."·

We believe that in the earlier years of this century there
was a sacredness in the benevolent movements which then
took their rise, and in the evidences of the true conversion
of a soul to God, which many of the young can now perhaps
hardly appreciate. The churches, after a long and fatal
slumber, had awoke anew to the truth that except a man be
"born again" by the power of the Holy Spirit, he must
perish, and to the duty of seeking the personal salvation of
"every creature." This gave rise to the formation, in 1810,
of the American Board of Foreign Missions, in 1816 the
Bible Society, in 1824 the Sunday-school Union, in 1825 the
National Tract Society, and contemporaneously many other
kindred institutions. Few men felt this inspiring impulse
more deeply than Mr. Tappan. Born in 1786, in Northampton, Mass., and passing seven years as clerk in a store at
Boston, his youth was spent in a dark period of the church.
He had a godly mother, Sarah Homes, a descendant of the
eminent William Homes, and intimate with the missionary
Mayhews of Martha's Vineyard—as she was also a relative of
the celebrated Benjamin Franklin ; but though her son's
moral character was spotless, we have no evidence of his conversion to God until, when at about the age of thirty, he
joined the church of the Rev. Dr. John M. Mason. Then,

"redeeming the time," he consecrated himself, body and soul, his power to accumulate wealth, his personal toils and prayers, all he had and all he was, in unreserved devotion to Him who gave himself a sacrifice for perishing men. He made princely gifts for many noble objects; for founding Auburn, Lane, and other theological seminaries; aiding young men in preparing for the ministry, and strengthening weak churches; he was himself a hard-worker in Sabbath-schools; his heart bled for the suffering and oppressed; there seemed no limit to his constant gifts or personal labors, though his business as a merchant was for many years as absorbing as that perhaps of any other man, in any land.

Mr. Tappan commenced business in Portland, Maine; was for a time in Montreal till the war of 1812; and in 1815 established himself in New York, where in 1817, in Hanover-square, he entered on that successful career as a silk merchant which made him for nearly twenty years one of the most prosperous and distinguished merchants of the city, having the confidence of all in his unbending integrity, and his business extending throughout the whole country. In the great commercial crisis of 1837 he suffered immense losses; and not long after turned his attention to other and more retired occupations, by which he obtained a comfortable subsistence for his family, and the ability still to contribute, though on a greatly diminished scale, throughout his protracted life.

"Our great system of benevolent institutions," says an able writer who knew him well, "owes its expansion and power in a great degree, to his influence. His example inspired the merchants of New York with the principle of enlarged benevolence, leading them to give their hundreds and thousands and tens of thousands where before they were accustomed to think it a great matter if they gave their tens or fifties. His wise counsels and energetic determination and munificent donations decided the formation and destiny of the American Tract Society, and gave it the strong and steady career on which it has advanced for so many years. His thoughtful mind planned the great enterprise of the American Bible Society of giving a Bible to every family in the United States, and his pledge of ten thousand dollars rendered it impossible but that the work should be undertaken—and done. Many others might be named of the great social movements of the last forty years, which owed their being or their power to his comprehensiveness of vision, sagacity of forethought, or largeness of liberality. Hardly any one can be named which did not become what it was, at least in part, through his agency and influence. It was a large heart, gifted with most extensive foresight, guiding a singularly effective will."

In 1827 he established, at the expense of tens of thousands of dollars, an able daily commercial newspaper which rested on the Sabbath, refrained from advertising theatrical licentious exhibitions and intoxicating liquors, and continues to be perhaps the first commercial paper in the country. From 1830 till his death in New Haven, July 23, 1865, in his eightieth year, he devoted his energies prominently to removing from this land the curse of slavery.

And when it appeared that pious young men were hindered from coming to Yale College for want of means, he assumed, in 1826, the responsibility of paying for the tuition of all beneficiaries in the college till the number should be more than a hundred.

In 1830, an event occurred which seems to have given a new direction to the main current of Mr. Tappan's future life. Mr. Garrison was then in prison at Baltimore for the non-payment of a fine imposed on him for an alleged libel as to the domestic slave-trade, and this being known to Mr. Tappan, he "promptly paid the fine and set him at liberty, getting the start of Henry Clay who was taking measures to do the same thing." This led Mr. Garrison to spend a week in Mr. Tappan's family, mildly and ably laying before him all his views of the abominations of slavery; and from this time onward the destruction of that system was evidently prominent in all Mr. Tappan's plans and efforts.

A most competent witness says of him : "As a business man he exercised a paternal regard for the welfare of the large number of clerks in his employ. While he avoided every thing obtrusive, he insisted that they should board in respectable families, regularly attend church on the Sabbath, abstain from sinful amusements, and shun vicious companions. He was unostentatious, simple in his habits, and hospitable. He had a profound reverence of God, and was a lover of good men of every denomination. He was an exemplary Christian, and looked forward to death as an introduction to an endless life of happiness, placing no reliance on any good deeds, but resting solely on the mercy of God through the atoning sacrifice of the Lord Jesus Christ. His prayers were peculiarly characterized by profound humility, tenderness, and child-like simplicity. In his last letter to one of his brothers he wrote, 'I feel that I can say, Lord, now lettest thou thy servant depart in peace, for mine eyes have seen thy salvation, and the emancipation of the poor colored people.' "

After fifty years of faithful service for Christ and the souls of men, Mr. Tappan, in his eightieth year, July 23, 1865, at his residence in New Haven, peacefully and thankfully entered into rest.

AUBURN THEOLOGICAL SEMINARY.

From the address of Prof. Hopkins of Auburn Theological Seminary, to the class graduating in May, 1866.

. . . At the opening of the year 1823, this seminary, then just beginning its career, was in a condition of peril threatening its immediate dissolution. It was a newborn child for which no nourishment or next to none, had been provided. Three professors indeed were on the ground : part of the present seminary building had been erected : two classes of students had entered. But there were no funds for the support of the professors : there was only a small library of second-hand books, and the trustees were already several thousand dollars in debt for current expenses. Efforts to raise money were almost wholly fruitless. To go on very long in this way was plainly impossible. The question had to be considered whether, for the time at least, the seminary must not be closed, the classes disbanded, and Professors Mills and Perrine dismissed again to the pastoral work.

In this crisis Dr. Lansing, pastor of the First Presbyterian church, who was also professor of sacred rhetoric in the seminary, visited New York city with some faint hope of securing assistance. Among other persons he called on Mr. Arthur Tappan, a young and enterprising Christian merchant doing business in Pearl-street. As the result of this interview he was led to hope that Mr. Tappan would perhaps endow a scholarship of $2,000 in the seminary: and this was all the encouragement he brought back from this visit.

But better things were in store for us. The Lord did not mean that this infant institution, founded with the most deliberate and prayerful regard to the wants of the church should perish so prematurely. From the address of Rev. John Keep at the installation of Dr. Richards, Oct. 23, 1823, I take the following statement of the change in its prospects :

"Although the friends of this seminary have not witnessed the pillar of cloud and of fire as a guide to their course, they believe that the 'still small voice' of Divine Providence has bidden them go forward. With mingled emotions of fear and hope, they still watch its infant struggles : and they are cheered as they already descry increasing light breaking in upon them from the retreating clouds. The circumstances under which we are convened are connected with the most pleasing hopes and associations. Especially should we be devoutly thankful in view of the recent interposition of Divine Providence which has laid the foundation for another professorship in this seminary. During the past season an unknown FRIEND in the city of New York has with a princely liberality made an endowment for the support of a professor of Christian theology. On this foundation the board of commissioners have duly elected the Rev. James Richards, D. D., as professor in this department : and he having accepted the appointment has been now inducted into office in the form prescribed by the ordinances of the institution."

This "unknown FRIEND" continued for many years after to be equally unknown to all but a very few persons connected with the seminary. With a Christian humility quite remarkable he refused to permit his name to be associated in any manner with his benefaction. He expressed his wish that Dr. Richards should be the incumbent of the chair of theology : and that it should be known as the "Richards professorship." The donation of $15,000, and all the arrangements connected with it, were carried on through the medium of the late Eleazar Lord of New York.

I am not aware by what means it finally transpired that this friend in need was Arthur Tappan, a name afterwards widely known for Christian philanthropy and for heroic fidelity to convictions of duty. For thirty years he was the mark for every weapon of insult and abuse oppression could wield. The man who but named *him* (at least if he was a Southern slaveholder or a Northern sympathizer) at once dismissed all mercy from his lips, and sneered and hissed ; "thief," "hypocrite," "incendiary," "fanatic," etc.—we all remember the vocabulary of abuse to which slavery accustomed us—were the epithets he was wont to be pelted with.

Since the last anniversary of this seminary Arthur Tappan has died. He had outlived his strength, his fortunes, his contemporaries : but he had also, thank God ! outlived that demoniacal iniquity which so long possessed this country, and which in going out has rent us with such an awful convulsion. He lived long enough to have the government and the North come over to his side, and to see half a million of men in arms champion his ideas to a successful issue. His eyes had seen the salvation of the Lord : and he was, no doubt, quite ready to say, *Domine—nunc dimittis !*

It is well-known that Mr. Tappan, while still in the prime of life, was overwhelmed by commercial disaster from which he never recovered. His fortune was swept away. But a part of it he had secured beyond the reach of mischance. What he kept he lost : what he gave, he saved. The $15,000 which endowed the "Richards professorship of Christian theology"—not a great sum indeed when compared with the splendid charities of far richer men at the present day, but for that time, and for a young business man to spare from his capital, truly "princely"—this $15,000, he had anchored safely where none of the blasts that wreck mercantile ventures could reach it—so carefully was the trust guarded that

18

not only has not a dollar been lost down to the present time, but it would seem well nigh impossible it ever should be lost.

With equal care the trust was guarded against theological perversion. The founder declared it to be "his intention and design in granting the said sum that the interest or income of said capital fund should be annually applied to the support of a professor of Christian theology holding the theological sentiments and faith which are required by the ordinances of the seminary now in force ; and if at any time hereafter any professor on this foundation shall in any important article differ from the said system of faith, and especially if such professor shall not fully believe and teach the true and proper divinity of the Lord Jesus Christ, the personality of the Holy Spirit, the total depravity of man in his natural state, and the eternal punishment of the wicked, then the founder of this professorship reserves to himself, his heirs, executors, and assigns, the right to reclaim and receive back the capital fund hereby granted," etc.

This benefaction marked the turning point in the fortunes of the seminary. . . . Friends plucked up courage : one good deed is apt to produce numerous echoes ; and this one repeated itself in welcome though lesser benefactions : students began to flock in. The next class that entered consisted of forty-eight members ; many of whom have preached the gospel with eminent success, and left their impress deep in the religious character of this and the Western states.

For forty years and more Mr. Tappan was permitted to witness such and similar fruits of his judicious liberality. Forty classes of students for the ministry drew their views of the system of divine truth from the chair he established, before he entered into his rest : happy above most other men in this, that in the prime of life and in the midst of his prosperity, he had laid up a good foundation for the time to come. It is at the request of the prudential committee and the faculty of this seminary, that I lay this chaplet on the tomb of Arthur Tappan.*

* See Appendix 10, for resolutions of the trustees, on death of Mr. Tappan.

APPENDIX.

GENEALOGICAL NOTICE.

ABRAHAM TOPPAN, ancestor of Arthur Tappan, came to America from Yarmouth, Norfolk county, England, October, 1637. The name was originally Topham, taken from the name of a place in Yorkshire, meaning upper hamlet or village. The pedigree, so far back as we have traced it, commenced with Robert Topham, who resided at Linton, near Palely bridge, supposed to be in the West riding of Yorkshire. He made his will in January, 1550.

His second son, Thomas Topham, was of Arncliffe, near Linton. He died in 1589. Edward Topham alias Toppan, eldest son of Thomas, was of Aiglethorpe, near Linton, and his pedigree is recorded in the College of Arms with armorial bearings. One of his sons was a lieutenant-colonel in the service of Charles I., and was killed at Marston Moor in 1644.

WILLIAM TOPPAN, fourth son of Edward Toppan, of Aiglethorpe, lived for some time at Calbridge, where his son Abraham was baptized, April 10, 1606. The family still exists in England, are now of Middleham, in the north part of Yorkshire, on the river Ouse. The crest is a Maltese cross.

As early as 1637, Abraham Toppan resided at Yarmouth. His wife was Susanna Taylor, a daughter of a Mr. Taylor and his wife Elizabeth. After the death of Mr. Taylor, the widow Elizabeth married a Mr. Goodale ; and after the death of Mr. Goodale she came to Newbury, where she died April 8, 1647. One of her daughters was Susanna, the wife of Abraham Toppan.

Among the records in London, where emigrants were obliged to register their names, and obtain permission to leave the country, is the following :

"May 10, 1637. The examination of Abraham Toppan of Yarmouth, aged 31 years, and Susanna his wife, aged 30 years, with two children, Peter and Elizabeth, and one mayd servant, Anne

Goodwin, aged 18 years, are desirous to passe to New England to inhabit."

In the first volume of the fourth series of the publications of the Massachusetts Historical Society, pp. 98 and 99, is the following :

"A register of the names of such persons, who are 21 years and upward, and have license to passe into forraigne parts from March, 1637, to the 29th of September, by virtue of a Commission of Mr. Thomas Mayhew, Gentleman," contains, among others, these : "Abraham Toppan, Cooper, aged 31, Susanna his wife aged 31, with their children Peter and Elizabeth, and one mayd servant, Anne Goodwin, aged 18 years, sailed from Yarmouth 10 May, 1637, in the ship Rose of Yarmouth, Wm. Andrews, Master."

In October, 1637, as appears by the following extract from the town records of "Ould Newbury," Essex county, Mass., Abraham Toppan was admitted to citizenship :

"Abraham Toppan, being licensed by John Endicott, Esq., to live in his jurisdiction was received into the town of Newbury as an inhabitant thereof, and hath here promised under his hand to be subject to every lawful order, that shall be made by the towne. "ABRAHAM TOPPAN."

The following year he was chosen one of the selectmen. He carried on his trade, and also engaged in merchandise.

Abraham and Susanna Toppan had eight children, the fourth of whom, SAMUEL, born 5th June, 1670, was a farmer, who settled at Newbury, and married ABIGAIL WIGGLESWORTH in 1702. Her father was minister of Malden, Mass., and her brother Edward was professor of divinity in Harvard College. They had ten children, of whom BENJAMIN was the ninth. He was born in 1720, graduated at Harvard College ; married ELIZABETH MARSH of Haverhill, Mass.; was settled in the ministry at Manchester, Essex county, in 1745, where he died, aged 70, greatly lamented. They had twelve children. The oldest, BENJAMIN, was born October 21st, "Old Style," equivalent to November 1st, "New Style." He was apprenticed to WILLIAM HOMES, Esq., the "honest goldsmith," as he was called, in Ann-street, Boston, and married his daughter SARAH HOMES, October 22d, "Old Style," 1770.

After the death of Rev. Benjamin Toppan, in 1790, his children, at a family meeting, agreed to change the spelling to Tappan, at the suggestion of the eldest son, who had for sometime adopted that way of writing it.

The Homes family originated in the north of Ireland. Rev. William Homes, great grandfather of Mrs. Tappan, was a Presbyterian minister there, emigrated to this country early in the eighteenth century; and was installed pastor of the church at Chilmark, Martha's Vineyard, Mass., in 1715 or 1716. He was the author of several publications, and was highly venerated by his contemporaries.

Robert Homes, his son, was master of a vessel that traded from Boston to Philadelphia. He married Mary Franklin, sister of Dr. Benjamin Franklin, who makes mention of him in his autobiography. He left two children, the oldest of whom was William, the father of Mrs. Tappan. He was born January 16, 1716, in Boston, where he served an apprenticeship in the goldsmith business, and afterwards, on his son's assuming the business, entered into trade, as a flour and iron merchant. His store was burned during the Revolutionary war. He then bought a farm in Norton, Mass., where he lived a short time, and died in Boston, July, 1785, in his seventieth year. He was buried with his wife in the Chapel burying-ground, Tremont-street, Boston.

SARAH TAPPAN was born January 2d, 1748, and died March 26, 1826. Benjamin Tappan was born November 1, 1747, and died January 30, 1831. They lived together fifty-nine years, honored in their day and generation. They had eleven children, seven sons and four daughters, and nine children survived them. Their grandchildren numbered seventy-two.

2.

THE CREDIT SYSTEM

THE following is extracted from a pamphlet published by Lewis Tappan, in 1869, entitled, "Is it Right to be Rich?"

"A few words with regard to the *credit system* that so generally prevails among men of business. The supposed gains, under this system, are very fallacious, while the net gains in the long run, under the *cash system*, would be much more lucrative to the individual and more beneficial to the community. Besides it is not easy to determine what one's income or actual gain really is, when the credit system so generally prevails. This uncertainty affords a pretext too often for giving as little as possible to the cause of God or man. If the cash system were generally adopted, more money would be paid into the Lord's treasury, and it would be a great restraint upon the feverish and almost insane spirit of speculation, interchange of indorsements, hazardous risks and wild expansion of business that harass business men, lead to bankruptcy, to neglect of families, to neglect of their own souls and the souls of others, and often to the ruin of body and soul. A merchant of remarkable industry and carefulness, now deceased, informed the writer that, during the thirty years he was in the wholesale importing and jobbing business in New York, as a dry-goods merchant, he had made a fortune of eight hundred thousand dollars *on his books;* but owing to bad debts, the amount had been reduced to so small a sum that he gave up trade, purchased a farm in the country, and, not succeeding very well, his sons are now clerks in New York. So much for the credit system."

The following statement of facts illustrative of the effects of the credit system, is worthy of consideration :

About the year 1832, Rev. David Nelson, M. D., subsequently author of the admirable work published by the American Tract Society, entitled 'Cause and Cure of Infidelity,' came to New York, to solicit aid to establish a college in Missouri. He wished to borrow the sum of $20,000 for the purchase of land, giving security therefor. After much inquiry and powerful effort, with the aid of a friend in the city, he succeeded in obtaining a loan for ten years, with annual interest at seven per cent. The money was borrowed from ISAAC BRONSON, Esq., one of the shrewdest financial men in the country. He required, 1. That the trustees of the college should mortgage to him the land to be purchased of the United States as security to their bond ; 2. That the forty merchants in New York who had expressed a willingness to loan their names to the amount of $500 each should unite in a guaranty ; 3. That five of the number, whose names he selected, should give a bond equivalent to indorsing the responsibility of the forty persons ; 4. That the friend who had negotiated the loan on behalf of Dr. Nelson, should give his obligation to hold Mr. Bronson harmless at all events. Having this fourfold security the money was advanced. It seemed strange that so much security should be required, but the far-seeing lender judged it necessary, and as will be seen acted with singular foresight in view of taking security of men engaged in the credit system.

When the ten years had expired and the trustees had proved irresponsible, No. 4 was applied to for payment. He acknowledged the obligation, but was pecuniarily unable to respond. No. 3 were then applied to, and four of them had become insolvent!

The only solvent person among them endeavored to collect their quota of the second class, but found that a large portion of them had also failed! He was therefore under the necessity of settling with Mr. Bronson, which he did in an honorable manner. This gentleman was Mr. RICHARD T. HAINES. When the loan was effected, those in the No. 2 list were all in prosperous circumstances, and each of the No. 3 list was rich. And yet, such are the uncertainties of trade, especially on the credit system, that in less than ten years nearly all these merchants became bankrupts.

3.

JOURNAL OF COMMERCE.

IN the Memoirs of David Hale, by Rev. Joseph P. Thompson, it is stated:

"In 1827, Mr. Arthur Tappan, with his princely liberality and zealous regard for the public good, resolved to establish in New York a commercial newspaper, to be conducted upon principles of sound morality and true independence, and with a scrupulous regard for the Sabbath. Some friends of Mr. Hale, learning of the movement, recommended him to Mr. Tappan as a suitable person to take charge of the commercial and business department of the paper, to which post he was accordingly invited. He entered upon his duties at the commencement of the enterprise, September 1, 1827; W. Maxwell, Esq., of Norfolk, Va., a gentleman of high literary reputation, being associated with him as the literary editor. The *Journal of Commerce* (as the newspaper was called) was then about the size of the New York *Tribune*, or one half its own present dimensions; and its daily circulation was only a few hundred copies—in fact much of its circulation the first year was gratuitous. Its editorials were generally upon literary subjects; but its columns were principally devoted to business and news, the latter being diversified every few weeks by the arrival of a vessel from Liverpool, Havre, or New Orleans.

"Such was the expensiveness, that towards the close of the first year, Mr. Arthur Tappan, who had already advanced upon the Journal *thirty thousand dollars*, determined to abandon it; and to rid himself of further responsibility he presented the entire establishment to his brother, Mr. Lewis Tappan, whom he had just associated with himself in business. Several changes followed this arrangement. Mr. Maxwell retired from the editorship, and Mr. Horace Bushnell (now Rev. Dr. Bushnell, of Hartford)—

who already evinced much of his peculiar spirit and power as a writer, and who had been an assistant of Mr. Maxwell—was employed some months as editor, while Mr. Hale, in whose name the Journal was published, continued to manage the business department. The paper was under the general direction of Mr. Lewis Tappan, who thus announced the principles on which it should be conducted:

It will be a primary object to render the Journal a first rate COMMERCIAL paper, worthy of this city. To this end an extensive correspondence will be maintained, the most ably conducted periodicals will be taken, and no pains nor expense will be spared to procure authentic reviews of the markets, prices current, etc. It will be necessary also to maintain a BOAT ESTABLISHMENT for the collection of marine news; and this must be done at our individual cost, as the public and our establishment will be benefited by a competition, and as it will be contrary to the principles of this paper, to be associated with similar establishments which devote Sundays to the collecting of news. By a vigorous competition we expect to prevent any deficiency arising from an observance of the Sabbath, by which we mean the hours consecrated as holy time by the general usage of Christians in this city, namely: FROM TWELVE O'CLOCK ON SATURDAY NIGHT TO TWELVE O'CLOCK THE NIGHT SUCCEEDING.

We shall avoid all participation in the gain of those fashionable vices which sap the foundations of morality and religion, on which the best interests of the nation depend. We profess to be friends of Christianity; not enthusiasts nor sectarians—and by a liberal and firm support of the moral and religious institutions of the country, we shall hope to merit the patronage of all good citizens. Nor shall we fear, for the Journal, the sneering imputation of its being a RELIGIOUS newspaper, because it will refuse to derive emolument from advertisements that are at war with the innocence, integrity, and moral weal of the community; nor because it will seek to promote the purity and elevation of public sentiment.

In short, it will be our endeavor to pursue an independent, courteous, and honorable competition; to COME OUT PLAINLY against moral delinquencies; while we hope to furnish a paper, which will instruct and gratify the merchant, the politician, the literary reader, and the moral and patriotic of all callings and professions. On the coöperation of such we confidently rely. Let the experiment be fairly made, and who can doubt that, in the metropolis of this great nation, a daily paper, striving to excel its contemporaries by a dignified discussion of all the leading topics of public interest, excluding vice in all its forms, will be extensively patronized.*

"Such," says Mr. Thompson, "was the original plan of the *Journal of Commerce,* as devised by Mr. Tappan. . . . The attempt

---

* Journal of Commerce, September 1, 1828.

to establish a paper on such a basis excited the opposition and contempt of mere men of the world. . . . As it was not the wish of Mr. Lewis Tappan to retain the control of the paper, he endeavored to procure an editor to be permanently associated with Mr. Hale. In a few months an arrangement was made by which Mr. Hale and Gerard Hallock, Esq., then editor of the *New York Observer*, became joint proprietors and editors of the *Journal of Commerce*. A guarantee fund of twenty thousand dollars was subscribed by several gentlemen for the support of the paper, and the editors were allowed two years to determine upon purchasing the property by returning principal and interest. This they subsequently did, and thus the Journal was established on a safe and independent basis."

NOTE.

The "expensiveness" was not the only reason my brother had for desiring to be rid of the concern. He was disappointed in regard to the expectations he had formed of the usefulness of the paper. It was more literary than commercial, and the moral effect had not been so great as had been anticipated. Besides, a large part of the editorial labor had been performed by two or three assistant editors, the office of chief editor being almost a sinecure—and that a very expensive one. At the same time the subscription list and advertising receipts were not increasing.

My brother felt that he had advanced as much money as it was convenient and proper for him to do, and he determined in the month of August to free himself from the necessity of sustaining the paper any longer than the expiration of the first year. Accordingly he informed me that he should not make any more advances after 1st September, and that the publication must then stop. I urged him not to sacrifice the property, and he replied, "I will then give it to you, on condition that you will examine into the concern, and put it on a right footing." I accepted the proposition, took leave of my mercantile business for a time, dispensed with the services of the chief editor, and, with the able assistance of Mr. Bushnell, assumed the editorship of the paper.

After several attempts, by correspondence and journeys, to procure a suitable person to succeed Mr. Maxwell, several gentlemen, at my invitation, supposed to be friendly to the enterprise, met at the Tract House to consult on the affairs of the Journal. Several of them attended. Messrs. Gerard Hallock and David Hale, to whom a proposition had been made, were also invited to the con-

18*

ference. I made a verbal statement of the concern—its situation on the 1st September; the efforts since made to sustain it; the present income and disbursements; and stated that if the subscription and advertising patronage continued as they had done for the past six weeks the income would at least equal the expenses. The proposition to Hale and Hallock and their willingness to accept it were laid before the meeting. Included in the proposition was a condition that a stated sum should be pledged to carry on the business for two years, and to allow Hale and Hallock to elect to purchase at the termination of that period or sooner. The gentlemen present spoke favorably of the paper, said it ought not to be discontinued, and that means for its support must be furnished. A subscription was opened, a considerable sum was subscribed, and after much painstaking the full amount was eventually obtained. At the end of two years Hale and Hallock decided to consummate the purchase; the advances of the friends were repaid; and six thousand dollars, the estimated value of the fixtures, type, presses, etc., on the 1st September, paid to Arthur Tappan. Although my brother acknowledged the ability and industry of the new proprietors, he did not approve the manner in which they conducted the paper, as it respected its political influence, and the stand it took on the anti-slavery question. Its pecuniary success has been very great.

It was demonstrated by the proprietors of the *Journal of Commerce* that a daily paper could be sustained in the city of New York without any desecration of the Lord's day. If successful then, it could be so now; and therefore there is no valid excuse for infringing on sacred time. There are multitudes of readers of such papers, many of them moral and religious men, who have it in their power to restrain such violation of the Sabbath. If they would refrain from purchasing a Monday's paper that is printed on the Lord's day, as many of them are, a check would be held over such issues, and the result would be that proprietors would find it for their interest to abstain from desecrating holy time. Editors, and all the employés, would doubtless be grateful for such acts of self-denial on the part of readers. *Is not a patron of a Monday's paper, on which work is done on the Sabbath, as culpable as the editor or proprietor?*

4.

COLONIZATION SOCIETY—RUM TRADE IN LIBERIA.

WHAT the cargoes of vessels trading to Liberia were made up of may be seen by the following advertisements, from the *Liberia Herald:*

No. 1. March 22, 1832.	No. 2. September 7, 1832.
C. M. Waring and F. Taylor offer for sale the cargo of the schooner Olive from Liverpool:	C. M. Waring offers for sale the cargo of the schooner Olive of Liverpool:
500 kegs of powder,	60 doz. blk. handled spear-pointed knives,
500 muskets,	
150 cutlasses,	10.000 best musket flints,
10 bags shot,	354 bunches dark straw beads,
10 puncheons rum,	223 pounds black pound do.
2 do. brandy,	245 do. white do.
20 casks ale,	1,197 gallons of rum,
10 do. brown stout,	350 kegs of powder,
etc., etc.	140 muskets.

BUYING THE GOOD WILL OF THE NATIVES.

The terms of one of the contracts may be seen in the society's eleventh report:

4th. The American Colonization Society shall have the right, in consideration of five hundred bars of tobacco, three barrels of rum, five casks of powder, five pieces of long baft, five boxes of pipes, ten guns, five umbrellas, ten iron pots and ten pairs of shoes, immediately to enter into possession of the tract of unoccupied land, bounded toward the West by Stockton creek, and on the North by St. Paul's river, etc.

The Sesters territory was perpetually leased to the Colonization Society on the 27th October, 1825, by King Freeman, "in consideration of *one hogshead of tobacco, one puncheon of rum,* six boxes of pipes, to be paid and delivered to [him] yearly, every year, the first to commence from the date of these presents," etc.

5.

JOSEPH STURGE'S STATEMENT.

WHEN Mr. Sturge visited New York, in 1841, on his return to England from his second visit to the West Indies, he made the following statement:

"In Jamaica a proprietor told him that it was considered a good day's work for a *slave* to clear seventy to eighty coffee trees of weeds, with a hoe, but by paying task work under the apprenticeship system, a man and woman cleared five hundred trees in a day, and a boy two hundred and fifty trees in one instance! So much for the free over slave labor.

"Mr. Sturge said that during his stay in the West Indies, he did not see a single negro intoxicated, and a practitioner of medicine told him that during all his practice he had never seen a negro woman drunk.

"In Jamaica the negroes contributed £2,000 currency, towards building a meetinghouse. On one occasion, the preacher told his congregation that if any of them were inclined to contribute towards repairing the chapel, they might leave their contributions in the vestry, and as he supposed that they had not come prepared, he would not send around the collection-boxes. A sum equal to £50 sterling was immediately left in the vestry."

6.

VICE-PRESIDENT COLFAX'S LETTER.

WASHINGTON, Feb. 25, 1870.

MY DEAR SIR: I remember very well going in 1835, when I was twelve years of age, to see the results of a mob attack on your property in Rose-street, caused by your anti-slavery principles; and I remember also that it made me prejudiced, even then, against the "institution of slavery," whose supposed interests caused that attack. I have no doubt that that early adverse impression caused me afterwards to range myself with the anti-slavery wing of the Whig party, though I remained connected with that party while it existed.

Yours very truly,

· SCHUYLER COLFAX.

LEWIS TAPPAN, ESQ.

7.

OBERLIN COLLEGE.

THE following resolution was unanimously adopted by the board of trustees of Oberlin College at its regular annual meeting in August, 1865, and ordered to be entered upon its records.

Arthur Tappan one of the oldest and munificent patrons of Oberlin College having departed this life, therefore, resolved, that in his death the college has reason to deplore the loss of one of its truest and noblest, and most valued friends. Yet, on the other hand, to rejoice that his great life was well done, and that so ripe in years and rich in munificence and toil, he has at length entered upon his glorious rest. Under the blessed influence of such a life, and such a death, we are quickened to fresh endeavor to follow him in the simplicity of his consecration to God and humanity, and in his steadfast devotion to the great principles of Christian benevolence.

The foregoing is a true copy of the records.

GEORGE KINNEY, Sec.

8.

LETTER FROM REV. C. G. FINNEY.

In a letter to the compiler from Mr. Finney, of a recent date, he says : "I regard Arthur Tappan as one of the best men I ever knew. He was as modest as he was good. I am happy to hear that you are preparing a sketch of his life. Will you lay aside all fear of being accused of too highly appreciating a brother, and let the church have the whole portrait ? Tell us all about his appropriations for Christ and humanity, and the opposition he met with on that account. Do you know that he paid the expense of getting up and running Sabbath-schools, by the students that left Lane Seminary? Mr. Streeter, one of them, mentioned the fact here at a public meeting two years ago, and said that until Mr. Tappan's death, the matter was, by his request, kept secret. Mr. Streeter spoke of the amount given as considerable. You are aware that just before I was invited to Oberlin, he was urging me to come West long enough to take that class through a course of theology. To furnish rooms and whatever was requisite, and he would defray the expense. . . . Many have since 'given much of their abundance,' but who among them as privately and of course as unostentatiously pledged his whole income for church and humanity. The magnificent donations of Peabody and others do not compare *relatively* with Arthur Tappan's. I see that Joshua Leavitt is requested to write a history of the anti-slavery movement. He will do as well as any man unacquainted with the influence of Oberlin on the whole Northwest. The fact is that Oberlin turned the scale in all of the Northwest. No man can tell the story right unless he knows this. Although Arthur Tappan failed to do for Oberlin all that he intended, yet his *promise* was the condition of the existence of Oberlin *as it has been.* God bless you.

"C. G. FINNEY."

9.

AMERICAN MISSIONARY ASSOCIATION.

THE following record of the executive committee was transmitted to the daughters of Mr. Arthur Tappan, after his decease.

NEW YORK, Aug. 12, 1865.

MY DEAR FRIENDS : By order of the executive committee of the American Missionary Association, I send you the following extract from the minutes of the last session :

The executive committee of the American Missionary Association, having learned of the decease of our esteemed Christian brother Arthur Tappan, the early tried and faithful advocate of the freedom of the slave, and the friend of the poor, for many years a member of our executive committee, and, since his removal from New York, a vice-president of the association, desire to place on record, and to express to his bereaved family and relatives, our high appreciation of his consistent Christian character, his distinguished liberality, and his earnest labors, and sacrifices, for the freedom of the slave, and the welfare of the oppressed. His benevolence, Christ-like, knew no distinction of race, clime, condition, or color, but was freely, joyfully, extended, wherever the Redeemer's kingdom or individual want indicated.

In his departure this association, the church of Christ, and the poor among men, as well as his bereaved family, have lost an earnest friend and faithful counsellor.

But while we record our sense of this great loss, we would humbly and gratefully express our thanks to Almighty God, that he was so long spared to his friends and the world, and permitted, before entering the heavenly rest, to witness with exultation and praise to God, the downfall of the accursed system, against which he had so long striven. And we would unite our prayers with those of his family, that even this so great affliction may be sanctified to their and our good, and that of the cause he so much loved.

A true copy from the minutes of the executive committee.

GEORGE WHIPPLE, CLERK.

10.

RESOLUTIONS ADOPTED BY THE TRUSTEES OF THE AUBURN THEOLOGICAL SEMINARY.

Whereas, It has pleased divine Providence, since the last regular meeting of this board, to remove by death Arthur Tappan, Esq., formerly of the city of New York, one of the earliest and most liberal benefactors of this institution: therefore,

Resolved, That the trustees feel called upon to place on record their grateful sense of the wise Christian beneficence of Mr. Tappan, and especially to praise God that he was led in the time of his worldly prosperity to endow by a donation of fifteen thousand dollars, the professorship of Christian theology, by this act giving life to the institution in its feeble infancy, encouraging other endowments, and securing for its first theological teacher, that wise, devout and faithful man of God, Rev. James Richards, D. D.

Resolved, That this act of Mr. Tappan furnishes a most instructive example of the wisdom of seasonable beneficence by Christian men, instead of postponing their charities till the time of their death, when the fluctuations of business may have stripped them of their means of doing good.

Resolved, That we record with devout gratitude the fact that Mr. Tappan was permitted, during the long period of more than forty years, to witness the fruits of his judicious charity in a succession of able and faithful teachers in the chair of Christian theology in this seminary, and in the education of so many hundreds of ministers of the gospel who have gone to all parts of our own and to heathen lands.

11.

BRITISH AND FOREIGN ANTI-SLAVERY SOCIETY.

WE extract the following from the London *Anti-Slavery Reporter* of September, 1865 :

The American papers announce the death in his eightieth year of Mr. Arthur Tappan (brother of Lewis Tappan) widely known for his benevolence and for the generous zeal with which he always advocated and supported any measures for the benefit of his fellow-men.

He was one of the early abolitionists, and cheerfully took a large share of the obloquy and persecution which were visited upon that despised class in its darkest days. When Garrison was imprisoned in Baltimore for an article in his paper upon the domestic slave trade, Mr. Tappan paid the fine and redeemed him from jail, and his name from that time forward was as notorious and almost as much hated at the South as Garrison's own.

Like most of the class to which he was known to belong, his whole life gave the lie to the assertion that the abolitionists were " men of one idea," for there was no charitable work or pious purpose to which he did not give the benefit of his great executive ability, and the support of his hearty and untiring devotion. Nor did old age cool his ardor, to the end of his days, his interest in good works never flagged, and for him certainly awaits the award, " Well done, good and faithful servant."

12.

LETTER FROM WM. LLOYD GARRISON.

BOSTON, March 3, 1870.

DEAR SIR : I am more than gratified to learn that you have prepared a sketch of the life of your lamented brother Arthur, for publication in a volume. He well deserves all that you or any others may say in his praise. With a sound understanding, a great conscience to the dictates of which he was inflexibly true, a genuine humility that did not wish the left hand to know what the right hand performed, a moral courage that could look any reproach or peril serenely in the face in the discharge of what seemed to be an imperative duty, a sense of rectitude commensurate with the golden rule, a spirit of philanthropy as comprehensive and universal as the "one blood" of all nations of men, a liberality rarely paralleled in the consecration of his means to deliver the oppressed and to relieve suffering humanity in all its multifarious aspects, and a piety that proved its depth and genuineness by the fruits it bore, his example is to me to be held up for imitation to the latest posterity.

The applications for his charitable assistance were legion ; but, notwithstanding his immense business, he gave no scope to an impulsive benevolence, but endeavored to examine each case upon its merits, and dispose of it upon principle. While always courteous, was there ever one who was less "a respecter of persons" than himself? No rabbi could command his attention more than the beggar in rags. But it is not for me to recite to you either his excellent traits or noble deeds. These you will record without flattery or ostentation, but solely in justice to his memory, and as incentives to well-doing on the part of such as may thus be made acquainted with his remarkable career. . . . The biography of your brother will be very timely.

Yours, to sing the song of jubilee,

WM. LLOYD GARRISON.

LEWIS TAPPAN.

13.

DEATH OF ARTHUR TAPPAN.

THE following tribute, by Rev. Joshua Leavitt, D. D., was published in the New York *Independent:*

"The venerable Christian philanthropist, whose name has

been, at one time, a word of power to all who love Christ's cause, and, at another, the song of the negro-haters throughout the country, as the representative of justice and mercy to the oppressed, has been gathered to his fathers in peace and honor at the ripe age of fourscore. Mr. Tappan died at New Haven, on Sunday, July 23, and was buried on Tuesday, in the cemetery of that place. Reserving for another occasion the fuller account which we hope to give of his life, and the services he rendered to his generation and to the cause of Christ in the world, we now only express the first emotions that arise at the event when we say that this world has parted with one of the truest Christians it ever knew. Sincerity as pure as crystal, and integrity as true as the beams of the morning, were the leading traits of his character. What he said, he believed; and what he saw to be right, he did. Those who differed from him most widely, and those who were most displeased by his action, felt and confessed that he was conscientious in his opinions, and honest in his conduct, to a degree never surpassed. He had no classification of principles or duties, by their times or relations. His piety was for every day, and his religion controlled his bargains as it did his devotions. A Christian indeed, he was a Christian everywhere, and in all his relations. He would no more wrong his closet in devotion than he would cheat a customer in trade. He believed the evangelical system of doctrine as honestly as the decalogue, and practised the duties of the second table as diligently as the first. He was a good man in whatever circumstances you tried him, and from whatever point of view you observed him. His character honored alike his profession as a Christian, his calling as a merchant, his position as a member of society. He was thought to be severe in judgment, but it was only because he judged others as he did himself, and he could not modify the decision, because he knew the law could not bend. He could not compromise in duty, because he could not alter the truth, which he believed because it was true. His whole life was eminently uniform and consistent, because it was wholly and always governed by one principle—the law of God. The life of such a man is a profitable study for all survivors, and its history needs to be written by one who is in full sympathy with the principles which governed him, and the objects for which he lived. His life consisted in what he believed and what he did—not in loud sentiments or florid imaginations. It had no lack of the essentials of faith and action, and he never sought for it the adornments of fancy or the excitements of overwrought emotion. Undoubting

belief, unhesitating submission, unremitting obedience, made up
a religion which he was resolved to live by, and which he was not
afraid to die by. The life of which it could be said in youth that
he never told a lie is completed and rounded out with a consistency as perfect as the circle of the sky.

"There is, probably, no man living whose influence upon the
destinies of the country is equal to his. Our great system of benevolent institutions owes its expansion and power, in a great
degree, to his influence. His example inspired the merchants of
New York with the principle of enlarged benevolence, leading
them to give their hundreds, and thousands, and tens of thousands
where before they were accustomed to think it a great matter if
they gave their tens or fifties. His wise counsels and energetic
determination, and munificent donation of five or six thousand
dollars in 1825, decided the formation and destiny of the American
Tract Society, and gave it the strong and steady career on which
it has advanced for so many years. His thoughtful mind planned
the great enterprise of the American Bible Society, of giving a
Bible to every family in the United States, and his pledge of ten
thousand dollars rendered it impossible but that the work should
be undertaken—and done. Many others might be named of the
great social movements of the last forty years, which owed their
being or their power to his comprehensiveness of vision, sagacity
of forethought, or largeness of liberality. Hardly any one can be
named which did not become what it was through his agency and
influence. It was a large heart, gifted with most extensive foresight, guiding a singularly effective will.

"In the slavery agitation, its beginning, its extent, its power,
its results, it may be said, without a question, that Arthur Tappan
was the pivotal centre of the whole movement. He supported the
Colonization Society for some years, because he believed it would
aid in the overthrow of slavery, and only abandoned it when he
became fully convinced that it was formed and was managed mainly in the interest of slavery, and for the purpose of strengthening
the system by removing its chief dangers. His decision and generosity released Mr. Garrison from his imprisonment at Baltimore,
and placed him in a position to commence the publication of the
Liberator. The formation of the Anti-Slavery Society in New
York, to be guided by those principles of religion and patriotism
to which his own soul held glad allegiance, hinged upon him, both
for its conception and execution. For years his contributions to its
treasury were its main reliance, amounting for successive years to

at least one-fourth of its yearly income. His generous response at that very juncture saved the *Liberator* from pending and instant suppression. And, in addition, he gave money and stirred up men to effort, right and left, to an extent which no earthly registry has recorded. In the darkest hours of mobs, and obloquy, and threatened assassination, he never quailed nor changed his course, nor doubted as to duties or results, but pressed right on, with steady step, toward the end which he was sure must come. For seven years he was the hinge on which a great nation turned to its new destiny. And he never let go, nor relaxed his energy, until he had seen the country so thoroughly aroused and so far permeated in all its ranks with the anti-slavery spirit as to make the final issue no longer doubtful, except as a question of time. He has been graciously permitted to remain among us until the great abomination has received its death-blow, and then departed in peace, to enter into the joy of his Lord. Well done, good and faithful servant! Thou hast been faithful above many, be thou ruler over higher interests in a world yet more exalted!

14.

EXTRACTS FROM A SERMON PREACHED IN THE FIRST CHURCH IN NEW HAVEN, JULY 30, 1865. BY REV. LEONARD BACON, D. D.

"With long life will I satisfy him, and show him my salvation."— Psalm 91:16.

A week ago this morning, a venerable member of this church, who had seen almost fourscore years, closed his eyes in death. He was one to whom the promise, "With long life will I satisfy him, and show him my salvation," had been literally fulfilled. There was much in his character and history which it may be profitable for us to remember.

Arthur Tappan was born at Northampton, Mass., in 1786. . . . When he was fourteen years old he was sent from home to learn that which was to be his business for life. . . . . At twenty-one years of age, he commenced business on his own account, with a partner, at Portland, Maine; but, not long afterward, they removed to Montreal. . . . . The commencement of the war between Great Britain and the United States, in 1812, made it necessary for them either to become British subjects or to close their business at a sacrifice, and return to their own country. His partner being like-minded with himself on that question, they did not hesitate. Though his judgment and sympathies as a citizen, and his personal interests, were adverse to the war, he loved his country, and would not be separated from it.

At the end of the war, in 1815, he removed to the city of New York, and commenced business there, as an importing merchant. The gains of the first year were more than balanced by the losses of the second and third, and a change in his arrangements became necessary. With a reduced capital, but with an unimpaired commercial character, he commenced, in the year 1817, the business in which he was, for about twenty years, eminently successful. Traders from all parts of the Union became his customers; his gains were steady and sure; he was rapidly accumulating a great fortune, and at the same time dispensing with exemplary liberality, when the commercial revulsion of 1837 produced, suddenly, an almost universal suspension of payments, and spread bankruptcy through all parts of the country. . . . Unable to obtain what was due to him from his customers, he was compelled to throw himself on the forbearance of his creditors; and, though the debts of the house were more than $1,100,000, he succeeded in making full payment within the time conceded to him. . . . . At the age of fifty-six, with nothing but his experience in business and his integrity, he began anew to earn a support for himself and his family. A few years of diligence and carefulness were sufficient to obtain by the favor of God's providence, a limited yet comfortable provision for his old age. Having lived here and worshipped in this congregation in his most prosperous days, from 1828 to 1835, he returned to this city about eight years ago, and became a member of this church. . . . .

Such is the outline of his life, with its leading dates, its labors and vicissitudes, its successes and disappointments, its domestic joys and sorrows. In all this there is little that is extraordinary; and if this were all that ought to be said about what Arthur Tappan has been and what he has done, and what he has seen and experienced, I might not have felt myself called to speak of him by name, or to describe his character. But, enclosed within this outline of his life, there is a story of self-consecration to the service of God, of earnest endeavor in the cause of truth and justice, of pertinacious sympathy with the poor and the wronged, of munificence, of conflict, of martyrdom, and of victory, which ought to be distinctly told, not for his sake but for ours.

. . . When he began to be prosperous in business, he began to show a liberality in giving, which was singular at that time, and therefore memorable, and which is rarely equalled among Christian merchants even now. . . . . In the year 1825, he was foremost among the founders of the American Tract Society, at New York. . . . . In 1827, a series of articles from the pen of Professor Morse directed public attention to the need of a daily commercial newspaper in New York, which should not be defiled with theatrical advertisements, and laudatory dissertations upon half-naked actresses ; and such a newspaper was established at his expense. A year or two later, he gave a new impulse to the work of the American Bible Society, by proposing in its board of managers that it should undertake to supply every family in the United States, within a limited time, with a copy of the Scriptures, and offering $10,000 as his contribution to the enterprise. He was, all this while, a free and constant giver to foreign and home missions, and to the American Education Society, then in the full tide of its greatest usefulness. And when it appeared that the young men, aided by that Society, were hindered from coming to Yale College, because there was at that time no fund, as at other colleges, for the payment of their tuition-bills, he assumed in 1828, the responsibility of paying for the tuition of all beneficiaries here till the number should be more than a hundred. Who can tell how much has been done for Christ by those whom he thus encouraged and helped on their way to the ministry of the gospel?

His New England principles and traditions ; the nurture of his childhood when the revolutionary enthusiasm for liberty had not yet subsided ; the keen sense of justice which predominated in his moral nature ; his ready sympathy with the wronged and suffering ; his religious belief that God hath made of one blood all nations of men, and the lesson which Christ had taught him in the story of the good Samaritan, caused him, from the beginning of his Christian course, to take a lively interest in efforts for the relief and emancipation of the African race, and especially for removing from our country the curse and shame of slavery. In common with other Christian and philanthropic men, he had favored the enterprise of the American Colonization Society. . . . . But in 1830, a young man who has since become famous, and who was then connected with a most uncompromising anti-slavery journal that had long been published without interference, in the mob-governed city of Baltimore, was thrown into prison there, by the sentence of a court, in default of the payment of a fine imposed upon him for an alleged libel on the good name of a slave-trader. Mr. Tappan . . . promptly paid the fine, and set him at liberty, getting the start of Henry Clay, who was taking measures to do the same thing. . . . . Then began the rage of the Southern people against Northern freedom of opinion, and of utterance, concerning slavery ; and many a dastardly attempt was made by Northern men to propitiate Southern fury by the sacrifice of sacred rights.

A meeting was called in the city of New York, in the autumn of 1833, to form a city anti-slavery society, which should act on public opinion for the abolition of slavery—a society to exist and operate by the same right by which similar societies had operated under the guidance of patriots like Jay and Franklin, in the days of Washington and Jefferson. At the demand and instigation of Southern men then present in the city, a mob was raised to defeat the purpose of the meeting. A few persons, however, assembled at a different place, and the proposed organization was effected. Thus was inaugurated the era of shameless servility to the arrogance of the slaveholding and slavetrading interest—the era of mobs for the suppression of all printing or speech against slavery. Before the close of that year, an American anti-slavery society had come into being and begun its work, defying the violence of mobs, trampling on every popular prejudice that was supposed to favor slavery, thriving on persecution.

From that time onward, Arthur Tappan was identified with the agitation against slavery. . . . . Of course his name in every part of the country, was associated with all terms of opprobrium. . . . . Yet nothing could move him from his course, for he was sustained by his own conscience, stimulated by his hatred of injustice and his pity for the weak and wronged, and strengthened by his confidence in God. The memorable anti-abolition riots in the city of New York, more than thirty years ago, raged with special fury against him, but no violence could move him from the course which he had deliberately taken in the fear of God. One night, the mob was in great force before his warehouse in Pearl-street, threatening to plunder and destroy it. . . . . A gentleman, who was at that time a clerk in the establishment, and who was one of the few who stood within the door with loaded muskets in their hands, waiting for it to be forced open, while the mob was thundering without—described to me, many years afterward, Mr. Tappan's characteristic quietness and firmness in that terrible excitement, and how calmly and thoughtfully he directed the defenders how to fire at the right moment, so as to repel the assailants most effectually, and yet to spare their lives. Fortunately a rumor went through the crowd, that a box or two of muskets had been carried into the building that day. One by one the rioters began to care for their safety in what might be a dangerous undertaking; and the mob was gradually dispersed.

In all the intensity of his zeal against slavery, he never lost his Christian sympathies. Though brought into coöperation with men whose views of Christ, of the church, and of the Bible, were widely different from his own, he was never carried into the dangerous current of their thinking. . . . .

Year by year it became more manifest that the churches of the North, and their ministry, whether right or wrong in their judgment concerning particular measures and expedients, were not apostate from Christ; and that the people of the North, however they might have been misled, and whatever sacrifices they had been willing to make for the Union, were not false to liberty. All this our venerable friend observed with growing thankfulness, till at last, when the slaveholding power in its madness had made war on the Union, he saw "the uprising of a great people" for union and liberty thenceforth inseparable.

I need not say in what steadfastness of love to his country, of confidence in God, and in the ultimate victory of righteousness, he has waited through these years of bloody conflict. Keenly sensitive to the sorrows and the horrors of the war, he has nevertheless seen the presence of God in it, and his faith has constantly foreseen the end, and the consequent openings for the progress of Christ's peaceful and spiritual kingdom. It was a joy to him that he saw in this house, last autumn, the annual assembly of the American Missionary Association, which had been instituted almost twenty years ago to receive the contributions of those who thought that older missionary societies were deficient in zeal against slavery, and which had found at last its predestined work in the millions of freedmen, and had been commended to that work by the common consent of the churches. And when the war was ended in the restoration of the national government to its supremacy, in the vindication of constitutional liberty, and in the sure and complete extinction of slavery, his joy was full. God had given him that for which he had prayed and longed, for which he had labored, for which he had endured so much of obloquy and hatred, and encountered so much of personal danger. Well might he say, "Now lettest thou thy servant depart in peace, for mine eyes have seen thy salvation."

The last time that he was present here was at our Tuesday

evening meeting, nearly three weeks ago. Our theme that evening was, "Here we have no continuing city, but we seek one to come." He loved such themes of meditation, and he told his daughters how much he had enjoyed that opportunity. Three days afterward, (Friday evening,) he lay down with his last illness upon him. In the intervals of consciousness or of partial consciousness which came to him he was heard faintly repeating some stanzas of a favorite hymn which was the dearer to him because he learned it in his childhood from his mother's lips:

"When all thy mercies, O my God,
    My rising soul surveys,
Transported with the view, I'm lost
    In wonder, love, and praise.

"When in the slippery paths of youth
    With heedless steps I ran,
Thine arm, unseen, conveyed me safe,
    And led me up to man.

"Through every period of my life
    Thy goodness I'll pursue,
And after death, in distant worlds,
    The glorious theme renew.

"Through all eternity to thee
    A joyful song I'll raise;
For oh, eternity's too short
    To utter all thy praise!"

With such thoughts, peaceful and thankful he passed away. God had satisfied him, and shown him his salvation.